A QUIET DEATH

Praise for Cari Hunter

Snowbound

"[*Snowbound*] grabbed me from the first page and kept me on the edge of my seat until nearly the end. I love the British feel of it and enjoyed the writer's style tremendously. So if you're looking for a very well written, fast paced, lesbian romance—heavy on the action and blood and light on the romance—this is one for your ereader or bookshelf."
—*C-Spot Reviews*

Desolation Point

"[*Desolation Point*] is the second of Cari Hunter's novels and is another great example of a romance action adventure. The story is fast paced and thrilling. A real page turner from beginning to end. Ms Hunter is a master at an adventure plot and comes up with more twists and turns than the mountain trails they are hiking. Well written, edited, and crafted, this is an excellent book and I can't wait to read the sequel."
—*Lesbian Reading Room*

"Cari Hunter provides thrills galore in her adventure/romance *Desolation Point.* In the hands of a lesser writer and scenarist, this could be pretty rote and by-the-book, but Cari Hunter breathes a great deal of life into the characters and the situation. Her descriptions of the scenery are sumptuous, and she has a keen sense of pacing. The action sequences never drag, and she takes full advantage of the valleys between the peaks by deepening her characters, working their relationship, and setting up the next hurdle."—*Out In Print*

Tumbledown

"Once again Ms. Hunter outdoes herself in the tension and pace of the plot. We literally know from the first two pages that the evil is hunting them, but we are held on the edge of our seats for the whole book to see what will unfold, how they will cope, whether they will survive—and at what cost this time. I literally couldn't put it down. *Tumbledown* is a wonderful read."—*Lesbian Reading Room*

"Even though this is a continuation of the *Desolation Point* plot, this is an entirely different sort of thriller with elements of a police procedural. Other thriller authors (yes, I'm looking at you, Patterson and Grisham) could take lessons from Hunter when it comes to writing these babies.

Twists and turns and forgotten or unconventional weaponry along with pluck and spirit keep me breathless and reading way past my bedtime."—*Out In Print*

No Good Reason

Truly terrible things, as well as truly lovely things, abound in the mystery-thriller *No Good Reason*...After visiting America for her last two books, Hunter returns to the land of hot tea and the bacon butty in her latest novel. Our heroines are Detective Sanne Jensen and Dr. Meg Fielding, best mates forever and sometimes something more. Their relationship is indefinable and complicated, but not in a hot mess of drama way. Rather, they share unspoken depths, comfortably silly moments, rock-solid friendship, and an intimacy that will make your heart ache just a wee bit.—*C-Spot Reviews*

"Cari Hunter is a master of crime suspense stories. *No Good Reason* brings tension and drama to strong medical and police procedural knowledge. The plot keeps us on the edge of our metaphorical seat, turning the pages long into the night. The setting of the English Peak District adds ambiance and a drama of its own without excluding anybody. And through it all a glimmer of humour and a large dose of humanity keep us engaged and enthralled."—*Curve Magazine*

"This novel is dark and brooding and brilliantly written. Hunter transports you right into the world she creates and keeps you firmly in the grip of the icy weather, craggy rocks and oppressive atmosphere." —*The Lesbian Review*

Cold to the Touch

"Right from the beginning I was hooked. Hunter never gives the reader a chance to get bored. This book is intelligently written and gives you an action-packed adventure with great characters."—*The Romantic Reader Blog*

"Hunter writes decidedly good stories. She combines excellent plot lines with crime drama and just the right amount of thriller to keep us on the edge of our seats. Each book feels distinctive, enjoyably new and refreshingly different to standard crime dramas. Fans of Sanne and Meg will love where she takes them this time. *Cold to the Touch* is more than strong enough to stand alone, but why miss an excellent series?"—*The Lesbian Reading Room*

By the Author

Snowbound

Desolation Point

Tumbledown

The Dark Peak Series:

No Good Reason

Cold to the Touch

A Quiet Death

A QUIET DEATH

by
Cari Hunter

2017

CREDITS
Editor: Cindy Cresap
Production Design: Stacia Seaman
Cover Design by Sheri (graphicartist2020@hotmail.com)

Acknowledgments

Thanks and a dish of butterscotch Angel Delight to the BSB gang, especially Sandy and Ruth for dealing with all the tricky behind-the-scenes stuff, and to my editor Cindy for her feedback and advice. To Sheri, for the lovely cover. To Alena Becker, for her knitting prowess, and to Nikki Smalls, for ensuring that our new nephews have their own dragons. To all the folks who've read these books, sent feedback, written reviews, and happily chatted about grannies sucking eggs. And to Cat, for the endless hours she spends as a beta, but mostly for making sure that I never get lost.

For Cat

Always

Prologue

They were getting closer. She could hear boots squelching in the peat and the crackle of grit and heather being crushed underfoot. Thin beams of light zigzagged across the moorland, picking out little in the driving sleet but keen enough to make her squeeze deeper into the tiny gap she had found. The rough surface of the stones bit into her skin and ripped her kameez. She pulled at the cloth, trying to cover her bare legs, her face burning with shame even as she shivered.

The men were shouting to each other, their words inaudible but weighted with fury. The taller one scrambled onto a nearby rock, his torch flashing within inches of her toes. He never thought to look down, though; never imagined that she might be huddled, with her fist stuffed into her mouth, not six feet from him. He jumped back to the path and swore as his trainers sank into the mud. She watched him walk away, the heaving bulk of his form quickly blotted out by the mist. The voices became less distinct, swallowed up by the wind and the drumming of her pulse.

A long time passed before she dared to unfurl her fingers and hold her hand out, catching drops of sleet and licking her dampened palm to ease her parched throat. She repeated the gesture, but seconds later, she couldn't remember why she'd done it, and she stared at her arm, baffled. The thrum of her heartbeat was slower now, the pain that had crippled her for days fading into a dull ache that might actually let her sleep. The rock felt warm when she leaned against it. She curled into a ball, feeling her mother run a hand through her hair and hearing Nabila sing the wrong words to an old tune. Reassured, she smiled and closed her eyes.

CHAPTER ONE

Taking the clatter of the Land Rover's engine as her cue, Meg Fielding sparked a match and lit the candles on the kitchen table. Secured to their saucers with Blu-Tack and melted wax, one wobbled and the other wavered, but neither toppled over. She blew out the flame as it began to singe her fingers, and then she adjusted the angle of a fork. Something was still missing.

"Aw, shit! Napkins!"

The turn of a key in the lock threw her into a tizzy. She flung drawers and cupboards open before giving up and tearing off sheets of bargain-basement kitchen roll instead, which didn't look too bad once she'd folded them into triangles and disguised them further by shoving them beneath the knives. Finally, she slapped a hand on the light switch. She'd sent Sanne a text making her promise to use the front door, and there was puzzlement in Sanne's voice as she called out, "Anybody home?"

Crouching in front of the oven door, Meg squinted at her reflection and wiped a smear of mint sauce from her forehead before chucking her apron in the vague direction of the washing machine. When she stepped into the hallway, Sanne froze, her coat still hanging off one arm.

"Oh no, what did you do?" She sniffed the air, her gaze straying beyond Meg. "Did you cook? In my kitchen? I thought we'd talked about this." She sniffed again, and her expression shifted from horrified to curious. "Bloody hell, something smells amazing."

Meg beamed, not offended in the slightest. It was a few years since she'd almost burned down her own house, but the memory lingered. "It's roast lamb. Your mum gave me strict instructions, and I've followed them to the letter." She kissed Sanne full on the lips. "Happy almost four-week anniversary. Now go and get your jammies on."

By the time Sanne came back down, Meg had started carving the leg of lamb. It was difficult to manage the knife whilst surreptitiously ogling Sanne, however, so she gave up on the slicing and devoted her efforts to ogling.

"You do look lovely," she said, watching Sanne sieve peas by candlelight. Still pink and damp from the shower, Sanne had towel-dried her hair, leaving it spiky all over, and thrown on her pyjamas and bed socks. A month of proper meals, restful sleep, and stress-free cases at work had restored some of the weight she had lost, and the sparkle was back in her eyes. When she smiled, Meg was tempted to swipe everything off the table and simply sit her on top of it.

"Meg?"

Caught somewhere between a naughty thought and an absolutely filthy one, Meg blinked and cleared her throat. "Yep? What?"

Sanne eased the knife from Meg's hand. "Dare I ask?"

"Probably best that you don't."

"Do you want me to finish the meat while you do something that doesn't involve a sharp object?"

"Okay," Meg said. "I'll get the spuds out. Your mum told me to roast them in goose fat."

Sanne's deft carving paused, the knife suspended motionless in mid-air. "God, I love you," she said.

❖

Dabbing her lips with kitchen roll, Sanne surveyed the empty dishes. The table looked as if a plague of locusts had ransacked it. The interview she'd led first thing that morning had overrun by several hours, thanks to the suspect's penchant for going off on fanciful tangents, and her lunch had been sacrificed to a detailed confession encompassing several major acts of terrorism and a murder committed in Denmark. When asked to point out Denmark on a map, he'd stuck his finger on Glasgow. The two Polo Mints she'd found in her coat pocket had only just kept her going on the way home.

"I had too many spuds. I think I might actually pop." She stretched her pyjamas away from her stomach.

"Can you squeeze pudding in?" Meg asked, beginning to stack the plates.

Sanne snapped the elastic back into place. "I'm assuming that was a rhetorical question."

As Meg added the final touches to a dessert she'd promised would knock Sanne's socks off, Sanne wandered into the living room and poked a fresh log into position on the burner. Spring might be just around the corner, but the brutal winter had yet to ease its grip on the Peak District, and she had driven home on roads slick with wet snow.

Leaning back against the sofa, she stretched her toes toward the fire. She had been looking forward to coming home since Meg's cryptic text. They hadn't arranged anything specific for their night off together, and she hadn't even been sure whether they would see each other, so the message had brightened an otherwise frustrating day.

She raised her head as Meg toed the door open and approached the sofa with her hands behind her back.

"Left or right?" Meg asked.

Sanne searched her face for a clue, but Meg's expression gave nothing away.

"Uh, left?"

"Ooh, good choice. You get more sprinkles." Meg handed her a glass bowl of butterscotch mousse and plonked herself down on the sofa.

Sanne laughed as she realised what the mousse was. "Angel Delight? You spoil me."

"It's Angel Delight with chocolate sprinkles, if you please." Meg daubed a blob onto Sanne's nose. "I would've made you something fancier, but peeling all those veggies took most of the afternoon."

"This is perfect." Sanne savoured her first taste. Angel Delight had been a guilty pleasure since childhood, and given that its preparation involved whipping a packet of powder into milk, even Meg could make it without incident. They ate in silence, their spoons ending up discarded on the coffee table as they observed the time-honoured tradition of cleaning the bowls with their fingers.

Still licking her thumb, Meg lifted her arm to let Sanne tuck into her. "How was your day?" she asked.

"Long. Uneventful." Sanne took a deep breath and felt every

tedious minute of her shift drain away. "But I can live with that for the moment."

"There's a lot to be said for uneventful."

"Aye."

Meg's arm tightened around Sanne, and her finger traced a thin white scar on the back of Sanne's hand, one of several that a multiple murderer had left her with. The three-month improvement notice attached to Sanne's personnel file at the start of that case had two weeks left to run, and she was ticking each day off on her kitchen calendar, if only to remind herself how far she had come since then.

Meg nudged her gently. "Penny for them."

Sanne squeezed Meg's hand, wondering how long she'd been quiet. "I was appreciating being happy. Nowt deep or meaningful, really. Just that."

"So you weren't composing romantic haikus or comparing me to a summer's day?"

"No, I was thinking that I'm dead snug and content and that you smell nice."

"I smell like lamb grease and goose fat, San."

"Don't forget the artificial butterscotch flavouring." Sanne cupped the back of Meg's head and kissed her. The sweetness coating Meg's lips would have made her squirm in anticipation if she'd had the energy to move. Instead she groaned and slumped against Meg. "It's no good. I am officially too full and too comfy to ravish you."

Meg, who'd always been better at drama in school, gasped like a swooning heroine. "Only four weeks and already we're victims of Bed Death."

"Oh, fuck off." Sanne poked a finger into her belly. "There's no way you want sex right now."

"Naw." Meg patted at the sofa until she found the television remote. "Right now I want to find something brainless to stare at while you fall asleep in my arms."

Sanne yawned. "That does sound lovely. But there's so much washing up to do."

Meg pulled a throw rug over them both. "Sod it," she said. "It'll keep till morning."

❖

Sanne woke just before her alarm to a room flooded with bright moonlight. Next to her, Meg was twitching in synch to a dream, but she shifted as if sensing that something had changed, turning to face Sanne, her fitful movements ceasing as she settled back on her pillow.

Sanne switched off the alarm, gifting herself the remaining two minutes beneath the quilt. Barely daring to breathe, she traced with one fingertip the silver light catching the arc of Meg's cheekbone and the pale throat where Sanne had so often pressed her lips. She had never really watched Meg sleep before, thinking it a sentimental thing, the preserve of proper couples, but although only four weeks had passed since she and Meg had decided to stop buggering around dating other people and simply date each other instead, it felt like a lifetime. A fear of ruining a friendship that had endured since childhood had kept them commitment-phobic for years, but moving into a relationship had been as easy as slipping on a well-worn pair of gloves.

Sanne stifled a laugh at her less-than-romantic simile. Despite their lack of experience in the art of wooing, she and Meg had given it a damn good crack, with exchanges of daft gifts, the undertaking of picturesque walks in the snow, and evenings out in local restaurants they'd always meant to try but never got around to. Five days into their fledgling affair, Meg had declared herself sufficiently smitten and had welcomed Sanne home from work wearing nothing but an old shirt and a smile. It was hardly their first time, but they'd compensated for a six-month separation with an enthusiasm that had yet to wane. The subject of living together had never been broached, and their irregular shift patterns gave them plenty of time apart. Whatever they had now, and however it might be defined, it seemed to be working.

Another check of the clock, and Sanne forced herself to edge out of bed, wincing as her stiff muscles resisted her attempts to sit up. She hobbled into the bathroom with her arms full of running gear, re-emerging minutes later to flick on her head torch, slip out of the front door, and tiptoe over her gravelled drive. Nothing was stirring in the chicken coop until she opened the gate, at which point Git Face the rooster crowed once in preparation and then let out a full-throated salute to the morning and everything in it. Leaving Meg to deal with him, Sanne set off at a sprint, easing down to a steadier pace once her lungs and quads began to burn. Frosty air rushed into her mouth and stung her cheeks. When she glanced up, the summits of the surrounding hills were outlined in moonlight, and Orion's Belt kept her heading in the right direction.

At the start of February, as soon as the snow had cleared from the valley, she had set herself a goal of running before work at least three times a week. Meg had told her she was bonkers, and Nelson had given it a month, but she'd relished the return to regular exercise, and she couldn't wait to get onto some of the higher routes.

The kitchen light was on when she got back to the house. Before she had a chance to take out her key, Meg opened the door.

"I throttled the little bastard, and we're having him for tea."

Sanne bent double, trying not to laugh as she panted for breath. "No, you didn't."

"Maybe not, but I was tempted." Meg rubbed her bleary eyes and surveyed Sanne's mud-splattered form. "Congratulations on not snapping an ankle."

"Thanks. You should come with me one morning."

"Mornings are for tea, toast, and bacon," Meg declared, turning the tap on and reaching for a glass. On odd occasions, Sanne had known her to go swimming, but most of her exercise came from hurrying around an Accident and Emergency department for forty-plus hours a week, and she was probably as fit as Sanne. She passed Sanne the glass and steered her toward the hall. "You shower all that crap off. I'll stick the kettle on."

CHAPTER TWO

Eleanor Stanhope waited for the lift to start moving and then turned to its mirrored wall. A quick adjustment to a hairclip repaired the damage inflicted by the brisk easterly wind, while a dab of lipstick covered a tooth-smeared patch. Having removed her coat and draped it over her arm, she smoothed her jacket and pencil skirt and checked her tights for ladders. It was a daily ritual unwitnessed by anyone in all her years as a detective inspector, and she'd got it timed to a T, standing ready to exit onto the fourth floor mere seconds before the ping signalled the lift's arrival.

She stepped out into darkness, the start of her day neatly poised between the departure of the domestic staff and the influx of the EDSOP detectives. Unless she was paged during the night, she aimed to hit the office by six a.m., giving herself an hour's grace to catch up on her e-mails and eat breakfast before the meetings and briefings and phone calls began in earnest. Her role as head of East Derbyshire Special Ops came with few perks, but at least her office had the luxury of its own kettle. She brewed her first mug of coffee and poured muesli into a bowl, topping it with grated apple and natural yoghurt. As the computer did its usual stutter and stall, she kicked off her shoes beneath the desk and managed to eat half the cereal before the system logged her on. Not that she was in any particular hurry: for the first time since late December, the EDSOP caseload was relatively light, as if the post-Christmas chaos had been so exhausting that the local criminal element was taking a break until the clocks went forward and the longer days created better opportunities for misbehaviour. EDSOP worked major crimes—murders, kidnappings, serious and sexual assaults—and the team of nine detectives had been a man down since a near-fatal attack on its only sergeant. Although Duncan Carlyle had assured Eleanor of his intention to return to work, Occupational Health were dragging their feet, and she had little inclination to expedite matters.

She prioritised her overnight e-mails as she listened to the voices drifting through from the open-plan office beyond hers. Sanne Jensen and her partner, Nelson Turay, were often the EDSOP early birds, beating the traffic and using the small kitchen to prepare their breakfast. They were arguing about something now, Sanne's voice laughter-filled but indignant, in contrast to Nelson's calm baritone. Sanne shouted across to Fred Aspinall for his adjudication and then invited them both to kiss her arse when she ended up on the losing side.

Eleanor finished her coffee, feeling like a headmistress snooping on unruly charges. She had worked with EDSOP for almost twelve years, and this was the most cohesive team she'd managed, especially with Carlyle away on extended sick leave. After battling through a rough winter, she was hoping for a chance to regroup, perhaps review training needs and see whether she could steer her brightest toward more specialised skills. That reminded her she had to organise further Taser courses, imperative for the team after several recent close calls. Sanne and Nelson were already qualified, along with Mike Hallet and Jay Egerton. Eleanor scanned the list of those remaining and bit the end of her pen when she reached Fred and his partner, George Torren. She'd be amazed if either of them could hit the side of a barn, but as the East Derbyshire diversity policy stated, ageism had no place in the modern police force.

"God help us all," she muttered, and added their names to the schedule.

❖

A glance at the Majors whiteboard told Meg all she needed to know about the previous night's shift. Of the nine cubicles, five were blocked by patients waiting for beds on the Medical Assessment Unit, and one by a patient who needed transferring to Urology at St. Margaret's. They had all breached the four-hour "admit or discharge" target, and the computer screens were blazing with red warnings. The breach manager, usually full of vigour and ready to do battle, appeared to be on the verge of tears, her designer jacket removed and her blouse untucked. If she'd carried a handkerchief, she would probably have been waving it.

"Welcome to another day in paradise." Liz, the nurse whose shifts often ran alongside Meg's, flung her arms wide to encompass the carnage. Behind a curtain, someone vomited, and a doctor so fresh-faced he looked shiny rushed toward Resus clutching a sheaf of printouts.

Meg stared after him. "Please tell me he's not been researching on Wikipedia again."

"He wouldn't dare," Liz said. "And Donovan's in there with him today, so we should be able to avoid another clinical incident."

"Terrific." Meg grimaced at the prospect of the chief consultant pecking her head for fourteen hours. Donovan had forgotten to mention he would be on duty when he'd phoned and persuaded her to work a long day. She tapped the board with a tongue depressor. "Who've we got in Three?"

"Rubina Begum. Thirty-eight-year-old, pseudo-unconscious with a bit of a temp. Brought in on an amber standby by a crew barely out of nappies."

"God love 'em." Meg's mood brightened as she snapped on a pair of gloves and collected the ambulance paperwork. "By 'eck, according to this she's comatose. We'd better fast-bleep Anaesthetics."

Liz headed in the opposite direction. "You know sarcasm is the lowest form of wit?" she asked over her shoulder.

"Yeah, so I've been told." Meg drew back the cubicle's curtain to find two people sitting beside the bed: a Pakistani man she assumed to be the patient's husband and a tear-streaked lad of no more than eight. "Morning, all. I'm Dr. Fielding. Is this your wife, sir?"

The man nodded slowly.

She turned to the lad. "And your mum?"

The lad sniffled and wiped his nose on his sleeve. "She won't wake up," he said.

Meg crouched in front of him. "I think she will, and I'm sure she's going to be fine. What's your name?"

"Mohammed." He straightened, emboldened by her attention. "And I'm seven and a half."

"Wow, that's really old. I bet you're dead clever." She looked across to his dad. "Do you speak English, sir?"

A shake of his head and a reluctant "so-so" gesture told her that she'd correctly identified Mohammed as the translator.

"I don't want to miss school," Mohammed said. Still in his pyjamas and slippers, he kicked against his chair.

Meg checked her watch, wondering how quickly she could revive, diagnose, and discharge his mum. "In that case, I'd better get cracking, eh?"

She pushed to her feet and surveyed her patient. A small, overweight woman, Rubina Begum was swaddled beneath two coats, and her eyelashes flickered when Meg lowered the bed's railing. With the exception of a mild temperature, her observations were normal, and she was no more unconscious than her son.

"Rubina." Meg shook her shoulder. "Will you open your eyes for me, please?"

Rubina screwed them closed instead, prompting a renewed bout of sniffles from Mohammed. Meg had never understood the willingness of some people to inflict distress on their own children, and it never failed to piss her off. Switching tactics, she pressed hard on the bony arc of Rubina's upper eye socket, maintaining the painful stimulus until Rubina tried to bat her hand away.

"Okay, that's encouraging," Meg said, loosening her grip.

Seeing his mum's miraculous recovery, Mohammed clambered onto the bed beside her. She blinked as if roused from a deep sleep and wrapped an arm around him, murmuring in Urdu, which he automatically translated for Meg.

"She says her back and her belly hurt."

Now almost certain that Mohammed would make his first class, Meg rummaged in a drawer and pulled out a plastic sample pot. "Can you ask her to have a wee in this for me?"

Mohammed giggled and turned pink. "You're a funny sort of doctor," he said.

❖

"I didn't do nothing. I don't know why I'm here, and I'm not saying nothing." Seamus Thompson drew a figurative line beneath his statement by rocking back in his chair and folding his arms. Immediately overbalancing, he thumped his legs down and made a grab for the table.

"That's fine, Seamus." Sanne took her time replacing the lid on her pen. "We'll go next door and carry on chatting to your brother. Remind me what he had to say about all this, Detective Turay?"

Nelson flipped to the correct page in his notepad and selected a choice line. "'Seamus was the one what had the hammer, and he done knocked that bloke's teeth in even after I told him not to.'"

Indignation made Seamus's eyes bulge, and his mouth dropped open to reveal a tongue bar bearing the legend "Male Slut." Ignoring his solicitor's attempts to placate him, he pushed at the table, sending his cup of water flying. "Did our Daragh tell you he stamped on the bloke's hands? Broke all his bones and laughed about it?"

"No," Sanne said. "Somewhat surprisingly, he left that bit out." She ignored the solicitor's scowl; it wasn't her fault his client had fallen for such a rudimentary ploy. These days most of the scrotes across the table in Interview One were well versed in the "no comment" drill, but Seamus and Daragh had obviously needed to watch more reality TV before they'd decided to put someone in the ITU for the sake of twenty-one quid and a crap mobile phone.

"Would you like to make a proper statement?" she asked. "Then we can have you tucked up in your cell by teatime."

Seamus wobbled his tongue bar between his teeth, considering the offer. "Do I have to write it?"

"No," Sanne said, well aware of his illiteracy. "I'll guide you through it and write it for you. Your solicitor will check it, and you can sign it."

"All right. Where do I start?"

"At the beginning."

That was the only cue he needed. "Well, see, it was all our Daragh's fault…"

It took more than two hours to untangle his testimony and wheedle out the pertinent points. As Nelson finally closed the door on Seamus and his solicitor, Sanne rocked her head from side to side, listening to the crunch of her vertebrae.

"What kind of genetic evil produced two of those?" Nelson asked.

"I think they're actually triplets," Sanne said. "Only, Paddy chooses to use his powers for good."

Nelson threw up his hands. "Do they have even a drop of Irish blood in them?"

"Nope. Apparently, their parents were so fond of Guinness, they named their brood in its honour."

"You made that up."

"I did not. I have it written down somewhere. Paddy told me the other day while you were in the loo."

Nelson's shoulders dropped as he began to laugh. "That would explain a lot."

"Aye." Sanne gathered her paperwork. "We can get the file off to the CPS first thing. I can't see them having a prob—"

A terse knock interrupted her. George pushed his head around the door.

"Boss wants us all in the briefing room. A hiker's called in a body up near Stryder Clough. First uniforms on scene have flagged it to us."

"Aw, bloody hell," Nelson said.

"Yeah." George held the door for them, his expression unusually grim. "The unis are saying it's a child."

CHAPTER THREE

The van juddered as the officer behind the wheel pulled out of a curve and misjudged the gradient. He dropped a gear, smoothing the ride, and Sanne eased her grip on the seat in front. All around her, the Peaks were beginning to gain height, their earthy brown slopes newly exposed by the recent thaw. Here and there, snowdrifts remained in shadowed gullies, but the sun shone on clear summits, the night's fall dispatched within hours. It was a perfect day for hiking, clear and crisp, with a breeze keen enough to keep people moving. Had Sanne not been on shift she would probably have gone up there herself, taking advantage of the weather window after so many weeks of poor visibility and freezing conditions. Some unfortunate sod who'd done just that was now a witness in a murder investigation, however, with his 999 call a jumble of location details stammered between retching. Black Gate Farm, the access point he had managed to identify, sat off a rough track a couple of miles before Sanne's cottage, and she knew this stretch of the Snake Pass like the back of her hand.

She began to fasten her coat, and her colleagues followed suit. With Mike Hallet busy in court, and Scotty and Jay out on unrelated door-to-door enquiries, there were six left from EDSOP, along with two uniformed officers to relieve those already at the scene. Eleanor ended a phone call and turned side-on in her seat to address them.

"The farmer, Ron Stanton, has offered to drive us as far up Stryder Clough as he can manage. He estimates a mile and a half hike from the drop-off point to the scene. The chopper is otherwise engaged for at least the next hour, but SOCO are hoping to commandeer it to bring in their kit and personnel. As we'll be on scene first, we'll make a start on the preliminaries. I need two of you to stay at the farm to get statements from the hiker and his wife."

Fred's hand shot up so fast that Sanne heard the click of his arthritic shoulder. All of EDSOP kept boots and wet-weather gear in their lockers, a sensible precaution given the semi-rural nature of their patch, but some were far more capable of a strenuous hike than others.

"I've got terrible blisters from last night's salsa," he said. "It's that Martha. She runs me ragged." He began to untie his laces, preparing to prove his point, but a chorus of dissent, and George slapping his hands, stopped him.

Eleanor raised her voice above the outcry. "Thank you, Fred. George can stay back to assist."

"Next right, mate. Just after the tree line," Sanne called to the driver. He waved to acknowledge her, spotting the turn in good time and easing the van off the Snake.

The cluster of stone buildings came into view after a bone-jolting crawl along a track more suited to four-wheel drives. To the frantic accompaniment of barking from the farm dogs in the yard, Sanne released her seat belt, keen to stand on terra firma and breathe something other than diesel fumes. She recognised Ron Stanton as he came over to greet Eleanor. Rarely seen without his flat cap and Barbour jacket, he was something of an institution in the area, a good-humoured man whom everyone wanted on their side in a pub quiz. Although in his early sixties, he was still lithe and fit enough to manage 250 hectares of land, winning prizes for the meat and sausage he supplied to Meg's local butcher in Rowlee.

From the doorway of the main house, his wife Trudy watched the team disembark from the van, and then clapped her hands to silence the collies and disappeared back inside.

"The Landie's fuelled and ready to go," Ron said. "Yon hiker and his missus are in the living room. It's a bloody shame what's gone on up at Greave, and you folks are welcome to co-opt anything you need for as long as it takes."

"We appreciate that, Mr. Stanton," Eleanor said.

He tipped his cap at her. "Ron, please. Oh, how do, Sanne? Here, let me get that for you." He strode across and took Sanne's rucksack before she had a chance to shoulder it. "Those girls of yours laying yet?"

"Not yet. It's still a bit dark for them." She fell into step with him as he led the way to his Land Rover. "I have high hopes, though."

"That's the spirit. I'll ask Trude to leave a dozen out for you if I remember." Ever the gentleman, he boosted her into the back of the Landie, where she shuffled onto the bench seat beside Nelson.

"I promise I'll share my eggs with you," she whispered to him.

The engine noise and the roughness of the ride curtailed any further conversation, and Sanne could only catch flashes of Stryder Clough through the canvas shell covering the rear compartment. She had run a similar route on occasion, following a lower path close to the clough's central stream and then joining the Pennine Way just beyond Greave Stones. Sitting proud at the top of the clough, the stones were ideal for picnics and scrambling, offering an excellent vantage point on a clear day, or shelter from the elements if the weather turned. She could only imagine the horror of finding a body hidden among them, although her imagination had ample source material thanks to two of her recent cases. Closing her eyes, she leaned into Nelson and felt his brief, reassuring grip on her forearm. They were approaching the two-year anniversary of their EDSOP partnership; by now, what he didn't know about her, he could probably hazard a good guess at.

A sudden lurch and dip brought the Land Rover to a halt.

"That's about as close as I can get you," Ron said, leaving the engine to idle and jumping down from the driver's seat. Sunlight flooded into the rear compartment when he unfastened the canvas flaps. Half blinded by the brightness, Sanne welcomed his guiding hand as she climbed out onto the plateau of stony ground that marked the end of the track. "You can join the path just there," he told her, aware of her familiarity with the area. "See? If I weren't so damn busy, I'd come with you."

"We'll be fine. Thanks." She hefted her rucksack and adjusted its straps. It was an old one she'd found stuffed into her own Landie, and Eleanor had filled it with logbooks, forensic clothing and markers, and recording equipment. She set off at a nod from Eleanor, leading without being asked and picking her way through the heather until she reached the narrow trail.

"One of these days I'll come up here when we're not on a case," Nelson said, taking in the view with wide eyes. "Bring Abeni and the girls, pack a lunch, and run wild."

Sanne smiled, the hills and fresh air irresistible despite the circumstances. "You should. They'd love it. Meg and I used to spend all our summer holidays outdoors, riding our bikes on the back field. Our mums wouldn't see us till we were hungry, and we'd have given our eyeteeth to get as far as the Peaks. There was none of this buggering about on Facebook or PlayStations."

"Tumblr," Nelson said. "I think that's where the cool kids are these days. Or is it Imgur?"

Sanne crossed her eyes at him. "Not being at all cool, I have no idea what you've just said." She slowed to gauge the best stepping stones as the path veered to the opposite side of the stream. Her first choice wobbled and capsized beneath her boot. "You can swim, right?"

Nelson looked dubious. "Yes, but I hate getting my feet wet."

"I suggest you avoid that one, then." She chose another and hopped across, waiting on the bank until everyone else joined her. "It's not far now," she told them. Looking up, she caught her first glimpse of the stern grey rocks, and she walked on without hesitation. Having assumed the role of guide and pacesetter, she couldn't shirk either responsibility even if she'd wanted to. She fixed her eyes on the path again, concentrating on where she put her feet and not what she was heading toward.

One of the officers guarding the scene met them at the spot where the path became less distinct, the clough giving way to peat hags and groughs undulating across the hilltop. He waited while they donned their Tyvek suits, masks, and booties, no doubt aware that his entire uniform would have to be sacrificed to SOCO for analysis.

"The vic's round here," he said. "We've been keeping to one path."

Eleanor nodded and gestured for him to lead on. They passed the flat table-like rock where Sanne and Meg had once shared lunch, soaking wet after a deluge but too happy with the views and homemade cake to care about their sodden socks, and Sanne was half-smiling at the memory when she noticed the foot. A small, frail thing, it protruded from between two stones, its toes almost submerged in the peat. She heard Chris O'Brien swear and Nelson draw in a sharp breath as they spotted it as well.

"Sanne, could you pass me the camera, please?" Eleanor asked. "Are you okay doing the video?"

"Fine." Sanne gave Nelson the rucksack to hold and withdrew both pieces of kit from its depths. She moved forward when Eleanor did, panning the camcorder in a wide arc and then narrowing its focus to a gap beneath one of the stones. The body revealed itself in increments: a tattered heel, a skinny leg, and a bottom bared by a crumpled-up dress.

"Fucking hell," Eleanor said, and the click of her camera ceased.

Ignoring Eleanor, Sanne squatted so low that her nose almost touched the peat, coming face-to-face with a young girl, her eyes half-lidded and her expression tranquil. This close, Sanne could see it wasn't a dress that she was wearing but a short, brightly coloured tunic with gold brocade decorating its purple cloth, missing the loose trousers that would have matched it. For some unfathomable reason the responding officers hadn't thought to mention that the girl was Asian, probably either Pakistani or Bengali, but Eleanor was already on the phone, breaking the news to the brass.

"Damn," Nelson said, stooping at Sanne's side. "What on earth is she doing all the way out here?"

Sanne lowered the camcorder. "I think that might be the sixty-four thousand quid question," she said.

❖

"Yes, sir, I'm aware of that." The peat was too wet for Eleanor to pace on, but that didn't stop her trying. Water gathered around her booties as they sank into the spongy layer, spilling over her bootlaces whenever she stayed still for too long. "I'm planning to call in a community liaison."

The wind forced her to hold the phone close, which aimed Detective Chief Inspector Litton's nervous breakdown directly into her ear.

"This is all we fucking need, with everything that's gone on in South Yorks," he said, his voice verging on a whine. "I don't want our force tarred with the same brush, and I won't have it said that we've wilfully neglected our duty."

"No, sir." Eleanor watched a grouse dart for cover as Nelson strayed into its territory, and she wished she could heed its "g'back" warning cry. Like several other police forces in England, South Yorkshire stood accused of ignoring evidence linking gangs of men to the sexual exploitation of young girls. That the men were mostly from ethnic minorities and their victims white had reignited racial tensions in the affected areas and raised suspicions that the police had been burying the cases for fear of appearing racist. The resulting media fallout had been considerable, and the issue was unlikely to fade from the headlines any time soon.

"Initial thoughts?" The snap of Litton's question startled Eleanor. She turned to face the stones again, finding less to distract her in their impassive mass.

"She's young," she said. "Perhaps thirteen or fourteen. No obvious cause of death. Her only visible injuries are minor and probably due to her being barefoot. The lower half of her clothing is missing, and her position suggests she may have hidden herself in the rocks rather than been concealed there by a third party."

"So we could be looking at rape not murder?" Litton sounded moderately cheered by the prospect, and Eleanor had to dig her nails into her palm to keep the anger from her response.

"It's impossible to say, sir. The body is still in situ. We'll know more after the PM."

"Yes, well, I expect to be kept apprised of any developments."

"Of course, sir."

He ended the call, and she dropped the phone into her pocket as if it had dirtied her fingers. Her team—well aware whom she'd been talking to—looked pensive as she approached. They weren't stupid; they all understood the implications for the department should one foot be set wrong on such a case.

"DCI Litton wishes us luck with the investigation," she said.

Nelson huffed in outright disbelief, and Sanne busied herself scratching peat from her eyebrow. Above them, the beat of rotor blades announced the impending arrival of SOCO.

"Now or never for your footage, Sanne," Eleanor shouted over the helicopter's din.

Sanne gave her a thumbs-up. "I've got loads already, and we took more photos."

Her enthusiasm made Eleanor smile. Sanne was in her element on the moors, but the hike and the increasing wind chill already had Eleanor craving a hot bath and a generous dram of Scotch. She couldn't feel her toes, her eyes were watering, and her nose kept running. While she appreciated the grandeur of the Peaks, she preferred to view them from the comfort of her car as she drove past. On the positive side, at least she wouldn't end up with second-degree sunburn this time around. "Do you want to stay and chat to SOCO?" she asked.

"Aye, so long as they don't try to chase me off with a big stick. I'll see if Nelson will keep me company. Safety in numbers and all that." Sanne shielded her eyes from the downdraught. "Are you on the next flight out?"

"That's the plan. Get what you can from them and brief me ASAP. Phone or e-mail is fine if you're late back."

"No worries, boss." Sanne grimaced as if realising what she'd just said. "Well, maybe a few, eh?"

❖

Still clad head to foot in forensic coveralls, but well beyond SOCO's newly established perimeter, Sanne used a thin crease on the flank of a suitable rock to boost herself upward. The gritstone bit a hole in her nitrile gloves and shredded the skin of her fingertip, but she managed to wriggle to the summit, where she found her balance and turned in a slow circle.

"Are you joining me?" she shouted down to Nelson, who stood squinting at her in the glare of the dipping sun. He briefly considered her proposition before nodding and starting to follow her route.

"Promise you won't laugh if I split my kecks?" he said, self-conscious as ever about the snug fit of his Tyvek suit.

"I promise I'll *try*." She held out a hand and helped him up, keeping a firm grip on him until he'd found his sea legs in the strengthening wind.

"Right," he said, once assured that his suit had survived intact. "What am I looking at?"

"For the most part, the summit of Brabyn's Tor. And that's the Pennine Way." Sanne nodded toward the only visible path. "From here it crosses the summit for about a mile before dropping down to the Smithy River. If you followed it south instead, it would dip to the Snake and then climb again toward Corvenden."

He grunted in recognition. "Bit of déjà vu about this, isn't there?"

"Yeah." She kept her eyes fixed on the horizon as a blush of pink began to highlight the dusting of clouds. She hadn't been anywhere near Corvenden Edge or Laddaw Rocks since the abduction case of the previous summer, and she didn't want to look at them now, though they were little more than a smudge in the distance. She hated that the actions of one man had tainted an entire area for her, but what had happened there was still too raw, and she wasn't sure when, if ever, she would be able to go back.

"Do you think this is a copycat, San?"

"Honestly?" She looked up at him. "I haven't a clue. From the state of the vic's feet I would say she'd been running, and it seems obvious she hid herself, but surely she's too young for someone not to have missed her? If she'd been up here with a group or her family, they'd have reported in by now, but local police and Mountain Rescue haven't been alerted. Besides which..." She hesitated, not wanting to offend him.

"Besides which, what?"

She decided to dive right in. "Well, you don't see many ethnic minorities in the Peaks. I've been running and hiking around here for years, and the vast majority of the people I meet are white. I could count on one hand the number of Asians I've seen, and they're never in traditional dress. Maybe in summer, having a picnic by the river, but never on the tops in crappy weather."

"Huh. So I'm a statistical anomaly, am I?" He sounded intrigued.

"That you are."

"Cultural thing?"

"I suppose it must be, but either way, I think we can rule out an abduction during a day trip."

"Okay." He scanned around, paying particular attention to a steep outcropping. "Any caves nearby?"

"No. The closest are those at Laddaw, but our vic would never have made it this far. Oh shit, I'll tell you what there is, though!" She shook her head at her own ineptitude and began to climb down. "There's a bloody road!"

Nelson spun in a three-sixty. "Where? I can't see one."

"You won't. It's a couple of miles north, over the lip of the hill. It connects up with the Snake eventually, but no one uses it much anymore except for local access. You can still get through to Sheffield that way, though, if you're idiot enough to try."

Nelson bounded back to the peat, ignoring the splash of black water that hit his suit. "Or if you want to avoid mobile speed cameras, police patrols, and anyone else who might remember you."

"Exactly." She weaved through the rocks until she could see Ted Ulverston, the Scene of Crime Officer who had worked their last major case and who had politely but firmly shooed them away from the girl's body.

"We're nowhere near finished yet," he called, spotting their approach.

"That's fine," she said. "I just wanted to pinch a couple of head torches, if you have any to spare."

Ted raised an eyebrow. "Why? Are you going potholing?"

"Not a bloody chance, but the sun's setting, and we've decided to toot around while you do your forensic thing." She wasn't usually one for subterfuge, but she didn't want SOCO tagging along when there might not be anything to justify the trek.

"Whatever floats your boat." Ted rummaged in a holdall and brought out a pair of torches. "I'll give you a shout when we're ready to move her."

"Cheers, Ted." The kit safely stashed, Sanne slung her rucksack over her shoulder. "We'll keep to the Pennine Way and bag or mark anything that looks like a recent discard," she told Nelson. "If she was out here in daylight, there's a chance she found the path."

"Aren't you going to tell the boss about the road?" Nelson's question held just the hint of a tease. Sanne was nothing if not by the book.

"I think she's got enough on her plate, and it'd take ages for anyone to drive over and meet us there." She puffed out her chest and held her head high. "I am seizing the initiative, Nelson. The boss made it my New Year's resolution."

"In which case, lead on."

❖

The swish of the curtain prompted Meg's seventeen-year-old patient to unplug her mobile from the wall and abandon the text she was in the middle of composing. Levi Collins had come to the hospital via ambulance with a half-hour history of abdominal pain that she hadn't attempted to self-medicate, and she swung her legs nervously as she awaited Meg's verdict. Meg spent a few seconds admiring her leopard-print onesie and fake UGG boots, standard local dress for a trip to the A&E, though the full-length tail was a novel touch.

"Well?" Levi asked. "Am I up the duff?"

"No. Your pregnancy test was negative." Ignoring Levi's triumphant whoop, Meg handed her a leaflet detailing various contraceptive choices. "Try to find something in there that suits you, eh?"

Levi stashed the leaflet in her bag. "What's up with me, then?"

"You have a UTI."

The colour drained from Levi's face. "Jesus, Mary, and Joseph. Is it chlamydia? God, me mam'll kill me."

"*U*TI, not *S*TI. You have a urinary tract infection. They're very common, and yours will clear up fine with a short course of antibiotics."

"Thank fuck for that." Levi toyed with her phone, as if the urge to update her status was too strong to bear. "Me mam says I'm dyspeptic."

"What, you're prone to indigestion?"

"No, I can't spell for shit."

"Ah, right." Meg bit her lip, trying not to laugh. "Okay, well, here are your antibiotics, and here's a leaflet that might help prevent another infection. Will you be able to read it?"

Levi plucked it from Meg's fingers. "Course I will. I'm not thick, y'know." She slid from the bed and untangled her tail from the railing. "Ta, Doc."

Meg jotted a note on Levi's chart, watching her wander into the X-ray department and then out again in search of the Majors exit.

"We should put trimethoprim in the bloody water supply," she said to Liz, as the tail vanished around a corner. "That's my fourth UTI of the day."

Liz rubbed her eyes as if she couldn't quite believe what she'd just seen. "I bet that one was your favourite, though."

"Oh, I don't know. Hers didn't come with a fake coma like Mrs. Begum's."

"Let's call it a tie." Liz proffered two charts. "Pick one. Belly ache with—you've guessed it—dysuria in Three, or drunk and doubly incontinent in Six."

"Please kill me…"

Meg was reaching for Six when she heard Asif call her name. She waved him over. "Saved by my favourite F2! Everything okay?" she asked.

Asif was a Foundation Year Two doctor who would be fully qualified in a matter of months, and he had flourished in A&E once he'd realised that 99.5% of his patients weren't suddenly going to drop dead on him. His expression was unusually troubled, however, and he ushered Meg farther away from the cubicle he'd just left.

"I'm not sure. I don't think so, but I don't really know what to do."

She read the cover of his patient's notes. "Anca Miklos. What's that? Czech? Polish?"

"Romanian. Her husband brought her in with scalds to both hands. He claims she dropped a pan of boiling water, but the history seems off, and she's not saying much at all."

"Does she speak English?"

"If she does, she's choosing not to. The translation service is swamped, and her husband is pushing for her to be discharged."

"Right." Meg snapped the notes closed. She hated bullies, and a long, frustrating shift had her itching for a battle. "How big is this chap?"

"About six two and well built. Why?" Asif's voice rose on the question.

She clapped him on the shoulder. "Go and grab Security in case he gets feisty, and I'll see you in there."

He went to find help, leaving Meg to enter the cubicle alone. The young woman on the bed tensed as Meg drew back the curtain, while the man at her side continued to eat a bag of crisps, stuffing them in by the fistful and crunching loudly.

"I'm Dr. Fielding." She deliberately positioned herself between Anca and her husband. "I'd like to examine your hands, Anca, if that's all right with you?"

She might as well have spoken to a statue. Unable to seek guidance or permission, Anca froze, her mouth falling open and her breath coming in rapid pants. She tried to see around Meg, and Meg sensed rather than heard the man get to his feet.

"We are ready to go," he said, standing close enough to Meg to make her flinch. Taking that as capitulation, he uttered a stream of Romanian, punctuated by gestures that needed no explanation. Anca nodded quickly, struggling to untie her gown with her bandaged fingers.

"No." Meg put a hand on her arm, stilling her efforts, and turned to her husband. "You can go, but Anca stays here. She needs to see a burns specialist. If you interfere with her treatment, I will contact the police. Do you understand me?"

The man's nostrils flared, and he clenched his fists. Meg stayed exactly where she was. Fuck him. If he hit her, that would just make it easier for the police to remove him, and it wouldn't be the first punch she'd ever taken. She managed not to react as his stance gradually relaxed, though the adrenaline coursing through her was making her legs shake.

Switching to a charm offensive, he smiled, oblivious to the blobs of crisp stuck between his teeth. "No police. Is not necessary. See?" He took Anca's right hand, presenting it to Meg; if he heard the whimper his touch provoked, he chose to ignore it. "You look. I will go like you say." Stroking Anca's cheek with his free hand, he spoke to her in a gentle tone. When Anca responded by nodding, he kissed her in obvious approval and stepped away from the bedside.

"You take good care," he told Meg. "One hour. Then I come back for her."

Meg checked her watch. "Shut the curtain behind you." She waited until his footsteps faded. Anca was staring at the gap he had left in the curtain as if expecting him to leap through and grab her by the throat.

"Hey," Meg said quietly. "He's not there. He's not—" She touched Anca's chin, encouraging her to make eye contact. "Do you speak any English?"

"No English," Anca whispered. "No English."

"That's fine. We can get around that." Meg took out her mobile and hit the app that had saved the department a small fortune in translator fees over the past few years. She selected Romanian from the drop-down box and typed her first question: *May I examine your hands?*

For a long moment she wondered whether Anca could even read, but then a tentative nod gave her the consent she sought. After donning a pair of gloves, she removed the burn dressings. It was immediately apparent why Asif had requested her opinion. Large blisters had formed across the dorsa of both hands, and each finger was red-raw where the skin had sloughed. The palms were just as badly damaged, with no sign of a splash pattern to support the history of a dropped pan.

The injuries were more consistent with someone taking Anca's wrists and forcing her hands into boiling water.

"Jesus." Meg ripped off her gloves and flung them in the bin. She wanted to run after the husband and slam his smug face into something hard until it knocked a confession out. Instead she typed: *Did someone do this to you? Did someone hurt you?*

"No." Anca's denial was instantaneous. "No, no, no."

"You're safe here. Aw, hell…" Meg typed out the reassurance, adding: *I promise he won't hurt you again.*

"No." Anca closed her eyes, sending tears streaming down her cheeks. "No, no."

Meg stuck her head out of the curtain. "Asif, get me an ETA on a translator, and I need Security to stop that bloke from coming back in here."

"Okay, I'll sort it," Asif said.

"What pain relief has she had?"

"Brufen and co-codamol. He wouldn't let me cannulate her."

"Fucking arsehole. Shake down Liz for the drugs key and grab me ten of morphine, will you?" She collected an IV tray and returned to the cubicle, where she typed out another message for Anca: *I'm going to put a little needle in your arm and give you a lot of good drugs through it. They'll take the pain away. Is that okay?*

Anca read the screen carefully. Then she looked at Meg and held out her arm.

In an attempt to reach the road before dusk, Sanne had pushed the pace hard, almost jogging along an easy paved stretch of the Pennine Way and then cursing as the slabs of stone abruptly switched to wet peat and rocky obstacles. Having found no litter and only two sets of fresh footprints, which probably belonged to the couple who'd discovered the body, she and Nelson hadn't needed to stop for long.

On the ridge of the hill, the wind was whipping the vegetation into submission, the slender stems of cottongrass bowed horizontal by the onslaught. Sanne pulled on the woolly hat she knew made her look ridiculous, and watched the final arc of the sun sink below the horizon. She heard the rasp of Nelson's breath as he caught up with her, and she let him tug her hat straight. The sun had snatched down the scant warmth of day, making him shiver and scan the barren moors as if for some kind of refuge.

"Our garden faces west," he said at length, now staring ahead. "Did I tell you I'd put a little pond in at the bottom?"

"Yes," Sanne said, unsure where he was going with this but wary of his tone. "You also confessed to pinching frogspawn from the park."

"Ah, so I did. Well, Nemy is obsessed with sitting there to watch the sun go down. She says it sets the water on fire."

"That's very poetic for a ten-year-old."

His smile was faint, almost an afterthought. "She reads a lot. She has more books than space on her shelves."

"Good for her." Sanne had been the same growing up, and her mum had always found the money for books, even if they were dog-eared second-hand ones from the charity shops. Being sent to her room had never worked as a punishment, as it was merely quiet time away from Keeley and Michael, where her dad couldn't belt her and she could read to her heart's content.

Nelson rubbed a hand across his face, and the troubled gesture jerked her back to the present.

"What the hell was she doing out here, San?" he said. "Hardly any clothes on, and no shoes. She was such a tiny mite, barely bigger than Nemy. How bad must things have been for her that running alone into *this* was the better option?"

"I don't know. Pretty damn awful, at a guess." Sanne could have kicked herself for not being more mindful of his reaction. Since setting off, she had devoted all her attention to their destination, leaving him to follow in her footsteps. Without needing to concentrate on the route, he had evidently been dwelling on the case. She touched his arm and felt the tension stiffening his body. Neither of them was stupid or naive enough to have overlooked the potential significance of the victim's missing clothing.

"Are you going to be all right to work this one?" she asked.

"I'll be fine."

He caught her eye as he answered, and her nod effectively drew a line under the conversation. Returning to practicalities, she indicated a dull grey strip on the opposite hillside, so obviously engineered that it stood prominent even in the failing light. "See that? That's Old Road."

Using the head torches to illuminate the steep descent, they picked their way down the hill and crossed Smithy River at the only bridge. Nelson eyed the remaining steep embankment in the manner of a knackered hero compelled to go mano a mano with the villain of the piece.

"Who put that there?" he asked in a passable imitation of a teenager's whine.

"Wicked, isn't it?" Sanne tried not to sound too cheerful. Her knees and hips far preferred going up to along or down. "Five minutes, mate, and it'll be all over. I promise."

It was rush hour, according to her watch, but no traffic had passed while they'd had the road in sight, and on reaching it, she felt safe enough to stand in its centre and gather her bearings. Facing back toward the river, she pointed west.

"The road starts just after Hawdale village, four or five miles from the end of the motorway. There's a couple of farms thattaway, and a sailing club at Smithy Reservoir. I think there might be another farm somewhere farther east, but nothing else until the road reconnects to the Snake."

"No crash barriers or fencing on this stretch," Nelson said. "I wonder how far it's open for."

"I'm not sure. The council have really let the maintenance slide. Given our vic's location, I think it'd be sensible to focus on this immediate area, for now at least." Sanne corrected the angle of her torch and stopped on the verge of teetering into a pothole. "It'd be easier if we could say she definitely used the bridge, but the river's shallow enough to ford in several places, and her chances of finding the Pennine Way were slim to none if she was running around in the dark."

Nelson paced a few steps, his light picking out a crumbling stone wall and forcing a bleat from a startled sheep. "How about we split and try walking twenty minutes in opposite directions?" he suggested. "Factoring in time for a cursory search, we should be able to cover a good half-mile."

"Sounds like a plan." Sanne glanced at her mobile. "I've got bugger-all signal. Call me on the radio if you find anything."

"Or if I trip over my own feet and wind up in a bog?" He didn't sound at all fazed by the prospect. He put his torch beneath his chin and stuck his tongue out. "I'm going to scare the pants off the locals, aren't I?"

"I hope not. Most of the farmers carry shotguns."

"Bloody hell." He instantly lowered his light. "Please come quick if you hear a bang."

"I'm sure you'll be fine. Just try not to creep up on any more sheep."

He gave a cub's honour salute. "East or west? Do you have a preference?"

"East? I think it climbs a bit in this direction, and I know your poor legs are tired."

"Thank you kindly," he said, not rising to the bait. "I make it ten past five. Shall we stop and turn back at half-past?"

"Yep." Suddenly unsure whether Eleanor would approve of their going-solo strategy, Sanne decided to put some sort of safety measure in place. "Buzz me after ten?"

"Will do."

Her worries assuaged, she started out, the crunch of Nelson's footsteps muted almost at once by the wind and by the road's curve. Moving her head slowly from side to side, she used her torch to scan the road and its verges but saw little except rough vegetation, more potholes, and the occasional sheep. The clear sky threatened an early frost, but she didn't feel cold, just an edgy excitement that combined nerves and anticipation into one jittery package. When her radio vibrated, it sent her pulse rocketing.

"Checking in as requested," Nelson said. "Are you having more luck than I am?"

"Nope." She kept walking, hoping to burn off the excess adrenaline by tackling the incline in front of her. "I'm probably having less."

"Great. See you in a bit."

She settled the radio on her belt and dug in for the climb, reaching the top without breaking a sweat. She stopped there to gauge the next stretch of road, which continued level for two hundred yards before hurtling around a hairpin bend. It was the sort of corner that killed bikers on the Snake: a fast approach into a sharp turn that was easy to misjudge. She'd had her fair share of near misses in the years she'd owned her cottage, most of them on her way home from fourteen-hour shifts.

The rumble of an approaching vehicle forced her off the road and into a thicket of grass and bracken. Keen to avoid being delayed by questions, she extinguished her torch and ducked low, scribbling down the number plate of the Range Rover as it passed. Its driver tore around the corner with a scant touch of the brakes, his confidence suggesting he was local to the area. By the time Sanne reached the bend, his rear lights were a pinprick in the distance, and they disappeared when he turned onto a side road without indicating. She recorded the road's approximate location and tucked her notebook back into her pocket.

With five minutes still to go, she adopted a more cautious position, sticking close to the soft verge on the left so as not to get minced by another speeding four-by-four. A sturdy crash barrier protected the opposite side, to prevent drivers from careering toward the river should they skid. Her attention was so focused on the road that she didn't see the carcass until she slipped in it.

"Shit!"

Her left foot slid out at an angle, and she dropped to her other knee to avoid falling onto her arse. Congealed blood and loops of bowel were gathered around her boot. She stared at the gore, unable to fathom its origin for the time it took her brain to kick into gear.

"Fucking hell," she whispered, quickly identifying fleece and hooves and a curved horn. "It's just a fucking sheep."

She pushed upright again and followed a faint smear that terminated six inches shy of the road's dividing line. Two distinct skid marks started twenty yards before the smear, the sharp braking consistent with a driver whipping around the corner and only seeing the hazard once it was too late to swerve.

Having carefully tracked to the end of the blackened lines, Sanne listened for traffic and then crouched on the tarmac. Orange, white, and blackened glass glittered in her torchlight, while several other fragments of debris, including the remains of the sheep, appeared to have been swept or dragged onto the verge. A metal screw rolled out from beneath her finger when she lifted a large section of silver plastic. Both looked as if they'd come from the vehicle's bumper, which would have been completely wrecked by such an impact, but she couldn't find the rest of it.

"Why would you only take half of it with you?" she murmured, her curiosity piqued. She could understand the driver clearing the road for the sake of other motorists or just to unblock it for themselves, but making the effort to remove a random piece, irreparable and covered in sheep splatter, seemed less logical. She walked along the verge again, pushing the bracken aside with her boots to ensure she wasn't mistaken. Then she keyed Nelson's code into her radio.

"Hey," she said to his weary greeting. "I might have something here." As she spoke, an incongruous splash of colour caught her eye. She released the talk button and wrestled a glove onto one hand. The sheep's entrails slithered apart when she delved into them, allowing her a tenuous hold on the yellow shard of plastic embedded in a soft sliver of organ. She swiped away a blood clot to reveal a "B" and a single straight line at the beginning of the number plate's second letter. Excitement banished her uncertainty, and she buzzed Nelson again. "I think I know where and how our vic escaped," she said.

❖

In the time it took Nelson to reach Sanne's location, she had formulated a convincing sequence of events and taken the plunge by requesting assistance from SOCO.

"Hmm." Nelson had stooped to examine the glass, and he drew the sound out, piling on the agony as she waited for his verdict. He walked back toward her, giving the crash site a wide berth. "How long did SOCO say they'd be?"

She felt a smile twitch at the corner of her lips. While she didn't need his validation, she always preferred to have it.

"At least an hour. They're still in the process of removing the vic, but Ted's getting someone to us ASAP."

Nelson displayed a cube of glass on the palm of his gloved hand. "Tinted rear window?" He passed it to her, and she turned it in her fingers. Unlike the jagged, random chunks of headlight and indicator glass, it bore the familiar square shape of shattered safety glass, the type often found in the clothing and hair of people involved in side-impact collisions.

"For argument's sake, let's assume the driver's a bloke," she said. "He stops to clear up the mess, collecting anything that might ID his car. Meanwhile the vic snatches the opportunity to break a window and run."

Nelson picked up the thread. "She heads downhill, toward the river. She might've seen the farms they'd passed, or perhaps it's just instinct to run down and not up."

Sanne spun around, picturing the child, unsteady and panicked, barefoot and already freezing as she tried to outrun her captor. "He must've heard the window smash and been right behind her." She swallowed and cleared her throat. Imagining such terror had made her voice catch. "So she crossed the river and went back up onto the moors, where it's easier to hide. If it was dark, that would've helped her to slip out of sight."

"He'd already hurt her by then," Nelson said quietly.

Sanne nodded. She couldn't think of any other reason for the girl to be missing half her clothing. "Most likely. Enough that she was desperate to get away from him. Maybe he was taking her to Sheffield, or maybe he'd just planned to kill her and dump her body out here."

Nelson kicked at the edge of the nearest pothole. "He left her out here anyway."

"Yeah," Sanne said, gazing across the vast black expanse of moorland. "But if he'd had his way, no one would ever have found her."

Chapter Four

M eg stood by the nurses' station, watching a porter steer Anca Miklos's bed toward the main corridor. Two steps behind, Anca's husband paused to look at Meg, his lips curling back like a dog's just before it goes for the throat. The translator had left over an hour ago, her attempts to gain an honest history stonewalled by Anca's refusal to deviate from the original story: she was clumsy, she had lost her grip on a pan of hot water, it was her fault. A specialist had admitted her onto the Burns Unit, and her husband—sweet and attentive at all times—had successfully petitioned Donovan for permission to return to her bedside.

A file thudded onto the desk in front of Meg, spilling its contents and making her jump. She hadn't heard Donovan approach.

"Why haven't you discharged Six yet?" he demanded, his pinched cheeks mottled white with anger. He never really had a colour to him, being either pallid or moribund, dependent on his mood, and right now Meg had seen corpses with healthier complexions. He shoved the file closer. "He's going to breach."

"He's intoxicated with a head injury, and he's vomiting." She spoke slowly, as if explaining something tricky to an impatient infant. "CT are backed up after a technical hitch, or I'd have flirted him to the ward for observation. I can't do that if there's a chance he's chucking off a subdural."

"He might've made it to CT had you not wasted half your shift interfering in your F2's case."

She clasped her hands together and clamped her jaw shut, which stopped her from smacking him in the mouth or suggesting precisely where he could stick his breach targets. She counted to three and then picked up the phone. "I'll chase CT and see if they can hurry things along."

He nodded, oblivious to how close he'd come to losing his front teeth. "The patient in Two needs a bladder washout before he goes over to Urology. Get a nurse to do it while you finish his chart, and book an ambulance on an eight-minute response."

She lowered the phone. "A washout will take longer than eight minutes."

"So we hold the crew until the patient's ready for transfer." Donovan's smirk made him even more cadaver-esque. "It's *our* targets I'm concerned about, not theirs."

"Right." She didn't have the energy to argue. At least the crew would be able to get a brew and put their feet up when they arrived to collect their "immediately life-threatening" enlarged prostate. Once Donovan had stalked out of earshot, she smacked her forehead with the phone.

"Ouch," Liz said, walking over. She gently peeled Meg's fingers loose and exchanged the receiver for a sandwich. "Here, eat this before you do anything else."

"I have to call CT," Meg said. The sudden switch from Donovan's bollocking to Liz's simple kindness made her want to lay her head on her arms and sniffle for a bit.

"The scanner's still buggered, and Clara's already doing the washout," Liz said. "You, meanwhile, are twelve hours into a fourteen-hour shift, and I know you've not had a break, so eat your damn butty."

Meg peeled back the plastic wrapper and took an obedient bite from the sandwich. Claggy white bread, limp lettuce, and rock-solid tomato, along with a salty layer that might have been ham, combined to taste like shit and stick to her palate. She devoured the first half in four huge mouthfuls.

"Better?" Liz asked.

"Craptastic."

"Only the NHS's finest freebies for you, Dr. Fielding." Liz's smile grew fainter the longer she looked at Meg. "You can't help someone who doesn't want to be helped, hon. You know that as well as I do."

"I know." Meg didn't state the obvious, that Anca Miklos would probably be too terrified or too brainwashed to seek the help she needed.

"How about you finish your butty and I'll book the ambulance?"

"Cheers, Liz." Meg picked up the remaining half. "I might take this outside, get a bit of fresh air."

"Hmm. You mean you're going to feed your crusts to the sparrows."

Meg kissed Liz's cheek. "It'll be nesting season soon, and spadgers are hungry little blighters. I'll be back in five. If Donovan comes snooping, tell him I've gone to kick arse at CT."

She took a roundabout route to the ambulance bay, where she arranged her crusts on top of the litter bin and pulled out her mobile phone. An absence of messages from Sanne probably meant she was on a new case, so Meg left her in peace and selected another name from the directory. A familiar voice answered within three rings.

"Detective Fraser, Domestic Violence."

Meg leaned against the metal grille of the oxygen store. It had only been a few days since she'd spoken to Fraser, and his assured manner always calmed her nerves.

"Hiya. It's Meg Fielding. Am I interrupting anything?"

"No, not at all. Are you okay?"

"Oh, I'm fine. I'm not calling about the case." She twisted her fingers around the thin metal behind her. "I was wondering if you could give me some advice about a patient, only there are images in her file, so it might be easier to discuss things in person."

"Are you on shift now?"

"Yes, till nine."

A knocking sound came over the line, as if Fraser was tapping his pen on a notepad. "Is this off the record, Meg?"

"Yes."

If he was perturbed by that, he hid it well. "Okay. Will Den's at nine thirty suit you?"

She chuckled. The diner was a complete shithole, but it did the best twenty-four-hour breakfast in Sheffield. "Only if I can treat you to the greasy spoon special."

The tapping stopped abruptly. "You got yourself a deal."

❖

At the end of the darkened EDSOP corridor, light was blazing through the window of Eleanor's office like a beacon. Sanne and

Nelson both raised their hands to knock on the door, until she stepped back and let him do the honours.

"Come in," Eleanor called. She sounded hoarse, as if every hour since she'd left the moor had been spent fielding phone calls. Given the nature of the case, the top brass would be keeping a close eye on the investigation, and with the time now ticking on for eight p.m., they would have had plenty of opportunity to offer their two penn'orth.

Sanne's ears pricked up at the sound of a boiling kettle, and as the door opened, she was greeted by the glorious sight of three mugs and a packet of biscuits. The scent of HobNobs made her mouth water. She'd hiked a good few miles that afternoon, and she couldn't remember the last thing she'd eaten.

"What the hell have you been paddling in?" Eleanor asked. She passed Sanne the first mug, arching an eyebrow as she caught a whiff of the thick matter coating Sanne's trouser hem.

"Dead sheep, boss." Sanne threw Nelson a dirty look. She'd changed her boots in the car park while he'd danced around and reminded her how cold he was, after which he'd persuaded her that no one would notice the muck on her trousers. Too busy warming his hands on his cup to feign sincerity, he shrugged in half-arsed apology and helped himself to a biscuit.

"Of course, how could I forget?" Eleanor leaned back in her chair. "What was the verdict from SOCO?"

"They concurred," Nelson said, picking crumbs from his knees and dropping them in the bin. "In all probability a vehicle hit the sheep and was forced to a stop. The broken glass on scene indicated two distinct areas of damage, which is inconsistent with a single head-on collision. Although most of the debris had been thrown aside or redistributed by subsequent traffic, the tech found ground-in fragments of tinted glass farther back from the point of impact, suggesting a rear window had been smashed. It also suggests that the car was travelling in the direction of Sheffield." He paused to sip his tea, allowing Sanne to conclude their summary.

"SOCO found no trace of the vic or the potential perp, but we'll need a fingertip search of the immediate area come daylight. They're optimistic they'll be able to get a make and model of the vehicle, and we have a tiny partial of the number plate."

"That's better than nothing," Eleanor said. "Even if you did have to dig it out of some poor creature's liver."

Sanne winced in remembrance. "Yeah, it's been a day of new experiences." She placed her HobNob on the table, her appetite waning. "SOCO removed the body just before we left. There was no obvious cause of death, but there were indicators of sexual assault. She looked about twelve, maybe thirteen."

Eleanor pushed her glasses up and rubbed the bridge of her nose. "I'll be observing the PM first thing in the morning, so I'll know more for the briefing. Full team at seven. Prepare a quick overview for presentation, and we'll sort the rest out from there. You can add the extra hours to your time owing. The brass has given me free rein with the budget for this one, for now at least." She tossed the biscuits to Sanne, who caught them neatly. "Here. I'll put these on the tab."

"Cheers, boss." Sanne stood, considering that a dismissal.

Eleanor dropped her glasses back into place as her phone began to ring. She raised a hand in farewell and reached for the receiver.

Meg peeled off her scrubs top with a sigh of relief. A last-minute cardiac arrest had pulled her into Resus in Donovan's stead, and she'd been forced to spend half an hour jumping up and down on the chest of a sixty-eight-year-old. Given that the alternative was having Donovan hang around to see out the end of her shift, though, she'd take the chest compressions any day.

Removing her clothes made her acutely aware of how bad she smelled. She dropped the thin cotton outfit into a linen skip and ran the locker room shower hot enough to cloud the mirror, so that she didn't have to see what multiple cycles of CPR had done to her hair.

Stepping beneath the spray and feeling it pepper her back with blissful needles of water, she closed her eyes and let hours of stress drain down the plughole. It wasn't as if today had been any different from the countless other shifts she'd worked. A&E departments across the country had been overstretched for years, as too many people used them for non-urgent complaints, and increasing longevity meant a rise in chronic and degenerative conditions. Add to that a high local rate of alcoholism, drug addiction, mental health crises, and young incapable parents, and it created the perfect storm twenty-four hours a day, seven days a week. Fortunately, Meg was a strong swimmer who rarely took her work home with her, even if the occasional case did sneak beneath her radar.

Mindful of her meeting with Fraser, she kept her shower far briefer than she would have liked, stepping out into a bathroom so chilly it made her hop on its slippery tiles. Her regular off-duty outfit of combats and a hooded top, selected only with driving home in mind, had spent fourteen hours screwed up in her locker. In deference to Fraser, she shook out their creases before throwing them on. Finally feeling warmer, she wiped the mirror and grinned at the state of her hair. It was short, shorter than it had been for the duration of her ill-fated, six-month relationship with Emily Woodall—F1 doctor, and lover of designer clothing, meat-free food, and not swearing—and all it took to create some semblance of a style was for her to run her fingers through it. In contrast to Emily's penchant for hair that needed pinning and clipping and buggering about with, Sanne had enthusiastically endorsed Meg's hassle-free style, and she had a real knack for taming the most rebellious bit. Meg grabbed her bag and coat, mentally adding "Hair Whispering" to her reasons for loving Sanne. "Good Sense of Humour" and "Shared Interests" were so passé these days.

Ideally placed for Sheffield Royal's multitude of shift workers, Den's Diner was a five-minute walk away, which left Meg just enough time to make a detour to the Burns Unit. She used her ID card to let herself in and followed the corridor to the nurses' desk.

"Hiya," she said to a bored-looking staff nurse. "I treated Anca Miklos in A&E and wondered how she was getting on."

The nurse selected a chocolate from the box in front of her. A collection of discarded wrappers implied this hadn't been the busiest of shifts. "She'll probably need skin grafts," she said. She bit into the chocolate and sucked out the filling. "Try explaining that to someone who doesn't speak a word of the Queen's. A translator was in with her for a while, so that's another three hundred quid of the NHS's budget down the Swanee."

"Aye." Meg was too tired to enter into a debate on the subject. "Is her husband still here?"

"No, he left at the end of visiting hours. She's in Side Ward Three, but she was asleep the last time I checked."

"I'll just pop my head round the door," Meg said. "I won't disturb her if she's out for the count."

The nurse was already rummaging for her next chocolate. "Yeah, that's fine."

The risk of infection meant that most patients on the Burns Unit were given their own rooms. Meg saw the flicker of televisions behind the blinds of those she passed, but Side Ward Three was in darkness. She tapped on the glass and pushed the door open a crack.

"Anca?"

The light from an IV showed that Anca was lying on her side, facing the door. She wasn't asleep, and she stiffened in response to Meg's voice. The device for self-administered pain relief sat beyond her reach, its syringe driver still full of morphine. It was a stupid thing to have given to someone with damaged hands, and as Meg approached the bedside she could see sweat beading on Anca's brow. The translator had probably left prior to the medication being prescribed, and the nurse clearly had better things to do than explain how the pump worked or suggest a more appropriate alternative.

"Here, like this. See?" Meg clicked the button. Operating the pump didn't require much pressure, and she hoped that a steady dose of morphine might dull the pain enough for Anca to be able to use it. Within seconds, the lines of discomfort disappeared from Anca's face, and she curled her left hand around the button. Meg tapped the timer on the pump.

"At zero," she said. She clenched her fist to indicate the number and mimed pressing the pump. "Yes?"

Anca nodded once. "Zero," she repeated.

"That's it. Good girl." There was more that Meg wanted to tell her, about shelters and helplines and the support network that existed for victims of domestic abuse, but Anca's eyes were already beginning to droop as the morphine took effect.

"Thank you," she whispered.

Meg smiled, even though she felt like crying. "You're welcome," she said.

❖

Caught in the lull between pre-pub customers and kicking-out time, Den's was mostly empty. The man himself brought Meg's order to the table, his trademark sweat-stained bandana a testament to the heat wafting from the kitchen.

"Hey, Doc." He smiled at Meg and nodded at Fraser. "Does Sanney know you're moonlighting with this fella?"

"Nope. San-*ner*"—Meg emphasised the correct pronunciation, even though she knew Den would never get it right—"has absolutely no idea." She bit the end from a rasher of crispy bacon and crunched it loudly.

Den laid a hand over his heart. "I don't know what she sees in you when she could have me." He set down the bottles of ketchup and HP sauce. "If you want more toast, give me a yell."

He returned to the kitchen, shutting the door and cutting off a blast of sixties music. Meg swapped the bacon for her glass of water, taking a couple of sips to rinse away the grease.

"Thanks for coming," she said to Fraser. "I didn't drag you away from anything vital, did I?"

Fraser was tucking in with gusto, and he wiped egg yolk from his lips before answering. "Nothing that can't wait, and you gave me a good excuse to call it a night. How've you been?"

"Not too shabby." She kept hold of her glass, resisting the urge to touch her face. Sanne wasn't the only one to bear scars from the winter months; the thin line marring Meg's cheek was still raised and pink around the edges. Her colleagues believed she had slipped on the ice, unaware that her brother Luke had punched her and then fractured her ribs by smashing her back into the kitchen sink. He was still in custody, pending trial, and Fraser—the investigating officer—had kept in regular contact with Meg to update her on the case.

She wiped her damp fingers on her trousers. Even after six weeks, remembering the hours she had spent bleeding and vomiting on her kitchen floor was enough to bring her out in a cold sweat. "Work has been the usual nightmare, which helps," she said. "And Sanne steps in if I get too mopey."

"Good for her." Like most emergency service employees, Fraser ate at record speed, and he had already finished his meal. He uncapped his pen and dabbed its nib on his tongue, the ink adding another spot to the day's tattoo. "So, this patient of yours…"

"Anca Miklos," she said, glad to change the subject. She spelled the name for him. "A twenty-four-year-old Romanian lady with burns to both hands, who was brought to the hospital by her husband. Both say the injuries were caused by her dropping a pan, but the pattern of the burns says that's a load of crap, and she was obviously terrified of him."

"Was she spoken to separately?"

"Yes, via a translator."

"And she supported his version of events?"

"Almost verbatim."

Fraser stirred a second sugar into his coffee. "Then that's a problem, Meg. I could arrange to have a word with her, but unless she changes her tune, the Crown Prosecution Service will never go for it."

"I thought as much." The admission left Meg deflated, as if she hadn't accepted defeat until that moment. "I don't even know why it's bugging me. It's not like we don't see it all the time."

"Maybe it's a bit close to home right now."

She had already considered that, and she easily conceded the point. "Aye, maybe. Would you try speaking to her anyway, just in case? She's on the Burns Unit, which has set visiting hours, so it'd be easy for you to avoid the husband."

Fraser checked the planner on his phone. "I'll call in tomorrow afternoon. Did you get his name?"

"Cezar." She gave him a scrap of paper with the details she'd gleaned from the computer. "That's everything I have."

"Thanks. It'll be enough to run him through the Police National Computer to check for any priors." Fraser folded the paper and capped his pen. "You look like you've had a long day."

"It's been a bit of a battle." Meg could barely sit up straight, and a yawn had just caught her unawares. "I really appreciate your help."

"My pleasure. It's just that I don't think I'm going to get very far. I'll call you tomorrow when I'm done, though."

"Great." She took out more than enough cash to cover the bill and passed Fraser her barely touched plate.

"As a doctor, shouldn't you be advocating a healthy diet?" he asked, taking up his cutlery again.

"Absolutely." She handed him the HP sauce. "But I won't tell if you don't."

❖

As much as Meg appreciated clean sheets and the hot-water bottle placed in readiness on her side of the bed, it was the sight of Sanne, fast asleep with a book resting on her nose, that finally made her forget about her shift. Kneeling on the bed, she leaned over to kiss Sanne's forehead and lift the book clear.

"I'm reading that," Sanne murmured. She sounded quite indignant for someone with drool on her chin.

"Yep, that's why it's stuck to you." Meg turned the lamp off and huddled under the quilt. Sanne didn't believe in going to bed with the central heating on, and her cottage could drop from tolerable to freezing in a heartbeat.

"I wasn't sure if you'd come." Still half asleep, Sanne threw one arm and one leg over Meg and rested her head on Meg's chest. She guided Meg's hand beneath her T-shirt. "Bloody hell, your fingers are like ice pops."

"It's nippy out there." Meg rocked her head back onto the pillow as Sanne's far warmer hand cupped her breast.

"Apparently so," Sanne said, and then chortled drunkenly at her own joke.

"I thought you were tired."

"I am." The answer was laden with regret. "And I have a briefing at stupid o'clock."

"New case?"

"Yeah. A bad one, up at Greave Stones."

Meg nestled her cheek against the top of Sanne's head, breathing in the familiar scent of own-brand shampoo. "Shh. Tell me tomorrow. Go back to sleep."

She heard Sanne snuffle in agreement, her breathing becoming deeper and slower. Then Sanne's eyes opened a crack.

"There's bread out for your lunch if you need it."

"Sanne…"

"And Ron gave me some eggs, so don't have jam butties again."

"Sanne!" Meg flicked her ear. "Sleep!"

Sanne nodded in apparent accord. Two minutes later, she was snoring.

Chapter Five

Eleanor couldn't count the number of post mortems she'd attended. In her junior detective years, she'd volunteered for the duty, not to curry favour with her seniors but because she'd found the process fascinating and because incontrovertible science had been far easier to deal with than duplicitous suspects and idiotic witnesses. Although the people part of her job had long since become second nature, she'd had no qualms about encouraging her daughter to study for a degree in forensic science.

Today's pathologist—known to everyone simply as Bedford— lifted the stomach clear and cut through it. Keen to learn the contents, Eleanor drew closer to the table. Her mask clung to her face with every inhalation, doing little to temper the smell of gut gases or the blood that was pooling around the small corpse.

"Not much in here." Bedford prised the bisected stomach apart as he spoke. "Small amount of water, no solids. Consistent with her malnourished state. She's underweight for her estimated age, and her teeth, hair, and skin are in poor condition. We took bloods last night, and the early results showed multiple vitamin deficiencies, low calcium, anaemia, and the presence of infection."

"Is the tox back yet?" Eleanor asked.

He set the stomach on the scales. "The basic screen was clear for all the usual suspects—opiates, common sedatives, alcohol. The remainder are still being processed."

"He would hardly have needed to use them, would he?"

The question was rhetorical, and Bedford ventured no response.

For an adult male perp, this child would have been easy prey, and the lack of ligature marks had already been noted during the rape kit.

"Do you ever get tired of it?" he asked quietly.

Eleanor raised her head in surprise. She had worked with him on numerous cases and couldn't ever recall a discussion beyond the body on the table. She waited as he stopped the tape recorder and peeled off his gloves.

"Yes," she said. It was six a.m., and she'd just watched the dissection of a child whom no one seemed to be missing. "Yes, I do. Sometimes I wish I didn't know what I know about people."

"I never tell my husband anything," Bedford said. "He works for a local charity, so we just talk about jumble sales and fun runs and kids who lose their legs but raise thousands of pounds."

Eleanor appreciated the need to separate work and home life. It was one of many reasons she was glad not to have married into the job. "Doug's a mechanic," she said. "I could probably recondition the engine on an MG if I was pushed. He's usually asleep in front of Sky Sports by the time I get home, but he'll always have cooked my tea for me."

"Sounds like a good bloke."

"He is," she said with genuine fondness. She watched Bedford replace his gloves and restart the tape.

"Removing the spleen," he said.

❖

Steam billowed from the shower when Sanne opened the bathroom door. Concealed behind the clouded screen, Meg continued to sing whatever tune she'd decided to massacre that morning.

"Oi! Are you paying my water bill?" Sanne shouted above the rumble of the boiler and the rowdy chorus.

A hand wiped at the glass, and Meg peered through the gap. "Wasn't planning to, no!" she yelled back. "And this relationship is far too young and fickle for us to be getting a joint account."

"Balls to that, sunshine!" Sanne said, squirting toothpaste onto her brush. "You have even less money than me."

Despite Meg's higher salary, once the cost of her mortgage, her mum's care home fees, her student loans and household expenditure disappeared from her wage, she had as little disposable income as Sanne, but long, scalding showers were something she refused to skimp on, which might explain why she rarely had the funds to buy new clothes.

"Are you on an early again?" Crouched on the toilet seat, Sanne began brushing her teeth. "I can never remember your shift pattern."

"That's because I don't really have one." Meg caught the towel Sanne threw to her. "Ta. Donovan keeps buggering me about. I suspect it's how he gets his jollies. Long day yesterday, early today, night tomorrow. At least, that's what I think I'm on. I usually just turn up and see whether I'm expected."

Sanne got up and spat into the sink. She leaned back as Meg came to stand behind her. Meg had dropped the towel, and her hot skin dampened Sanne's shirt.

"You need a diary," Sanne said, trying to focus on the discussion at hand.

"I'd only lose it, and then someone would know all my secrets."

"'Dear diary…'" Sanne looked in the mirror, watching Meg kiss the soft skin beneath her ear. "'Today I made Sanne late for work again.'"

"You're never late." Meg nipped at Sanne's earlobe, her fingers busy with the shirt buttons. "You're far too principled."

"Unlike you."

"Well, yeah." She dropped out of view, and seconds later, the play of her tongue across Sanne's midriff made Sanne's knees wobble.

"Shit." Grabbing the sink with one hand, Sanne used her other to halt Meg's progress. "Not on your nelly. You know what happened last time."

"What, when you lost your balance and slipped onto your arse?"

"Yes, well remembered." She tugged Meg up and steered her into the bedroom. At some point, Sanne's trousers had been unfastened, so she let them drop and stepped out of them en route.

"Christ." Meg gulped as Sanne—now clad only in a gaping shirt, bra, and knickers—turned to face her. "That's a good look on you."

"I don't think I'd get away with it at the office."

"Their loss." Meg clambered onto the bed, lay flat on her back, and beckoned Sanne closer. "Lose the kecks before you get up here. Leave the rest on."

Unable to argue with that kind of instruction, Sanne did as she was told, allowing Meg to guide her into place and gripping the headboard at the first touch of Meg's tongue.

"Jesus Christ," she whispered. Her head fell forward, thudding into the wall.

"No, he definitely had more principles than me," Meg murmured. "Now be a love and don't break my nose."

Sanne nodded convulsively. "I'll try."

"That's all I ask."

Meg kissed the inside of Sanne's thigh, nudging it wider before pushing up deeply inside her. Sanne's mouth fell open, her chest heaving as she tried not to hyperventilate. Meg swapped her tongue for two fingers and sent Sanne's head into the plaster again. Sanne groaned as Meg established a hard, smooth rhythm, her tongue joining her fingers, until Sanne didn't have a clue what was where, only that she wasn't going to last for long. Somewhere in the garden, Git Face crowed as if to protest the debauchery, and Sanne came with enough force to rattle the headboard.

"Aw, fuck." She could barely hold herself in position, and she felt Meg steadying her. Still shuddering, she peeked down. "Fuck. Did I break anything?"

"Possibly a land-speed record, but other than that, no."

"Oh. Good." She shook her head, waiting for coherence to return. She shuffled backward and sagged into Meg's arms like a sack of spuds.

"We shouldn't do this in the morning." Meg stroked Sanne's sweaty hair away from her forehead. "The rest of my day is doomed to pale in comparison."

Sanne tipped Meg's chin. "Morning is perfect for this," she said. "Now, where do you want me?"

❖

The thump of Sanne's bag on the desk brought Nelson's head up from his paperwork.

"Traffic bad?" he asked, watching her rummage through files and knock things over.

"No, it was fine." She found the right folder but not the memory stick that went with it. Her chest felt tight and panicky. She wasn't late, but she had a pre-presentation routine she liked to keep to, and running in with her shirt all to cock and her bullet points missing wasn't part of it. "Where's the stuff from last night?"

"Here." He waved the stick at her. "Did you oversleep?"

"No."

That wasn't quite a fib. She'd gone *back* to sleep, true, but she hadn't overslept in the strictest sense. When she dared to look at Nelson, he was laughing softly.

"It's not what you're thinking," she said. "Okay, well, yes, it probably is—"

"San..."

She put a hand to her burning cheek. "What?"

"Take your joy where you can find it, that's what my granny always used to say." He passed her the memory stick. "And I don't think we're going to get much joy in here today."

"No, I doubt we are."

The mood in the EDSOP office was unusually sober, with heads down and conversation muted. In the corner, Fred's kick to the photocopier was a half-hearted effort at best.

"The boss got in from the PM about twenty minutes ago, with Litton right behind her," Nelson said. "She's not been seen since, but we're assuming the briefing's going ahead."

Sanne nodded, her attention fixed on her computer screen. With the right file opened and apparently intact, she breathed easier. "Shall I give the location overview while you focus on the evidence?" she asked, aware that his sense of direction was next to nonexistent.

"Yeah, highlight that section for me so I can go through it."

They worked quietly until Litton departed, with an underling scurrying behind him, and Eleanor went into the briefing room. An EDSOP-only briefing meant no need to rush for seats, but the team was gathered around the tables, pens readied above notepads, with plenty of time to spare.

No one reacted overtly when Eleanor dimmed the lights and filled the overhead screen with photographs of the girl's body, but the air in the room seemed to still. Out on the moors, most of the corpse had been obscured by shadows and rocks, enabling Sanne to view it with a degree of equanimity. By contrast, the stark lighting of the morgue accentuated every detail in the photos. Blood had pooled on the right side of the girl's face, giving it the look of a Halloween mask, unmarred on one half and grotesque on the other. Exposed for the examination, her body appeared even more fragile, her skinny limbs and prominent ribs and hips emphasizing how underweight she was.

Sanne noted her observations down, printing them in a careful hand until she could focus on the photographs without fear of losing her breakfast. In the next chair, Nelson was employing a similar tactic, though his complexion, usually a healthy dark glow, had noticeably paled.

"Everyone should be familiar with the circumstances surrounding the discovery of this body yesterday," Eleanor said, forgoing opening pleasantries. "Bedford has estimated her age at between twelve and fifteen years. Her size and the ambient temperature have played hell with pinpointing the time of death, but taking into account the recent overnight frosts and the unreliability of rigor in a child, he's given us a window of twenty-four to thirty-six hours, around February the twenty-first and twenty-second, which at least narrows things down somewhat. Lividity was fixed to the right of the body, confirming that it wasn't moved post mortem." Abandoning her traditional briefing spot—front and slightly off-centre—she perched on a desk closer to her team. She switched to a photograph of the child's lower legs and tattered feet. "Other than a small laceration on her right wrist, these were her only external injuries, most likely a result of running across the moors, but the rape kit was positive, and she'd suffered significant internal injuries, not all of them recent." She paused to let that sink in.

Mike Hallet cleared his throat. "What was the cause of death?"

"Primarily hypothermia, but Bedford has also recorded hypovolaemia, anaemia, and possible sepsis as contributory factors."

"So some arsewipe of a defence lawyer will be able to bargain this down to rape and manslaughter?" Fred asked.

"Yes, in all likelihood, but we'll worry about that later. For now, we have an unidentified minor with nothing found during the PM to change that." Eleanor brought up an image of a purple tunic and a plaited woollen bracelet. "These were the only items she was wearing, and beyond saying that she's Pakistani or Bengali, we can't be more specific about her ethnicity, so we'll focus the house-to-house within those communities."

She moved on to detail the area of moorland and Old Road that would be covered by fingertip searches, and then handed over to

Sanne and Nelson, whose summation of the previous night's findings passed smoothly and—possibly due to Carlyle's absence—without interruption.

"I've spoken to Greater Manchester's Traffic sector this morning," Nelson said. "Bearing in mind that this vehicle could have come from the motorway, they've agreed to examine any relevant camera footage once we have an idea of make and model."

"Greater Manchester Police are also in full cooperation regarding the wider enquiry," Eleanor added. "They'll be carrying out their own door-to-doors and getting the vic's photograph into the relevant areas. Her body may have been found in our patch, but that doesn't mean she's local to us."

Casting about the room, Sanne saw numerous eyes roll at the prospect of a multi-force investigation, and there was a general shuffling of bums and paperwork. While she didn't lack ambition, at times she was happy her role was junior, and this was certainly one of them. Trying to organise and delegate across two police forces would add an extra layer of aggravation to an already complex case.

"Initial thoughts?" Eleanor looked round at her team.

"Honour killing?" George said, glancing at the screen and scratching the whiskers on his chin. "She seems young for that, though."

"She is," Eleanor said. "Most, though not all, violence around so-called honour is committed against women in their late teens or early twenties."

"Opportunistic abduction and rape?" Jay suggested.

Sanne raised a hand. Briefings always made her feel like she was back in the classroom, but at least she spoke up without waiting for a teacher's permission. "A white perp trawling Asian neighbourhoods for a victim would probably have been noticed by someone. I'd be surprised if it hasn't been called in."

"Definitely something to check," Eleanor said, adding it to the bottom of her notes. "Given local tensions, it would be remiss not to consider a white-on-Asian revenge motive, which means that the usual idiots—English Defence, 212, the Infidels, et cetera—will need speaking to. But if we're looking at a stranger abduction, then why hasn't anyone reported our vic missing?"

"That seems to point to family involvement," Nelson said. "It may not be honour-related, but it's being covered up for some reason.

Perhaps our perp is a wayward son or husband who's been abusing his sister or daughter for a prolonged period, and things have come to a head. The family take the decision to protect one at the expense of another."

"She's school age, but that doesn't necessarily mean she's ever been to school," Sanne said, not looking up from her scribbling. One of these days she'd teach herself shorthand. "You would hope that a teacher or friend would have spotted her malnutrition, or that her behaviour or sickness record would have triggered concerns about abuse."

"They don't always see it, San," Nelson said.

"I know." As a child, Sanne had noticed the bruises that Meg regularly sported at school, though the teachers had turned a blind eye. "But they are more attuned these days to the warning signs. This child could have been a family friend shipped here for a better life. I mean, look what happened in Salford with that lass in the cellar. She was about the same age when she was brought over, and the couple who enslaved her kept her hidden for…twelve years, was it?"

"Yes, about that," Eleanor said. "We'll have to speak to border agencies at Manchester, Liverpool, and Leeds Bradford airports." She threw up her hands at the massive scope of the task. "And who the hell knows, we might as well chuck in Heathrow and Gatwick. She could've entered the country from anywhere."

Fred cut through the murmurs of disquiet. "On the bright side, boss, the Pakistanis are a pretty tight-knit bunch, and so are the Bengalis. If this lass was from one of the larger communities, someone outside the family loop might recognise her. Photos of dead kids do tend to prick the conscience."

"That's the spirit," Eleanor said. "Okay, I don't need to tell you that we have a lot of people pushing for a speedy and satisfactory resolution to this one. DCI Litton has approved my request to keep things within EDSOP, for the preliminary investigation at least. We'll be getting unis to help with the door-to-doors and the fingertips, but nothing from outside agencies unless we choose to involve them. I appreciate that most of you have ongoing cases, but this has to be everyone's absolute priority. I've got your briefing notes here with your initial assignments. So," she folded her arms and looked at each of her team in turn, "let's try not to fuck it up."

A smart rap on the door sent her across to answer it. She returned with a middle-aged Asian woman whose traditional salwar kameez, rendered in shades of turquoise and pale green, stood out like an oasis among the crowd of grey and navy suits.

"This is Meera Ahmad, our community liaison," Eleanor said. "She's here to assist with any language or cultural issues we may encounter within the Pakistani communities, and she'll be with Sanne and Nelson today, so radio them if you need to speak to her. Any problems with those who speak Bangla, you'll have to use Language Line."

Sanne caught Nelson's raised eyebrow and returned it with interest. While someone fluent in Urdu would undoubtedly be useful, given that they'd been tasked to the Sharcliffe area, having to babysit a civilian on a ride-along would be a pain in the arse. She caught Fred's shit-eating grin and mouthed "fuck off" in response. Then she fixed a smile on her face and went over to meet the civvie.

❖

Indicating left, Sanne pulled the pool car into the filter lane and braked for the lights. Heavy rain had forced the traffic to a crawl, and the driver of the bus three cars in front seemed disinclined to exceed fifteen miles an hour. Behind her, Nelson wriggled, trying to find a comfortable position for his long legs. She usually navigated while he drove, but, chivalrous to a fault, he had insisted Meera take the passenger seat and surrendered the car keys to Sanne for once. Having a third party in the car put Sanne and Nelson on their best behaviour. Their usual rock-paper-scissors battle to choose the radio station had been forsaken in favour of no music at all, neither of them had so much as sniggered when they passed a pub called "The Dandy Cock," and the conversation had erred on the side of polite "getting to know you" exchanges with Meera.

"Were you both patrol officers before EDSOP?" Meera asked. She spoke perfect English, clipped by a Pakistani accent, and had surprised Sanne by spending most of the journey chattering in Urdu on her mobile phone.

"Yes," Sanne said. "We worked North Sector, but Nelson's far older than me, so we didn't know each other back then." She lurched into the steering wheel as Nelson kicked her seat. Catching his eye in the rearview mirror, she poked her tongue out at him. "Careful. You'll put a hip out, bending like that."

Meera indulged them with a smile. "You'll know Sharcliffe quite well, then."

"We used to get up here a fair bit." Sanne inched the car forward a couple of yards, missed the green light again, and swallowed the tirade she'd been about to launch at the bus driver. She only realised how much she normally swore when she was doing her utmost not to. "The usual stuff, mostly—domestics, burglaries, car theft—but the last few years have seen an upsurge in drug offences and drug-related violence."

"The young men," Meera said. "I would always worry about bad influences on my sons. They're at university now, though. They're good boys, very bright."

Sanne accelerated and sped through the light on amber. Stuck behind the bus again, she turned to Meera. "Have you just got the two lads?"

"No, we have a daughter as well, Saeed's twin. She should be marrying in spring. It was difficult to find a husband for her. She's very fussy."

"Right." Sanne didn't know what else to say. The decision to get wed might well have been the girl's own, but Sanne was curious as to whether she'd shown any desire for a university education or resisted the notion of an arranged marriage. Propriety, however, made her bite her tongue.

Nelson broke the awkward silence. "Any news from Keeley yet, San?"

Back in familiar territory, Sanne relaxed her hold on the steering wheel. "Not yet, but she's due any day now. That's my sister," she added for Meera's benefit. "She's pregnant with her fifth. God only knows what she'll call this one." She didn't mention Keeley's sterling efforts to vary the Halshaw gene pool by procreating with a different bloke each time. Keeley's idea of commitment was producing offspring numbers two and five with the same fella.

"Do you have any children yourself?" Meera asked.

"Uh, no. I think being an aunt will be enough for me." Sanne could feel herself getting hot as she sensed Meera checking her finger for telltale rings, and she waited for the inevitable follow-up question. She loathed coming out to strangers, not because she was ashamed of being gay but because she hated making people feel uncomfortable. She had seen the shutters come down too many times during polite conversations with little old dears after they'd given witness statements, or with people at university she'd thought were friends, or with her family doctor when he'd broached the subject of birth control. For all she knew, Meera's sons were raging queers and Meera herself a fully paid-up member of FFLAG, but she doubted it.

"Sanne has enough to do growing veg and keeping her hens in line, don't you, San?" Nelson said, leaning between the seats and holding out a bag of Werther's Originals.

"Yes, I do." She took a toffee and unwrapped it. "Cheers, mate."

"Any time." He showed Meera his wallet, the leather folded back to display a small photo. "These are my two terrors. That's Nemy, she's ten, and the little one, Tia, is five."

"They're beautiful," Meera said. "They look so much like you!"

With their guest successfully distracted, Sanne sucked her sweet and concentrated on weaving through the outskirts of Sharcliffe. A maze of narrow, tightly packed terraced streets, Sharcliffe was identical to all the other dirt-poor, rundown neighbourhoods in Sheffield, except that the pound shops, Chinese chippies, and payday loan suppliers gradually gave way to supermarkets selling catering-sized sacks of onions and barrels of cooking oil, the butchers were halal, and there was scarcely a white face to be seen.

"First right, second left," Meera said, not realising Sanne had memorised the route before setting off. "I grew up around the block, on Calder Street."

"Do you still live local?" Sanne asked. Not many of Sharcliffe's young people went to college, let alone university, but Western materialism was creeping in, largely funded by drug crime.

"No, we moved to Broomhill when my father expanded his business, but I still have relatives here."

Sanne pulled into the car park of a Cash and Carry whose owners had agreed to its use as a rendezvous point. A police van was already there, and the uniformed officers beside it were drawing curious glances from passersby. One of the officers, standing blond head and shoulders above her colleagues, waved as she saw Sanne parking the car.

"There goes the neighbourhood," Nelson murmured, in a voice low enough that Meera didn't hear him.

Sanne waited until he got out of the car on her side. "I forgot to tell you, Zoe texted me this morning and asked me to wear something gorgeous."

Nelson considered her attire. "That shirt *is* a very fetching blue."

"Why, thank you," she said, though she vaguely recalled her original choice being quite different. "I'm officially off her hook, at any rate. She's dating a bloke from Tactical Aid, and she sounds totally smitten. They go to boot camp classes together."

"Really? How sweet."

Zoe Turner had set her sights on Sanne around the same time that Luke Fielding had beaten the living daylights out of Meg, throwing the proverbial spanner into a situation that hadn't needed additional complications. Bearing an uncanny resemblance to something out of Norse legend and with a personality to match, she had eventually taken no for an answer and then surprised Sanne by sticking around and becoming a good mate.

"Morning, all," Nelson said, once the officers had gathered within earshot. "Thanks for your patience. I know the weather's not been the best. Detective Jensen here has a grid breakdown of our sector showing your assigned streets. A colour photo of the victim's face in profile, an artist's impression of her entire face, and a shot of her clothing are also attached."

"People are obviously going to have questions," Sanne said, handing out the paperwork. "Try to keep your answers as nonspecific as possible for this initial door-to-door, and use your instincts. If someone is a little too interested or knowledgeable or raises alarm bells in any way whatsoever, note the name and the address and give us a shout on the radio. We have Mrs. Ahmad with us as a liaison today, so direct any general questions or concerns to her."

"Right, then." Nelson rubbed his hands as fat drops of rain began to splatter the tarmac. "Let's get cracking."

While the group checked their maps against their allocated streets, Zoe strode over to Sanne.

"Why, Detective Jensen, the black in your coat really brings out the brown in your eyes." She held out an umbrella for Sanne to duck beneath.

Sanne batted her eyelashes, mainly to get the rain off them. "Oh stop, you flatter me. I did contemplate a swanky pink number, but it didn't go with my boots."

"Pink is so last season, darling." Zoe studied her list. "Where've you ended up?"

"Over near the market. There's a school, two mosques, three or four residential streets. If we're lucky we'll be done by midnight."

At the edge of the car park, she saw the lone remaining officer look pointedly at Zoe and tap his watch. Zoe groaned.

"I better get going. My old mate went off to Firearms, and they've paired me with someone new and enthusiastic." She took a step and then paused. "Married life agrees with you, San. You're all aglow."

Sanne kicked the heel of Zoe's boot. "We're not married, you silly sod."

"Not yet." Zoe waggled a finger. "But your Meg's a keeper."

"Aye, she is. You can be my flower girl if we ever get hitched."

"Lunch will do for now, one day when we're all off. Y'know, after you've solved this case."

Sanne left the cover of the umbrella as the patter of rain grew more sporadic. "Oh, I'm not solving this one," she said, raising her coat collar. "I thought I'd let someone else do all the hard graft. Speaking of which…"

"Sharcliffe awaits," Zoe said. "Be careful out there, Scrapper. I know what you're like."

Sanne refused to dignify that with anything but a single-fingered salute, which she swiftly turned into a scratch of her nose when she saw Meera waiting with Nelson.

"All set?" he asked, his face admirably straight.

"Yep. Milton Street's closest. Do you want to take the evens with Meera, and I'll do the odds? We can meet back up for the school before we go to Crooke Road."

"Sounds good. There's a mosque just off Crooke. What time are we best going there?" He kept the question general, but it was Meera who answered.

"Most mosques hold evening classes. Tajweed, Fiqh, some segregated, others mixed. You should be able to find the times online, and speaking to the imam would be a good place to start."

"Fiqh." Sanne held her pen poised. "How are we spelling that?"

"F-I-Q-H."

"Okay, got it," Sanne said, hoping she wasn't looking as clueless as she felt, and intending to do a spot of research when she got a spare minute. Religion fascinated and appalled her in equal measure, leaving her slightly tongue-tied when conversing with a genuine believer. While she found the traditions, language, food rules, and dress codes interesting, part of her always teetered on the verge of enquiring whether the world would be better off without any of it. It was a debate that had enlivened many a traffic jam and stakeout with Nelson, though they'd never arrived at a satisfactory conclusion.

"I've got the number for the mosque here." He showed her a website he'd Googled. "I'll give them a call and see if we can arrange something for later."

A brief burst of sunshine welcomed them onto Milton Street, not that it did much to improve the general ambience. With no space for front gardens, unkempt patios two paving slabs wide provided the only buffer between each terraced house and the street. A few enterprising spirits had shifted slabs to plant a rose bush or a sickly hydrangea, but most of the entrances had been used as dumping grounds for dead car batteries, derelict toys, and pieces of household junk too large for the wheelie bins.

Balancing on a wobbly front step, Sanne knocked at the first door, sparking a chain reaction of energetic shrieking and scolding from within. The security chain prevented the door from opening fully, but a woman wearing a headscarf peered out.

"Yes?"

"Morning. Sorry to disturb you." Sanne held up her ID card. "My name's Sanne Jensen. I'm a detective with the East Derbyshire Police. Would you mind if I asked you a couple of questions?"

"Police? Why?" The woman's eyes widened, and Sanne wondered how much she had actually understood. She was in her early twenties, and her traditional dress bore no trace of Western influence. Given her age, she had probably been raised in Pakistan and brought over to England once married.

She opened the door wider to reveal a baby perched on her hip and a toddler clinging to her tunic. "Jabir!" she shouted, adding a stream of Urdu to the name, and a lad trotted out from the front room to stand shyly by her side.

"Hey," Sanne said. "Is this your mum?"

He nodded.

"Is anyone else at home? Your dad? Grandma?"

He shook his head. "I've got chicken spots, so I'm off school."

"Oh dear, I hope you're not too itchy." Sanne glanced across the road, but Nelson and Meera had obviously fared better and been invited inside one of their houses. She reintroduced herself for Jabir's benefit and gave him her ID. He studied her mugshot, his expression sombre, and then passed it back. Although using a child to translate wasn't ideal, she suspected this visit would set the theme for the day. She held the first photograph above his eye line. "Jabir, can you ask your mum if she recognises—" She saw Jabir's nose wrinkle in confusion. "Sorry, ask her if she's ever seen this girl before? Do you understand?"

"Yes," he said, and he must have gleaned a rough idea because, on his prompting, his mother took the photo from Sanne's hand.

After giving her time to study the image, Sanne replaced it with the artist's impression and then the picture of the clothing. The woman's lips moved, but Sanne couldn't catch the words.

"Does she know her?" she asked Jabir.

"No." He tilted his head. "She is saying a prayer for her."

Sanne waited for the woman to finish before collecting the photographs. "Thank you both for your time." She handed Jabir her card. "If your mum needs to speak to me, tell her to call that number."

"Sar-ner Jensen." He sounded the words out, watching for her approval.

She gave him a thumbs-up. "Aye, that's not bad for a first try."

Wary of the loose step, she let the woman shut the door, so that if she wrecked anything she could repair it in secret. The cement just about held, however, and she waved at Nelson as they all changed houses.

Progress through to number twenty-seven followed a similar pattern of incomprehension, and eventual apologetic headshakes. No one answered at four of the houses, and the heavens opened somewhere in the mid teens. Consequently, the middle-aged woman who opened the door of number twenty-nine took one look at Sanne's bedraggled state and ushered her into the hallway.

"So cold!" The woman clucked her tongue. "Would you like juice? Chai?"

"Chai would be lovely, thank you." Sanne had never been one to look a gift horse in the mouth and was particularly fond of the spiced tea. She had declined several earlier invitations, but that had been before the downpour snapped two of the spokes on her brolly.

Having hung Sanne's coat on the banister, the woman steered her past the ubiquitous collection of paired shoes lining the hall, and into the front room.

"Sit, please." She indicated a pristine sofa covered with clear plastic.

"No, no, I couldn't. I'm all wet." Sanne's trousers squelched as she patted them. She wasn't sure whether it was her obvious mortification or the threat to the soft furnishings that changed her host's mind, but the woman clucked again and escorted her into an adjoining room where the seats were well worn and where four pairs of curious eyes latched on to her.

"Hiya." Sanne waggled her fingers at the two toddlers playing in front of gas fire and nodded to acknowledge the elderly man in the bed against the wall. A younger woman sitting on the sofa shifted to make space, so Sanne perched on the edge of it, still conscious of her soggy clothing. "Thank you. Sorry, I didn't mean to barge in on you."

The young woman waited until the elder had gone into the kitchen and begun to clang pots about. "My mother-in-law. You can't say no to her once she's set her mind. It's best just to do as she tells you."

"Yeah, I got that impression." Sanne put her paperwork on the sofa arm and displayed her ID. "I'm Detective Jensen, and I work for East Derbyshire Special Ops. We're investigating the death of an Asian girl whose body was found yesterday."

"The one up on the moors? I saw it on the news this morning."

"Yes, that's right—"

"Parveen!" The shout from the kitchen sounded as if it had come through a loudhailer. Parveen shook her head in apology and obeyed the summons, leaving Sanne with one child encroaching on her bootlaces and the other using a plastic hammer to tap her knee. She scooped the boot-botherer onto her lap and gave him her keys to jingle, as animated conversation and the sizzle of oil drifted into the room.

The family had extended the house into their backyard, the addition of a galley kitchen halving the concrete square. Above the fireplace, an ornate gilt frame held a photograph of the Hajj, while the television was tuned to a soap opera on Dekho TV. The smell of spices soon replaced that of hot oil, and Parveen reappeared bearing a laden tray. She passed around mugs of milky tea and swapped the toddler for a plate of onion bhajis.

Raised on a diet of English-only fare, thanks to her dad's refusal to eat "bloody foreign muck," Sanne had spent years catching up for lost time by sampling food from as far away as she could, and bhajis were a favourite of hers. She reluctantly declined a second and took her time wiping her fingers on a napkin, loath to break the easy hospitality with a blunt return to business. Parveen, however, switched the subject for her.

"The girl under the rocks, she was Pakistani?"

Sanne set down her mug. "As best we can tell, but it's not an exact science."

"You have her picture?"

"Yes."

Mindful of the children, she passed the images across. Parveen studied each in turn, her lips thinning in anger and her fingers tight on the margins. Her mother-in-law murmured "Allah" as she looked over Parveen's shoulder en route to the kitchen, but she showed no sign of recognition.

"This was all she wore? No salwar?" Parveen indicated her own trousers.

"No, no salwar, just the kameez."

Swearing beneath her breath, Parveen returned the photographs. "She's so young."

"Between twelve and fifteen, we think." Sanne slid the images out of sight, trying not to show her frustration. She wasn't sure what she'd expected from the morning: some sort of key development or vital clue? A sudden revelation followed by a positive ID? From her time as a patrol officer, she knew that Pakistani families often extended over entire streets and that unrelated neighbours tended to be good friends, sharing personal and official business. Perhaps that had led her to hope for an early breakthrough, when realistically the victim was unlikely ever to have set foot in Sheffield and the entire day would turn out to be a waste of time.

"Do you have a copy of the sketch?" Parveen asked. "My sisters are still at school, and they don't miss much. I can show them the sketch but not the other pictures."

Sanne gave her one of the duplicates she'd intended to take to the mosque. "Please show it to as many people as you can. My number's on this card if you do hear anything." She finished the last of her tea and stacked the mug on her empty plate. "Shall I take them—" She pointed to the kitchen, but Parveen raised a hand.

"I think you're busy enough without volunteering to wash up."

"Yes, I should get back out there." It was still raining. Sanne could hear it hitting the roof slates, and the wind had set a gate banging in the alley. Leaving the cosiness of the sitting room, she went into the hall and was pulling on her damp coat when Parveen's mother-in-law bustled toward her, proffering a tinfoil parcel.

"For later," she said, thrusting the package into Sanne's hands.

Common sense told Sanne not to resist. "Thank you, you're very kind." She opened the front door to a wet gust that slapped at her face and played hell with her hair. Across the road, Nelson paused between houses to throw her an enquiring look. She shook her head as she pulled up her hood and made a beeline for number thirty-one.

CHAPTER SIX

The human body was never designed to survive a fall of two storeys onto concrete. Its bones snapped far too easily, its organs ruptured, and its arteries sheared. If the victim was lucky, a combination of these things happened upon impact, and death was instantaneous. Meg's twenty-five-year-old patient hadn't been so fortunate. Still conscious on arrival in the shock room, he had battled and screamed and would no doubt have kicked, had his pelvis not resembled a shattered eggshell.

"Any word on his parents?" Meg asked for the umpteenth time.

"ETA was fifteen minutes." Liz watched the monitor calculate his blood pressure. Her eyebrow arched as the numbers appeared on the screen. "Christ. Will he last that long?"

Meg hung another bag of fluid and closed the door on the rapid infuser. "I don't know. I'm surprised he hasn't arrested already."

Everything she did now was aimed at reaching that deadline. It was an hour since Maxwell from Neurology had taken one look at the CT scan and advised that the patient be treated with TLC in a side ward. His stark verdict meant that nothing else would be fixed either, so blood was continuing to pour into the lad's pelvic cavity, and his lungs were filling with fluid despite the drains. Meg wasn't sure which would kill him first, his failing heart or the swelling to his brain. Sedated and intubated, he was at least clean and warm and comfortable, with bandages soaking up the haemorrhage from his open skull fracture, and the rest of the damage hidden under blankets. His scaffolder's boots and overalls were folded neatly in a property bag, and the Resus doors had been marked with laminated pictures of butterflies, warning ambulance crews and department staff that someone within was dead or dying. The only thing missing was his parents.

"I'll go and keep an eye out in the ambulance bay," Liz said.

Meg nodded, using a fresh piece of gauze to wipe the blood trickling from the lad's nose. Barry, she reminded herself. "Bazza" to his mates. Single, hardworking, liked footy and playing darts. His shell-shocked colleague had offered these personal details in apology for knowing nothing of his medical history.

Meg raised her head hopefully when the curtains around the bed rustled, but it was only the organ donation coordinator.

"Aren't they here yet?" he asked.

"Ten minutes," Meg said. "An officer's blueing them over from Leeds."

"How's he doing?"

"Shite. At this rate, there'll be nothing left to salvage."

"Bloody hell." The coordinator squeezed Barry's hand. "Your mum and dad are coming, mate. Try and stick it out till they get here, okay?"

For a long, silent moment, Meg watched the rise and fall of Barry's chest as the vent breathed for him. Every breath encouraged his heart to beat, killing him in increments by pumping more blood into the void.

"Never know the minute, do you?" she said quietly. It was something she tried not to think about; those who dwelt on the subject didn't last long in emergency medicine. "He got up this morning, ate his breakfast, tied his boots, probably swore at the traffic like the rest of us. Then one slip of his foot, and his brain's mush and he's circling the drain in here."

"I never leave the house on an argument," the coordinator said. "No matter how annoyed I might be."

Meg primed another bag of fluid. "I doubt any of us do." She hesitated at the sound of approaching footsteps.

"His parents are here," Liz said, panting as if she'd run a marathon. "The car's just pulled up in the bay."

Meg tore off her plastic apron and checked her scrubs for blood. Satisfied that she was presentable, she turned to the coordinator. "Do you want to wait in the Rellies' Room? They should come and see him first."

Accustomed to the routine, the coordinator gave a curt nod and hurried out of sight.

"Shit, Liz, can you just…?" Meg mimed wiping her nose, and Liz grabbed some gauze to clean Barry's face. "It's the basal skull fracture. I can't stop it bleeding, but I don't want to plug his damn nostrils."

"I'll keep him tidy. You go."

Meg met Barry's stricken parents at the Resus door. A couple in their mid-fifties, they were clinging to each other like passengers on a sinking ship. Meg shook their hands in turn, but they were already looking past her at the door that barred their way.

"I'm Dr. Fielding. I've been taking care of Barry."

Barry's mother sobbed, and her husband tightened his hold on her. "The officer told us it didn't look good," he said, phrasing the statement almost as a challenge. "But he'll be all right, won't he, Doc?"

Even though Meg had expected the question, it still felt like a sucker punch.

"No," she said, providing the answer immediately, because everything else she said was likely to be lost. "I'm very sorry, but his injuries are so severe he won't recover from them."

She spotted the warning signs in Barry's father at once: his rapid breathing, clenched fists, and altered stance.

"What the fuck does that mean?" he demanded. "Are you letting him *die*?"

"No, sir. We've done everything we can to keep him alive. It just isn't going to be enough."

This admission knocked the bluster out of Barry's father. His posture sagged instantly, making him look smaller and more frail. Seeming to remember his wife, he wrapped an arm around her, supporting much of her weight as her legs shook.

"Can we see him?" he said.

"Of course." Meg led the way into Resus, explaining about the vent and the sedation, and deciding it would be kinder to lie when Barry's mother asked if he would be able to hear them. "He might," she said. "We'll never know for sure. Don't be scared of touching him or holding his hand."

Liz had silenced the monitors so that Barry's parents wouldn't be greeted by a cacophony of frantic alerts. His blood pressure had plummeted in the minutes Meg had been away, and his heart had given up trying to compensate. Standing at a discreet distance, she checked her phone as it vibrated: Fraser. She dropped it back into her pocket. Much as she wanted to speak to Fraser, he would have to wait.

❖

The local secondary school was emptying out by the time Sanne met Nelson and Meera at the far end of Crooke Road. Groups of teenagers were swaggering along the wet pavements, sharing bags of toffees or chips, their conversation a polyglot of English and languages Sanne could only guess at. Here and there among the black hijabs and the navy blazers she spotted a skirt rolled up above the knee or a pair of brightly coloured trainers, a rebellion against the strict dress code, but the kids were far better behaved than the foul-mouthed, dope-smoking rabble she had shared her own school classes with.

Conscious of sticking out like a sore thumb, she returned a few curious smiles, but the majority of the kids she passed were far more interested in their mobile phones and iPods, only noticing she was there when they had to step out of her way. Earlier that afternoon, the school's head teacher had taken copies of those case photos suitable for display to his young charges and promised to broach the subject in the morning assembly. Neither he nor the available staff members had recognised the dead girl, and Sanne approached the entrance to the Al Amin mosque resigned to ending the day with nothing to show for it.

Situated within a row of three-storey terraces, the mosque's sole distinguishing feature was a string of tattered bunting. A middle-aged man met Sanne and Nelson in the entrance, where, accustomed to the procedure, they removed their boots and added them to the assortment of flip-flops and moccasins left by the door. The man nodded his thanks before leading them along a hallway carpeted in pristine Axminster and rapping on a door at the far end.

Sanne hung back, allowing Nelson and then Meera to precede her into the room. The imam left his desk to meet them halfway, shaking Nelson's hand and returning Meera's greeting. Sanne introduced herself but knew better than to offer her hand.

"Please, sit. Would you like something to drink?" He directed them into chairs and retook his own, nodding at their polite refusals. "Of course, I'm sure you're very busy. May I see the photographs?"

Sanne watched his reaction closely as he considered the images. He was younger than she had expected, and his hands were trembling when he returned her file.

"I don't recognise her," he said, with a slight catch in his voice. "I wish I could be of more assistance, but no one has approached me recently with any concerns."

"Would you be able to ask your"—Nelson floundered for the right word—"congregation?"

"Yes, of course. Tomorrow would probably be best, at Jumu'ah—Friday prayer. Do you have a card with your details? Thank you." The imam tapped the card on the desk, looking as uneasy as a perp in a line-up of one.

"Was there something else, sir?" Sanne asked.

"No, not really. Well, yes, but I'm not sure it bears any relevance to your investigation. I've already reported the matter on the 101 helpline, and an officer is supposed to be coming to collect the letters at some point."

Sanne's ears pricked up, and she sensed Nelson lean forward.

"What letters, sir?" Nelson asked.

The imam opened the top drawer of his desk and withdrew two envelopes. "The first came on Monday. Then a second arrived yesterday. We receive mail like this on a weekly basis, even more so following the exploitation cases in Rotherham. We try not to make a fuss, but you said on the phone that this child had been assaulted sexually, so…" He pushed the letters across the desk.

Sanne and Nelson donned latex gloves before taking an envelope each. Sanne opened hers, noting the local postmark, and unfolded a sheet of lined paper on which someone had scrawled an itemised list of unimaginative threats: burning down the mosque, destroying all the "Paki" shops, and highlighted in capitals at number one, "WE WILL RAPE YOUR DAUGHTERS." As if afraid that the emphasis might be lost, the word "your" was underlined in red several times. Both letters were signed EISD: English Infidels, Sheffield Division.

"Seriously?" Sanne said, forgetting where she was for a moment. "They actually signed it?"

Nelson swapped his letter for hers. "They also spelled mosque with a K, San."

"This is true."

"Central Masjid and Etter Street Masjid have received identical correspondence," the imam said.

"We'll speak to them this evening." Sanne made a note of the two mosques and dropped the letters into an evidence bag. "Thank you, sir. You've been very helpful."

"Do you think this group might be connected to the girl's death?" he asked.

"I'm not sure," she said. "But we'll certainly be paying the EISD a visit. Can you contact us immediately if you receive any further threats?"

"Certainly. We've warned people to be extra vigilant."

"Good." Nelson stood to leave. "We won't take up any more of your time."

Back out on the street, Nelson made a radio call to reallocate their remaining house-to-house streets and asked one of the nearest groups of officers to pick up Meera. Relieved to be off the chaperoning hook for a while, Sanne dug out her parcel of bhajis as she and Nelson walked back to the car park.

"How the heck did you manage to wangle these?" he asked, his cheeks bulging.

"Charm, wit, but mostly by being small and getting rained on." She was stuffing in a last mouthful when her mobile buzzed. She smiled as she read the text. "Oh, hey, I'm an auntie again!"

He slung an arm around her and gave her a quick hug. "Boy or girl?"

"Girl. Seven pounds four, safely delivered at home."

"No name?"

"Not yet." She looked up at him. "Keeley's probably still trying to decide how to spell it."

"Don't keep me in suspense. Meg persuaded me to put a fiver on Kayci."

"Only a fiver? She conned a bloody tenner out of me!"

Nelson laughed. "Your girlfriend could sell coals to Newcastle."

"She could," Sanne agreed easily, but then stopped walking. "Y'know, I've never called her that before."

"Well, now you have. And look, the world's still turning."

Sanne gazed up at the darkening sky and took a deep, elated breath. "Yes, it is," she said.

❖

"What do you mean, she walked out? How the hell could she just *walk out*?" Meg paced to the far end of the ambulance bay, away from the crew coaxing an elderly gentleman into a wheelchair. She swapped her phone to her other ear as if that would somehow change what Fraser was telling her.

"Apparently, she asked to go for a cigarette," Fraser said. "When I arrived at the ward, the nurse on the desk had already alerted Security, but Anca had been AWOL for over an hour by then." He delivered the facts calmly, but that did little to placate Meg.

"It took them that long to realise that she wasn't coming back? What the hell were they playing at?" Meg didn't have the energy to stay angry for long, however. She slumped onto the bench near the hospital's main entrance. Below the "No Smoking" sign an emaciated twenty-something, trailing a drip and sporting a stump where his right leg should have been, sparked up a cigarette and inhaled as if his life depended on it. Another man in hospital-issue pyjamas asked him for a light and lit his own cig. A woman with her hands swathed in bandages wouldn't have stood out in this crowd.

"She timed her request to coincide with shift handover," Fraser said.

"You mean her husband timed it," Meg countered. "There's no way she planned this herself. Her injuries would stop her from driving, so she'd have needed a lift."

"I know." Fraser paused to speak to someone else and sounded brighter when he came back on the line. "Do you want a bit of good news?"

"Yes, please."

"Okay, well, the Burns Unit has reported Anca as vulnerable and missing, so my team can officially get involved with trying to find her. Security are sending us the CCTV from the hospital grounds. Hopefully, that'll shed some light on who met her and what that person was driving."

"She probably came out round the back. What few cameras there are don't work very well." Meg didn't want to rain on his parade, but an ongoing staff campaign to increase CCTV coverage around the hospital's satellite buildings had highlighted how shoddy and dysfunctional the current system was.

"O ye of little faith," he said. "Security estimated they could pull the footage and get it across to us by tomorrow afternoon. In the meantime I ran Cezar Miklos through the PNC, and he doesn't have a record."

Sleet began to fall, sending the amputee and his fellow smoker scurrying for cover. Meg stayed where she was, in a foul enough mood to welcome the gloomy weather. "He gave a false address when he booked Anca in to A&E, didn't he?"

"Yes," Fraser said, with obvious reluctance. "A patrol unit went round there today. It's a private property owned by a Pakistani family who don't have any Romanian friends or lodgers. I think we can safely assume that all the details he gave, including the names, are bogus."

"Little wonder, if he gets his kicks pinning his wife's hands in boiling water." Meg stalked back toward the ambulance bay before she could upset any of the relatives streaming in for visiting hour. "I bet he only brought her to the hospital because he was worried she wouldn't be able to do the fucking housework."

"That's a distinct possibility. Abuse victims rarely get medical treatment unless something goes badly wrong."

"Yeah, I know." Meg slowed her pace. She felt sick, and her back was aching in sympathy. A van with tinted windows pulled up in the bay, and two hospital porters began to unload an empty stretcher. Despite the best efforts of the coordinator, Barry's parents had refused permission to harvest his organs, and the van was here to transport his body to the morgue. It had, Meg decided, been one of those days. "I have to go," she said, following the stretcher into the corridor. "Sorry for being arsey. I really appreciate everything you're doing."

"I'll keep you updated," Fraser said. "I just wish I had better news."

She ended the call as the porters neared the Viewing Room. From behind the closed door, sobbing was clearly audible. Barry's family was large and devoutly Catholic, and they had arrived en masse half an hour too late.

"Hang fire, lads." Meg put a hand on the stretcher, waylaying the porters. "I'll see if the family are ready for you."

The men steered the trolley to the side, grateful to have an intermediary. Meg wiped the sleet from her face with her sleeve and knocked on the door.

❖

Eleanor paused in the middle of the sentence she was typing. She had left her office door ajar, and she went to meet Sanne and Nelson as soon as she heard their voices in the corridor.

"You might want to leave your coats on," she said, catching Sanne in the middle of unfastening hers. Sanne's eyes widened in expectation, and Nelson stopped trying to unpeel his wet scarf. They smelled like cold air, bracing and fresh compared to the fustiness of the office.

"Did you find something, boss?" Nelson asked.

Eleanor sat at the closest desk and waited while they found temporary perches.

"I spoke to a contact at Special Branch, and he confirmed that the EISD are on their current watch list," she said. "They've mainly been responsible for the more obvious extremism-related offences: vandalism, racially aggravated assault, one attempt to torch a corner shop that failed when the perp set fire to his own trousers."

Sanne swung her legs to and fro. She was always in motion when she was thinking, although she didn't seem aware of that. "So the kidnap and rape of a minor would be a big departure for them," she said.

"Very much so. Special Branch keep an eye on them, but they're not rated as a high threat. Their numbers dwindled after a leadership battle that saw a few punches being thrown in the Dog and Duck pub."

"Oh no," Nelson said, making the leap a split second before Sanne hid her face in her hands. "Are these idiots based on Malory Park?"

Eleanor displayed the information she'd printed out. Occasionally, she missed not spending her shift out in the field, speaking to witnesses or knocking on suspects' doors, but she was happy to pass on this one. "Forty-three Phelot Walk is the current HQ of the EISD, or the Beswick family, as they're more commonly known. Sid Beswick, the paterfamilias, has previous for GBH and possession, and one of the lads is serving three to five at a young offenders' institute."

"Dare I ask?" Sanne said.

"Burglary, mostly." Eleanor checked the sheet. "And nicking cars, only he can't drive, so he started his stretch with a broken leg."

"Outstanding," Nelson said. "Are we going to need Tactical Aid for our house call?"

Eleanor had discussed a risk assessment with Special Branch and accepted her contact's conclusion that the family, though unpleasant, were unlikely to pose a serious threat. "I think the two of you will be fine. Just remember to give a clear warning before you Taser anyone." She handed the paperwork to Nelson. "I doubt they have anything to do with the girl's death, but it'll be worth having a chat with them about the hate mail, at least. Besides which, if we drop the ball on a lead and it comes back to bite us on the arse…"

"Say no more." Sanne already had her woolly hat out of her pocket. "Has anyone made any headway today?"

"Not as yet." Eleanor tried to avoid looking at the clock on the wall. Litton was expecting a progress update at six p.m., and unless a miracle occurred in the next ninety minutes, her report would be brief to the point of nonexistence. Despite the negatives coming in from every possible line of enquiry, she knew she would stay late on the off chance that something came up, and undoubtedly go home empty-handed to a family already in bed. "There was no manufacturer's tag on the vic's clothing, but Forensics found traces of animal faeces, which have been sent for further analysis. In all likelihood they came from the moors, though, so it's not exactly a breakthrough. Other than that, we have nothing from the house-to-house or the fingertip, nothing from the airports, and nothing from the hotline."

"What about the vehicle?" Nelson asked.

"There's a team working on the partial plate and the analysis of make and model. I've been advised not to hold my breath." This time she did glance at the clock and immediately wished she hadn't.

"We'll let you get back to it, boss," Sanne said.

"Keep in touch." Eleanor listened to their chatter fade as the lift arrived. Then she turned back toward her office and the telephone that had already started ringing again.

❖

A muscle at the corner of Sanne's jaw began to twitch as Nelson left the bypass and entered the Malory Park housing estate. She'd had the twitch on and off for a while—stress-related, Meg reckoned—and her sweaty palms seemed to confirm the diagnosis. She hadn't been back to Malory since the afternoon in January when she and Nelson had inadvertently tracked down a serial killer and she had offered her own life in exchange for that of a six-year-old boy.

"You okay, San?" Nelson asked.

"Yep." She dried her hands and looked out at Balan Road through the sleet.

Nothing had changed. The council estate was as dour and derelict as ever, the anaemic glow of its streetlights not enough to conceal how bad things were. A school bus stopped in front of their car, and Nelson let the engine idle as a handful of teenagers got off. In an effort to improve attendance, the council had launched a free route from the estate to the local secondary school, but the bus had been almost empty by the time it turned onto Balan. Three bobbing orange dots marked the kids' progress along the pavement. They had all lit cigarettes the instant they'd left the bus.

"Next right," Sanne said, directing from memory.

Nelson slowed as she counted the numbers for him. "Maybe we should stop and say hello to Ma Burrows," he said, recognising one of the worst houses on the walk.

Sanne shuddered at the prospect. "You go right ahead. I'll wait here for you."

"I think I'll pass as well."

No one had bothered to take down the Christmas lights at number forty-three. The wind had knocked a moth-eaten reindeer loose from its fixings, leaving it swinging at an angle like a welcome sign at a haunted motel.

"Well, this looks to be a fine establishment," Nelson said. "I absolutely cannot wait to get inside."

A fierce wind drove the sleet into Sanne's eyes as she stepped out of the car, but not even that could make her hurry to the front door. Pausing by a hole in the fence where a garden gate should have hung, she listened to an argument between two children of indeterminate age, their shadows moving behind threadbare curtains. An adult yelled at the kids to shut the fuck up, and the sharp sound of a slap was followed by wailing.

"Home sweet home," she muttered, reminded of those rare occasions when her dad had copped for babysitting duty.

The wailing softened to muted sobs, giving Nelson's knock a chance to be heard. A dog responded more quickly than the other occupants, barrelling up beneath the front curtains onto its hind legs and barking.

"Just when you thought things couldn't get any worse." Nelson—definitely more of a cat person—eyed the dog with unease. "Is that a Staffy or one of those banned monsters?"

"Staffy," Sanne said. "Still capable of taking a chunk out of your arse, though. Oh, aye up." She nodded at the small figure peering through the door's single glass panel and held out her ID. "Police. Can you open the door, please?"

The figure scarpered, returning seconds later trailing an adult male who opened the door a crack.

"Yeah?" he said.

"Mr. Beswick?" Sanne redisplayed her ID. "Police, Mr. Beswick. We need to ask you a few questions."

The man spat and hoiked his jeans beneath his sagging beer belly. His nose had been broken so many times it resembled a malformed potato. "'Bout what?"

Sanne sighed. "Would you prefer we came back with a warrant and the Tactical Aid Unit? Only, they tend to make a mess."

"For fuck's sake." He yanked on the door and stood in the gap, his arms folded. "Happy now?"

"Delirious." She made a point of glancing over her shoulder, where, true to form, curtains in the houses opposite were starting to twitch. "Do you really want to do this on the doorstep?"

Instead of answering, he stepped aside with a sarcastic little bow.

"After you," she told him, preferring not to have him at their backs. "Could you put the dog somewhere secure, please?"

Mumbling a string of obscenities, he paused at the first door and yelled through it. "Spud! Stick that fucking dog in the kitchen, then fuck off upstairs!"

They waited as boots stomped across a hard floor and a connecting door banged, muting the dog's yips. Spud made an appearance seconds later, scowling at Sanne and regarding Nelson with an expression traditionally reserved for shit on the bottom of a shoe. Genetics had not been kind to Spud. A short lad of about fifteen, he had oversized lips that dominated his face, drawing attention away from beady eyes and ears like the handles of a Toby jug. That he was overweight and stank of grungy teenager was almost incidental.

"Fuck do they want?" he asked.

Sid clouted him over the back of his head. "Shut your trap and take our Peggy with you."

Peggy, tear-stained and much younger than Spud, with pigtails and missing teeth, was the child who had first come to the front door. She scampered upstairs ahead of her brother, hesitating midway to throw another furtive glance in Nelson's direction.

"Why's Dad let a Paki in?" she whispered to Spud.

Spud's answer was lost as they vanished into the gloom at the top of the stairs, but Sanne hoped that some rudimentary form of ethnology would be included in his response. She entered the living room a step behind Nelson and almost slammed into him when he stopped abruptly.

"Mrs. Beswick?" he said, and Sanne heard the ripple and slap of flesh, as if something immense had attempted to move. Coming to stand beside Nelson, she realised how accurate her conjecture had been.

Mrs. Beswick's girth was spread across two sofa cushions. A rancid smell and the food wrappings strewn around her ulcerated legs implied that she hadn't changed position for some time.

"What've yer done now, yer numb twat?" she asked, digging her hand into a family-sized bag of cheesy puffs.

"Dunno yet." Sid grinned at Sanne and settled onto the sofa's remaining cushion. "What've I done now, officer?"

Sanne didn't bother to correct him. She pulled photocopies of the Al Amin hate mail from her file and gave them to him. "Do you recognise these?"

He made a show of reading the letters, his lips moving unconsciously. "Nope," he said at length.

"But you are a member of the EISD?" She gestured at his right forearm. "Your tattoo would certainly suggest that."

He scowled, probably regretting his decision to wear a T-shirt. His George Cross tattoo had *EISD* running through the centre of it. "Yeah, so what if I am?"

Nelson stepped forward, narrowly avoiding the ham toastie smeared across the uncarpeted floorboards. "*So*, our information tells us that you're the group's current boss, which means letters like this only go out with your approval." He shrugged at Sanne. "Unless one of your members has gone rogue, of course."

Hitting Sid's ego proved a sound tactic. He bristled visibly, caught between admitting culpability and appearing vulnerable as a leader. "I didn't send 'em, but I might know who wrote 'em," he said, his eyes flashing in defiance. "And those Pakis deserve everything they get, the mucky bastards."

Sanne toed the toastie aside and swapped the letters for a photo of the girl's body. "Do they deserve this?"

"Wh—?" He stared at the image and then up at Sanne. "You think I did *this*? I didn't. I never. I mean, come on!"

"'We will rape your daughters,'" Sanne read from the letter. "This child was sexually assaulted, Mr. Beswick, and left to die. So yes, whoever sent this threat to the mosques is obviously a suspect."

"But it wasn't me!"

"It wasn't him." Mrs. Beswick shook her head, setting her chins wobbling. "He's always home with me, on account of my disability."

"Give us a name, then," Nelson said. "If it wasn't you, who was it?"

A sudden clatter and a yell from upstairs made Sanne jump. She whipped around to face the door just as Sid leapt off the sofa.

"Run, Gobber! Go, lad!"

"Oh, you stupid bollock," Sanne spat, hurtling out into the hallway. She took the stairs two at a time and kicked the back bedroom door open. As she crossed the threshold, she was greeted by the sight of an older lad disappearing through the window, and Peggy slugging her thigh with a baseball bat.

"Jesus Christ," she hissed, hopping on her good leg and grabbing the bat before Peggy could use it on Nelson. Spud whooped as the lad cleared the opening, where Sanne saw him teeter on a ledge before jumping across to a flat-roofed shed. "Find a way round the back!" she yelled at Nelson, who had Peggy by the scruff of her cardigan as she pinwheeled her fists at him. He certainly wouldn't fit through the window, but Sanne thought she might.

"Please don't break your neck," he shouted.

Pumped up for the chase, she hauled herself onto the sill. The window was small enough to act as a burglar deterrent, but as a kid she had sneaked out of her bedroom on Halshaw more times than she could count, and the principle of "legs first, let the body follow" held true. Standing on the rain-slickened ledge, she caught her breath as Gobber performed a clumsy high wire act on the garden wall. He swore when he saw her land on the shed, his left foot slipping and his arms flailing. He didn't fall, though, and he dropped out of sight again as Sanne ran toward him. Using her momentum, she leapt for the wall, managing to launch her upper half over it and swing her legs up. She sat atop the bricks, gauging Gobber's inelegant egress and her own route down.

"Nelson, he's heading south, south!" she shouted into her radio. An upended wheelie bin made an improvised stepping stone, and she hit the ground in a crouch, her knees groaning at the impact.

Phelot Walk sprawled in all directions, the backs of houses overlooking the fronts of others, with a car park forming a central space. Gobber ducked out from behind a Ford Fiesta and sprinted across the car park, aiming for the next maze of terraces and almost coming a cropper on a stray dog. He kicked at the mutt, giving Sanne a chance to close the distance. Water hit her knees as she dashed through puddles in an effort to sidestep the snapping dog.

"Crossing Balan!" she yelled into the radio. "He's heading for the playing field!"

"Right behind you," Nelson replied. Engine noise in the background told her he was driving.

She reached the edge of the grass seconds before she saw the headlights, the high beams arcing to catch Gobber square in the back. Now close enough to hear his rasping breaths, she dug in and increased her pace. Her fingers brushed his jacket but lost contact when he dodged.

"Just stop, mate," she told him. "We've got a bloody car."

"Fuck you," he gasped, barely able to speak for wheezing. Although not as plump as his brother, he wasn't slim. "Fucking dyke pig!"

Estimating Nelson's position, she swerved to the opposite side, hemming Gobber in and herding him toward the car. Realising what she'd done, he spun to face her, his fists already raised, a glint of metal in one of them. Sanne didn't think; she barely even knew the Taser was in her hands until its red dot lit up the centre of Gobber's chest.

"This is your one and only warning," she said. "Drop the knife or I drop you."

He was bigger than her, and his nostrils flared as he considered his options. He tensed at the slam of a car door.

"I didn't do nothin'," he said. He opened his hand, and the blade stabbed into the grass by his boot.

"Step away from that and put your hands behind your back."

He did as she instructed, but she kept the Taser sighted as Nelson cuffed him, only deactivating it once Nelson had turned him around.

"There's a van on the way." Nelson was all business, but the relieved look he gave her spoke volumes.

"Great, thanks." She grabbed Gobber's shoulder, steering him across to the blue lights that were approaching at speed. "You're a bloody dickhead," she said, and began to read him his rights.

CHAPTER SEVEN

S anne clicked to the next section of the computerised pro forma and nibbled the chocolate off a KitKat as box after box of free-text options loaded.

"Bollocks," she said, catching sight of the numbers at the bottom of the screen. "There's five bloody pages of this."

Nelson stirred his coffee with his own KitKat. "Just be glad you didn't fire the damn thing. The form for that is three times as long."

Taser drawing, it seemed, was a serious business, requiring a dissertation-length explanation of the hows, whys, and wherefores.

"I suppose it could be worse." She rethought the line she'd just typed and erased all but the first word. "We could be fingertip-searching the Beswick abode."

He raised his mug to salute her "glass is half full" disposition. "There's always a bright side, San. How's your leg?"

"It's throbbing." She resisted the urge to rub the aggrieved area. Peggy Beswick had one hell of a right arm for a seven-year-old, and the bruise was now a hot, swollen lump. "What were they doing with a baseball bat anyway? None of them struck me as the sporty type."

"Self-defence, at a guess, although I'm sure Sid won't admit to that. Things have been a bit fraught on Phelot since the punch-up at the pub. He dropped the nines a couple of weeks ago after a brick was chucked through their front window."

"I bet he chucked it right back." Sanne frowned. "Should 'big fuck-off knife' be hyphenated or not?" .

"Definitely hyphenated," Nelson said and then coughed, alerting her to Eleanor's presence, but she had already heard the tap of heels on the carpet and was busy typing again by the time Eleanor reached her desk.

"I'm assuming you don't need medical attention or counselling after your close encounter with a seven-year-old and her knife-toting brother." Eleanor set Sanne's first report back on her desk.

"No, boss. I'll live," Sanne said.

"And using the back door to access the garden was out of the question?"

She squirmed a little under the scrutiny. In the heat of the moment, shinning out of the window had seemed a perfectly logical choice, although with hindsight perhaps things could have been done differently.

"There was a dog in the kitchen," she said.

"Huge, nasty thing," Nelson added. "I don't think the family would've moved it even if we'd asked nicely."

"Fair enough," Eleanor said. "Make sure you mention the dog as well, Nelson." She turned her attention back to Sanne's screen.

"I should have this finished soon," Sanne said, pre-empting the enquiry. "How are things down in Custody?"

"Lively." Eleanor read over Sanne's shoulder but didn't offer a comment. "Sid Beswick is screaming blue murder at anyone within earshot because he thinks his family is being persecuted, Spud's moaning about the food, and Gobber's complaining of chest pain and a twisted ankle."

"He ran fast enough for someone with a bad ankle." Sanne slapped her mouse and accidentally deleted a paragraph. "No! Come back! How do I make it come back?"

"Right click, undo," Nelson said, well accustomed to her computer-induced tantrums. "Are any of them being interviewed tonight?" he asked Eleanor.

"No. They're all waiting for their regular solicitor, who, surprise surprise, won't be able to attend until tomorrow morning." Eleanor raised her glasses and settled them on her head. "At least that'll give us a relatively early night. Get everything submitted and then go home."

"San's not going home," Nelson said. "She's got a brand new niece to visit."

All the stress fell from Eleanor's face, and her broad smile lit her eyes. "Congratulations! Does she have a name yet?"

Sanne tried not to react at the unintentional tweaking of a sore spot. "Uh, no. Keeley hasn't quite decided on one."

"Be sure to let me know." Eleanor nodded at them both. "I'll see you tomorrow for the briefing."

Five minutes after Eleanor's departure, Nelson switched off his computer. Sanne stopped typing and listened to him rearranging things on his desk.

"Go home, mate," she said. "I'll be ages yet." That wasn't strictly true, but he had already missed putting his children to bed, and she didn't want to delay him further.

"You sure?"

"Absolutely."

"Give my love to the tiddler."

"I'll send you a photo. And her name, if it's printable."

"Oh, I'll be waiting up for that. Night, San."

She waved at him and cracked on with her report as the office fell silent. All being well, she would be meeting Meg at Keeley's at eight. Right on cue, her phone buzzed. Meg: *Sweet and sour chicken, or beef in black bean?*

Both, Sanne replied, and clicked onto page four.

Television light was flickering behind the front curtains when Sanne neared her parents' house on Windermere Avenue, but she drove past without stopping. She knew her mum was round at Keeley's, and she had no intention of speaking to her dad. The sleet had turned to thin rain, swirling the mist beneath the streetlights and casting an eerie cloak over the back field. She had always thought fog the kindest weather for Halshaw, blurring the grimmer details. Like those on Malory Park, the majority of Halshaw's houses and flats were council owned, their residents mostly unemployed or the working poor. Sanne had grown up a couple of streets over from Meg, the two of them determined to break the Halshaw cycle of exam failure, underage pregnancy, benefits dependence, and addiction.

After bouncing her Land Rover through a pothole, she braked hard to allow a stooped man to cross the road. He tipped his cap at her, his hand quickly returning to support the bag of booze he'd bought at the precinct. She recognised him as one of her school classmates, although she couldn't remember his name. She took a left at the bus shelter, which for once still had its glass in it, and parked behind Meg's car three minutes early. Meg met her on the pavement, wearing the same clothes she had left Sanne's cottage in and smelling of hospital soap. Sanne pulled her close and kissed her.

"Hey." Meg breathed the word against Sanne's lips. She looked pale and weary.

"Hey yourself. Did you not make it home?"

"No, but it's a long, depressing story that I'll tell you later." She squeezed Sanne's hand and ducked into her car, bringing out a bulging bag from the Chinese chippy and a present wrapped in "Happy Birthday" paper. "Technically it *is* her birthday," she said, plonking the gift into Sanne's waiting arms.

Sanne linked arms with her and led her to the front door. "At what point did you realise you'd forgotten to buy wrapping paper?" she whispered.

"About ten minutes ago. Fortunately, the chippy is right next to Kumar's, and he sells everything. Well, everything aside from 'It's a Girl!' paper." Meg rang the bell and winced at the excited screeching that ensued. "Jesus, it sounds like a zoo in there. Why aren't the little bleeders in bed?"

Behind the door, two of the lads had entered into a pitched battle, rattling the plastic intermittently as they fought. Sanne opened the letterbox and peered through it.

"Oi! Don't make me come in there and arrest you."

Both lads froze, and a small hand waggled out of the gap. "Hallo, Aunt San."

"Hiya, Kyle. Where's your Nana?"

The paw withdrew as the door opened.

"She's right here," Sanne's mum said. She kissed Sanne's cheek and then Meg's. "Come in out of the rain. You'll catch your deaths." Her rolled-up sleeves and the bubbles in her hair told of an interrupted bath time, and sure enough, Kiera—slippery wet and naked as a jaybird—darted down the hallway and wrapped herself around Sanne's leg.

"Hallo, poppet." Sanne scooped her up, bubbles and all. "Where's this new sister of yours?"

Herded toward the living room, Sanne tiptoed around abandoned toys and school bags. A roll of carpet still sat along the edge of the stairs, and the unpapered walls were covered in crayon scribbles. The council had finally crumbled beneath Keeley's constant mithering and moved the family to a four-bedroom house well over a year ago. Keeley had been in the process of "decorating" ever since. Holding court on the sofa, surrounded by pink balloons and teddies, she was maternal bliss personified—pint of cider in one hand, Mars Bar in the other. It took Sanne a moment to spot the baby, tucked in a bassinet beside the massive telly.

"Hi, you two," Keeley said, through a mouthful of Mars. "Did you bring food? I'm bloody starving. Ooh, is that Chinese? Fab." She plucked the bag from Meg's hand and waddled into the kitchen, leaving her mum to swap Kiera for the latest addition.

Meg put her chin on Sanne's shoulder and considered the baby. "She's quite cute for a new 'un," she whispered. "No cone head. Good bit of hair. Face isn't too squished."

"Doesn't look like Wayne," Sanne added.

"No. That's a bonus." Meg made a point of surveying the room. "Where is the doting dad, anyway?"

Sanne's mum paused in the middle of wrestling a nappy onto Kiera. "He's wetting his new daughter's head down the Crown and Horses. He came by earlier to see her, but he moved back in with Sheryl Hopworth about four months ago."

"Ouch." Meg wiped macaroni from one of the armchairs and steered Sanne into it. "I'll go and help Keels."

With the lads playing upstairs and Kiera dozing in front of the gas fire, peace descended on the living room.

"You look tired, Mum," Sanne said as her mum sagged onto the sofa and took off her slippers. "You can't run after six kids and Dad all day. You'll make yourself ill."

Her mum's brow knotted. "Five kids."

"Yeah, but I'm counting Keeley." Sanne stroked the baby's palm, smiling at the instinctive grip around her finger. "Is Dad okay?"

"He's been a bit up and down. Some pain with his stomach, but he won't go to the doctor."

"Because the doc would tell him to stop drinking." She tried to quell the anger that surged whenever she considered the impact of her dad's miserable existence on her mum. She'd wished him dead since her childhood, and nothing had happened to change that as she'd grown up.

"There was blood in the toilet the other day." Her mum opened her hands helplessly. "I don't know what to do, Sanne."

"I'll speak to Meg. Don't worry, okay? You've got enough on your plate. Speaking of which…" She resettled the baby in her bassinet as Meg and Keeley returned from the kitchen to distribute brimming dishes of Chinese takeaway.

"Come on, then. Don't keep us in suspense." Meg sat on the floor by Sanne's feet. "What've you called her?"

"Oh, I love it!" Keeley said. "You'll love it, too! It's *so* exotic."

Meg gripped Sanne's ankle, shifting slightly so she could watch Sanne's reaction. "I can't bear the excitement!" she said in a fair approximation of Keeley's pitch. "Do tell!"

"Khaleesi!" Keeley clapped her hands. "Isn't it adorable?"

Meg coughed so hard that Sanne thought she'd choked on her sweet and sour. Her eyes filled with tears, and her shoulders began to shake. "Where've you hidden her dragons?" she spluttered.

"Huh?" Keeley said.

Sanne thumped Meg on the back. "It's certainly original."

"I'm already calling her Kally," her mum said.

"But why would she have dragons?" Keeley asked.

"Have you not read the books?" Meg said.

"I quite like Kally," Sanne muttered.

Keeley eyeballed Meg. "What books? I stole the name off Janice Jones. Her baby's not due till March, and Tilly Price says she's fuming now."

"George R.R. Martin's epic series of swords and gratuitous nudity," Meg said. "It's quite famous. It's on the telly and everything."

"Sounds like crap." Keeley stabbed a piece of beef. "I've not read nothin' since *Fifty Shades*."

Meg nodded in sympathy. "I think *Fifty Shades* ruined reading for a lot of people. Ow!" She rubbed her bum where Sanne had kicked her.

"Sorry. Cramp," Sanne said, flicking a grain of rice at her.

From the corner, Khaleesi let up a thin wail, her little hands punching above the bassinet sides.

"I'd cry too, love," Meg said. She set her plate on the floor and went across to commiserate with the new arrival.

❖

Despite the mortgage that occasionally brought her out in a cold sweat, Meg loved everything about her house: the stream that ran along the bottom of its garden; the Belfast sink and bay windows; the blackbird that nested in its tallest conifer; but, she decided as she slid through a deep froth of bubbles into red-hot water, the oversized double-ended bath she'd treated herself to at Christmas was now her favourite thing of all.

"C'mon, San, it'll get cold!" She ducked her head beneath the suds, rinsing away the stink of the soap she'd used in the staff shower. When she resurfaced and opened her eyes, Sanne was gingerly dipping a toe.

"Bloody hell. At what point in the next millennium is this going to get cold?"

"Fine." Meg stretched the full length of the bath as Sanne withdrew her reddened digit. "But you'll get all goose pimply waiting for—hey, what the hell happened to your leg?" She beckoned Sanne closer and laid a careful hand over the black and blue contusion at the midpoint of her thigh. It must have been sore, but Sanne didn't react to her touch.

"I had a run in with a seven-year-old." Sanne eased Meg's fingers away, keeping hold of them as she lowered herself into the bath. "At a house full of white racists."

"Did you arrest him?"

"Her." Sighing, Sanne wriggled lower, arranging her legs either side of Meg. "And she was seven years old, Meg."

"Old enough to know that clobbering coppers is wrong."

Sanne's eyes slid shut, and she answered through a yawn. "Given her upbringing, I'm not so sure. Anyway, enough about me. How crappy was *your* day?"

"On a scale of one to ten?" Meg squirted gel onto a sponge and swirled it around as she debated her score. "If ten is being battered by my brother and spending the day on the kitchen floor, this was maybe an eight."

"Was Donovan being an arse again?"

"No, he's on leave, but we had a young lad who fell from scaffolding and landed on his head. Plus, remember that Romanian lass I told you about?"

"Domestic violence with the burns?"

"Yeah. She"—Meg made her fingers into air quotes—"'left the ward for a cigarette' and never came back."

"Christ." Sanne pushed herself upright, all signs of sleepiness banished. "Does Fraser know?"

"He was the one who told me, and he's working the case now, so fingers crossed he'll find her." Meg tugged Sanne's foot until she slid beneath the bubbles again. Though they sometimes discussed their work, neither tended to dwell on the details for long, and she didn't want Sanne distracted when EDSOP was in the middle of a major investigation. She began to soap Sanne's toes with the sponge.

"Did your scaffolder die?" Sanne asked, apparently not as relaxed as Meg had hoped.

"Yes, about ten minutes after his parents arrived."

"At least they were with him." Sanne provided her other foot when Meg tapped it, but her eyes were still wide open, and her finger was drawing patterns on the side of the bath. "I climbed out of a window today, and a lad pulled a knife on me." She spoke hurriedly, as if afraid that she might lose her conviction. "I wasn't going to tell you, but I hate keeping secrets, and I had my Taser, so it was okay and probably not as dangerous as I just made it sound."

Meg tweaked Sanne's big toe, reminding her to take a breath. Sanne's chest rose and fell rapidly as she tried to compensate.

"Did you actually zap the little shit?" Meg asked.

"No, I didn't need to, but I did go a bit Dirty Harry on him." Sanne rubbed her reddened face, a slight smile beginning to form. "I've not climbed out of a window in years."

"It's Eleanor's fault for telling you to grow a pair and then giving you a sodding Taser," Meg said, though she wasn't as exasperated as she made out. In the last few weeks she had become rather fond of this new, more assertive Sanne.

The water rippled from end to end as Sanne shifted to lie with her head on Meg's chest. "I won't do anything daft." She kissed the soft swell of Meg's breast. "I promised I'd be careful."

"Yes, you did." Meg smoothed Sanne's hair from her face. "I've put enough stitches in you to last me a lifetime."

"No more stitches." Sanne kissed Meg's breast again, her tongue flicking out to tease the nipple. "I'll be good and behave myself."

Meg opened her legs as she felt Sanne's hand glide lower. "I'm not entirely sure that I believe you," she said, pretty damn sure that she no longer cared.

Sanne blew bubbles across Meg's chest. "For you, I'll make an exception."

❖

Lying snug beneath the quilt, with lassitude making her bones feel like jelly, Meg watched Sanne thump her pillow and wriggle around until she found exactly the right spot. It was a ritual reminiscent of a cat bedding down for the night, the resemblance helped by her habit of kneading the air with her toes as soon as she got comfortable. She switched out the light, cueing Meg to sidle closer until they were spooning.

"Remind me again why we waited so long to do this," Sanne said. She'd snagged Meg's T-shirt in her fists and was holding on tightly.

"Idiocy, denial, and a healthy dose of cowardice," Meg offered, and felt the gentle puff of Sanne's answering laugh. "But I think we're doing okay, aren't we?" She chewed on her lip, waiting for a response. If something wasn't working for Sanne she would rather know now before she fell any deeper.

The verdict came in a flurry of kisses to the back of her neck.

"I'm taking that as a yes," she said, as the butterflies stopped dancing in her belly and Sanne nibbled her earlobe. "Whoa. That makes my knees feel weird."

Sanne released her ear with a wet pop. "We absolutely cannot have any more sex," she said. "I have to get up in five hours."

Her decisive tone made Meg smile. "That's fine. Just note it for next time."

"Will do."

The grip on Meg's shirt slackened as Sanne began to doze. Meg closed her eyes, allowing herself a few more minutes before she returned to her side of the bed. She was about to make a move when Sanne jerked and the rhythmic movement of her toes ceased.

"Shit, I forgot to tell you about my dad," she said, with her usual uncanny ability to snap back to wakefulness.

"What about him?" The last time Meg had seen John Jensen he'd called her a "faggot" and launched a can of cider at her head. His attempt had fallen well short, but the exchange epitomised their relationship, and whenever she called at Windermere Avenue she avoided the front room.

"My mum says he's had bellyache and there's been blood in the loo. He won't go to his doctor."

Meg mentally ticked off the most probable causes—peptic ulcer, Mallory-Weiss tear, cancer—and wondered which would be the easiest on Sanne's mum. Something sudden and unfixable, she supposed. He'd had several life-threatening bleeds from oesophageal varices in the past, but he'd always bounced back, against the odds.

It was too dark to see anything, so she turned over and cupped Sanne's face in both hands. "Do you want me to pay a house visit? Take some bloods and try to put the frighteners on him?"

"Could you? For my mum's sake?"

"I'll go tomorrow before I start work. I think I have an old biking helmet stashed in the shed, so I should be safe enough."

Sanne covered Meg's hands with her own. "Thank you."

"Not a problem. Go to sleep, love."

Meg went back to her cold half of the sheets and settled onto her pillow. She was almost asleep when Sanne's voice cut through the darkness.

"Maybe this time he'll do us a favour and fucking die."

Chapter Eight

Interview One, EDSOP's main interrogation room, might have boasted top-notch recording equipment and a one-way mirror, but it hadn't been designed for comfort. Its austere colour scheme and hard-backed chairs were intended to focus the attention, encouraging perps to keep their time within its walls as brief as possible.

Slouched in his chair with his arms folded, Jordan "Gobber" Beswick didn't seem to have grasped this. He'd yawned in the middle of confirming his name for the tape, giving Sanne a good idea of how the interview would play out. Bearing that in mind, she decided to kick off the proceedings with an easy one. She slid the hate mail across the table until it sat beneath his nose.

"Jordan, can you take a look at this letter and tell me whether that's your handwriting?"

He glanced down and shrugged. "No comment."

Sanne gave no outward reaction. The interview would continue as planned, and all of their questions would be asked, regardless of whether he answered in full or stonewalled.

"When we searched your bedroom, we found several more of these letters, stamped and ready to post. Can you explain that for me?"

"No comment."

She took a grubby, tattered book from her file and opened it at random. "This is one of your school exercise books. Would you say that this handwriting, *your* handwriting, is a match for the handwriting on the letters?"

Another shrug. "No comment."

She withdrew the book. Her question had been moot anyway; the remedial scrawl of what little schoolwork Gobber had ever completed was an unmistakeable match for that used to threaten the mosques, right down to the football-sized blotches with which he dotted every "i." The only unexplained aspect was that he'd chosen to keep an essay about pig farming.

She sensed Nelson lean forward and saw the tension in the set of his shoulders and the stiffness of his posture. EDSOP had been at this for hours now, first with Sid Beswick, whose own "no comment" interview had been prolonged by multiple requests for toilet and cigarette breaks, and then with Mrs. Beswick, who'd spent fifty minutes complaining about the chair aggravating her bad back before she'd finally succumbed to a dramatic bout of vertigo.

"You do understand," Nelson said, "that regardless of your solicitor's advice, refusing to answer these questions removes your opportunity to offer an explanation for your actions and may actually harm your defence when your case comes to court?"

Merely by moving, he had managed to catch and hold Gobber's attention, possibly due to the sheer novelty of being in the same room as a black person. Gobber opened his mouth to respond, and for the briefest moment Sanne thought they might be getting somewhere.

"No comment," he said and picked the head off one of his spots.

"Can you drive, Jordan?" she asked. The PNC had confirmed that he did drive, mainly cars that he'd pinched. "Come on, where's the harm in telling us that? It's a simple enough question, with a simple answer."

"No comment."

"Because I was wondering whether you ever took a car out for a spin up over the moors?" she continued in the same pleasant, conversational tone. "Maybe tried your hand at the corners on the Snake or the Woodhead Pass? Old Road?"

If he recognised the significance of the questions, he hid it well, showing no signs of stress or subterfuge as he gave his standard response.

"No comment."

"Ever been up here?" She shoved a photo of Greave Stones toward him, before slapping a second, wider shot alongside.

"No comment."

She waited a beat, letting him wonder what might be coming next.

Then she set down their most graphic image of the dead girl's face, the one with the mottled purple side uppermost and the clouded eye half-open.

"Because we found her right under those rocks," she said. "Someone had raped her repeatedly and left her to die, and the letters you've been sending out have made you our prime suspect."

Gobber reacted then, even if he didn't intend to. He swallowed so violently that his Adam's apple bobbed like a cork on choppy water. He looked at his solicitor, who shook her head once.

"No comment." He choked on the words, his mouth still flapping afterward.

"You remember what Detective Turay said, don't you?" she asked. "That we can't help you unless you start to help us?"

"Yes…I mean no," he stammered. "No comment." He shook his head, his face suddenly pale and clammy. "I think I'm gonna puke."

❖

With three and a half years as a patrol officer under her belt, and almost two years working on EDSOP, Sanne had seen enough death and destruction to inure her to most things, so she was mildly perturbed to realise that the gout of curdled milk and cornflakes Gobber had regurgitated all over Interview One had been enough to put her off her tuna butty.

"I can still smell it," she said, giving her sleeve a surreptitious sniff. "Are you sure he didn't get me?"

Nelson stopped typing. "I'm sure. I think his legal fees will have to include the cost of a new outfit, though."

That made Sanne smile. Most of Gobber's vomit had landed in his solicitor's lap. She nibbled the corner of her sandwich, sure she'd be hungry later if she threw it away. The office was mostly empty, as everyone not involved in the morning's interviews had headed back onto the streets to continue door-to-door or chase up the meagre leads from the hotline. While Gobber recovered in his cell, and Interview One underwent a deep clean, Sanne and Nelson were planning to visit the Beswicks' neighbours to try to glean an idea of the family's recent movements.

"Almost set?" Nelson asked.

She logged off from her computer and smoothed the tinfoil over the remnants of her lunch. "Ready when you are."

Restored to her usual co-pilot position in the pool car, she stuck her feet on the dash.

"I e-mailed the boss and updated her," she said as Nelson paused at the car park barrier. "I'm sure the CPS will authorise an extension on Gobber's custody, but I think we're barking up the wrong tree with the Beswicks."

Nelson pulled away from HQ, joining the rest of the midday traffic, a volatile combination of pensioners heading for the supermarket and tradesmen speeding to their next call. He tapped the steering wheel, mulling over her statement. In the rush to complete their paperwork and arrange for medical assistance, they hadn't had a chance to discuss the interview.

"I suppose Gobber's response can be read one of two ways," he said at length. "One: he's guilty as sin but suffered a genuine gut reaction to being confronted by his handiwork, or two: he likes to carry a knife and run his mouth off but is too squeamish to follow through on his threats. There's no record of violence in his priors."

"Difficult to know which option to go for, isn't it?" Sanne realised she was using her toes to accompany Nelson's beat on the wheel and forced herself to stop. "Our vic was abused over a period of days, though, and possibly longer. It might not take much nous to snatch a child off the streets, but keeping her concealed for any length of time points to a level of planning and premeditation that I don't see Gobber being capable of."

Nelson glanced at her, his expression bleak. "Maybe the whole family were in on it. That's not without precedent, San."

"No, it's not," she said. Although none of the Beswicks owned a car, it wasn't inconceivable that they'd abducted and molested the child as a team. The possibility made the small amount she'd eaten churn in her stomach. Gobber had only just turned eighteen, Spud was still at school, and their little sister wasn't much younger than the victim. Sanne grasped the one straw that threw doubt on the theory.

"That doesn't explain why no one's reported our vic missing," she said. "If this is a typical stranger abduction, where are her parents? Why hasn't anyone called it in? There's been nothing that fits her description in the local or nationwide missing persons." She took refuge in her frustration, letting it blot out every other emotion. "It'd be easier if the Beswicks would fucking speak to us. They've probably got alibis we could confirm, but instead they fall back on the 'no comment' routine and leave us all pissing about."

Nelson smiled at her rant. "Feel better now?"

She cocked her head to one side, taking stock. "I do, actually. Give me five minutes and I might be able to finish my sarnie."

"That's the spirit."

It took longer than her estimation, but she was just screwing up her tinfoil as Nelson parked on Phelot Walk, and the fresh air fortified her even further. She stepped around a shattered bottle sparkling in the winter sunshine and contemplated the afternoon's task.

"Pick a side, any side," she said, but then reconsidered. "Actually, I might start opposite. There was a fair bit of curtain-twitching going on last night."

He locked the car and rattled the handle just to be sure. "I'll try the immediate neighbours. The walls on this estate are so thin, I bet people can hear every word that's said."

"Right-o."

She readied her ID as she crossed the road. A flutter in the grey nets at the window suggested her presence had already been noted, and sure enough the front door opened before she'd raised her hand to knock. A woman who must have been eighty if she was a day peered through the narrow gap permitted by her security chain and added an extra defence by thrusting her walking stick toward Sanne's knee.

"Police, ma'am," Sanne said, holding her ID closer. "I wondered if I could ask you a few questions about the family at number forty-three."

"That bunch of layabouts? What do you want to know? They're dirty, noisy, lazy, flea-bitten ragamuffins, and I've complained to the council about 'em till I'm blue in the face." The woman sniffed and slid the chain from its latch. "I suppose you'd best come in before one of them throws dog shit at my window again."

Sanne followed her into a living room apparently decorated by a myopic lover of flock wallpaper. Every wall clashed with the next, each patterned like a psychedelic Rorschach test.

"What did you say your name was?" the woman asked. She flopped into a tilted chair and used a remote control to lower its position.

"I didn't. It's Sanne, Detective Sanne Jensen."

"Swedish?" The woman frowned, scrutinising her from top to toe. Sanne almost expected her to reach for the binoculars on the window sill, but she refrained. "You're too short to be Swedish."

"I'm not Swedish."

"Danish?"

"No, ma'am. I was born just down the road."

"Huh. Bloody silly name, if you ask me."

Sanne declined to comment. Her mum had chosen the name, and Sanne rarely divulged the reasoning behind it. Although it caused endless mispronunciations and misspellings, she wouldn't have swapped it for anything.

She sat on the edge of the sofa opposite the woman. "And you might be?"

"Mrs. Mary O'Donnell." Mary nudged a sepia-tinged wedding photo with her walking stick. "Widowed for nigh on twenty years now, the good Lord rest his soul."

Sanne picked up the photo, genuinely interested in the man who had been brave enough to wed Mary. He looked ordinary, neither especially handsome nor likely to stand out in a crowd, but then people might say similar about Meg, and Sanne thought the world of her.

"He were worth a damn sight more than that shower of shit over there," Mary spat. "Out at all hours, screaming and shouting, that mutt and those kids of theirs running riot. Did you arrest the lot of 'em? I hope you throw away the bleedin' key."

Sanne had opened her mouth to respond at several points in Mary's diatribe, shutting it again when she missed her chance. She let Mary run out of steam and carefully replaced the photograph as Mary sucked on an inhaler.

"Be a love and make me a brew," Mary said. "There's some bourbon biccies in the tin."

As the interview was clearly going to proceed at Mary's pace, refreshments sounded like a good idea, and the kitchen, though decorated in the same dubious taste as the living room, was clean enough that Sanne treated herself to a mug of tea. Having waited until Mary had given her seal of approval by dunking her first bourbon, Sanne uncapped her pen.

"We're investigating the death of a young girl, Mrs. O'Donnell. Perhaps you've seen something about it on the news."

"The Pakistani lass under the rocks?" Mary slurped overspill from her saucer. "What's she to do with the Beswicks? They hate all the coloureds."

"Yes, well, we're wondering whether that might have been a motivating factor." Sanne found a clean page in her notepad. "You said the family were 'out at all hours.' Have you noticed anything unusual about their comings and goings? Particularly between last Saturday and Wednesday?"

Mary sucked her biscuit through what few of her teeth remained. "Can't say as I have. The one with the ears had a scrap with the stupid one in the middle of the road a couple of nights back, but that's par for the course. They get up late, the young lass toddles to school on her own, they have chippy three times a week, the dad and the eldest go to the Dog and Duck every other night, and they all go to bed past midnight. I never see the mum, but that's hardly surprising given her size."

Sanne took dutiful notes of the Beswicks's routine, running out of room and flipping over to a new page. Although Mary hadn't intended to, she'd started to establish an alibi for Sid and Gobber, should the staff at the pub confirm their presence over the last week.

"What about vehicles? Have you seen any of them driving a silver car or van with a B at the start of its registration?"

"Absolutely not." Mary shook her head. "Hardly anyone on this side of Phelot has a car, and that lot have never driven anything unless they've nicked it. I'd remember if I'd seen them in one, because I usually take the reg for when the coppers turn up." She smirked, displaying chocolate-smeared gums. "The local bobbies know to come here first."

"I'll bet they do." Sanne could imagine her posted by her window, binoculars in hand, television remote primed to mute the programme the instant anything occurred in the street. She was a one-woman Neighbourhood Watch, the only problem being that everything she'd said assisted the Beswicks far more than the investigation.

Sanne finished the last of her tea and placed one of her cards by Mary's saucer. Her phone buzzed as she slipped her notebook into her pocket, the caller ID showing Zoe's name. "Sorry, do you mind if I get this?" she asked Mary, who waved her consent with a bourbon. She ducked into the hall and answered the call before Zoe gave up.

"San? Can you talk?"

The straight-to-business nature of the question put Sanne on alert. "Yeah. Everything okay?"

"I'm not sure," Zoe said, sounding uncharacteristically rattled. "Is there any chance you could come out here to take a look at something?"

"Where are you?" Sanne didn't have a clue what Zoe's assignment had been that day, but she assumed they were still working the same case.

"We're in a barn. It belongs to Nab Hey Farm, just off Old Road. Our sarge sent us, and it sounded like nothing at the time, just a woman who thought she'd seen lights one night while she was driving home and eventually called the hotline when she read about the body at Greave."

"And?" Sanne asked. All the hairs on her arms were standing up.

"And someone's been here, San." Zoe's voice dropped a notch. "They tried to clean up, but we've found stuff they missed. I didn't know who else to call. I don't want to set all the bells and whistles off and then have it turn out to be a waste of everyone's time."

Sanne checked her watch, trying to plan for an unanticipated detour. It was 2:15 p.m. If Nelson wanted to stay on Phelot, she could pick him up on her way back or arrange for someone to collect him.

"I can be with you in about an hour, hopefully less," she said. "Treat it as a scene, if you think it might be one, and preserve as much as you can." She went into the kitchen and closed the door. "Zoe, do you think the vic was held there?"

Zoe took a shaky breath. "Not just her," she said. "San, we might be wrong about this, but it looks like several women have been kept here."

Chapter Nine

As her profession required her to render aid should she happen across a medical emergency, Meg always carried a bag of kit in her car, which left her well-equipped to make an unofficial house call on thirty-two Windermere Avenue.

"Thank you so much for coming," Teresa Jensen said, giving her a quick hug on the doorstep. That she kept her voice to a whisper implied she hadn't told her husband anything about Meg's visit. The house, as usual, smelled of fresh baking, her cheeks were dusted with flour, and two children could be heard squabbling in the kitchen.

"I'm minding Kiera and Kerby while Keeley has a rest," she said. "We've been making buns."

Meg put an arm around her shoulders. "When do *you* get a rest?"

"When they're all in bed. Are you going to see him now?" Teresa nodded at the first door on the right. It was always shut, keeping the children out and the smell of John Jensen in.

Meg nodded, keen to get it over with. "Aye. Wish me luck."

As Teresa went back to referee the kids, Meg tapped on the door and opened it without waiting for permission. The room was dark, with its curtains drawn against the daylight, and the television on standby. She stood on the threshold and allowed her eyes to adjust. She crinkled her nose at the stench of an unwashed body and stale alcohol, but beneath that was something more troubling, a smell she recognised from work.

"Shut that fucking door, Teresa. How many times do I have to fucking tell you?" John growled from his usual corner.

Meg did as he demanded, able now to discern the empty cider

bottles and cigarette packets littering the carpet. Several darkened patches amid the detritus suggested he had failed to reach the toilet on numerous occasions.

"It's not Teresa, John. It's Meg Fielding." She walked over and set her bag on the coffee table. "Sanne asked me to come. She said you've not been well." Meg hoped he might be too addled to connect any of this back to his wife. Even in the dim light, she could see that Teresa's concerns were well founded. He was jaundiced and emaciated, with a belly so distended that he looked nine months pregnant. The bucket by his side was a quarter full of coffee-ground vomit and cigarette butts.

He glared up at her, his yellowed eyes alive with spite. "Sanne can fuck off, and so can you. I don't need nobody checking up on me or telling me what to do." He lit a cigarette with trembling hands and exhaled the smoke toward her.

She let the cloud dissipate and then leaned down low. "I'm not here for your sake," she said quietly. "I don't give a flying fuck if you want to drink yourself into oblivion and stroke out in this miserable room in your shitty little chair. I just don't want Teresa to come in here one morning and find your body. So let me take some blood tests and examine your belly. I can already see you need admitting to hospital, but whether you let me arrange that is up to you."

He drew on his fag again, though he directed the smoke away from her this time. "I'm staying here. Do your fucking tests, but I'm not going nowhere."

She shrugged. He was lucid enough to have mental capacity, so he could make his own decisions, however ill-advised. "That's your choice. At least I'll be able to give Teresa an idea of what to expect and when to expect it."

His baseline observations, when she took them, were predictably deranged: pulse too high, blood pressure too low. His temperature was fine, but that was scant consolation. She found a vein at the third attempt and drew off multiple samples.

"How often are you being sick?" she asked.

"I've not been counting."

When she tilted the bucket, he flicked his cigarette into it, making the vomit sizzle and sending up a smell of raw liver.

"Does it always look like this?"

"Yeah, mostly. So what?"

"So it's blood, that's what." She palpated his abdomen, noting where he was tender and guarded. "You probably have an ulcer that's bleeding, but I won't know for sure unless you go to the hospital."

"You got wax in your ears?" He tried to shove at her but could barely keep his arm raised long enough to make contact. "I'm not moving from this chair."

She began packing her kit away. "Fine. I'll run your bloods and send the results to your own doctor. Maybe he'll be able to talk some sense into you."

John unscrewed a fresh bottle of cider, slopping it over the arm of the chair as he tried to aim it into a pint glass. "You finished?"

"Yes, I'm finished."

Opening the door was like finding a gateway to the Promised Land. She took her shoes off at the threshold, not wanting to trek anything down Teresa's spotless hallway. Teresa was watching from the kitchen, Kiera in her arms and Kerby hanging on to her apron.

"Will he go to the hospital?" she asked.

Meg shook her head. "I'll speak to his doctor this afternoon. Perhaps John will listen to him."

"He won't," Teresa said. "The only person John listens to is John."

"I think we might be past the point of changing that." Meg placed her shoes on the mat by the door and took Kerby's hand. "C'mon, kiddo, how about we do the washing up with Kiera and let Nana have a sit down?"

Old Road was slightly easier to navigate in daylight than darkness, but Nelson—no fan of the Peak District's serpentine passes under any conditions—had handed Sanne the car keys mere seconds after deciding to accompany her to Nab Hey Farm. A sharp shower had slicked the frost-pocked tarmac, forcing Sanne to concentrate on her driving rather than admire the fresh covering of snow on the hilltops. Although travelling in the opposite direction from last time, she recognised the stretch where she'd found the crash debris and the mangled sheep, and she slowed for the bend that followed.

"The farm is about a mile before the start of Smithy Reservoir," she said, accelerating out of the curve and clipping a pothole that rattled her teeth. "If I remember rightly, it's stood empty for more than a year, though I'm not sure why. Ron Stanton might be a good one to ask about it. He's usually clued up on the local gossip." She glanced left toward Brabyn's Tor, but she couldn't see the stones on its summit, just a layer of white fading in and out of low cloud.

Nelson had followed her eye line and noticed the weather rolling in. "What's the forecast for tonight?"

"More snow over the tops. Rain and sleet in Sheffield. Lows of minus three," she said, reciting what she'd read on the BBC website.

"Crikey. Do you think we'll get home?"

"I bloody hope so. I don't fancy bivouacking out here."

Indicating right out of habit, even though there was no one behind her, she eased the car onto the farm's access lane. Empty fields bordered both sides of the track, large sections of them overgrown, with floodwater in the dips. It was obvious that no stock had been grazed there for months, nor had anyone bothered to maintain the approach road. Unkempt hawthorn squealed against the car's paintwork.

"Here we go," Sanne said, spotting the patrol car parked by the first of the farm buildings.

As Sanne manoeuvred around a puddle and into a space, Zoe climbed out of the patrol car, raising a hand in greeting. She barely managed a smile, though, and her hair—usually held in an immaculate twist—was falling from its clips and blowing in her eyes.

"Hiya," she said. "We've been trying to make some notes while everything's fresh. My mate's going to stay here and finish them off, if that's okay?"

"That's fine." Sanne grabbed torches from the car boot. Neither she nor Nelson had speculated much upon what Zoe might have found, preferring to see the evidence instead of formulating wild theories en route. Now, listening to the wind rushing through the narrow gaps between the empty buildings, she felt a thudding at her temples as her blood pressure rose.

"Best suit up," Zoe said. "We've already tromped in a load of shit that we shouldn't have." She donned the forensic clothing that Sanne gave her and set off without further explanation, leading them along another track that curled and climbed beside a stream, eventually tapering out at the entrance to a field. She pointed to a large stone barn with a smaller building a few yards away from it. "It's this one."

"How many other buildings are there?" Sanne asked.

"I'm not sure. We checked here first because you can see it from the road. Then I called you, and we decided to stay out of the rest in case we buggered something up. The door wasn't locked, just held by string looped over a nail. We figured anyone needing shelter could've gone inside, so we didn't try to get permission."

The door started to open when Zoe pushed on it, but it snagged on an uneven section of floor, leaving them to squeeze into the space beyond. They stood shoulder to shoulder, the darkness ahead alleviated only by a single dirty window and the tiny cracks in the mortar between the stones. An unpleasant smell hung in the air, nothing that Sanne could readily identify, though it seemed to crawl along her skin. She and Nelson switched on their torches almost in unison, Sanne aiming hers at her boots, reluctant to direct it anywhere specific until she had an idea of what it might illuminate.

"Over here," Zoe said. "We marked out a path." She used her own torch to highlight a thin walkway, its edges created by scraping two lines in the hardened layer of muck that covered the floor. The smell became stronger the farther into the barn they went, and Zoe paused just as Sanne resorted to covering her nose with her sleeve.

"We think this was the toilet. Someone's tried to dig it over, but they only did half a job." Zoe indicated a small pen with low stone walls and a lip where a gate could have sat. The beam of her torch picked out the shreds of tissue paper still visible amid the churned-up filth.

"What the hell has been going on here?" Sanne asked.

"Nothing good." Zoe moved on to another walled section, twice the size of the first, with its gate still in situ.

Sanne stepped through the gate and panned her torch around.

"Right-hand side, about twelve inches up," Zoe said. "See where the daylight's peeking in?"

"Yeah." Treading in the fresh boot prints, Sanne crossed the pen and crouched by the wall to examine the stone that Zoe had picked out. It sat at an odd angle, the crumbling mortar around it and its neighbour mostly scraped away. She touched her gloved fingers to the block. Dots of crimson had splattered its surface where bare skin had torn on it. Although someone had managed to loosen and nudge it, they hadn't been strong enough to force a way through. "Fucking hell," she whispered. "They were so close to getting out."

She could hear Nelson on the radio. Apparently convinced by the findings, he was requesting EDSOP backup and SOCO.

"Look on the floor, in the corner." Zoe came up behind Sanne and took hold of her torch hand, guiding the beam to the right place. "My mate caught it when the sun shone."

Sanne caught it as well, a flash of yellowed metal, almost completely buried, the earth around it newly disturbed.

"He dug a bit before I could tell him not to." Zoe pulled two small evidence bags from her pocket. "We think they might have hidden something from each of them."

Sanne raised the bags into her light. The first bore a strip of patterned cloth edged with red brocade, the second a scrap torn from a photograph. The woman in the image wore a hijab and had averted her eyes from the camera. She was older than the girl found on the moors, perhaps in her early twenties. The dusty rural setting suggested the photograph had been taken overseas.

"There's a partial print on the back," Sanne said, passing the bags to Nelson. "Her hands must have been bleeding when she ripped it."

"What are you thinking, San?" he asked.

"I'm not sure." She turned again to the corner with its potential register of victims. "We'll need SOCO to confirm whether more than one person really has been held here, but it does seem that way, doesn't it?"

He nodded. "Judging by that picture, trafficking is the most feasible explanation. The demographics aren't typical, though."

"True, but it marries up with our vic's absence going unreported. Her family could still be waiting to hear from her." Sanne shook her head, imagining the news they would be receiving instead, and then had a minor attack of the collywobbles as she considered the potential implications of their findings. Three people struggling in the dark with crap equipment were nowhere near adequate to perform an effective search. They needed forensic expertise, and Eleanor to be there calling the shots. "Did the boss give an ETA?" she asked.

"An hour. SOCO said ninety minutes."

On the other hand, she thought, Eleanor would wonder what the hell they'd been doing wasting precious daylight if they called it quits after one barn. "We should check the building next to this one," she said. "Our perps can't have been in here all the time or they'd have heard the attempts to break through the wall, but they were probably close by."

"Why choose this place?" Zoe asked as they walked single-file toward the door.

"Sorting house?" Nelson suggested. "Pakistan International flies into Manchester or Leeds Bradford, and this is a good halfway point between the two."

"Secluded and abandoned, and off a road that barely anyone uses," Sanne said. "Perfect as a stopover. Well, perfect until one of your lasses escapes and the police start sniffing around."

The sudden brightness of the sun made her stumble on the first clod of grass she encountered. Shielding her eyes, she started toward the neighbouring barn. A more recent adjunct to the first, its roof was sound and its stone walls showed no signs of degradation. A shiny, heavy-duty padlock secured its door.

Nelson turned the padlock in his fingers and pressed on the hinges, assessing their worth. "There's reasonable suspicion, it's doable, and we'll be able to preserve the lock," he concluded.

Sanne had no problem with that, and Zoe was already limbering up. They took turns to kick at the lowest hinges, their boots pounding against the metal. The brackets gave way almost simultaneously, the door collapsing inward as Nelson shoulder-charged it.

With one hand on her Taser and the other aiming her torch, Sanne yelled "Police!" into the void. When nothing stirred or responded, she crept forward, scanning for signs of life or recent inhabitation. She found the latter almost immediately: an upended Calor gas stove and empty food tins. Leaving them untouched, she headed for the largest of the barn's pens. A gas burner had been placed in this one as well, carefully positioned between two single mattresses.

"So we could be looking for at least two perps," Nelson said.

"Yeah," she agreed absently, her attention focused on the dirt and straw adhering to the surface of each mattress. "Nelson, help me flip this over."

He gave her a puzzled look but did as she asked. As the mattress fell back into place, they stepped away from the thick cloud of dust and let it settle.

"Oh God." Sanne froze, her torch beam fixed on the vivid stains that had made her catch her breath. Behind her, Nelson swore with rare vehemence, and Zoe kicked something solid. Sanne turned to face them. "We should get out of here and leave everything for SOCO. We can't risk making a mess of this."

She switched off her torch, relying on the threads of daylight to guide her exit. She'd seen enough.

CHAPTER TEN

The forensics tent blazed with LEDs, the background rumble of the generator giving DCI Litton the perfect excuse to raise his voice at Eleanor, not that he ever needed one. Having arrived at Nab Hey Farm an hour after her, he'd declined her invitation to walk up to the buildings now established as crime scenes, probably because he didn't want to get cow shit on his expensive shoes, and he'd spent much of his time attempting to use his phone in an area renowned for unreliable mobile coverage.

"Fucking stupid godforsaken place!" He jabbed at the screen of his iPhone and thrust it back into his pocket. "You need to liaise with GMP's Modern Slavery Team. If they start bitching about their budgets, tell them that Manchester is your probable entry point, and get as many of their boys on board as you can."

"Yes, sir," Eleanor said, tolerating his patronising "teaching your granny to suck eggs" approach only because she hoped it might expedite his leaving the scene.

"With luck this will turn out to be the work of our friends from the Eastern Bloc." He rubbed his hands, his expression suddenly jovial. "That mob are up to their eyes in this sort of shit, and we'll be able to avoid any messy confrontations with the Pakistanis."

"Yes, sir." By this point she would have agreed to pretty much anything to get him to shut up and go.

"Right, well." He drew his coat collar closed and eyed the sky beyond the tent. Thick clouds had obliterated the stars, driven by a northerly wind that was making the canvas billow. "I'll be issuing a brief statement to the media tonight, with a view to scheduling a full press conference once the forensics begin to yield results. Keep me informed."

She gave a curt nod, hoping he would chair the press conference himself. Although media involvement was crucial, he had a love for grandstanding that she didn't share.

"Will do, sir."

He marched away, but his escape was hindered by a SOCO tech at the entrance, and they performed an awkward two-step dance before Litton resorted to shoving his way past. The tech stared after him for a moment and then headed across to Eleanor.

"That's everything from the barn, ma'am."

"Thank you."

Eleanor took the evidence bags from him and arranged them side by side on the trestle table. There were seven in total: five new ones to add to the two that Sanne had given her earlier. As before, their contents were distinct, each suggesting the presence of a separate individual: three more shreds of cloth, one brightly patterned and the others faded cotton; a fragment of cheap, gold-plated jewellery; and a Pakistani rupee coin. Running out of space, she nudged the bags until they overlapped, keeping them apart from those containing a selection of discarded condom wrappers. It didn't seem right, somehow, to let them touch.

"Fucking hell," she said, too quietly for the departing tech to notice. It wasn't the crime that she took personally; anyone with an ounce of humanity would be repulsed by what appeared to have gone on here. But the thought that someone operating in her patch had stored people like animals, had kept them in pens and abused them, and then managed to herd them on to who knew what future? That really did piss her off.

"Boss?"

She spun around, grateful for Sanne's cautious interruption. Sanne hadn't moved beyond the entrance of the tent. Looking starved with cold and dead on her feet, she seemed oblivious to the mud on her trousers and the flakes of fresh snow dotting her hat. Eleanor forced herself not to comment. She had never treated Sanne any differently to the men on her team, but still there were moments when she had to bite her tongue and let Sanne tough it out.

"All the other buildings are clear," Sanne said. "They've only used those two. SOCO have just removed the second mattress. I spoke to a tech, who said blood typing would be done overnight. DNA comparisons will take longer to run, but they'll have the samples gendered by tomorrow."

"Hair and fibres?"

"We've got both, as well as tissue samples from the wall. No semen, though. I guess everyone used protection." She came across to the table as she answered. She glanced at the array of multicoloured packaging and picked up the bag with the coin in it. "I spoke to Nelson. He got back okay, but he's struggling to trace the current owner of this place. I wondered about calling in to see Ron Stanton on my way home. He ought to know who lived here, at the very least. Nelson left me the pool car, so it wouldn't be a bother, and I have to order some chicken feed from Ron."

That last detail made Eleanor smile. "Okay, then, but only if you need to go there anyway," she said, knowing damn well that Sanne—like herself—would rather be heading straight home to a hot meal and bed.

"I'll set off now, before the snow really kicks in." Sanne put the coin back in its place. "Briefing's at seven tomorrow, right?"

"That's right."

Neither commented on working the weekend. All leave had been cancelled as of that afternoon. While it didn't happen often, it was simply assumed that everyone would be on shift or on call until the investigation concluded.

"I'll e-mail you when I get in." Sanne tugged her hat lower. "Night, boss."

"Drive safely, Sanne."

Eleanor waited for the tent's flaps to fall into place behind Sanne and then took out her mobile. With the signal hovering at one dubious bar, she dialled the number from memory, her mood brightening as a long-familiar voice answered.

"Russell Parry, MST."

❖

Never sure when the local pub quiz was, Sanne had phoned ahead to check Ron would be at home. She parked beside his Land Rover and jumped out into a thick layer of slush.

"Bollocks."

Cold water seeped into her boots, refreezing toes she had just managed to thaw. Her empty stomach rumbled, and the wind biting at her cheeks made her sneeze.

"Sanne? Good Lord, girl, get in here and sit by the bloody fire!" Ron shouted. He was standing at the kitchen door, not daft enough to venture outside, but one of his collies trotted across to greet Sanne and subtly shepherd her in the right direction.

The heat from the AGA set her shivering, and Ron plucked off her hat as she worked on unzipping her coat with numb fingers.

"Sorry to call round so late," she said, shocked to see the wall clock ticking past a quarter to nine. "I won't stay long."

He hung her wet coat by the door. "Don't worry, love. Come into the living room. Trudy's just made a pot of tea."

Almost falling over her socks in her haste to get to the open fire, Sanne waved at Trudy, who was plating up thick slices of fruit cake.

"You can adopt me any time, y'know." Sanne accepted a mug and settled onto the sofa with the collie. Steam rose from her trousers as she pushed closer to the fire. "Well, maybe we could arrange a part-share with my mum."

Ron laughed into his mug but then sobered. "So what's happened at Nab Hey?"

"We're not entirely sure yet," she said slowly, deliberating on how much to disclose. "An organised gang might have been using it, but SOCO—sorry, Scene of Crime Officers, like the CSI off the telly—are still working on the details."

"Has it to do with the child at Greave?" Trudy asked.

"Quite possibly." Sanne sipped her tea. "She may have been held in one of the farm buildings for a while."

Ron's mug clattered as he set it down on his plate. "Bloody hell! Why the devil would they go up there?"

"Good question, and one I was hoping you might be able to help answer."

He scratched the coarse growth of his beard, anger sending a tremor through his hand. "I don't get over that way, San. I don't have any reason to use Old Road."

"No, I didn't think so. That's not why I came here." She fished out her notepad. "We're having trouble tracking down the present owner of Nab Hey, and I thought you might know."

"That'd be the Burkes." Ron scoffed. "Burke by name, berks by nature, if you catch my drift."

She raised an eyebrow. "I take it you're not close friends?"

"We got on fine with Marvin Burke," Trudy said, cutting another slice of cake and sliding it onto Sanne's plate. "But he's been dead eighteen months or more now, and his children aren't worth the cowclap on his boots, the grasping little misers."

"Ah, right," Sanne said, beginning to get the picture. "Well, you know what they say. Where there's a will, there's a relative."

"Aye," Ron said. "They all moved out of the area, and none of them wants to take the farm on, so they're bickering over their piece of the pie. It's been tied up in probate since Marv passed."

"That explains a lot." Sanne tapped her pen on her teeth. "Don't suppose you have any contact information for the children?"

"Not as such, but I know the law firm handling the probate, if that'll be any use." He went to the telephone table and flicked through an address book. It took him a while to find the right page, but he eventually scribbled a name and number down and handed her the slip of paper. "Here you go."

"Thanks, Ron. I'm sure this'll be a great help."

"No problem. Now, what about them chickens and that miserable little bastard of yours? Do you want the same as usual?"

She stuffed in the last of her cake and nodded until she'd swallowed. "Yes, please." She followed him back into the kitchen.

"Fox not got him yet?"

"Not yet." She began to pull on her boots, her toes recoiling from the damp insides. "I live in hope."

He waited for her to fasten her coat and took the twenty-pound note she dug from her wallet. "Should have it in by Thursday. Have you got enough to see you through?"

"Yep, Thursday's fine."

He walked with her across the yard, patting the roof of her Landie fondly as she fastened her seat belt. "Take it easy. I doubt it's done snowing yet."

"So long as it holds off for half an hour. Tell Trudy thanks for the cake."

"Will do."

She ground the gears into reverse and gave Ron's toes a wide berth. As the warm glow of the kitchen receded in her rearview mirror, she concentrated on reaching the Snake Pass without fishtailing into a hedge. She wasn't in any rush to get home. With Meg on nights, her cottage would be cold and empty. No supper waiting on the table, and no warm body to share the bed.

She changed down a gear as the engine began to whine, reminding herself that she'd spent years on her own and that this was what she usually came home to. Besides which, it would be nice to have some alone time. Pausing at the junction, she decided this carefully constructed argument was a right load of crap. After a day like today, alone time was the last thing she wanted.

Wrapped in a blanket and with a belly full of soup and toast, Sanne was trying not to fall asleep onto her book again when the phone rang. Fearing an EDSOP summons to drag her back out into the snow, she checked the caller ID through her fingers, only exhaling when she saw Meg's name.

"Hey, you," she said. "How goes it?"

Meg's response was interrupted by a siren, indicating she was hiding in the ambulance bay as usual.

"Everyone is very very drunk tonight," she said, once the background din had subsided. "Except for me, of course. And Horny Keith. He was sober as a judge."

"Horny Keith?" Sanne closed her book, suitably intrigued. "I'm assuming there's a story behind that name."

Meg crunched something before she answered. "Nice old chap got himself a new girlfriend, only she's forty-eight and he's eighty-four. He pops three Viagra in a pre-coital fit of nerves and promptly faints. Thinking she's killed him, she snaps two of his ribs performing over-enthusiastic CPR like she's seen on the telly."

"Oh, dear God. You couldn't make this shit up, could you?"

"Not a chance." Meg slurped a drink and laughed at the same time. "Sorry, this is the first break I've had. You've not been waiting up for me, have you?"

"No, not at all. This book I'm reading is really good." Sanne didn't put much effort into the fib. She knew Meg would see through it in a heartbeat.

"You're a daft sod. Are you in again tomorrow?"

"I am now." The log burner's flames were throwing patterns onto the chimney breast, and Sanne let her eyes unfocus as she watched them. "Zoe called in a lead at a farm off Old Road. It looks like a gang have been trafficking women through the area and using one of the barns as some kind of holding station. We were out there most of the day."

"And most of the night by the sound of you," Meg said. "No wonder you're not asleep. Are you okay?"

Sanne hesitated; her statutory "I'm fine" never washed with Meg. "I'm as okay as I'm going to be." She drew up her knees, sending her book thudding to the floor. "But it's so fucking frustrating, Meg. We've no idea how long it's been going on for, or how many people are involved, and we'll probably never trace all of the victims. They have no identity over here and no one to protect them, and they'll just vanish into the worst kind of life imaginable."

"At least you know now that it's happening. You have a place to start."

Sanne hugged her knees with her free hand. "Aye, but a child had to die first. Jesus, we're complacent around here. It's like everyone walks about with their eyes shut, smug in the belief that bad stuff only happens in the city."

"Till some arsehole comes along to disprove that."

"Yeah, there's been a few of those recently." She sighed, aware that she'd have to let Meg go soon. "Speaking of arseholes, did you manage to see my dad?"

"I did, and I got his blood results about ten minutes ago."

"How bad are they?" she asked, alerted by Meg's careful tone.

"If I were his doctor, I'd be dragging him into A&E by his ear. He's been vomiting blood, so he's anaemic, and his liver function is diabolical, which means he's not clotting properly. I've e-mailed his

GP, and I'll phone the surgery first thing Monday morning. My hands are a bit tied, with it being the weekend."

"Any idea what's causing the bleeding?" Sanne wasn't asking for her dad's sake; she just wanted to warn her mum if the prognosis was likely to be poor.

"Probably an ulcer, but I have no way of knowing for sure. He won't let me do anything about it." Meg cursed beneath her breath as someone in the background shouted her name. "I've got to run, San. Try not to worry about your mum," she said, effortlessly pinpointing where Sanne's concern lay.

"I'll try," Sanne said, though she knew she'd fail. "Night, love."

Chapter Eleven

Eleanor didn't look up from her paperwork when someone rapped on her door. Confident that it was too early for Litton, she shouted, "Come in!" and turned a page, frowning at the scarcity of the detail in the forensics report.

"Morning, ma'am."

The Mancunian accent and the scent of fresh coffee had her smiling before she raised her head, and she left her desk to greet her visitor with a warm handshake.

"Hey, stranger. It's been far too long."

"I know." Russ Parry planted a wet kiss on her cheek. "I tried to work it out last night. Is it really five years? That conference in Nottingham?"

"Integrated Offender Management? Bloody hell, that was a fun day." She watched him take the chair in front of her desk and set out napkins and polystyrene boxes. Five years had put a couple of inches on his waist and left his dark hair peppered with grey, but he'd weathered better than some of her colleagues, and she was genuinely glad to see him. He slid one coffee toward her and then changed his mind, swapping the two cups.

"There's a shot of espresso in mine," he said. "Getting up at four a.m. damn near killed me."

He'd brought their usual breakfast from Den's: bacon and egg barmcakes with mushrooms. Eleanor debated cutting the fat off her bacon rasher but decided it was too much trouble and tucked straight in. He grinned at her, taking obvious delight in leading her astray.

"Are you still in Didsbury?" she asked.

"No, Altrincham. We downsized after Ed went to uni. Doug and the kids okay?"

"They're all fine. Anna's in her second year at York, and the lads are both in sixth form."

"Great stuff. Give them my best." Russ dabbed egg yolk from his chin and gulped down half his coffee. "Ah, that's the ticket. Right, where are we at?"

"These are the overnight forensics from the barn," she said, gathering the pages and handing them over. She would have liked to spend more time catching up, but with an early team briefing scheduled, she knew they didn't have the luxury. "Did you manage to read through everything I sent you?"

"Yes, and I've copied a few recent case studies into the main directory to give your team an idea of what they might be dealing with." He pushed aside the remnants of their breakfast to make space for his laptop. He'd always been adept at switching from small talk to business, a trick that frequently wrong-footed perps during interview. "We have a number of individuals under surveillance, but none of them seem to be stepping out of area, and none have known links to your patch."

"That would make our job far too easy, wouldn't it?" She stirred sugar into her coffee, grinding the spoon against the base of the cup. "Despite everything we found yesterday, we're no further ahead. These bastards imprisoned and raped multiple women and left barely any trace of themselves. At some point they even had the balls to go back and attempt to clean house, probably after realising we had no fucking clue what type of crime we were even investigating."

"How were you to know?"

His sensible question allayed some of Eleanor's exasperation. She shook her head, grateful for a fresh point of view. "I suppose we weren't, but we should at least have considered it a possibility."

"Unlikely age and ethnicity, El." Russ exchanged one file for another. "Most of the female vics we've been seeing recently are brought in from Eastern Europe, Africa, China. Believe me, it's a growing market. I sign on to a mile-high pile of new shit every morning."

"I can imagine." She raised her coffee in appreciation. "Thank you for coming here to wade through some of mine."

❖

"Oi! Hold it, San!"

Still half asleep, Sanne slapped a hand on the wrong button, prompting the lift doors to close on Fred's desperate lunge. She hit the next button instead, and he limped in as the doors changed course.

"What the devil happened to you?" she said, dodging his dramatic collapse against the far wall.

"I put my bloody back out last night." He mopped his sweaty brow with a handkerchief and then used it to blow his nose.

"Salsa again? You need to give that up, mate. It's bad for y— oh…" She trailed off as he turned cherry-red and shook his head. "Ah, right. Say no more."

He scuffed the floor with his boot like a lovelorn adolescent. "I think I'm falling for her, San. She makes me want to write poems and buy her teddies and stuff."

They squashed closer together as the lift stopped and three SOCO got on.

"I'm very happy for you." Sanne hugged Fred's arm, wondering whether a wedding might be on the horizon. She'd missed out on his first three. "Would you like some ibuprofen?"

"Yes, please, and the name of that fancy restaurant you took your doctor missus to."

She kept hold of his arm as they exited the lift. "Sine Qua Non," she said.

"Bless you." He offered her his hanky.

"That's the restaurant, you pillock. It's a little place in Hawdale." "Italian?"

"The name's Latin, but it was all a bit fusion. Lovely, though." She steered him to his desk and dropped two painkillers into his palm. "Keep moving or you'll seize up."

He gave a filthy laugh. "Funny, that's what Martha told me last night."

Sanne's mouth dropped open. "I'm going to pretend I never heard that," she said as he winked at her and knocked back the pills. She stuck her fingers in her ears and made a beeline for her desk in case he decided to embellish his tale. Once out of the danger zone, she raised a pre-emptive finger to cut off Nelson's enquiry. "Trust me, you don't want to know."

"That bad?" Nelson looked beyond her, watching Fred adjust his chair.

"Much worse. I may never recover." She started her computer and logged on to the main case directory. As was customary at the weekend, it took an age for the system to process her request, and people were filing into the briefing room before the last icon appeared. Leaving everything running, she picked up her notebook. "How many are we expecting?" she asked Nelson.

"I'm not sure. From the overtime register, SOET are coming on board, plus anyone else who wanted to work this weekend."

Uncertain of protocol, the uniformed officers parted to allow Sanne and Nelson through, only filling the gaps in the seating once EDSOP and the SOET detectives had found places. Eleanor entered the room five minutes early.

"Good morning, everyone," she said, cueing silence. "I'm going to keep this as concise as possible because we have a lot to get through and even more to be getting on with. The labs have pulled an all-nighter to analyse the samples obtained from the two barns, primarily the blood found on the mattresses, plus the blood and tissue from the barn wall. So far they've isolated four blood types, and all the samples have been gendered as female. DNA profiling is ongoing, and only that will give us a real idea of how many victims we could be dealing with. Obviously, we still need to confirm whether our victim from Greave was held at Nab Hey, but we are operating on that assumption."

She paused to change PowerPoint slides, selecting a shot of the mattresses in situ at the second barn. The sight of them, even without the accompanying smell or the darkness, was enough to make Sanne chew on her thumbnail.

"Despite extensive searches, we have almost nothing from our perps," Eleanor continued, once the murmurs had died down. "Two partial fingerprints were lifted from two separate condom wrappers, but neither belongs to anyone with a record, and there was no semen on the mattresses. A half-empty box of latex gloves, and the condom use, suggests that everyone who came into contact with the victims was well protected. Several fragments of tyre treads were noted in the yard, but the poor weather rendered them impossible to cast. However," she smiled faintly, "it's not all doom and gloom. SOCO have confirmed the make and model of the crash debris found on Old Road as a Toyota Previa minivan. Here you go." She flicked to the relevant slide, her smile broadening at the ragged cheer that went up from her audience. "We're going to focus on the M67 cameras, particularly where that motorway terminates just before Hawdale, and GMP are helping us out with the cameras around Manchester airport. Although the dates closest to the vic's estimated time of death are our priority, the timeframe has necessarily been extended to account for the business at Nab Hey, so quite a few of you are going to be staring at a lot of blurry footage. Take regular breaks. I'd rather you nipped for a fag every half hour than fade out and miss something vital."

She stepped to the side and handed the remote to a man Sanne didn't recognise.

"This is DI Russell Parry from GMP's Modern Slavery Team. While we'll also have input from our own Sexual Offences and Exploitation Team, the MST was created purely to investigate cases of human trafficking."

"Thank you, DI Stanhope." Parry gave Eleanor a formal nod, but the pause he'd left between her title and surname suggested he rarely used them. He selected his first slide and let it sit without commentary for a long moment.

Sanne stared at the pieces of cloth and jewellery, the scrap of photograph, and the coin. Someone had brushed them almost clean and laid them out like the eccentric collection of a proud magpie. They reminded her of personal effects salvaged after some natural disaster, when everything else had been swept away and no one knew how many were lost. None of the material matched the clothing the dead girl had been wearing, but it was impossible to be sure when they had only found half her outfit.

"We're probably looking for a well-organised and well-connected group in conjunction with this crime," Parry said. "Blood typing has identified at least four victims, and their ethnicity is as yet unknown. These items suggest seven, and that could be the tip of the iceberg. From victim testimony in previous cases, we know that trafficked women are lured to the UK by promises of education, employment, your basic better-life bullshit. These women are some of the most vulnerable you will ever encounter—poor, uneducated, desperate. Most don't speak a word of English. Once across the border, the traffickers seize the victims' passports, leaving them entirely dependent on the gang. The women are subsequently coerced into prostitution, domestic slavery, marriage, and in some cases pregnancy. The going rate for a trafficked victim is around three thousand pounds."

As Parry took a sip of water, Sanne scribbled the number down and underlined it, repulsed by the notion that she could buy another human's freedom for less than two months of her wage. She quickly turned to a blank page when he began to speak again.

"Given the various condom sizes recovered from the second barn, it would appear that multiple males visited this property. Perhaps—and I apologise for my choice of phrasing—the perps set up a 'try before you buy' agreement, or perhaps they were prostituting these women from the premises. Either scenario points toward an extremely bold operation and one that could have been ongoing for some time. They didn't manage a thorough clean-up, but they did supply disposable gloves and condoms, suggesting an awareness of basic forensics and perhaps a certain level of bravado, along the lines of 'we've left this for you to find because we know you'll get nothing from it.'"

Nelson stopped writing and raised his hand. "Does that imply a gang with no priors?"

"In all honesty, it's difficult to say." Parry clicked off the overhead. "These people don't tend to come from squeaky-clean backgrounds; they've usually racked up a record by the time they're well enough connected to pull off something of this magnitude. It's more likely to mean our perps were just damn careful, while the men they were doing business with are the ones with no criminal history."

Sanne mulled that over, trying to imagine a regular bloke driving to an abandoned farmhouse in the middle of the Peaks to assault a woman for an agreed fee. It was prostitution amplified to a whole new degree, and it had taken place practically on her doorstep. She held her pen up. "Sir?"

"Go ahead."

"How do the buyers find out about any of this? I mean, it's not like the perps run an ad in the local paper." She hesitated, suddenly unsure. "Is it?"

"You'd be surprised, but no, most of the business is touted online. Forums, message boards, dating sites, social media—the usual suspects.

I suspect any messages relating to Nab Hey will have been removed by now, but they were probably just a phone number and a keyword or code that wouldn't mean anything to a layperson."

Eleanor returned to the front, a stack of papers in her arms. She gave them to the first available officer and indicated he should send them around the group. "Assignment sheets, forensics summary, and hard copies of a couple of case studies that DI Parry has also uploaded onto the system. If you have any further questions, please feel free to pick his brains. That's what he's here for."

"And for the coffee," Parry added. "You have far better coffee here than we get in Manchester."

Sanne flipped through her handout until she found the day's tasks. "You're contacting the Burke family," she told Nelson, who was still wrestling with the pages. "I've got local agents dealing with agricultural land sale, and then we're both on CCTV and any follow-up house calls."

Nelson mimed hanging himself with his tie. "Something tells me this is going to be a very long day."

❖

Sanne added another sheep to the doodle she had started during her first phone call. Eight estate agents later, all of whom had placed her on hold, her sketch of Kinder Scout and its surrounding hills boasted a unicorn prancing beside a waterfall, along with a pair of winsome shepherdesses corralling an impressive variety of livestock.

"Celine Dion," she whispered to Nelson. "Makes a change from Ed-fucking-Sheeran."

"A change for the better?"

She held the phone away from her ear as the ballad reached its crescendo. "No, just a change. Any joy with daughter number two?"

He glanced at his notes. "Nope. She's a new media consulting executive—whatever the heck that is—in Shoreditch, and she hasn't been to Nab Hey or had any direct dealings with it since her dad died. Her main concern was whether our investigation would adversely affect its value."

Sanne drew an angry face on her sheep. "It's good that she has her priorities straight," she said, and then abandoned her doodle for her checklist as the agent returned to the line. "Oh, hello. Right, so you don't keep any record of enquiries? No note of interested parties, on the off chance that something suitable comes up for them? And you can't recall anyone asking about vacant or available farms in the last twelve months?" Her list rapidly filled with crosses as the agent equivocated. Passing client details to the police was apparently bad for business, because Sanne's entire morning's work had gleaned only three names, and one of those was a septuagenarian living in California. Although Nab Hey had never been on the market and consequently never sported a "for sale" sign, the gang who had utilised it must have heard about it from somewhere.

"Okay, thank you for your time." She hung up and rubbed a couple of her knuckles. The finger she'd once broken punching a murder suspect got stiff in damp weather, and rain was currently battering the office window.

"Is that all of yours done?" Nelson asked.

"All the ones on my list, at least." Never having smoked, she awarded herself an e-mail break instead. "Did you see that Gobber Beswick has been charged with racially aggravated harassment and released on bail?"

"No, I didn't. What about the rest of them?"

"Released without charge. Still, one out of four's not bad." She stood and stretched, ignoring Fred's shout of "show off!" when she bent to touch her toes. Despite being shortened by an extra half hour in bed, her morning run had left a pleasant ache in her muscles and cleared the stuffiness of a late night from her head. It had also, as usual, left her famished. She rummaged through her desk drawer and found a cereal bar that was only a few weeks out of date.

"These things don't go off, do they?" She held it aloft for Nelson to see.

"Naw, they're hermetically sealed. It'll last till the apocalypse."

"Good to know." Chewing a passable concoction of oats and apricot, she opened the CCTV directory and signed for the first unallocated file: M67, Hawdale exit, February 21st. "Wish me luck, I'm going in," she said, and pressed "play."

❖

Swinging on her chair, Sanne watched the Micra get into the wrong lane at the roundabout and cut up a taxi. If the footage had come with sound, brakes would have squealed and horns blared. The Micra moseyed around again at low speed and headed away from the motorway with a queue of cars behind it, none of which was a silver Toyota Previa.

"Nelson, I'm bored." Sanne underscored her whine by throwing a balled-up piece of tinfoil at his head. He caught it neatly and returned it with interest, skimming it off her shoulder and onto Fred's desk.

"Oi!" Fred yelled. "That nearly took my bleedin' eye out."

"On the bright side, it's taken your mind off your aches and pains," Sanne called back, as the driver of a minibus tried to race an Audi and ended up embarrassing himself. She slapped her feet onto the floor. "This is useless! Shouldn't we be out *detecting* or something?"

"It's the best lead we've got, San." Nelson's reasonable tone only aggravated her further. She knew he was right, but she wanted someone to share her frustration and slam stuff about with, not try to placate her. A soft "pfft" made her look down, and she smiled in spite of herself.

"Perfect, thank you." She grabbed the stress ball he had tossed in front of her and squeezed it hard, mashing its little face until the urge to smack something had passed.

A fuzz of grey marked the end of her current tape. She closed the file and eased her grip on the ball, torn between going for a wee or making a brew. Hell, maybe she'd do both. For the past six hours and thirty-four minutes, tea and the toilet had been her only respites from the monotony, and the list of outstanding CCTV files didn't seem to be getting any shorter.

"Coffee?" she asked Nelson. When he held out his empty mug, she offered him the ball in exchange.

"Better keep hold of it." He pressed it back into her hand. "If nothing happens overnight, we'll be at this again all day tomorrow."

Her groan was smothered by Fred's excited yelp.

"I got one!" He beckoned them over. "Just passing junction four."

Sanne crouched by his chair as he replayed the footage.

"There!" He freeze-framed a shot of a Previa, its registration clear: BX07 6UF.

She and Nelson shook their heads in unison. "Doesn't work, mate," she said. "Second letter has to start with a straight line."

"Huh?"

On the other side of the desk, George sniggered.

"Like an L or F or N, not a C or Z or X." She wrote the letters in thick felt pen as she spoke, because Fred didn't seem to be catching on.

He looked aghast. "Now you bloody tell me."

"It's here in the briefing notes, you pillock." George displayed the relevant page. "Right beside a photo of the partial plate."

"Ah, bollocks." Fred threw his notes in the air, scattering them about his desk. The gesture dislodged the hot-water bottle from his back, and he grabbed at it. "Ouch!"

Sanne offered him her hand and the stress ball. "Come and walk it off with me. We'll nip downstairs and pretend we smoke."

"I thought I had the bastards," he murmured, allowing her to lever him up. He wobbled when he stood, looking his age for the first time since she'd known him.

"We'll get them." She added emphasis by tightening her grip on his hand, but she wished she believed what she was saying.

Chapter Twelve

Meg sucked at the lolly her favourite porter had just given her and scrutinised the Majors whiteboard.

"Let's see. Three UTIs, two chest infections, three generally unwell, and oh, you are shitting me." She pointed the lolly at the name in cubicle four. "I thought he was dead."

Liz sighed. "Sadly, rumours of his demise were greatly exaggerated."

"That explains why the department smells like mouldy cheese." Worried about contaminating her lolly, Meg stuck it back in her mouth and grinned at Liz. "I was told to pick a nurse to work in Resus with me. For a small fee, the job is yours."

Liz checked her pocket. "I've got a quid and half a Curly Wurly."

"That'll do."

At seven thirty on a Saturday night, the only available space in Resus was the shock room, its bed kept for cardiac arrests or similar dire emergencies. Meg headed for the central desk, where Asif sat writing on a chart.

"Hey, what've you got for me?" she asked.

"Hi, Dr. Fielding." He pushed a set of notes toward her. "Vera Aster, eighty-nine. She's in bay two with her daughter. Came in via ambulance from Pennine View."

Meg arched an eyebrow. The facility was one of several notorious nursing homes in the area. "How long had she been ill before they realised?"

"Half an hour, or so they claimed." Asif set the blood results on top of the chart. "Her lactate was four point six. She was hypothermic and hypotensive, and her urine output was nonexistent."

"Christ. I'm guessing there's not been much improvement."

"No. She has advanced dementia, and ITU won't touch her. We're waiting for a call from Medical Assessment, but they're at capacity."

"She'll die in here, then, the poor sod." Meg glanced at the cubicle where Vera lay unmoving, swaddled in blankets, with her daughter holding her hand. She shuffled the notes, searching for the familiar lilac pro forma. The last thing she wanted to do was start jumping on the brittle chest of an eighty-nine-year-old. The "Do Not Attempt Resuscitation" was already signed and dated, however. "Thanks for getting this sorted."

"The daughter is very sensible," Asif said. "She just wants her mum to be comfortable."

Meg nodded, intimately familiar with the sentiment. Early onset Alzheimer's had kept her own mum in nursing care for the past two and a half years. "I'll go and introduce myself. Is everyone else okay for the time being?"

"Yep, all stable and rather boring, really."

"Lovely."

Monitors flashed at her as she approached the second bay, all of their numbers in the red. Every breath Vera snatched rattled through her chest, but her kidneys had succumbed to the sepsis first, and the catheter bag hanging from the side rail was empty. Vera's daughter dried her eyes before shaking the hand Meg offered.

"I'm Dr. Fielding. I'll be looking after your mum tonight."

"She keeps asking for her dad." The woman's voice cracked. "I don't know what to do for the best."

"Tell her that he loves her and that he's on his way here," Meg said without hesitation.

The assurance seemed to allay the woman's uncertainty. The fear eased from her expression, and she stroked a hand through her mum's thin hair.

"Will it be long now?"

Meg looked again at the monitors, ignoring the shrill peel of the bat phone. "I don't think so. Is there anyone you'd like me to call?"

"No, there's only me left. Thank you, though."

Vera stirred, her voice rising in distress and then falling away when her daughter spoke to her. Meg drew the curtains as she left, affording them a modicum of privacy in a department ill-suited for end-of-life care.

Liz had answered the standby phone in Meg's absence. She handed over the details of a red pre-alert for Meg to read. *Male, fifty-eight, haematemesis, GCS nine.*

"Great, that's just what we need." Meg yanked fresh gloves and an apron from the wall holder. "ETA?"

"Ten. There's nowhere to ship anyone out to. We'll have to stick him in the shock room." Liz reached for the phone again. "Anaesthetics?"

"Yeah, might as well. Fluids, O-neg, and another candidate fast-tracked onto the tranexamic trial."

Liz gave a thumbs-up. "Bonus."

Once Meg was satisfied with her preparations, she went to wait by the ambulance doors. The sound of sirens lured her outside, and she hugged her arms across her chest to fend off the bitter cold. Timed to perfection, the blue lights she'd seen approaching were extinguished just before the ambulance hurtled beneath the canopy. She recognised the EMT driving, and opened the vehicle's back door to greet his regular mate.

"Hey, Kath—" She stopped dead as a woman in the passenger chair turned at the sound of her voice. "Oh shit. *Teresa?*" She looked at the man on the stretcher, his gaunt face half-hidden by an oxygen mask. What little she could see of him was soaked in crimson. Teresa sobbed and covered her mouth with bloodstained hands.

"Shock room. *Now,*" Meg told Kathy. She unclipped Teresa's seat belt and guided her down the steps. "Are you hurt anywhere?" she asked, aware of John's propensity for lashing out.

Teresa shook her head. "It's all his." Her eyes widened as she watched the crew rush by. "I need to tell Sanne," she whispered.

"I'll call her," Meg said. She co-opted a passing nurse to escort Teresa to the Relatives' Room, and kissed Teresa's cheek. "Sit tight, and I'll come and see you as soon as I can."

She sprinted across to the shock room and grabbed hold of the sheet either side of John's feet to help slide him onto the bed. The abrupt motion made him vomit, and he coughed, splattering the bedding with frank blood.

"Get him on his side!" She tipped the sheet with Liz, flipping him over and arranging him into a rough recovery position. The anaesthetist, appearing with impeccable timing, started suction to clean up the mess.

"Thanks, Sahil." Meg listened to Kathy's handover with half an ear, trying to order her priorities, number one of which kept coming back to phoning Sanne, even though she couldn't, not right now.

"IV access?" she asked.

"Left ACF," Kathy said. "He's had a litre of saline."

The fluid hadn't done much to improve matters. John's blood pressure was unrecordable, his heart rate fast and irregular. He barely reacted when Meg stuck a large-bore cannula in his other arm. It was unnerving to see him so compliant, when he'd spent his adult life being a complete tosser.

"Liz, get his details up on the computer. I ran some bloods for him last night. He'll be typed and crossed, so order six units." She hooked up a bag of O-neg, setting it running as Liz gaped at her. "It's Sanne's dad," she said in an undertone.

"Right." Liz's only outward reaction was a slight double-take before she collected the ambulance paperwork and ran to the desk.

Meg finished John's baseline obs and began to inject drugs that would—on a good day—help him to clot and then stabilise any clots he managed to form.

"Shall I fast-bleep GI and see if they have an endoscopist on call?" Liz shouted, anticipating the worst-case scenario and reminding Meg that this really wasn't a good day.

"Yes, please. Sahil, can you manage his airway until then?"

"Just about."

"Let me know if that changes." Meg watched the suction tubing fill with another stream of bright red gore. The duodenal ulcer that John had ignored had probably chewed a hole in a neighbouring artery. "How long on the blood?"

"Ten minutes max, and GI are on their way." Liz began to help her prep for an arterial line, their heads close together as they worked. "Is he a drinker?"

"At the last count it was five litres of crap cider a day." Meg shrugged and wheeled the trolley to the bedside. "There was no telling him."

"Let's get this done," Liz said. "I'm guessing you have a phone call to make."

❖

Sanne dug a tissue into the corners of her eyes, trying to stop them from watering. She'd spent nine hours trapped within this surreal EDSOP binge watch: endless silent footage of cars driving aimlessly, rendered in grainy black and white. The desks around her were empty, her colleagues having given up one by one to stagger home and remind their families they still existed. She had set herself a target of two more files, and her latest was three-quarters through when her mobile rang. Eager for distraction, she prepared to listen to an automated sales pitch and was delighted to see Meg's name instead.

"Hiya." She clicked "pause," feeling brighter than she had all day. "Did you manage to sleep all ri—"

"San, your dad's been brought in," Meg said, cutting her off. "He's lost a lot of blood, and he's really unstable."

Holding the phone between her ear and shoulder, Sanne closed the video and marked it as incomplete. "Is my mum okay?" she asked.

"Yes, she's sitting with him. A specialist stopped the bleeding, but he's still waiting for an ITU bed."

Sanne logged off and collected her belongings, her movements stiff and automatic. "Tell her I'm on my way."

"Sanne." Meg used her schoolteacher voice, guaranteeing Sanne's undivided attention. "Drive carefully."

"I will, love."

The weather, as indecisive and moody as a teenager, chose to favour Sanne with clear skies this time, and warning signs on the bypass informed her that gritting was in progress. Mindful of her promise, she concentrated on the roads, keeping well away from the boy racers and speeding taxis. Waiting at a red light, she tried to remember the last time she'd seen her dad and what he'd said to her, but she couldn't. She couldn't remember him ever saying anything she'd want to keep hold of.

With visiting hours long since finished, the car park in front of the Royal was almost empty. She chose a bay close to A&E and flung enough money into the ticket machine to cover her till morning. Meg met her at the main reception, guiding her through the clamour of Minors before stopping in the deserted ambulance corridor to pull her into a hug.

"You all right?"

Sanne closed her eyes for a moment, reluctant to move, though she drew away almost at once. "I'm fine. What happened?"

"Arterial bleed from a stomach ulcer. Your mum found him, but he'd lost about half his volume by then."

Sanne nodded, wondering vaguely whether half would be enough. "Will he wake up?"

"I don't know. He's so battered by the drink that it's hard to say. If he has a rebleed, then no, he probably won't."

"Is he on a ventilator?" she asked, hesitating at the shock room. She knew from past experience that a vent would mean anaesthetising drugs and no chance of her dad regaining consciousness without prior warning.

"Yes, he's vented." Meg touched Sanne's cheek, encouraging Sanne to look at her. "He won't know you're there, San."

Emboldened, Sanne opened the door. Her mum was alone at the bedside, both hands clasped in her lap as she stared at the bed. Evidently used to medics coming and going, she didn't react until Sanne spoke.

"Hey, Mum."

"Sanne." She rose then, meeting Sanne halfway and brushing her fingers through Sanne's windblown fringe. Her hands were red-raw where she had scoured them, but flakes of blood remained beneath her nails. "Were you at work?"

"Yes, I've come straight from the office."

"Oh, love, you must be tired out."

They sat together in the hard wooden chairs.

"Have you had any tea?" Sanne's mum asked.

Sanne huffed a small laugh. "No, but I'm not hungry. Honest."

From her position, she could see her dad's thin face in profile, with its dirty growth of whiskers and the spiderweb bursts of veins on his cheeks. His teeth were slack against the tube from the vent, as if he would be gnawing on it were the drugs not keeping him placid.

"Have you called Michael?" she asked.

"I tried, but there was no answer on the last number he gave me. He could be anywhere." Though her mum managed to keep the disappointment from her voice, her furrowed brow betrayed her pain. Her only son had declared himself born again some five years ago. The last Sanne had heard, he was trying to spread the word in Tower Hamlets.

"Keeley knows," her mum continued. "But I don't think she'll be able to come."

Sanne listened to the vent forcing oxygen into her dad's lungs and watched his chest move with each artificial breath. A pile of crumpled antiseptic wipes sat on the overbed table, but although her mum had done her best to clean his face, she could do little to alleviate the foul smell coming from the rest of him.

"I was watching *Strictly* in the back room." She shook her head in apparent despair at her frivolous behaviour. "I only had it on low, because he hates the music, but I didn't hear him shout or anything. I took him a couple of crumpets when it finished, and he was on the floor. There was blood everywhere."

Sanne gripped her mum's hand. The last time they had been here, she remembered being steered into the A&E shower and then shivering in oversized scrubs as doctors rushed about and used words she couldn't understand. She had found her dad collapsed in the bathroom and slipped on the clots when she'd tried to help him.

"I knew he wouldn't touch the crumpets," her mum whispered. "But you have to keep trying, don't you?"

Sanne didn't know how to answer that, so she said nothing. With a fortuitous sense of timing, a nurse bustled in to check monitors and adjust fluids. She closed the door again as she left, shutting out the tumult of Saturday night in Resus, and restoring the room's strange, confidential atmosphere. Sanne rarely had a chance to see her mum alone. Sunday lunches meant Keeley talking about Keeley, and kids running riot, while Sanne's shifts left few opportunities for long phone calls.

She stood and took the two steps to the bedrail, wrapping her hands around the metal so that she wouldn't act on her instincts to shake her dad and convince herself he really was oblivious. As a child she'd been terrified of his unpredictable rages and his tendency to lead with his fists or his belt. He didn't scare her now; he just reminded her of the pathetic gutter-dwelling scrotes she dealt with on a daily basis.

"Did you ever love him?" she asked, turning back to her mum.

There was no answer for a moment, and the flicker of her mum's eyes toward the bed implied she shared Sanne's apprehension.

"I'm not sure," she said slowly, as if she'd never dared to give the matter any thought. "I was fond of him at first, when we were courting. Believe it or not, he was funny and quite handsome, and he had a steady job at Bradshaws, so your grandma approved."

"Bloody hell, the battleaxe actually liked him?" Sanne laughed in disbelief, and her mum smiled with her.

"Aye, as much as she liked anyone. I never told her about the drink, though, and she died before he really hit his stride."

"Did you know about that before you married him?" It was something that had always bothered her: why her mum—usually so astute and sensible—would commit to a man on the verge of alcoholism.

"Yes, I did." Her mum toyed with the wedding band on her finger. "But it was…it was complicated, Sanne."

It wasn't much of a clue, but Sanne's career relied on her ability to read people, to gauge their expressions and tease the meaning from their evasive replies. In the end it was such a simple deduction that she wondered why she'd never worked it out before. Perhaps she had, but had never wanted to acknowledge it.

"You were pregnant," she said. "With me, before you married him."

A nod from her mum confirmed it. "He wanted me to get rid, but I couldn't, and my mum would've washed her hands of me either way; all her side were staunch Catholics. I was only six weeks gone, so we pretended I'd caught on the honeymoon, and no one batted an eyelid."

Sanne felt as if a load of rocks had been dumped onto her chest. It hurt when she breathed, and tears began to cloud her eyes. Her mum held out a hanky and then dabbed Sanne's cheeks for her when she blinked and stared at it.

"You were a tiny, perfect baby," her mum said. "And beautiful, and I wouldn't change a thing. Please don't cry."

There had been countless days during her childhood when Sanne had railed against her lot: the toys she'd wanted for Christmas and never received; the gang of girls who'd smacked her around the playground; coming home to Keeley screeching and her dad full of beer. But there had also been long, lazy summers mucking about on the back field with

Meg, and stealing kisses behind the bike shed, and reading beneath the covers by torchlight. And propping up all of that was a mum who had always loved her unconditionally. Sanne leaned over and kissed her mum's cheek.

"Thank you for not getting rid of me," she said.

Chapter Thirteen

Nelson didn't say a word as Sanne draped her coat over her chair and set her notepad beside her computer. He merely rested his chin on his steepled fingers and watched her every move like a hawk.

"Nelson…" The glare she attempted made her a bit squiffy. "Pack it in. I'm okay. I slept at my mum's."

She didn't mention that they'd only got home at four thirty, or that she'd spent the next three hours tossing and turning in the bunk bed that she and Keeley had once shared. Having just glimpsed her reflection in the locker room mirror, she was sure he would read between the lines.

He didn't labour the point. "How's your dad?" he asked.

"The nurse I spoke to this morning said he's poorly but relatively stable. I left plenty of taxi fare for my mum so she can visit him, and I'll go and see her when we finish here." She logged on to the case directory. "Any developments overnight?"

"Yes, actually. Hang on a tick." He lifted a file to check beneath it, setting it down when he failed to find whatever he was looking for. His desk drawer banged shut, and Sanne lost sight of him as he chased something he'd dropped. "Aha! Here we go." He reappeared, brandishing a blurry image of a Toyota Previa. "Our mission for the morning, courtesy of an eagle-eyed officer at GMP."

"Ooh, nice." She nodded her approval. "Do we have a registered keeper to go with it?"

"I'm glad you asked that." He held up a typed report. "Put a bit of spit and polish on yer boots, San. We're off to leafy Thirlow."

The early morning cloud cover had split and thinned, allowing fingers of sunlight to break through and dazzle the Sunday drivers, none of whom seemed to be in any hurry whatsoever.

"You're taking a right onto Thirlow Court Road, once this dozy bugger finds second bloody gear." Sanne rapped her knuckles against the passenger door of their pool car. Lack of sleep and the constant parade of bimbling idiots clogging up the roads were setting her teeth on edge.

"Shall I find us something soothing to listen to?" Nelson reached for the radio.

"I'd rather you didn't."

"I can sing if you prefer?" He filled his lungs in preparation but blew it all out when she walloped him in the gut. "Hey! That wasn't very nice."

She tried to keep her face straight. "Every time you sing, your god murders a kitten."

"That's a rotten fib, Sanne Jensen."

She snorted with laughter and had to clamp a hand on her nose while she found a tissue. "Aw, fuck. You made me snot on myself."

"Serves you right."

"Shit. Speaking of rights," she watched their junction sail by, "you needed to turn there."

As Nelson muttered and made a U-turn, Sanne peered out at the huge, gated, detached houses lining the road. Lying southwest of the city centre, Thirlow was one of Sheffield's most affluent suburbs, and not somewhere that she and Nelson often found themselves.

"Maybe the Previa was bought for the nanny, who uses it to take little Tarquin and Delilah to school," she said, only half joking, as she counted the Audis, Jags, and BMWs in the driveways.

"Perhaps." He pulled onto the verge by the house she indicated. "But then there are some people who have no desire to be ostentatious about their weal—Ah." He spied the brand new Range Rover and the Porsche 911 flanking the approach to their destination. "We should've called ahead, shouldn't we?"

"Naw." She left her finger on the security buzzer a few seconds longer than necessary. "It's more fun when we catch people off guard."

A disembodied voice asked them to state their business. Sanne responded by holding her ID in front of the fisheye lens, and the wrought iron gates opened with studied indifference, as if daring them to sully the spotless resin-bound gravel.

"Okay, then." She kept hold of her ID as she broached the threshold, always more nervous about dealing with moneyed folk than scrotes. "Is that actual marble?" she whispered, when they reached the faux-Georgian pillars and steps at the front of the house.

"Probably just fancy plastic," Nelson said, and surreptitiously kicked the first step. "Ow, no, it's marble."

The doorbell resonated around the porch, bringing to mind every BBC costume drama ever made, replete with liveried footmen and mob-capped scullery maids. Her imagination running riot, Sanne was disappointed when a balding forty-something chap in a Superdry hoodie opened the door.

"Can I help you?" For a Sheffield inhabitant, he was remarkably accent-free.

Sanne redisplayed her ID, immediately on her best behaviour. The man might have been dressed casually, but his outfit and Rolex watch didn't look like eBay knock-offs.

"Morning, sir. Sorry to call around so early. I'm Detective Jensen, and this is my partner, Detective Turay. We're with East Derbyshire Special Ops."

The man nodded in obvious confusion. "Neil Caulfield. Would you like to come in?" Despite having no close neighbours, he was peering over Sanne's shoulder, and although he relaxed slightly when he saw their unmarked car, he still seemed keen to conduct his business in private.

"Thank you. This shouldn't take long." Sanne tried not to sound too enthusiastic. While she was content with her own life, nosing around posh houses was undeniably a perk of the job.

Caulfield escorted them through an expansive entrance hall and into the first reception room, where a wall-mounted living-flame fire formed the centrepiece, and a lad was playing a first person shooter on a cinema-sized television.

"Skedaddle," Caulfield told him as he removed his headphones and gawked at Nelson. "And find your mum." Caulfield gestured for Sanne and Nelson to sit, before taking a seat on the matching white leather sofa.

Sanne slid the CCTV image from her file and laid it face-down on her knees. So far she had no opinion of the man's innocence or guilt, but he was certainly wealthy enough to have the right connections.

"Mr. Caulfield, are you the registered keeper of a Toyota Previa, registration plate BM15 GXR?" she asked.

He had been sitting ramrod straight, every inch of him on guard, but the question made him sag like a deflated balloon.

"What did she do this time?" He rubbed his forehead, where drops of perspiration were forming. "Is it compensation they're after? Because clearly I can pay."

"Huh?" Sanne glanced at Nelson, who gave her a "your guess is as good…" look in return. "Who are you talking about, sir?"

"Jessica, of course." He stood up and bellowed "Michelle!" out the door. Seconds later, a woman with waist-length blond hair and a tan so false she reminded Sanne of an Oompa Loompa entered the room.

"Where's Jessica?" Caulfield demanded.

"Upstairs, with Chelsea." She suddenly noticed their guests and rolled her eyes. "Oh, bloody hell, Neil. What's she done this time?"

Much as Sanne wanted to grab a box of popcorn and let the drama play out, it wasn't getting them anywhere. "Just…" She raised a hand for silence. "Right. Who is Jessica?"

"Our nanny," Michelle said.

Sanne hoped she didn't look as smug as she felt. "And she's the only one who drives the Previa?" The Caulfields appeared to consider that a rhetorical question, so Sanne continued. "Am I to assume she's not the best of drivers?"

Neil Caulfield scoffed. "I don't know why we bought her anything bigger than a Punto. She can't park for toffee, and she's lost three wing mirrors and a headlight in four months. Bloody hell, she's not put anyone in the hospital, has she?"

"No, she hasn't," Nelson said. He leaned forward, notes at the ready. "Why might she have been at Manchester Airport on the twentieth of February at 7:05 p.m.?"

Michelle entered a code into her mobile and navigated its screens with a manicured finger. "She was picking up Granny Caulfield," she said. "The flight arrived at 6:20, direct from Tenerife. I can forward you the itinerary if that'll help."

"Yes, please. This has my e-mail on it." Sanne gave her a card. "Would it be possible to speak to Jessica?"

"She's doing Chelsea's hair."

Nelson tilted his head, a movement so subtle that no one but Sanne realised things were about to get awkward. "No problem," he said. "We'll hang on here and take her down to HQ when she's finished."

The prospect of losing the help for several hours brought about an immediate change of heart.

"Why don't you go upstairs and see her right now?" Michelle said. "It's the first bedroom on the left. The pink one, you can't miss it." She didn't seem inclined to escort them, and she shut the door behind them as soon as they had gone into the hall. Sanne heard a series of fierce whispers but couldn't distinguish more than the odd word.

"They've got nothing to do with our case, have they?" she said to Nelson.

"Nope."

She eyed the balustrade encircling a landing bigger than her bedroom. "But in the interests of being thorough, we should at least confirm the airport trip with the nanny?"

Nelson nodded. "Yes, exactly. We're just being thorough." His poker face began to slip. "But mostly we want to see what else is up there."

She grinned. "Now you're talking."

They took their time on the staircase, a grand sweeping affair that made Sanne long for a crinoline dress in which to swish down it. Forgetting Michelle's directions, she accidentally poked her head into a state-of-the-art wet room boasting a shower so high-tech that a laminated instruction manual hung off its dial.

"I just have tepid and 'fucking hell!' on mine," she said.

"I live with a wife and two daughters," Nelson countered. "I'm lucky if I can get near ours."

Heading away from the rap music and automatic gunfire clattering behind a pale blue door, they made a beeline for the only pink one, its panels bedecked with glitter and fairy decals.

"Sweet merciful Christ," Sanne whispered. Expecting to interrupt a pamper party, she peeked round the door and was surprised to find the girl—Chelsea, she remembered—curled up on her bed, listening to her nanny read her a story. They both started at the intrusion, and the nanny slammed the book shut.

"Who are you?" Chelsea asked. Sanne guessed her age at no more than six, and her question combined a precocious child's curiosity and her indignation at having her private space encroached upon by strangers.

"Apologies," Sanne said formally. "I'm Detective Sanne Jensen, and this is Detective Nelson Turay." She shook Chelsea's hand. "You must be Miss Chelsea Caulfield."

Chelsea nodded. "And this is Jessica."

Jessica had gone a funny shade of pale. "I got it fixed myself," she said. "They promised they wouldn't tell anyone if I paid for the repairs."

"It's okay. We're not here about that." Nelson picked up the book she'd dropped. "Oh, this is a good one," he said, and Chelsea beamed at him. "Which page are you up to?"

With Chelsea distracted, Sanne perched on the bed beside Jessica. "Is this your car?" she asked, displaying the CCTV print.

"It's the one I drive for the Caulfields, yes. Am I in trouble?"

Sanne refolded the image. "No, I don't think so. We think a car similar to this was used in a serious crime. Could you confirm why you were at Manchester Airport on the twentieth of February?"

"I collected Mr. Caulfield's mother," Jessica said, without equivocating. "She was drunk as a skunk on duty free. I did ask them to buy me something smaller, but Mr. Caulfield said the Previa was safer for the children."

"Knock off a few more wing mirrors and he might change his mind." Sanne watched Nelson blow out his cheeks like a puffer fish and cross his eyes. Chelsea, sitting next to him on the rug, was hanging on his every word.

"Her hair takes me about five minutes," Jessica said. "We use the rest of the half hour for a story. Ms. Caulfield would have her out shopping or dancing or horse riding otherwise."

"Don't worry, your secret is safe." Sanne caught Nelson's eye, and he returned the book to Chelsea, who ran back to the bed and dived on the mattress.

"Hurry, we're nearly at the end!" she cried, and Jessica resumed the tale as Sanne and Nelson left the room.

Sanne's mobile rang halfway down the stairs, the caller ID showing Eleanor's name. She took it outside to answer it while Nelson went to speak to the Caulfields.

"Hey, boss," she said. "We're just finished in Thirlow. No joy on the Previa. The airport visit was a simple granny pickup."

"Well, it seems GMP are on a roll. They called Fred with another one," Eleanor said. "Might be a bit more promising. The registered keeper is a Mohammed Rafiq Sadek, who owns a small supermarket in Sharcliffe."

"Great. Did you want us to meet Fred there or something?"

"No, he can barely stand up this morning. Apparently, salsa classes are very bad for you."

"Aye, so I've heard." Sanne coughed and changed the subject. "Are we going to Sharcliffe in his stead, then?"

"Yes. I'll send you the address and the images. No priors for Sadek. He's owned the shop for three years, and his wholesale website states that he's lived locally all his life. We have the car joining the M56 from Manchester Airport at 4:21 p.m., which would tally with the arrival of a PIA flight from Lahore. It's next seen at 10:52 p.m., leaving the M67 at the Hawdale junction."

"I wonder why that took so long," Sanne said. Even in rush hour, the journey was a couple of hours at most.

"Good question. Perhaps he went for a meal or to visit family, or perhaps he waited until he was damn sure no one else would be using Old Road."

"Could make for an interesting chat," Sanne said, falling into step with Nelson on the driveway and mouthing "the boss" as he shot her a questioning look.

"Indeed," Eleanor said. "Meera came in to see how we're getting on and offered to help smooth the way if necessary. She'll see you there in about an hour."

"All right." Sanne didn't think they'd need Meera's assistance, but it seemed rude to decline. "I'll let you know how we get on."

"Where are we off to?" Nelson asked as she ended the call.

"Sunny Sharcliffe, to see a chap about another Previa."

He nodded his approval. "Cooking on gas now, aren't we?"

"The boss certainly sounded more cheerful." She waved at the sensor on the electric gates, scowling when nothing happened. "Course, we might be stuck here for the rest of the day."

"Open Sesame!" He snapped his fingers, and the motor whirred into life.

She gazed at him in awe. "It's true what they say. You really *do* have superpowers."

"Naw, just an uncanny sense of timing. Are you ready for my next trick?" He zapped the central locking on the car. "Ta-dah!"

"Wow. Not just a superhero but a *god*."

He chuckled. "Get in, you silly sod. I might be all-powerful when it comes to opening stuff, but I can't do a thing about the traffic."

❖

Sheffield Royal was the last place Meg wanted to go on her day off, but with Sanne at work she knew Teresa would be alone in the ITU. Her head was swimming pleasantly after her night shifts, the world weaving around her as if it was drunk and she was the only one sober. Having left the house without her bag, she sat in her car for several minutes before she figured out where she was supposed to be going. The journey passed in a stop-start haze, and as she pulled into a parking spot her pocket began to buzz.

"What the hell?" Eventually, she recognised the sound of her mobile and answered the call. "Morning."

"Technically, it's afternoon," Fraser said. "Did I wake you?"

"No, but I've been on nights, so I don't know my arse from my elbow. What's up?"

"Could you look at a photo and tell me if it's our man?"

For a perplexing moment she thought he wanted her to identify her brother again, but then she remembered Anca Miklos and the hospital security footage that Fraser had requested.

"Yes, of course. Are you going to e-mail it?"

"It's already on its way," Fraser said. "Give me a shout back on this number."

He disconnected, and Meg opened the e-mail, tapping her foot as the download stalled repeatedly. Although the images were by no means clear, Cezar Miklos had been captured in a series of freeze-frames as he opened his car's rear door, and Anca was recognisable thanks to her mitten-like bandages.

Meg called Fraser back. "It's him," she said. "Did you get the car reg?"

"Afraid not. We have the make and model, but the footage never gave us a good enough angle on the plate."

"I'm shocked." She couldn't summon the energy to be truly sarcastic. She rubbed a bit of sleep from her eye. "Is that it, then? Dead end?"

"No, we'll keep looking, and the case will stay open, but the car was potentially our best lead."

"And it's come to nothing."

"Yeah, so it would seem," he said. "Thanks for the ID, though. It helps to know for sure who we're trying to find."

"Not a problem. Keep in touch." She hung up and walked toward the hospital entrance, getting halfway there before she remembered to aim her car keys over her shoulder and press the lock. Snowflakes were swirling around the tarmac, melting before they had a chance to settle. She shivered and pulled her collar closed. Along with her memory, night shifts destroyed her ability to stay warm.

The doctor at the ITU desk greeted her by name, and he winced when she asked after John's condition. He leafed through John's folder and found the latest lab results for her.

"He's had another three units of blood," he said, "but his last count had dipped to nine point two."

"Which means he's bleeding again."

"It would appear so. I've scheduled him for another scope"—he checked the clock on the wall—"in about fifty minutes. Is he a relative of yours?"

"He's my partner's dad," Meg said. "Okay if I go and sit with her mum for a while?"

The doctor tripped a little on the unexpected pronoun but nodded his assent. "Room two."

She walked through the main bay on her way to the individual cubicles, its patients all elderly, the cutting-edge technology around them a stark contrast to their wizened faces and wasted bodies. Vera

Aster had never made it this far; she had died minutes after Sanne's arrival in the shock room.

Catching a glimpse of Teresa dozing by John's bed, Meg tiptoed into the room and scanned his observation chart. He was hanging on by a thread, his organs teetering on failure as his blood pressure failed to stabilise. Teresa stirred when she sensed Meg's presence, and she tried to make herself presentable by patting her hair into place.

"It's only me." Meg dragged a chair alongside hers. "I thought you might like some company."

Teresa laid a hand on Meg's arm. "You should be in bed."

"So should you."

"And poor Sanne's gone into work. There's no telling any of us, is there?"

Meg stretched out her legs and settled into her seat. "I fear we may be cut from the same cloth."

"That's as may be." Teresa copied Meg's position. "But is it polyester or silk?"

"Silk," Meg said. "Definitely silk."

❖

Situated at the end of a shabby precinct, Sadek Foods was doing lively trade for a Sunday afternoon. Beneath its striped awning, crates of fruit and veg were stacked against multipacks of fizzy drinks and toilet roll. A neon sign reading "Fresh Halal Meat" occupied the front window's prime spot, with adverts for mobile phone cards and money transfers to Pakistan battling for the remaining space. As Meera was running late, Nelson had squeezed into a parking spot almost opposite the shop, from where he and Sanne could watch people meandering in and out.

"All very ordinary," Sanne said.

Nelson peered through the misted windscreen. "And those loo rolls are a bargain," he said, with a tinge of envy. "Hey, there she is." Reacting faster than Sanne, he ducked out of the car to head Meera off before she could go inside to look for them.

"Sorry, I thought I'd missed you," she said as Sanne caught them up.

Pausing on the pavement, Sanne straightened her coat and

readied her file and ID badge. She motioned for Nelson to lead the way, conscious that their presence had immediately been noted by the customers milling among the groceries.

The clocks didn't exactly stop when they walked inside, but conversations became muted, and a child stuffing sweets into his mouth lost a couple as his jaw dropped. The lad behind the butcher's counter, almost obscured by the lamb carcasses swinging around him, pointed his knife toward the rear of the shop when Sanne asked for Mohammed Sadek. The customers' reactions must have acted as a tip-off, however, because a smartly dressed Pakistani man came and met Sanne and Nelson in front of the main counter.

"Mohammed Sadek?" Nelson asked.

"Yes, but I go by Rafiq." The man offered his hand as Nelson made the introductions, and he greeted Meera in Urdu. "Would you like to come through to the back? There's not much space out here."

He opened a section of the counter, swapping places with a slightly younger man who took over the till. Boxes of wholesale stock lined the walls of the room Sadek took them into.

"Please sit." He indicated a pair of wooden chairs and a sofa with sunken cushions. "Can I get you something to drink?"

He provided refreshments regardless of their polite refusals, snapping open cans of mango Rubicon and pouring the juice into mismatched mugs that he set on the low coffee table. Sanne watched him move around the cluttered space, clearly unperturbed by their unannounced visit and keen to play the gracious host. According to Eleanor's information, he had just turned thirty and lived two streets from the shop with his wife and three young sons. Although he was dressed traditionally, the cloth of his kameez was stretched taut across his broad chest and prominent biceps, and his accent owed a lot more to Sheffield than to Pakistan.

"So," he said, once satisfied that everyone was catered for. "How may I help?"

Sanne opened the image Eleanor had sent to her phone and passed it to him. "Are you the registered keeper of this car?"

"Yes, I am. It's taxed and insured, and I have the logbook at home."

"Has it been involved in any accidents recently?"

"Not to my knowledge." He returned her phone and sipped his

drink straight from the can. "Unless Kadri's trashed it. Is that why you're here? Has he done something stupid?"

Sanne made a note of the name, but she had a sinking feeling that she knew where this was going. "Who's Kadri?"

"My cousin. He borrowed the car for a trip to London."

Nelson shifted slightly, his knee rattling the table. "When would that have been?" he asked, stilling the metal frame with his hand.

Sadek fetched a calendar from the wall but didn't seem to find the answer on it. "I'm not too sure. Wednesday, I think. It was all pretty last-minute." He looked at Meera as if she would understand. "You know how it is with family. They ask and you give."

Sanne interrupted before Meera could steer them off topic. "We'll need the address Kadri is staying at in London."

Sadek opened his hands. "Sorry, but I don't have it. He has a ton of friends down there, and he didn't tell me any specific place."

Despite his apparent sincerity and willingness to cooperate, red flags were popping up all over for Sanne. She drew a line beneath the cousin's name and decided to push a little harder. "Can you confirm why the car was at Manchester Airport on the nineteenth of February at four thirty p.m.?"

Again Sadek glanced at the calendar, but Sanne had already noted that every date was blank.

"What is this concerning?" he asked.

"And then in Hawdale off the M67, some six hours later?" she continued, as if he hadn't spoken.

"I think I know what this is concerning," he said quietly. "I saw in the paper that you couldn't pin it on those racist idiots from Malory, so you're looking for someone else to blame." He stood and moved toward the door. "If we're going to continue this conversation, I would like to have legal representation present."

She nodded slowly, trying not to infer anything from the request. Few people these days, guilty or innocent, were comfortable talking to the police, and the wariness was heightened within minority communities.

"Would tomorrow morning at nine suit you?" She placed her card on the table, overriding any dissent. "We're based at the main Sheffield HQ. The officer on the desk will direct you when you arrive." She smiled to smooth the edge from her instructions. "Ask for 'Sann-er' Jensen, but it won't matter if you cock up the name."

"'Sann-er.' Right." He gestured at the door. "I really have to get back to the shop."

"Thank you for your time," she said.

She and Nelson walked to the car in silence as Meera hurried in the opposite direction. A covering of wet snow had left the pavements slippery and deserted, and lights began to appear in windows. Nelson started the car but didn't put it into gear. Sanne waited for his verdict, curious to see whether it matched her own.

"Hmm," he said.

"Hmm, indeed."

"A missing car and a half-arsed story."

"And then no story at all for the airport trip," she added.

"Summat's off."

"Yep." She set her wet boots on the dash. "Let's go and see what the boss has to say about it."

❖

In the middle of pouring a cup of coffee in lieu of the lunch she'd not even had a chance to unwrap, Eleanor ground her teeth as someone knocked on her door. Loath to sacrifice her drink, she crossed the carpet with cup and spoon in hand. She would have expected Litton to enter straight away, or for one of her team to respond to her hail, but Meera, obviously unsure of protocol, waited until the door was opened for her.

"Come in." Eleanor glanced down the corridor. "Are Sanne and Nelson with you?"

"No, I set off before them." Meera declined the offer of coffee with an agitated wave. When she wouldn't sit, either, Eleanor stayed in front of her desk, resting against it.

"What can I do for you?" she asked, already uneasy. The timing of Meera's arrival in the office earlier that morning, shortly after GMP had picked out the second Previa, had been so uncanny that Eleanor suspected Litton's involvement. Having decided that Eastern Europeans—the current, acceptable bogeymen in the eyes of the popular press—would turn out to be the culprits in this case, Litton had thrown a conniption fit down the phone when she'd told him the Previa belonged to a Pakistani lad from Sharcliffe.

"Rafiq Sadek is a good family man," Meera said in a rush. "He's worked hard to build his business and—"

Eleanor cut her off. "Do you know him, Meera? Personally?"

"No, not really. But his auntie is related to my husband, and she says he wouldn't be involved in anything illegal."

"You should've disclosed your relationship before accompanying my detectives today." Eleanor put her mug down harder than she had intended. She was annoyed at herself more than anything for not seeing this coming. Meera had been born in Sharcliffe and had made no secret of the fact that she still had relatives in the area.

"I'm a community liaison." Meera enunciated the words clearly, as if addressing a child. "The role assumes I am familiar with the people in that community."

"I'm aware of that, and ordinarily it wouldn't be a problem. But you said you'd spoken to the aunt. Did you tell her about today's visit?"

"No." The muted reply suggested Meera had told *someone*, but when she looked up again her eyes were blazing. "It's too easy for you to lay the blame at our doorstep, to say that one of us is responsible for this crime."

"*Nothing* about this case has been easy." Eleanor managed not to snap, but it took all of her self-control. Meera's inclusion as a liaison was testament to how carefully and respectfully EDSOP had tried to tread, yet it seemed their efforts would still be deemed inadequate. "Watching the body of an abused child being cut up on the slab wasn't easy, nor was walking through the barn where that child and several other women were probably imprisoned and raped. My team and I are following the best leads we have, which isn't saying much, and if one of those brings forth a Pakistani suspect, then so be it, but don't think for a second that Rafiq Sadek is a convenience."

"You don't understand how much this will taint him," Meera said. "It will shame his entire family. That boy has worked his way up from nothing."

Eleanor had heard enough. "Did Sanne and Nelson question Sadek in public?" she asked.

"No, but—"

"Did they disclose their business within earshot of others?"

"No, they didn't."

Eleanor felt better for that confirmation, though she hadn't doubted their conduct for a second. "Was Sadek able to explain why he'd been at the airport and the subsequent delay in getting to Hawdale?"

"No," Meera said quietly, but then seemed to collect herself. "He requested legal representation, which is only sensible."

"Very," Eleanor agreed, her interest piqued. The delay would also give him time to get his story straight. "When is he coming in?"

"Tomorrow morning."

Eleanor pushed up from the desk and returned to her chair behind it. "You won't be permitted to attend that interview, and I would strongly advise you against any further contact with the family."

Meera bristled but offered no rebuttal. "I'm going home," she said.

Eleanor nodded. "Close the door behind you, please."

The EDSOP Brainstorm was an informal event that usually involved hot drinks and snacks of some sort, a huddle around a spare table, and bullet points on a good old-fashioned, low-tech flipchart. Awarded the title of special guest, Russ Parry had provided the cake and assumed the role of scribe. He wrote *RAFIQ SADEK* at the top of the first page as Sanne finished handing out plates. With energy to burn, despite scant sleep and a long day, she sat on one of the back tables so her legs were free to swing.

"To summarise briefly," Eleanor said, once everyone had settled. "While Rafiq Sadek doesn't fit the bill for a suspect, he is certainly a person of interest. His Toyota Previa has allegedly taken a rather convenient trip below the Watford Gap to destinations unknown, and it seems he may have needed more time to think about why said car was spotted at Manchester Airport and then Hawdale, because he terminated the interview at that point. A married man with three children and no priors, he owns a thriving business and would appear to be a pillar of the community. Given the general mistrust of the police within that community, it may be remiss to read too much into his request for legal assistance. So, initial thoughts on how to proceed?"

When Sanne raised her hand, Parry scribbled his first bullet point and hovered by it, pen poised.

"How about ANPR cameras, now that we have a full registration to play with?" she asked. More than eight thousand of the traffic cameras fixed around the country had the capability to recognise number plates. Any passing "vehicles of interest" were immediately flagged for investigation, but a record of every other vehicle was also taken and stored in case of future need.

"A request is being processed," Eleanor said. "There are no ANPRs on the Snake or Old Road, but an idea of Sadek's movements in general would definitely be useful. The post mortem estimated the twenty-first or twenty-second of February for time of death, but the date we currently have Sadek's car at Hawdale doesn't tally with that. It's a couple of days too early."

Sanne had already been pondering the discrepancy. "He could conceivably have been collecting from the airport or another holding place on that day and transferring the women to the barn at Nab Hey."

Her supposition sent a few dissenting murmurs through the team.

"He might just have played airport taxi for a relative and gone home on the Snake," George said. "You join both roads from Hawdale, and the placement of the camera doesn't tell us which route he took."

"In which case, why not give us the specifics when we asked?" Sanne countered. "It's not us putting him under the spotlight; he's doing it to himself. And if we can confirm that his Previa was in Hawdale again around the twenty-first or second, that would be a more conclusive link to the body at Greave."

Eleanor intervened before things became too heated. "We would need the car and forensic evidence to establish that beyond doubt," she said. "But obviously we're still going to be working on the CCTV footage around the estimated TOD. Good. Anything else?"

"Check for local body shops, garages, or possible storage for the Previa, if we think that the cousin story is a load of codswallop," Fred said. "And personally I do."

"Me too." Mike Hallet waved his slice of cake, sending crumbs flying. "Maybe we should put the EDSOP 'ayes' on one side and the 'nays' on t'other, like they do in Parliament."

Sanne chewed her pen, firmly on the side of the "ayes" and encouraged by Fred and Mike's accord. The fact that Sadek had gifted himself hours to establish an alibi for his airport visit was gnawing at her. He was probably racking up his phone bill right now, contacting relatives willing to attest to whatever story he concocted and verify that he had loaned his car to a needy family member.

"For fuck's sake," she muttered, and accidentally kicked George's chair. "Shit. Sorry, mate."

"S'okay, love," he said, shuffling beyond the line of fire.

The exchange drew Eleanor's attention. "Something to add, Sanne?"

Sanne skimmed the flipchart, making sure she'd not missed anything while she'd been assaulting George. "Will we be speaking to Sadek's family?"

"That depends what comes up during his interview." Eleanor walked to the board and faced her team. "It would be an understatement to say that these developments have made DCI Litton apprehensive. Obviously he can't stop us pursuing this line of enquiry, but he has requested that we proceed with the utmost caution."

"No calling round to interview Sadek's wife while he's in here tomorrow, then?" Nelson said.

"Absolutely not, unless you're curious to know what happens when our DCI's blood pressure reaches critical level. I do want eyes on the shop, though. If Sadek is running a second business, that's as good a place as any to do it from. I want to see if any of those coming and going are known to us or to Manchester's MST. DI Parry is going to provide us with a rogues' gallery from his patch, and I'll get a surveillance rota drawn up by tomorrow." Eleanor managed a weary smile. "Okay, that's enough for today. Go home. You all look shattered, and I need a Scotch."

"Excellent idea," Fred said. "Pub, anyone?"

There were plenty of "ayes" this time around, but Sanne shook her head when he called her name.

"My dad's in the hospital," she said. "I'm going to see him, and then I'm going home."

Fred put his arm around her. "Will someone be at home for you when you get there?"

She looked up at him. "God, I hope so."

❖

A persistent fall of snow had covered the Snake Pass, not enough to shut it but enough to slow Sanne's journey to a bum-numbing, clutch-foot-aching crawl. The driver of the truck in front was struggling for control on the corners and skittish on the descents. When he almost jackknifed on a blind bend, she began to consider the pros and cons of stopping where she was and hiking the rest of the way. Knuckles white around the steering wheel, she managed to stay the distance, pulling into the lay-by at the top of her access road and murmuring a heartfelt thank-you when she recognised the car she had parked behind.

Wellies and winter woollies donned, she embarked on the home stretch with a bounce in her step, the memories of her dad as still as a corpse—though steadfastly refusing to become one—banished by the wet flakes landing on her tongue and by the promise that Meg would indeed be waiting for her. Her small cottage was lit like a beacon, Meg using every lamp at her disposal to ensure Sanne didn't miss her turn and end up in the henhouse.

Sanne entered the kitchen to a rush of warmth and the sight of most of her fridge's contents arranged on the countertop. Before she had a chance to wonder about the food, Meg ran from the living room and skidded across the tiles toward Sanne with her arms outstretched. Underestimating the lack of traction on the bed socks she'd stolen, she overshot her mark and almost ended up in the sink.

"Well, that was dignified," Sanne said.

"Thanks." Meg rubbed her offended belly. "I was aiming for romantic enthusiasm, like in the films, where the reunited lovers bound into each other's arms."

"Don't they usually do that in flowering meadows and slo-mo?"

"I chose to exercise a degree of artistic licence." She kissed Sanne's frozen nose. "Your dad still chugging along?"

"He is. Thanks for giving my mum a lift home." Sanne laid her cold cheek against Meg's flushed one. "And for being here."

"My pleasure." Meg turned to stand shoulder to shoulder with Sanne. "Now, you may be wondering about the mess."

"I assumed you'd be getting to that," Sanne said, flipping off her wellies and hanging her wet coat on a chair by the wood burner.

"I was fully intending to cook you something complicated and delicious," Meg said. "But then I started to watch this nature documentary, and a fluffy baby seal was being chased by a polar bear, so I muted it and shut my eyes, and when I woke up it was two hours later. How does soup and toasties grab you?"

The ingredients on the counter—leftovers ideal for stuffing in sandwiches—suddenly made sense to Sanne. "Sounds great."

Meg lit the gas burner, above which a pan sat in readiness. "The soup is all homemade."

"Meg, it's Heinz tomato." Sanne held up the empty tin she'd spotted in the recycling pile.

"To which I have added extra pepper and a spoonful of Bovril, thus rendering it homemade." Meg ignored Sanne's look of disgust. "Try it before you pull that face. And, by the way, you need a new sandwich toaster."

Sanne's disgust quickly changed to horror. "You haven't—have you destroyed my toaster?"

"No, but look at it! It's already knackered!" Meg pointed her wooden spoon at Sanne's beloved Breville. It was one of the first things Sanne had bought herself on leaving home, and, although ancient and missing a leg, it toasted the most perfect sandwich. She patted it reverently and plugged it in.

"Thank goodness. Wreck this, and it could spell the end of a beautiful relationship."

"Yeah, yeah," Meg said. "Make yourself useful and butter that bread."

They ate on the sofa, balancing their plates on lap trays, with the television on low. Such a lack of decorum would have horrified Sanne's mum, but they had long since fallen out of the habit of sitting at the table.

"Tell me something I don't know," Sanne said, mopping up the last of her soup with a piece of sandwich.

Meg crunched her toastie, deliberating. Then she raised her index finger. "In Alaska it's illegal to whisper in someone's ear when they're hunting moose."

"Fuck off!" Sanne dropped her spoon into her bowl. "You made that up."

Meg crossed her heart. "BBC documentaries do not lie. Your turn."

"I don't think I can top that." Sanne tried to remember her day, to pick out something unusual or interesting, but then she realised that she wanted to leave it at the office where it belonged and that she had nothing to say about her hospital visit. She put her tray on the floor and curled her legs beneath her. "I like coming home to you," she said. "I thought it might bug me because I'm used to being on my own after work, but I was so happy to see all the lights on tonight, and then there you were."

"Sliding gracefully across the floor," Meg said.

"In my jammies and my bed socks." Sanne tugged the waistband of Meg's pilfered pyjamas, encouraging her to sidle closer. "How's your belly? Any bruises?"

"Only to my pride." Meg arranged the blanket over them both. "But do feel free to check later, when I don't taste of Bovril and corned beef."

Sanne kissed her regardless. "You mostly taste of tomato," she murmured.

"Sanne Jensen," Meg said, "that kind of flattery will get you anywhere."

❖

The measure of Scotch reflected the glow from the open fire, amber twisting brightly in the glass as Eleanor swirled it.

"Cheers." She tapped Russ's pint pot and took a mouthful of her whisky, enjoying the heat it tracked down to her stomach. They had outlasted the rest of her team, the snow forcing most to retire earlier than they might otherwise have done. The inclement weather was keeping the pub quiet, and Eleanor had kicked off her heels and tucked her legs onto the seat by the inglenook.

"Our taxi reckoned he'd be about forty minutes." She held up her glass. "Plenty of time for you to get another round in."

Russ took the hint and the empties to the bar, returning with fresh drinks and two packets of scampi fries.

"I seem to recall you having a bit of a thing for these." He tossed her a packet and placed her drink on a damp beer mat.

"Only when I was drunk enough." She sipped the Scotch first, reluctant to obliterate its flavour with that of ersatz shellfish and lemon. "God, I needed this."

He swiped froth from his upper lip. "Here's to one of those days that can only end in vast quantities of alcohol." He opened his crisps. "And scampi fries."

"It has been a bit of a shitter," she said. "I almost lost it with Meera. For her to have the audacity to get on her high horse, when she'd all but confirmed she'd warned the family that we were heading over there. We've bent over fucking backwards not to tread on anyone's toes, but nothing we do will ever be good enough. And then I've got Litton sticking his oar in every which way."

Russ chewed and swallowed while he contemplated. "Fear makes people lash out, El. And there's plenty of that going around, thanks to fuck-ups in Rotherham and the like. I suppose there's a concern that the police will go all out in an attempt to overcompensate, that we'll come down hard on suspects from ethnic minorities rather than risk further accusations of negligence."

"That won't be happening on my team."

"No, you've got a good bunch here, and you've had some cracking cases of late. I recognised Sanne from the papers." Russ washed his final crisp down with half his pint. "She's smaller in real life."

Eleanor opened her fries and propped the bag within reach of them both. "Don't underestimate her. She packs a mean punch. She gave our Sheffield Slasher such a clobbering last month that she's got a couple of fingers she can tell the weather by."

"You're shitting me." When Eleanor shook her head, Russ laughed loudly enough to disturb the lone drinker at the end of the bar. "Remind me not to piss her off."

"We'd had words beforehand," Eleanor said. "She has a tendency to be a bit of a shrinking violet. Three days later, she's tackling an armed psychopath on her own."

"A shrinking violet, eh?" He gave her a wry look. "Sounds like someone I used to know."

"Christ, don't remind me. I had to order spare shirts that first week of training. I'd sweat through them before we even started a class."

"And then, four months out, there was that weird bloke we did for stalking his ex. Remember him? He wouldn't stop trying to nuzzle your hair."

"I remember he walked into his cell with a limp," she said.

Russ stole the last fry, speaking around its crunch. "I knew right there and then that you'd go far."

She flexed her toes as the alcohol and the heat from the fire combined to alleviate the strain of the day. "And here we are."

"And here we are," he said. "And hey, here's Doug." He waved to catch Doug's attention, meeting him halfway across the snug to shake his hand.

Eleanor put her shoes on the wrong feet and spent a few seconds trying to work out why she couldn't walk in them.

"Bollocks," she mumbled. Barefoot again, she shrugged into her coat as Doug held it open for her. She kissed his cheek, breathing in his familiar smell of motor oil and aftershave, and hugged his arm for balance. "Thanks for coming to rescue us. I'm a bit tipsy."

"Let's get you home," he said. Then, to Russ, "Hotel or our spare room?"

"I'm booked into the Victoria, if it's no trouble." Russ took Eleanor's other arm. "Come on, El, put your best foot forward."

Her shoes finally on, Eleanor did just that.

CHAPTER FOURTEEN

The officer on the front desk kept his phone call succinct.

"He's on his way up," he told Sanne.

"Ready?" she asked Nelson.

"Whenever you are."

They'd been ready for the last hour: notes written, questions compiled. Determined not to sacrifice any further advantage, Sanne had gained permission to record the interview's audio and to question Rafiq Sadek under caution, although she'd tempered that somewhat by booking Interview Two. She always enjoyed wrong-footing potentially hostile subjects, and nothing was quite as disconcerting as expecting to be interrogated by a pair of hardnosed arseholes and then being shown to a room bedecked with cheerful upholstery.

As requested, she paused at Eleanor's office. "We're just going in, boss."

Eleanor pushed her chair back, giving herself breathing space from the computer, if only for a minute. "DCI Litton would like a copy of the audio as soon as the interview concludes."

Sanne had expected that, but it still sent a shiver of anxiety through her. "I'll e-mail it to you," she said.

Eleanor rewarded this subtle defiance with an approving nod. "DCI Litton stated a preference for the interview to be conducted by a Pakistani detective."

"Well, he's got a lesbian and a black bloke, so I don't think we can be accused of lacking political correctness."

"My response wasn't quite as blunt." Eleanor rolled her chair forward, amusement glinting in her eyes. "But it went along similar lines. Good luck."

"Cheers, boss."

The lift doors opened just as Sanne met Nelson outside Interview Two. Showing no sign of indecision, Rafiq Sadek turned in the right direction and strode toward them, two steps in front of another Asian man in a crisply pressed suit. He introduced his solicitor and declined the offer of a hot drink, pouring himself a glass of water instead and getting comfortable on the chair that Sanne indicated. Accustomed to interviewees tapping their feet and fidgeting, she was rattled by Sadek's composure. He sipped his water, his eyes never leaving her as she activated the tape recorder and proceeded through the caution and the preliminaries. Had this been a poker game, he would have taken even Nelson to the cleaners.

Keen to establish the pace and tone, she opened her file and gave herself time to reread her initial questions before she asked her first one.

"Mr. Sadek, yesterday afternoon you confirmed you were the registered keeper of a silver Toyota Previa, licence plate BL58 WCZ. Is that correct?" She placed the CCTV image in front of him.

Sadek topped off his glass and set the jug precisely in the centre of its coaster. "My solicitor would like to read from a prepared statement," he said, and Sanne's heart sank. There was little wonder he looked so smug if he'd decided to play that card.

The solicitor produced a typed sheet and cleared his throat. "My client, Mohammed Rafiq Sadek, loaned the aforementioned Toyota Previa to his cousin, Kadri Afzal, on the morning of February the twenty-fourth. Mr. Afzal has taken the car to London for an indeterminate period, and my client is unsure of his exact whereabouts. As my client owns a second vehicle, he did not consider Mr. Afzal's request to be an inconvenience. On February the nineteenth, my client collected a friend from the viewing park at Manchester Airport, leaving at approximately four thirty p.m. and travelling to Levenshulme, Manchester, where he and his friend ate dinner at a restaurant. He returned home later that evening via the Snake Pass.

"My client has provided the names and addresses of friends and family members who can corroborate these details, but unfortunately he does not have contact information for Mr. Afzal, following a recent change of mobile phone. The route taken to and from the restaurant in Levenshulme is also provided. I have advised my client to say nothing further during the course of this interview."

The solicitor marked the end of the statement by presenting Nelson with a copy.

"Thank you," Nelson said, his tone commendably free of sarcasm. Had the solicitor given the statement to Sanne, she would probably have rammed it down his throat. She skimmed her notes again. Even if Sadek took the "no comment" route, they still needed to ask all of their questions and give him the opportunity to answer.

"You say you travelled home on the Snake Pass," she said. "Have you ever used Old Road instead? Perhaps to avoid the traffic?"

Sadek looked impressed that she was even bothering to try. He sipped his water, evidently in no rush to conclude matters. "No comment."

Sanne wrote this down, underlining it twice to make him wonder what she'd read into it. She and Nelson were in no hurry either. They had a statement to pick apart and a DCI waiting to cast judgement on their efforts. Nelson removed his jacket, settling in for the long run and prompting Sanne to do likewise. If Litton wanted to spend hours listening to a "no comment" interview, she was more than happy to oblige him.

❖

It wasn't often that Eleanor allowed herself to get really pissed off, but she'd been in the office since six and missed her lunch again. A meeting scheduled by Litton to last an hour had overrun by two, giving her a headache in addition to the mild hangover she'd started the day with, and the cherry on top of it all was now filling the screen in the briefing room.

"This isn't worth the paper it's typed on," she said, leaving Rafiq Sadek's statement up there for those members of EDSOP who'd not yet seen it. "At this juncture it's impossible to say whether he's involved in our case, but he's pulling out all the stops to be an obstructive little arsehole, so I think it's only fitting that we follow his example. I want every person named in his statement pulled in for interview and questioned under caution. Don't just visit them at home: bring them in here and let them stew for a few hours. If they're inconvenienced, all the better. It might make them think twice, the next time they're asked to support some bullshit alibi."

She paused to drink from a bottle of water, half expecting someone to challenge her or question the wisdom of a gloves-off approach, but no one uttered a word of dissent. If anything, they seemed heartened by the reversion to standard tactics.

"We'll need translators on standby, boss," George said.

"Thank you for volunteering to arrange that." Eleanor made a note on the whiteboard, writing his name alongside the task and turning a deaf ear to his epithet-heavy reply. "Fred, while he's busy wrestling with Language Line, can you request ANPR records for Sadek's current car and for the likeliest route Cousin Kadri might have taken down south?"

She had already thanked Sanne and Nelson for not pressing that latter point in the interview; the less informed Sadek was, the more chance they had of catching him unprepared.

"GMP are going to deal with the Levenshulme friend," she continued. "Jay and Scotty, you're on family members or friends with automotive expertise or garages, lock-ups, et cetera. I don't believe that that Previa is in London, so it's probably stashed somewhere local. Check if any of his known associates are in car sales. Ask to see diaries, receipts, VAT invoices, anything that might make them twitchy." She spotted Sanne's raised hand. "Go ahead."

"What about a search warrant for Sadek's house and shop?" Sanne sounded far calmer than she had post-interview, when she'd walked into Eleanor's office apparently on the verge of throttling someone.

"Not yet," Eleanor said. "Given the sensitive nature of the investigation, DCI Litton has set the bar quite high for those, and at the moment we barely have reasonable suspicion."

Sanne nodded, the flush back in her cheeks. For almost two hours, Sadek had ignored his solicitor and Nelson, and directed every one of his "no comment" responses at her. She had mentioned it to Eleanor in passing, just as an observation on his behaviour and attitude, but her damp hair and fresh shirt suggested she had been unsettled enough to shower shortly afterward.

"I've drawn up a surveillance rota." Eleanor brought up the schedule on the overhead. "Low-key, and only on the shop at this point, but I have managed to cadge a knackered, unmarked van complete with tinted windows and a camera so foolproof that even Fred could operate it."

"Huzzah!" Fred raised his arms in triumph but let out a yelp when his back went into spasm. "Oh, God. Help."

As Sanne and Nelson each lowered one of his arms, Eleanor quickly amended the rota, moving him to a later date. Then she brought up her final slide, letting it sit for a couple of seconds while her team regarded it—and her—with sombre expressions. She kept her voice low when she spoke again, guaranteeing her their full attention.

"In an investigation like this one, that heads in a direction we weren't anticipating and comes with so many external factors to consider, it's easy to lose our focus." She tapped the screen with the back of her hand, and the photograph of the dead girl beneath the rocks undulated gently. "*She* is our focus. This morning the labs matched her DNA to blood found in the barn at Nab Hey. They have also isolated DNA from nine different women, which is two more than we found items for. Now, I'm not naive enough to think we will ever track all of these victims down. Our objective is to prevent any more women from sharing their fate." She clapped her hands together, breaking the tension and making George jump. "Okay, enough of the motivational crap. Everyone know what they're doing? Excellent. Check in when necessary, and be careful out there."

She stayed behind as they filed from the room, until there was only her and the dead girl in the darkness. Six days after the body was found, the image hadn't become any easier to bear, yet it seemed wrong to snuff it out by turning off the projector. She raised her glasses to the top of her head, smudging the finer details, as she gathered her paperwork and straightened the chairs. Once there was nothing remaining for her to do, she finally flicked the switch, and the girl disappeared.

❖

"Why are you arresting him? Why are you arresting him? He's done nothing wrong. *Leave him alone!*" The voice of Hasan Faraj's sister rose to a scream on this final demand, and she yanked on the arm Nelson was using to guide Faraj from the house.

"Enough!" Sanne stepped between the girl and Nelson, breaking the contact and giving him a clear path to the front door. In the corner of the living room, Faraj's mother was weeping and beseeching Allah for intervention. "He's not being arrested," Sanne told the girl. "Make sure your mum understands that. We're taking him to our headquarters to question him about your cousin's car, after which—all being well—he'll be coming home."

"'All being well'?" Bitterness rolled off the words. "You mean, if you can't manage to fit him up for something."

"No." Sanne stood her ground, despite the girl's proximity. "I mean that if he cooperates he'll be back here in a few hours."

The girl folded her arms, her foot tapping in a blunt staccato. "And if he doesn't?"

Sanne kept her own body language open, non-combative, but she wasn't going to sugar-coat things. "Pack him some pyjamas."

She expected a clout, or fingernails coming straight for her eyes, but the bald suggestion took the wind out of the girl's sails.

"I'll phone Dad. Don't tell them nothing!" she shouted past Sanne, as Nelson opened the door. Then she gripped Sanne's biceps. "What's your name? I want to make a complaint."

"Move your hand." Sanne waited out a count of three. "*Move it.*"

The girl startled and released her, snatching Sanne's proffered card instead, as if to compensate for her lack of nerve.

"That has all the details you'll need," Sanne said. "Search online for the IPCC to make your complaint."

"Stop taking the fucking piss!"

Unwilling to get into a slanging match with a fifteen-year-old, Sanne followed Nelson onto the street, where a crowd of onlookers had gathered to glare at them. She walked right past them, unable to understand the mutterings and murmurs aimed in her direction but gleaning a good enough idea.

Nelson waited for her at the car. "You okay?" he asked.

"Fine. You?"

"Yep. Shall we get out of Dodge while the going is moderately bad?"

She nodded and continued round to the passenger side. Faraj let her fasten her seat belt before he booted the back of her seat.

"So, are you a fucking dyke then, or what?" he asked.

She locked eyes with him in the rearview mirror. "I'm a fucking dyke," she said. "Now get your feet off my seat and shut your mouth."

❖

With no room to pace in the EDSOP corridor, Eleanor sidestepped a sweating teenaged interviewee whose complexion was more acne than skin, and checked her watch again.

"George, use Interview One for Hasan Faraj when Sanne and Nelson get here with him. He's another of Sadek's relatives who's corroborating the Kadri story."

"Will do." George saluted and tripped over the teenager's flip-flops. "Anything else you need?"

"No, just them. Send them straight in." She returned to her office, where Russ was sitting beside the Tactical Aid sergeant, their heads bowed over building plans. "Ten minutes," she told them. "The traffic's bad on the bypass."

"Should only take us an hour or so to get over there on blues," Russ said. "We can hang on and brief everyone together."

"How many entrances?" she asked, taking the remaining seat.

"Three: front and back, plus a fire escape into the adjoining alley. To say it's a logistical nightmare would be understating things somewhat." He marked crosses on the plan and grinned at her. "Thanks for the loan of your team."

"I'm hoping this will turn out to be mutually beneficial," she said. "Besides which, DCI Litton is very keen to foster a strong working relationship with GMP."

"And muscle in on the credit, should things go well."

"Cynic."

A knock on the door made them look up.

"Showtime," Russ said. "Have you still got a vest that fits, DI Stanhope?"

"Sod off." She opened her office door to Sanne and Nelson, en route to collecting her jacket and stab vest. "Tactical briefing will be held at Longsight nick, but I have some notes for you to read on the way over there," she told them. "Mike and Jay are on board as well. Are you all set?"

They nodded, the gleam of excitement in their eyes mirroring that in Russ's.

"Okay, then." She shrugged into her vest. "Let's get going."

❖

The interviewees segregated along the corridor shuffled aside or gaped as Sanne led the ten-strong team toward the lift. She had to rein in her instinct to break into a sprint, sure that every minute wasted getting across to Manchester might result in the raid being cancelled. Outside, the TAU van was parked in the drop-off bay with its engine running. Sanne bagged a window seat and looked out at the vivid line of orange splitting the darkened sky, the sunset carving the storm clouds into layers, like a cake with a filling of flames.

She turned on the torch attached to her vest, sharing a set of notes with Nelson as the TAU driver cleared the car park barrier and sparked up his blues. Due to the time constraints, Eleanor had only outlined the bare bones of the assignment, and Sanne was keen to know what she was letting herself in for. Tuning out the blare of sirens, she read quietly, waiting for Nelson's murmured assent before turning each page.

According to the précis, Greater Manchester's Sexual Offences and Exploitation Team had been surveilling a three-storey terraced house in Longsight for the past fortnight, recording the different men who visited the property each night and noting the arrival of two women, herded out of a van and taken inside the house via the rear entrance late on 19th February. Neither woman had left the property since.

"Jesus, have you seen the date?" Sanne asked.

"Yep." Nelson checked the next page. "Looking at the vehicle details, it wasn't Sadek's Previa doing the drop-off, but still, that's one heck of a coincidence."

"Why the hell wasn't it flagged to us sooner?" Sanne said, incredulous at the lack of dot-joining.

Nelson had continued to read, and he used his own torch to highlight a name. "Apparently GMP were at cross-purposes. They were planning to raid the brothel, but then this Bashir chap showed up out of the blue, so SOET alerted Parry, who recognised the significance of February the nineteenth, and here we all are."

"Parvez Bashir." Sanne sounded the name out. "You ever heard of him?"

Nelson shook his head. "But we don't really travel in the same circles, do we?"

Bashir—mid-forties and mixed race, with a Pakistani father and an English mother—had a criminal record showing steady progression through possession with intent, to sexual assault and battery. He had upped the ante after a spell in jail, culminating in a charge of controlling prostitution for gain. When several witnesses retracted statements or refused to testify, the case collapsed, and Bashir, who allegedly made a living as a taxi driver, now resided in a detached house in the wealthy suburb of Didsbury.

"Ambitious fella, isn't he? No wonder Parry's looking like a cat that might get the cream." Sanne reached the section of the briefing that detailed Bashir's suspected involvement in the trafficking of women across Europe to the UK. He had made an unforeseen appearance at the Longsight property at about the same time that Sanne was arguing with Hasan Faraj's sister. According to the team on site, he was still inside.

"Longsight borders Levenshulme." Nelson was peering at an A-Z. "Sadek would have known he could get away with saying one but heading to the other."

"Especially if he'd swapped vehicles." Sanne grabbed her armrest as the van chicaned through the rush-hour queue at a traffic light. Typically, one driver did precisely the wrong thing and blocked the entire lane. Unwilling to force cars through a red light, the TAU driver muted his sirens, the rhythmic flash of his blues far more sedate than the thrum of Sanne's heartbeat. She pulled out her phone, intending to send Meg a text, but faltered, unsure what to say. The screen returned to sleep mode as she stared at it.

"Do you tell Abeni about things like this?" she asked Nelson. "Because I've never...Well, I've never really thought about it with Meg."

He shut the map, giving her his undivided attention. "Feeling more responsible now that you're officially a couple?" he said, not teasing, just curious.

She nodded slowly. "I worry about her more, too. Y'know, little things, like her driving home on the Snake after a night shift, or some of the idiots she has to deal with in A&E. I mean, I worried before, but everything seems different these days."

He patted her hand, probably to stop her from massacring a fingernail. "Tell her about it afterward, when everything's fine and there's no reason for her to fret. That's what I do. I suppose I have it easier with Abeni, though, because she's sheltered from all of this, the things we see and have to deal with. Meg's not; she has a far better idea what you'll come up against, which will only make it harder for her."

"So if we're in one piece later, I tell her then?" Sanne tilted her torch until it illuminated Nelson's face. "I told her about climbing out of that window."

"But only after you didn't fall and break your neck."

"True." She settled into her seat, feeling better for his advice. "Thanks, Nelson."

He sat back as well, watching the city pass by in a blur of rain and neon. "Any time."

❖

Had Sanne not known better, she might have mistaken Longsight for Sharcliffe. An inner-city district built up around a strip of mini-markets and Asian speciality shops, it had a similar crisscross of terraced houses encircling it, and most of its residents were from ethnic minorities.

The east Sheffield TAU van was now travelling in convoy with Central Manchester's, their blues and sirens off as they crawled along Stockport Road amid a mob of taxis and buses. The tinted window to Sanne's left framed the odd curious glance, but the majority of the passersby appeared indifferent to the police presence.

"We should be turning off any minute," Nelson said. He adjusted the angle of the A-Z, struggling to keep track of their progress via vandalised street signs and his own rubbish map-reading. He hadn't spoken much since the briefing at Longsight police station, his attention, like Sanne's, focused on the photocopied schematic for fifty-eight Cheviot Road. The end-terrace extended over three floors, with three means of access, two of which opened onto unlit alleys.

Closing her eyes against the glare of reflected streetlights and fluorescent takeaway signs, Sanne tried to visualise the layout from their assigned entrance through to the point where her team would call clear: middle floor, two rooms to the right of the landing and three to the left. The stairs dog-legged before continuing to the upper floor, so one of her team would be stationed to intercept anyone trying to flee down them.

Balancing her notes on her lap, she moved a hand to her Taser, reassuring herself that it was there. The procedure for drawing and activating it had been ingrained by hours of training, not to mention a recent practical refresher courtesy of Gobber Beswick. She hadn't anticipated a need for carrying one after transferring to EDSOP, but two of her recent cases had brutally disabused her of that notion.

"Here we go," Nelson murmured as the van took a left and his finger inched closer to the X he'd marked on the A-Z.

As if a switch had been flicked, the Sheffield TAU lads stopped chucking someone's sandwiches around and quietened, donning the last of their kit. She recognised one of them from a raid the previous month. Balding and built like a brick shithouse, Graham popped a bubble in his gum and winked at her before pulling on a balaclava. Although his IQ was largely confined to his biceps, he excelled at putting the boot in, and the edginess that had beset her since the briefing abated somewhat when she rechecked her notes and realised he was the TAU lead on their floor.

The van thudded over a speed bump, sending up howls of protest and knocking her into Nelson. He righted her, leaning in without thinking to brace her for the next one.

"Cheers, mate," she said, and then lowered her voice to a whisper. "Are you sweating as much as I am?"

"Probably more. I can't tell whether it's nerves or impatience."

"Both." Usually the one in charge of route finding, she hated not knowing where she was going. "I think he's having a laugh and driving round in bloody circles now."

The road they were on was a carbon copy of the one they'd just left, fronted by Victorian terraces, many with boarded or smashed windows. Cobbles demarcated the alleys, and the front doors opened directly onto the street.

"Nope, Cheviot's the next one." Shining his light on the map for her, Nelson sounded a quiet fanfare when he spotted the sign. Sanne's applause was muted, her eyes fixed on the window again, counting down the houses until the van pulled into the alleyway after number fifty.

Eleanor got to her feet. "Okay, GMP are already in position in the east alley," she said. "And nothing's changed since we left the nick, so let's get going."

The TAU moved first, sliding open the van doors and jumping down into the alley. They were hefty men, but the stamp of their boots landing on wet cobbles, along with a muffled cough, were the only sounds Sanne heard them make. After the oppressive heat of the van, she welcomed the sudden shock of cold air. Feeling a sneeze coming on, she sniffed in a breath to get it out of the way before following Nelson toward their designated TAU members. Drizzle had veiled the passageway, leaving its far end murky and indistinct, but an unfamiliar voice in her earpiece confirmed the Manchester TAU were heading for the front door and ready to take the top floor via the eastern fire escape.

"Alpha and Bravo to the rear," the Sheffield TAU sergeant said. "My lot with me to the front."

They divided efficiently, Sanne and Nelson keeping a few paces behind Graham and the rest of Bravo team as they weaved around wheelie bins and the discarded household junk cluttering the alley. A dog set off barking at number fifty-four, its claws scrabbling on the concrete as its bulk sent a shudder through the gate. A floodlight hit the yard, but it was angled too acutely to reach the alley. Ducking instinctively to hurry past, Sanne smelled dope and dog shit, and for once appreciated not having eaten in a while.

In keeping with their neighbours, the owners of fifty-eight Cheviot had taken no chances with security. A four-digit combination padlock secured the solid wooden gate, and rolls of illegal razor wire topped the high brick walls.

"All teams go." Eleanor's taut command, carried across the comms.

"Camera," Sanne said, spotting the small CCTV fixed to a corner post. "Better get a wriggle on."

One of the two TAU officers wielding enforcer rams waved to the lens and then smashed the steel rod against the gate, rattling hinges which shook but held. Cursing, he adjusted his stance until he and his mate could batter their target in tandem, stealth sacrificed for expediency as the wood imploded and their boots finished off what little resisted. They sprinted for the back door, making short work of the uPVC and catching an Asian man by the scruff of his neck as he tried to launch himself out of the gap, wielding a piece of metal like a samurai. Sanne ducked beneath it, and an officer jerked the man's collar to slam him up against the yard wall.

"Fuckin' drop it!"

A barrage of Urdu and further struggling followed, but the metal went flying seconds later, and Sanne had to leapfrog his legs as the officers pinned him face-first on the concrete paving and then sat on him.

"You do not have to say anything, but it may harm your defence…"

The mantra faded to nothing as Sanne sprinted after her team into the house. Tracking the flashes of torchlight, she passed through the kitchen to the first flight of stairs, taking them two at a time until she caught up with Nelson. With the chaos over the comms reaching fever pitch, her team left one man poised at the bottom of the next flight and paired off, advancing along a narrow carpeted corridor whose doors were all fitted with sliding bolts.

Shouts of "Police!" and the occasional shriek or guttural yell punctuated the crashing of wood and the grating of locks. Sanne approached the farthest room with Graham and stood well clear of the door as he kicked it open. The impact set a light bulb swinging, its squalid glow picking out a middle-aged man crouched on an unmade double bed, naked apart from the leg he'd shoved back into his trousers. As Graham moved to secure the adjoining room, the man abandoned his clothing and his common sense to dash toward the window. His belly slapped the glass and his fists rose to smash it just as Sanne grabbed his arm and pivoted him round. He clawed at her with his free hand, his teeth bared in a snarl like an animal prepared to chew off its own limb to get away. She felt his nails rake her cheek, but he was already off balance, and he tripped over the leg she shoved between his.

"Fucking bitch!" He kicked her as he fell, and then screamed when she planted her foot in his bollocks and dropped her full weight onto his torso.

"Hands behind your back!" she yelled, digging her heels in to stop him bucking her off. "*Now!*"

Graham smoothed out the negotiations by smashing the man's face into the carpet, and the man complied with Sanne's instructions, allowing her to cuff him and recite his rights. Moaning incoherently, he curled into a ball, and she threw a blanket over him so she didn't have to look at his arse.

"Detective Jensen?" Graham's voice undercut the rasp of her breaths and the ongoing row in her earpiece. He wiped his sweaty face with his balaclava as he gestured at the adjoining room. "I think you'd be better in there than me."

She straightened slowly, only now seeing the shredded pink nightie and the Formica-topped table strewn with sex aids and condoms. Bright spots of blood dotted the crumpled bedding. Lightheaded with adrenaline and trepidation, she walked across to the second door and pushed it gently. As she stepped inside the tiny bathroom, two pale hands shot up to hide the face of the young girl cowering under the sink.

"No, please, please," the girl said. "No, please."

"It's okay." Sanne knelt but kept her distance. Even in the dim light, she could see the welts and bruises that marred the girl's body. "I'm a police officer. I'm not going to hurt you."

"No, please." The girl began to sob, pressing closer to the porcelain as if that might be enough to protect her. Sanne couldn't place her accent but guessed at Eastern European.

"I'm not going to hurt you, I promise. Here, you must be cold." She shrugged out of her jacket and touched the girl's hand with its sleeve. When that didn't seem to make anything worse, she carefully draped it around the girl's shoulders. "Do you speak English?"

Shaking her head, the girl lowered her arms a fraction, her mouth still covered as she answered. "Just. Little."

"What's your name?" Sanne set an open palm on her own chest. "I'm Sanne. Sanne Jensen."

The girl pulled the jacket tighter, her bare feet scuffing the floor as she tried to cover her legs. Blood was trickling from a split in her bottom lip, and a deep purple bruise had narrowed her left eye to a slit. She was fifteen years old at the most. She winced as she took too deep a breath. "Grieta," she whispered.

Sanne managed to smile, tempering her urge to go back next door and kick the shit out of Grieta's assailant.

Grieta reached out to her with a shaking hand. "Police?"

"Yes, police." Sanne closed her fingers around Grieta's and activated her comms. "Boss, we're clear far room, middle floor. I need medical assistance for one female vic, approximately fifteen years of age, conscious and breathing, multiple minor injuries."

There was a slight delay before Eleanor responded. "Roger that," she said, her tone too tight to give anything away. "If she's mobile, bring her to the ground-floor living room. Medics are en route."

"Wilco." The formal exchange restored Sanne's composure. She released her mike and squeezed Grieta's hand. "How about I find you some clothes?"

Evidently understanding some if not all of the question, Grieta nodded. Still huddled in the corner, she watched Sanne move to the door.

"Fourteen," she said, using her palm to mimic Sanne's earlier gesture. "Not fifteen, fourteen."

❖

Sanne's feet felt weird against the clammy leather of her boots. Unable to find any shoes for Grieta, she'd offered her own socks, sliding them onto icy toes as Grieta fumbled with cardigan buttons. In the time it had taken Grieta to dress, the raid seemed to have run its course. Floorboards were still creaking, but the traffic over the comms had subsided, and the only other noise reaching the bathroom was the sound of a woman weeping.

"Ready?" Sanne asked.

"Yes," Grieta said. She had kept hold of Sanne's jacket, pulling it over her cardigan and zipping it all the way up. It obviously hurt her to move; she bit her swollen lip as she crawled from beneath the sink and allowed Sanne to help her stand. She shrank back when Sanne opened the door.

"He's not here, Grieta. He's gone." Sanne stepped aside to reveal the empty room. She watched Grieta's eyes flicker from the bed to the table and finally to the corridor.

"I can go?" Disbelief underscored Grieta's question, as if she still expected to have the rug pulled from under her. She began to cry when Sanne nodded, big rolling tears that she fisted away until Sanne gave her a wad of toilet paper. Blood streaked the tissue as she blew her nose.

"It's all right," Sanne said. "Come with me."

The corridor and stairs were deserted, the doors busted on each room they passed, letting loose a foetid smell of sex and inadequate plumbing. Walking stiffly by Sanne's side, Grieta bowed her head and stared at the floor. If Sanne's jacket had come with a hood, she would undoubtedly have raised it. Eleanor met them at the foot of the stairs, her hair falling from its tie, and her coat askew.

"She's our fifth," she said to Sanne in an undertone as she guided them to the living room. "The eldest is twenty-two. Paramedics are waiting, and the TAU are shipping out with the arrests."

"Bashir?" Sanne asked.

"He went in the first van. There were seven arrests in total, and a mass of paperwork and computer files confiscated." Eleanor's reply lacked inflection, a coping mechanism Sanne could relate to. Later, Eleanor might show satisfaction or relief or even sorrow, but not while the job remained unfinished. She stopped at a frosted glass door with white paint flecking from its frame. The hallway had widened, and two ugly chenille sofas sat either side of an irony-free welcome mat. Floorboards were visible through holes in the carpet, but Sanne supposed no one visited the property for its ambience.

A paramedic answered Eleanor's knock, and Grieta's face brightened when she glanced into the room. A young woman cried out, meeting Grieta halfway and wrapping her in an ambulance blanket.

"She was asking for her sister," the paramedic said. "I think she might've found her."

Not wanting to embarrass herself, Sanne ignored the lump in her throat and turned away from the reunion. She started to shiver as the draught whistling down the hall dried the sweat on her shirt. "What now, boss?"

"Do you want a medic to clean your face?" Eleanor asked.

"Huh?" Sanne touched her cheek, finding three crusted lines of blood that stung when she pressed them. "No, they're just scratches," she said, unsure how they had occurred.

"Right, then," Eleanor said, apparently deciding not to pull rank. "SOCO are taking the bedrooms, GMP are taking the arrests, and the vics are going to St. Mary's in Manchester."

Sanne folded her arms, not appreciating being thrown out of the loop. "And EDSOP?"

"DI Parry has given us first crack at the office. Nelson and Mike are in there trying to sort whatever may have relevance to our case, with a view to leaving the rest for Manchester's MST or SOET."

"Do they need a hand?" She craved the distraction of a mindless task, and sifting through a pile of paperwork sounded ideal.

Eleanor seemed to have no difficulty reading between the lines. "I think they'd appreciate that."

❖

No one had bothered to proofread the brochure. Its grammar and spelling left much to be desired, and the ink had faded and smudged in places. The photographs were held in plastic sleeves, easy to switch or update. It was a job done on the cheap: why waste money on niceties if you were the only supplier able to meet the demands of your particular niche customer?

If Sanne tilted the images a certain way, her light caught occasional fingerprints, sometimes one on each edge of a photograph as if someone had taken it out to examine it in detail. These she set apart for SOCO. Using the names pencilled on the backs, she crosschecked the rest against an inventory found on the brothel's computer, categorising them by country of origin and then subcategorising by age: Bulgaria 22, 23; Latvia 14, 18, 21; Pakistan 16, 20, 22; Poland 17, 21; Romania 16, 17, 18. Multiple images of the five young women currently undergoing treatment at St. Mary's specialist sexual assault unit occupied pride of place in the most recent brochure. Preliminary statements obtained at the hospital by a SOET officer had confirmed that none of those women had ever been held in the barn at Nab Hey.

Sanne withdrew the final picture of a blank-faced Pakistani girl and held it beneath her desk lamp. She looked without seeing, her focus on the periphery and not on the explicit central pose. On the other side of the desk, Nelson swore and banged something down, his choice of epithet so out of character that Sanne stopped what she was doing, her light and the photo frozen inches apart.

"Nelson?"

"What?" he snapped, throwing all his emphasis on the "t." His fingers were so clenched that she wondered whether his nails had drawn blood.

"Hey," she said softly. "If you want me to take that one instead, pass it over here." She dreaded to think what he'd found, but he obviously wasn't coping with it. That he pushed it between their computers without arguing set even more alarm bells ringing.

"Sorry, San. I didn't mean to bite your head off." He rubbed his face with both hands. "I just want to go home and see my girls."

"So go," she said. "I won't be long either, and I think we're the last ones standing, apart from the boss. I can get these off to SOCO or finish scanning them into the case file."

He deliberated for a moment but then logged off and picked up his bag. "I'll see you in the morning," he said, pausing at her desk and kissing the top of her head. "Thank you."

"Give my love to Abeni and the terrible twosome," she said. "Drive safe."

"You too."

She listened to him leave, waiting out the tread of his boots across the carpet and the rattle of his locker. When the lift pinged and began its descent, she switched off her lamp and retrieved the stapled A4 sheets from the side of her monitor. The itemised tariff ran to two pages, price in the right-hand column, description of specialities in the left. It was clear that the proprietors of Cheviot Road prided themselves on their "No Boundaries" ethos; if the client could pay, then his requests— however extreme—would be fulfilled.

She reached the midpoint of the second page before she had to stop reading. The water she gulped down was lukewarm and made her feel even worse, her fingers sliding around in her sweaty gloves and threatening to lose their grip on the glass. A piece of chewing gum fished from the depths of her pocket settled her nausea, however, allowing her to scan in the last of the photographs and enter the tariff into the evidence log.

Eleanor's office stood in darkness as Sanne carried the box of paperwork down to Evidence. Having already collected her bag and slung on a spare sweater in lieu of her coat, she didn't return to the fourth floor. Her Landie started on the third attempt, coughing its disgust at the late hour, but she forced herself to turn toward Sheffield instead of home. The roads were quiet, the corridors of the hospital even more so, and the blare of the ITU security buzzer felt like a drill bit punching into the headache that was building over her left temple.

She walked to her dad's room without drawing the attention of the doctor at the main desk, and ducked inside, glad to be out of sight. No one was sitting vigil by her dad's bed. Two empty chairs were positioned in expectation of visitors, and a handmade "Get Well Soon, Granddad" card suggested Keeley had made an effort of sorts, but those were the only signs that anyone knew he was here. Sanne perched on the farther chair and tried to establish whether anything had changed. Although the blood transfusion was missing, the drips and feeds seemed the same, and the vent was continuing to give fourteen breaths a minute. A new growth of beard marked the days since his admission, and the smell of sanitising alcohol had replaced that of stale cider. Even bed-bathed and clothed in a hospital gown, the cleanest she'd seen him in years, her dad still stank of alcohol.

"Hello there. Are you John's daughter?"

Sanne's head flew up, and a check of the clock told her she'd dozed off for ten of the thirty minutes she'd allotted for her visit. Seeing her confusion, the nurse dropped a bag of saline on the storage unit and squeezed her shoulder in misplaced understanding.

"You must be exhausted, love. It's been a stressful few days, hasn't it?"

"Yes, it has," Sanne said, not lying, just not on the same page as the nurse.

"But hopefully we've turned a corner now." The nurse patted Sanne's dad on the forearm.

"What corner?" Sanne leaned forward, scrutinising the monitors again, searching for clues but seeing nothing she could make sense of. Her throat closed as if to prevent her next question. "Is he getting better?"

"Well, he's got a long way to go, but the doctor was really pleased with his last bloods and might try lifting the sedation tomorrow morning."

"Lifting the sedation," Sanne repeated, too numb to give the phrase meaning.

"Yes, love." The nurse pulled a sympathetic face, clearly pegging Sanne as an imbecile. "If everything goes to plan, we'll be able to wake your dad up."

The arc of headlights across the living room wall sent Meg into the hallway. She stood at the bottom of the stairs, giving Sanne a chance to let herself in, but Sanne fell back on old habits and knocked.

"Jesus Christ," Meg hissed as she opened the door. "Get in here."

The phone call should have been warning enough. Sanne hadn't said much, merely asking where Meg was and whether it would be okay to call round so late. She'd sounded hollowed out, as if every aspect of her personality had been beaten into submission. Meg hadn't been prepared for her to look that way as well, though, and she could only begin to guess what might have caused it.

"Are you hurt?" She touched Sanne's cheek, avoiding three fresh gouges and checking for fever. Although Sanne never had much colour in winter, she was ghostly even by her standards.

"No, I'm okay." Sanne laid her hand on top of Meg's. "I'm knackered, that's all."

"Mm-hm." Meg walked her into the living room and sat her in front of the fire. "What happened to your coat?"

Sanne shook her head, sending a tear flying onto the upholstery. Her eyes were swollen and bloodshot, but she didn't seem aware that she was crying. "I don't think you want to know."

"San." Meg didn't continue until Sanne looked at her. "If it'll help, tell me." Reluctant to pressure her into a decision, she switched her focus to the fire, poking a log into place as Sanne deliberated. They had always confided in each other, using each other as sounding boards or simply as an ear to rant into, but perhaps that had been helped by the distance of a non-relationship; perhaps Sanne would now start worrying about offending her sensibilities. Meg returned the poker to its spot and was about to reassure Sanne that she really didn't have many sensibilities, when Sanne began to speak.

"We raided a suspected brothel in Manchester." She wiped her face and righted her posture. "We arrested a bloke in one of the rooms, and I gave my coat to the fourteen-year-old Latvian girl he'd just raped and beaten. He'd had to pay extra to leave marks on her—almost five hundred pounds—because that'd put her out of commission until she healed. He was a fucking accountant, Meg, and he picked this child from a catalogue as if he was shopping in Argos."

"Did he do this, too?" Meg's finger fell just shy of the scratches.

"Yes, but I kicked him in the nuts, so he came off worse."

They smiled at the same time, and Sanne closed her eyes as Meg stroked her cheek.

"He had children of his own, still in school," she said. "What's their life going to be like now?"

"Awful," Meg said, "for a while at least, but they'll get support and counselling, and their dad won't be able to hurt them or anyone else."

"That's true. That's good." Sanne's head bobbed in agreement.

Assuming that covered the worst of it, Meg was about to offer supper when Sanne threw a final spanner in the works.

"I went to see my dad tonight," she said. Exhaustion deadened her voice, but she persevered. "The nurse told me that he's getting better. That they want to wake him up."

Meg's stomach did a sick little lurch. The longer John had remained in the ITU, the more confident she had become that something—infection, a rebleed, multi-organ failure—would finish him off. She wondered briefly whether Sanne's tenacity came from him, but she'd be damned if she'd give him the credit.

"Try not to worry, love," she said. "You've got enough on your plate as it is."

"I'm not worried, not really. Whatever happens, happens."

Meg left the lie unchallenged and held out her hand. "Come on. Shower and bed for you, unless you want something to eat first."

"I'm not hungry." Sanne made the admission like a first-time criminal confronted by a jury of disappointed family members, and then yawned so widely that Meg heard her jaw crack. "I promise I'll have breakfast. Eggs or porridge or something filling."

"Eggy bread?" Meg suggested as they reached the bottom of the stairs. "Best of both worlds."

"Fabulous. And you know how to cook that."

"Oh, I'm getting up with you, am I?"

"I thought you might." Sanne tripped on the bathroom threshold and stumbled to the toilet seat. "Six hours' sleep is more than enough. It said so on the telly."

"In that case, it's a date."

Six hours would have been plenty, but Sanne got up after just three, throwing the covers back and walking out of the bedroom. Woken by the cold, Meg heard her bypass the bathroom and go downstairs.

"Bloody hell, San." Too befuddled to make sense of anything, she yanked on the quilt and then sat bolt upright. "Shit." She threw on a sweater and slippers, straining for a clue as to Sanne's whereabouts. She hadn't heard either of the main doors unlock, so she tried the living room first, checking each corner before dragging the throw rug from the sofa and taking it into the kitchen.

"San?" She left the light off, grateful for the full moon that showed her Sanne sitting on the floor behind the table. "Thank you for not making me chase you outside," she whispered, wrapping Sanne in the rug and sacrificing her own slippers to Sanne's bare feet.

She had only seen Sanne sleepwalk once before, back in summer when her stress levels had been similarly high and she'd ended up at the bottom of the garden. That night it had been warm enough for Meg to take the time to coax Sanne inside, but the cold tiles weren't doing either of them any favours, and the chatter of Sanne's teeth forced Meg to lug her up. Pliable as a doll, Sanne followed Meg to the bedroom, her face expressionless as she lay down. Instinct seemed to kick in then; her eyes drifted shut and she nestled against Meg. Meg put an arm around her, ready to react should she decide to wander again, and tried not to think about the father of two who had used a brothel where he could rent children from catalogues.

CHAPTER FIFTEEN

"You weren't kidding about the coffee, were you?" Eleanor took another sip from the polystyrene cup, reluctant to admit defeat.

Russ toasted her courage with his own brew. "Horrible, isn't it? I've seen it make grown men weep."

"What about the women?"

"They're sensible and stick with tea." He turned up the volume on a small monitor as its screen flickered into life. "We must be through the preliminaries, then."

She pushed her coffee downwind and opened her notepad in its place. She'd never been inside the interview room at Longsight Police Station, but even on a dodgy live feed it bore a depressing resemblance to EDSOP's. A warning light informed Parvez Bashir that his interview was being monitored remotely, and all that separated him from the two MST detectives was a plain metal table with its feet bolted to the floor.

Dressed in a well-fitting but inexpensive suit, Bashir was doing his utmost to appear humble and attentive. Keeping his hands open on the table, he confirmed his details and maintained eye contact as the detectives explained the interview's objectives. The lead detective eased him into the questions, discussing the areas he covered in his taxi and the hours he worked.

"Weekends are the very worst," Bashir said. "All of the drunk young people. I charge extra if they vomit, which is only fair if I'm the one to clean it up."

"Absolutely." The detective smiled, but nothing reached his

eyes. "Could you tell us why you were at fifty-eight Cheviot Road, Levenshulme, yesterday evening?"

Bashir answered without missing a beat. "I had a fare to pick up, booked for five thirty, but the traffic is always terrible on the A6 so I set off early."

"Why did you go inside?" the detective asked. "Don't you chaps usually stay on the street and hoot the horn?" He looked at his colleague, who nodded her agreement.

"I needed the toilet," Bashir said. "I knocked, and someone kindly let me in."

Eleanor put out a hand and stilled the pen Russ was tapping on the table.

"Sorry," he said. Irritation had brought vivid blotches to his cheeks. "I testified against him at his last trial, the one that went to shit. He had one of my witnesses battered so severely that her own dad couldn't ID her in the ITU."

"He's fucked this time," she said. "He just doesn't know it yet."

"I've been here before, El. Had him on the hook, and the bastard managed to wriggle off it." He fiddled with the contrast on the monitor, more for want of something to do than because there was a problem.

"Can you explain why you were in the main office at the time of your arrest?" the detective asked Bashir.

Bashir threw up his hands at his own incompetence. "I got lost. I think the man said 'third on the left,' and I must have counted badly." He turned to his solicitor, who passed him a slip of paper. "This is the receipt for the taxi booking. The receptionist at my company will be able to confirm it as well. Honestly, sir, this is just a misunderstanding."

The detective nodded. "Are you saying that you had no idea as to the nature of business taking place at fifty-eight Cheviot Road?"

"Of course not." Bashir sounded appalled. "Even now I only know a little. I do not think that I wish to know the details."

The detective set a photograph of Rafiq Sadek in front of Bashir and invited him to take a closer look.

"Do you recognise this man?"

Bashir shook his head. "I've never seen him before."

"What about her?" the detective asked, exchanging the photograph of Sadek for one of the dead girl from the moors. Her image hadn't been found in any of the evidence examined from the raid so far.

Despite the poor quality footage, Eleanor caught the disquiet threatening to undermine Bashir's carefully choreographed performance. He recovered quickly, though, to spin his reaction to his advantage. "That's a terrible thing to show me." He loosened his collar as if it chafed. "You should have warned me about that."

"Nicely done," Russ muttered.

"Just to recap, Mr. Bashir," as the detective spoke, he returned the photos to his file, "You had never set foot in fifty-eight Cheviot Road prior to yesterday evening."

"That is correct."

"And you had no idea that a large-scale forced prostitution ring was operating from the premises."

"No, none at all. I am happily married, sir."

"I'm not suggesting you were a client, Mr. Bashir."

Bashir bristled. "No, you think I am involved in the business. That I somehow organise it, despite having no ties to any of it, and despite the legitimate company that I do run. Tell me, where exactly would I find the time for such an enterprise? There are hardly enough hours in the day as it is." He directed his appeal to the detective's colleague, as if there was a chance she would rally to his cause. Instead, she handed her partner a sealed plastic bag containing a photograph. Eleanor recognised it immediately; she had booked it out of Evidence that morning and brought it with her to Manchester.

"We'll take a break in a minute," the lead detective said. "First, though, I'd like you to clear something up, if at all possible."

"Of course," Bashir said, his eyes straying to the bag.

"I'm going to show you another photograph, and I have to warn you that it is sexually explicit." The detective paused for Bashir to nod his consent and then turned the bag around.

Bashir squinted at the image, taking his time like a well-behaved, cooperative witness. "Am I supposed to know this girl as well?" he asked.

"I'm not entirely sure." The detective tucked the bag away again. "One of our colleagues in East Derbyshire removed that photograph from a brochure gathered as evidence in the raid last night. Now, there are two things that I'd really like to know. The first is why you happened to arrive at fifty-eight Cheviot, not for five thirty p.m. as you claim, but at eleven minutes past three." He slapped a surveillance shot in front of Bashir but continued without pause. "The second is why your fingerprints were found on the photograph of this girl."

He did pause then, sipping his water, an eyebrow raised. Bashir threw a wild glance at his solicitor, who shook her head.

"No comment," Bashir said.

Eleanor muted the video feed as the solicitor demanded time to consult with her client.

"Got you, you little fucker," she said.

❖

Kneeling by her locker, Sanne arranged an extra sweater on top of everything else she'd packed in her bag, wedging it in like the last beach towel layered over holiday clothes.

"Crikey, how long are you planning on going for?" Nelson asked, the holiday analogy clearly on his mind as well.

"Eight hours, at the last count." Her tongue poked out as she fastened the zip on an outside pocket. "But I might get cold or too hot, and we'll definitely get hungry, so I've tried to cover all our bases."

Nelson lifted his far smaller bag. "By packing for a week."

"Naw." She hefted the rucksack on one shoulder, almost tipped over, and quickly shoved her arm in the other strap. "I've left my pyjamas and my pillow at home."

He laughed, setting off for the lift at a slow walk to allow for her heavier load. Fred saluted as they passed him, his desk buried under a pile of Cheviot Road paperwork. Sanne managed to exit without breaking into a trot, but she stabbed the lift button repeatedly, dreading a last-minute summons to waylay them or change their assignment, and she only began to relax once the doors glided shut and the EDSOP corridor disappeared.

"Thank goodness for that," Nelson murmured, unconsciously echoing her sentiments. The shadows beneath his eyes suggested he hadn't slept well, and he'd been subdued through the morning as they'd continued to process their allocation of evidence from the raid. Compared to that, eight hours of surveillance in an unheated Ford Transit with no toilet sounded like a plum gig.

Bright sunshine and a pool car that didn't smell of stale farts or fags put further ticks in the bonus book. Not only had the car's last occupants been hygienic, they'd even left toffees behind. With the bag of sweets primed on her lap, Sanne set her feet on the dash and turned the radio up, howling along to a song whose lyrics she half-improvised as Nelson shook his head in despair and accelerated toward the bypass.

"You'll make it rain," he said, undermining his warning by fishing for his sunglasses. She opened them for him and held them out.

"Not today," she said, craning her neck to examine the sky. "It's going to freeze hard tonight, and more snow's forecast for tomorrow afternoon."

"Great. Don't suppose you've got blankets and hot water bottles in your luggage."

"Nope," she said, ignoring his dig. "You'll have to do star jumps if you get chilly."

"A fourteen-stone black man bouncing around in the back of a Tranny van. I'm sure that wouldn't attract anyone's attention!"

She contorted herself into the footwell as she dropped her map. "Hey, if the van's rockin'…"

"Exactly." He slowed the car a touch. "You okay down there?"

"Yep, never better." She wriggled back into the seat, the map fortuitously falling open to the right page. "Okay, Scotty said he'll reverse into this side street for the changeover. We can leave our car there and nudge the van forward a tad until it's back in position. I thought the damn thing might stick out like a sore thumb, but apparently there are so many crappy vans parked up around there that no one's batted an eyelid so far."

"But no one's done anything remotely useful in terms of the case, either," Nelson said.

She unwrapped him a sweet in an attempt to forestall any negativity. "We've only been watching the shop for—what? Twenty-four hours or so? Sadek seemed pretty savvy to me. If he is involved, he's probably decided to lie low for a while."

"I suppose that begs the question: why bother with the surveillance?"

"Well, he's also a cocky little shit, which means there's a chance he might slip up." She chewed her toffee, enjoying it even more when it turned out to be banana flavoured. "And it lets us get away from our desks and spend this beautiful afternoon in the charming suburb of Sharcliffe."

Nelson slammed on the brakes as the concept of a roundabout suddenly outwitted the driver in front. "If we ever get there," he said through gritted teeth.

"If we ever get there." She gave him another toffee, carefully selecting his favourite. "I think this might be treacle."

"I knew there was a reason you were my best ever partner," he said, his cheek bulging like a hamster's.

"You won't be saying that by eleven o'clock tonight. You'll be turfing me out on the street and making me walk home." Spotting the surveillance van on the corner, she began to scan the road for a parking space. The van had originally been impounded for lack of insurance, its rear doors proudly advertising "House Clearences. Any Job's Big or Small."

"Oh, the shame." Nelson winced, the dodgy grammar distracting him from his parallel parking and forcing him to try again. "It's a good thing we're incognito."

"Adds to the authenticity," Sanne said, nodding at Scotty and Jay as they left the van and went to retrieve their car. From beneath the brim of the cap she'd just put on, she watched a lady walk by, her tartan shopping trolley fraying at the seams to reveal its load of bread and vegetables. The woman passed the van without giving it a second glance, clearing the way for Sanne and Nelson to make a move.

"Right-o," Nelson said. "How do I look?"

Sanne tweaked the collar of his navy blue overall. Her outfit was identical, except that she'd had to turn up its legs and sleeves. "Like a man ready to collect a load of shite from someone's house."

"Splendid."

Scotty had left the keys in the van's ignition, half a packet of chocolate digestives and a puzzle book on the passenger seat, and a small kettle that could be plugged into the lighter.

"Very civilised," Sanne said, overlooking the half-eaten Pot Noodle and trying to become accustomed to the tang of sweaty feet lingering in the back. "Jay's had his bloody shoes off, hasn't he?"

"Yep." Nelson started the van and manoeuvred onto the street until the frontage of Sadek Foods could be observed via the side window.

"You're fine there," she called, preoccupied by her efforts to figure out the camera. She snapped a candid of Nelson and checked it in the viewer. "Not sure I got your best side." She displayed a shot mostly featuring crotch and midriff.

"Annie Liebovitz must be quaking in her boots." He held out his fist in the traditional rock-paper-scissors fashion. "Loser gets first watch," he said, and cracked his knuckles.

❖

"Noisy, confused situation." Nelson chewed his pen, concentration creased into his brow. "Eight letters, starts with a B."

"Boist—oh wait, no, that's too many letters." Keeping the shop in sight, Sanne stood and stretched her arms above her head. Her left leg tingled, the pins and needles in its foot making her stamp it. Six and a half hours into their stakeout, Sadek Foods was still busy, its customers unperturbed by the frost forming now that the sun had set. As the feeling returned to her foot, she aimed the camera through the tiny gap in the window covering and photographed a random male to recheck her settings. Despite the camera's shoddy appearance, it worked well, compensating for the lack of daylight to produce a clear image. She blew on her fingers to warm them and put her gloves on.

"Third letter's an L," Nelson said, reminding her of her crossword duties.

"Bul...Bel...Bal..." She poured bottled water into the kettle, inspiration striking as she fixed its lid into place. "Ballyhoo? Bloody hell, that's an arse of a clue."

He whooped. "It fits, though, so I'm having it."

The tea and coffee made, she passed him his mug and resumed her seat at the bench.

"'Expected successor,' four letters, ends with an R." His breath clouded as he spoke, mingling with the steam from his brew to veil him in a pea-soup fog.

"Hmm," she said, but her attention was focused on the window, not the clue. "They're a little out of place around here. We'll have them for posterity on the way out."

"Who are we having?" he asked, wafting away the mist.

"Two white blokes. The only white blokes I've seen so far."

He set his pen on his puzzle book. "There's a Polish enclave a few streets out, isn't there?"

"Yes, but they don't tend to mix with the Pakistanis."

"Maybe they've acquired a taste for the local cuisine." He sipped his coffee, his eyes back on his crossword.

"Yeah, maybe." From her job-related forays into Sharcliffe and from the local news coverage, Sanne knew that the recent Polish immigrants had opened their own speciality stores and church, and that their gradual encroachment into the Asian-dominated area was a source of growing tension. "It's probably summat and nothing," she conceded, though she readied the camera regardless.

Her brew went cold as she waited, an unpleasant layer of grease settling on its surface. "For fuck's sake, what's taking so long?" she muttered, and then swore again when the men reappeared, each carrying a laden shopping bag.

"Can't win 'em all, San," Nelson said, offering her a digestive.

"Bollocks." She took their photo for the hell of it and lowered the camera as a woman in a niqab chivvied three young children across the street. She watched the woman sling a large box of nappies on top of her pram and slap the eldest child's hand to stop him biting on an apple. He began to howl, his face distorted with indignation, and the woman pulled him inside the shop by one arm in the manner of put-upon mums everywhere.

Sanne nibbled her digestive, amazed to think how ignorant she'd been when she'd started her career as a response officer. Her first calls to ethnic minorities had left her so out of her depth that she'd put in hours of research to try to glean an understanding of the different religions and customs she might encounter on the job. She had barely scratched the surface, but at least she'd stopped offering Muslim witnesses refreshments during Ramadan.

"Y'know, Nelson, you're the only black friend I've ever had," she said, embarrassed enough to brush the crumbs from her knees so she wouldn't have to look at him. "The council tried to move a Pakistani family onto Halshaw once, in the late eighties, and my dad thought it was the end of the world. He ranted on about it every bloody teatime and banned any of us from going down their street. He could've saved his air. They were moved straight off again when someone firebombed their house."

"No black kids at your school, then?"

"Nope, not a one. There were a few at my sixth-form college, but within the first fortnight someone kicked off a rumour that Meg and I were lesbians and told everyone we were from Halshaw, so most people left us alone. Which was fine, I suppose. Not having social lives meant we managed to get plenty of work done." She raised her head and met Nelson's eyes, remembering how crushed she'd felt when her hopes of turning a new leaf at college—away from the estate and the gang of girls who'd plagued her through school—had been obliterated. Nelson took a biscuit for himself and slid the packet in front of her.

"A boy at my school put a banana on my desk every Monday for a month," he said. "He called it 'Monkey Monday.' The teacher knew, but she didn't do a damn thing to stop it."

"Fucking hell."

Nelson shrugged, quite sanguine about his revelation. "Good thing I liked bananas, eh? I'd take them home, and my mum would put them with custard for me."

Sanne broke the last digestive in two and gave him the bigger piece. "I think your mum would have got on well with mine."

"Two very fine ladies," he said. "Now, 'Expected successor,' four letters, ends with an R."

"Heir." She aimed the camera toward the window, framing a middle-aged Asian man in the viewer. "That bloke's been in twice in the last hour. Think it means anything?"

"Probably means he forgot to get sugar," Nelson said, refusing to engage with her conspiracy theory. "Or that he left his phone on the counter."

"Aye, probably." She checked the man's photo against the mug shots Parry had provided, and then added it to her growing folder of people they would never be able to identify. With the novelty of the stakeout long faded and her back stiffening up again, she held the camera out to Nelson. "Come and take over here for me," she said. "I'm going to do some sit-ups before I lose the feeling in my arse."

❖

Crouching by the pushchair in cubicle six, Meg high-fived the toddler she'd just discharged. His little paw, sticky with paracetamol syrup, left a smear of pink goo on her palm.

"Cheers, pal." She wiped her hand on her scrubs and stood, putting her on the level with his painfully young parents. "Okay, here's more paracetamol to take home. One spoonful every four hours if he's still warm and grizzly. And what *don't* we do if he's so hot he's started to shiver?"

"Wrap him in a blanket and put him in front of the fire!" The dad almost shouted his answer, as if determined to beat his girlfriend to the title of Star Pupil.

"Excellent." Meg rewarded his progress with a *Feverish Child* leaflet. "Any problems, phone 111 for advice," she said, choosing not to add that the call-takers manning the helpline would most likely dispatch an ambulance to return the child to A&E.

Completing her paperwork made Meg half an hour late, not too bad for a twilight shift, the end of which coincided with closing time at most of the local pubs. She changed in the staff room, swapping scrubs for clothes that didn't smell of strawberry medicine and baby sick, and leaving the rest of her belongings in the locker to collect on the way out.

After buzzing to no avail, she used her ID card to let herself into the ITU, passing the empty nurses' desk on the way to John's room. Frantic activity and shouts of "Clear!" at the far end of the main bay explained the dearth of medical personnel. The door to room two sat ajar, an irregular clicking sound replacing that of a ventilator. She took a moment to curse every deity known to man, plus a few more she'd made up, before she went any farther. The clicking stopped as she stepped inside, Teresa lowering her knitting so she could pay attention to her visitor. Given the late hour, she had probably expected a nurse, and her face brightened when she saw Meg instead.

"What on earth are you doing here, love?" She stood to hug and kiss Meg, holding on tightly until her grip faltered and she began to cry.

"It's okay. It's okay," Meg murmured. She could see John over Teresa's shoulder, his vent removed, a thin oxygen tube resting beneath his nose as he breathed for himself. "Come and sit down."

They sat together, still holding hands, and stared at the bed.

"I promised Sanne I'd come up after my shift," Meg said. "She was on a surveillance job until late, and she barely slept last night."

"She phoned earlier, but I didn't answer." Teresa shook her head, guilt stark in her eyes. "I didn't want to tell her."

"I'll tell her," Meg said. "Don't fret about that."

"He woke for a few minutes. I don't think he recognised me, and I know I should've reassured him, but I couldn't bear to say a word." Teresa spread the tiny half-finished sweater across her knees, her fingers pulling at a thread. "Look at this. I keep dropping stitches."

Meg took the sweater and folded it away. "Come on. I'll give you a lift home."

It was over an hour later that she crawled into bed at Sanne's, chilled to the bone and woozy with fatigue. Sanne nudged into Meg's arms, mostly asleep but generous about sharing her warmth.

"Everythin' okay?" she mumbled.

"Everything's fine." Meg kissed her forehead. "Shh, go back to sleep."

CHAPTER SIXTEEN

The frozen ground sent shockwaves through Sanne's calves as she pushed her tired legs into a sprint. She cut left, leaving the path and relying on the sky for navigation. Keeping Orion's Belt on her right, she traversed a section of no man's land, cracking the ice on frosty bogs and using the thicker patches of heather as stepping stones. The exertion cleared her head, forcing her to focus on her route and not on the simple, half-stupefied exchange that had sent her out running in the first place.

She found the homeward path without difficulty, lengthening her stride as the terrain became less tricky. An owl glided silently in front of her, its wings outstretched in the moonlight. She stopped to track its flight, losing sight of it when it swooped behind a dry stone wall, the early morning so still that she heard the terrified squeak of its prey. Continuing at a less frantic jog, she let Rigel guide her home, the bumps and dips on the path familiar enough that she could admire the shadowy hills without fear of falling.

She'd left her kitchen light on and set a towel and a glass of water in readiness by the back door. She drained the glass and tiptoed upstairs in the darkness, trying not to make any noise as she showered and dressed. Notification of her failure came in the form of warm hands helping her to tug on her sweater until her head popped out through its narrow polo neck.

"Hey," Meg said. She scratched her scalp, obviously troubled. "Are you okay? I found your note, but I feel like I missed something."

Sanne walked her back to bed and tucked her in. "I'm all right. I woke up early and asked whether my dad was off the vent. You said yes, and I went for a run so I didn't stick my fist through a wall, that's all."

"Fuck." Meg got caught in the sheets as she struggled to sit up again. Conceding defeat, she thwacked her head onto the dip in her pillow. "Shit, San, I'm sorry. I meant to break it gently, but I don't...I don't even remember speaking to you."

Sanne ran her hand through Meg's bed-tufted hair. She hadn't intended to blindside her, and Meg's blunt answer had been preferable to any attempt at beating around the bush. "It's not your fault. You were pretty much asleep, I think."

"Yeah, I got in late." Meg checked Sanne's knuckles just in case. "Don't punch walls. Nothing good ever comes of it."

"I won't," Sanne said, crossing her heart. "Have another hour or two in bed. I'm not leaving for a while yet."

"Mm, I'm getting up." Meg yawned, her eyes already drifting shut. "I'll just hang on till you're done in the bathroom."

"That'd be a first." Sanne toed her slippers from their hidey-hole beneath a chair and hopped into them on the landing. Famished, and finding herself spoiled for choice when she opened her fridge, she decided on sausage and eggs and started her laptop while the grill warmed.

She hadn't realised how many photos she and Nelson had amassed the previous day until she accessed the camera's memory card and saw more than a hundred thumbnails begin to open. Her eggs were scrambled in readiness and the sausages sizzling before everything had finished downloading. For convenience's sake, she loaded her breakfast onto toast, eating it left-handed so she could operate the computer with her right. She deleted the blurred or poorly lit images and sorted the remainder by gender and age, comparing them again to Parry's gallery of rogues in case anyone had been overlooked. The kitchen grew lighter as she worked, although clouds were quickly rolling in to cover the patches of blue sky and dull the sunshine. Squally showers of sleet were pattering against the window by the time Meg came down, dressed in so many layers she could barely fit through the door.

"Central heating, San," she said, rubbing her upper arms with gloved hands. "I thought we had an agreement about this."

"Bugger, yes, we did. I meant to set the timer before I went to bed.

Sorry." Sanne left the table to stack another log onto the burner and refill the kettle.

"At least the shower was hot. I'll check the thermostat for you and see if it needs tweaking." Meg's voice faded, as if she'd abruptly lost interest in the topic.

Sanne glanced up from the stove. "You all right over there?" She tapped the spoon on one of the mugs, trying to attract her attention. "I saved you some sausages, if you fancy them for breakfast."

Meg didn't answer. She had sat in Sanne's seat and was peering intently at the computer. "What are you doing with his picture?" she said.

Abandoning the mugs, Sanne went to crouch by Meg's side. The image she had been about to file now filled the screen. She tilted the laptop, blocking out the window's glare so she could see the person properly. It was one of the two men assumed to be Polish. "Do you know him?" she asked.

Meg nodded. "It's Cezar Miklos." She slapped the table impatiently as Sanne hesitated. "You know, that Romanian shithead from A&E."

"Christ. The one who brought his wife in with the burns?"

"Yes, and then disappeared with her. Where did you get this?"

"From our stakeout," Sanne answered slowly, her brain working ten to the dozen. "Did Fraser ever find proof that Miklos was actually married to the woman you treated?"

"No. Every detail he gave was false—the names, her date of birth, their home address—and then they vanished into thin air."

"Apparently not." Sanne clicked to the next photograph, hoping to find a car in the shot. She remembered the men parking close to the shop, but she'd never thought to capture the vehicle. The edge of a Saab had been caught in frame, but none of its plate was visible. "Fucking hell!" She shoved away from the table and paced to the window.

"You think Anca Miklos was trafficked, don't you?" Meg said.

Sanne leaned against the sink, its edge chilling a line across her back. "I think there's a very good possibility of that, yes. And if she was, then this bloke showing up at this particular shop is one hell of a coincidence."

"Unless he simply went there to buy food." Meg folded her arms, rocking her chair onto two legs as she spoke. "This Romanian chap, with his friend, at almost nine p.m., in an area that's pretty much one hundred percent Pakistani."

Sanne grinned and picked up the phone. "Precisely."

❖

"Bloody Nora." Fred swung his chair around, eyeing Sanne as she walked toward him with Meg. "No one told me it was 'Bring Your Girlfriend to Work' day."

"That's because Martha's already got you in enough trouble." Sanne paused for introductions. "Meg—Fred Aspinall." She lowered her voice to a stage whisper. "The dancer with the dodgy back."

"Oh, salsa man!" Meg shook the hand he proffered. "Try a dollop of Brufen gel, mate, and maybe some warm-up exercises next time."

Sanne steered her away before Fred could start comparing notes on Meg's preferred type of warm-ups. Nelson met them by Sanne's desk, setting his paperwork down so he could hug Meg.

"The boss and Parry are waiting in the briefing room," he told Sanne.

"Right, cheers." She bit the inside of her lip, but her teeth relented slightly when Meg leaned into her.

"Best not keep them," Meg said.

Unable to get hold of Eleanor on the phone, Sanne had left a message and immediately hot-footed it to HQ with Meg in tow. Word of a possible development had obviously got round, because most of the EDSOP detectives tagged along to the briefing room, where Eleanor waved them all inside.

"Detective Fraser is caught up in an interview and asked that we start without him," she said. "And for those who don't know, this is Dr. Meg Fielding from the A&E at Sheffield Royal."

"Morning, all." Meg smiled at her audience, clearly in her element. She found a USB port for Sanne's memory stick and opened the first image, a cut-and-paste composition of Cezar Miklos outside Sadek Foods plus the hospital CCTV photograph that Fraser had sent to her mobile phone. The two men were unmistakeably one and the same.

Sanne stepped forward when she saw Nelson's double take. "For the past week, Domestic Violence have been trying to find this man—a Romanian national—in connection with suspected non-accidental injuries inflicted on a young woman he claimed to be his wife. He booked her into A&E using a forged European Health Insurance Card and false details, and he took her from the Burns Unit the following day before she could be properly treated. DV have been unable to locate him since."

"What was the nature of her injuries?" Parry asked.

"Extensive partial thickness burns to both hands," Meg said. "If I had to guess, I would say that someone held her by the wrists and forced her hands into hot liquid. She supported his story of a dropped pan, but the wounds didn't tally with that, which is why I spoke to Detective Fraser."

"I took the second photograph during our surveillance last night," Sanne said. "This man and another white male spent approximately twenty minutes inside Sadek Foods."

"Looks like they did their weekly shop," George said.

"Yes, it does." She adjusted the image to show Miklos's carrier bag. "But then it looked like he'd brought his wife to A&E after a simple accident, and that turned out to be a load of crap."

"There were three Romanian women in the Cheviot Road brochure," Nelson said. "And we've never established the nationality of all the vics held at Nab Hey. If Rafiq Sadek is involved in any of this, it would make sense for him to have Eastern European connections."

Parry turned in his chair so he could address the whole room. "I don't recognise either of these chaps, but there's a large market for women trafficked from Eastern Europe, and thanks to the EU's freedom of movement policy the logistics are far simpler than shipping in women from Asia. My team are still attempting to trace all the women in the Cheviot brochure who weren't found in the house, plus the ones recorded as having passed through the property and shipped elsewhere, but the majority of them were EU nationals."

"Perhaps Sadek started small but fancied establishing a multinational organisation," Eleanor said. "Especially now we've taken Bashir out of the loop and potentially created a power vacuum." She looked at Parry, who raised an eyebrow and blew out his cheeks.

"Bollocks, I didn't think of that," he said.

"At any rate," she continued, "it's enough to bring Sadek in again. Sanne and Nelson, if you could do the honours, please?"

Sanne nodded, having already prepared herself for the request.

As the meeting splintered into smaller groups, Eleanor excused herself from a conversation with Parry to approach her and Meg.

"I appreciate you coming in," she said to Meg. "I've booked Interview Two for you, if you're still sure about doing this."

"I'm sure." Meg's eyes flickered to Sanne's for a split second, the only hint that she wasn't as indomitable as she appeared. As one of the few people to have seen Anca Miklos in person, she had agreed to look through the photographs from Cheviot Road to establish whether Anca was among them.

"I don't know what would be worse," she said as Sanne escorted her down the corridor. "Finding her in there, or not finding her and never being able to trace her."

Sanne changed the sign on Interview Two to "In Use" and held the door for Meg. "This investigation has gone off on so many tangents that Cheviot Road might be completely unrelated," she said. "A date matched, that's all. The raid opened up a can of worms, but they might not connect to anything—not the body at Greave, nor the women who were kept in that barn."

"You sound fed up," Meg said, taking a seat on the main sofa. "You like all your ducks in a row, don't you?"

"Aye." Sanne sat next to her, close but not touching, wanting for all the world to simply lock the door and forget what was happening beyond it. "In a row, and getting fat on that can of worms. I should know better by now, but I always hope there'll be a resolution, that someone will be held accountable. With this case, though, we're just wandering into grey area after grey area."

Meg turned on the lamp, throwing a mellow spotlight onto the file in the centre of the coffee table. She moved it toward her but stopped short of opening it.

"Emergency medicine is far simpler," she said, toying with the edge of the binder. "If it's broken, we can try to fix it or drug it into submission. If that doesn't work, the patient either gets better on their own or slips off the plate. I couldn't do your job. It's far too messy."

"Says the doctor who regularly ends up elbow-deep in gore." Sanne leaned forward and stilled the motion of Meg's hand. "Do you want me to stay?"

"No. Don't you have an arsehole to arrest or something?"

"We have a person of interest to bring in for further questioning," Sanne declared in clipped Queen's English.

"The same person of interest who decided you were his very favourite detective the last time around?" Meg asked, her tone suddenly serious.

Sanne regretted telling her about that. "Yes, that's the one. I'm sure he'll be delighted to see me."

"No doubt." Meg patted Sanne's jacket, using one hand and then both when she didn't find what she was searching for. "Where's Sparky?"

"Locked up safe and sound, and that is not its name."

Meg shooed her away. "Just be sure to take him with you."

"I always do," Sanne said. "Call me if you need me."

Meg nodded and picked up the file. "I always do."

CHAPTER SEVENTEEN

Sanne leaned over the bathroom sink, turning her face toward the far wall and checking her hair in the mirror. She couldn't see anything amiss, but she dampened a handful of tissues regardless and blotted the side of her head, gently at first and then with more force until the area felt well and truly sanitised. She used her fingers in lieu of a comb and straightened her shirt collar.

Rafiq Sadek smiled at her as she walked into Interview One and took her place beside Nelson. The tape recorder was already running, the introductions concluded. The same solicitor as before had accompanied Sadek to HQ, the delay incurred by contacting him being largely to blame for what had happened outside the shop.

Sanne sipped from the mug Nelson had set by her notes, disinclined to start the interview until she was ready. She'd offered to take the lead again, given that Sadek would probably address all of his responses to her anyway. Blowing on her tea, she regarded him over the brim of her mug. The small radiator behind him packed a punch, and a thin film of sweat gave an unflattering shine to his face. Failing to conceal his irritation this time around, he changed position restively, taking several sly glances at his watch.

"Sorry to drag you away from your shop," she said. "I know you're a busy man."

"I am," he snapped, surprising her by abandoning his "no comment" ploy. "I don't appreciate being back here, nor do I appreciate this department harassing my family and friends."

"Aye, that came through loud and clear less than an hour ago." She had a list of questions about Cheviot Road and Parvez Bashir, questions that Sadek would no doubt be expecting were he at all involved in the business there, but she tucked that sheet to the back, opting for a different approach. "Were you working in the shop last night?" she asked.

"Yes."

"On the till?"

"Yes. We have CCTV installed, if you need to verify that."

"That's good to know." She caught sight of Nelson scribbling a note decorated liberally with asterisks. She paused to jot one of her own, letting Sadek stew over why he needed to establish an alibi. "You work long hours, don't you? Keep the shop open till late?"

He turned to his solicitor, who shrugged. "We open at six thirty a.m. and close at ten thirty p.m. I was there past midnight, cashing up and restocking." He folded his arms. "I had a colleague helping me."

With Sadek's presence in the shop confirmed far more easily than she'd anticipated, Sanne pushed the photograph of Cezar Miklos and his companion across the table. "Do you recognise these men?"

Sadek picked the photo up, bullish enough to allow his fingertips to brush against hers. "No, I don't," he said, but his face seemed to pale slightly, and he was still staring at the image as he answered.

"Take your time," she told him.

He shook his head in apparent regret and returned the photograph. "I don't know what else to say. I've never seen them before."

She swapped the shot for its unedited version, one in which the backdrop of Sadek Foods could clearly be seen.

"Try again," she said. "Think back to about nine p.m. last night. These men appear to have bought quite a lot, and I would imagine they'd stand out in a shop whose clientele that same day was exclusively Asian."

The room fell so quiet that the rotation of the tape recorder sounded like an angle grinder. The colour rose again in Sadek's cheeks, and he gripped the photograph tightly enough to crumple its edge.

"You've been watching my shop?"

"Yes," Sanne answered without hesitation. "And you've just told us you were serving on the till when these men came in, so I'm a little puzzled as to why you would claim never to have seen them before."

"I serve a lot of customers," he said, his voice growing in confidence. "And I don't tend to make a note of their colour. Besides, aren't you lot happy to see integration between diverse communities?"

"Oh, we're all for integration. But the gentleman on the right of that photograph isn't someone you'd particularly want to integrate with."

"I'll have to take your word on that. I don't tend to check a customer's credentials before I serve him." He tossed the photo onto the table, sending it skidding past Sanne. She put a hand out to stop it going over the edge.

"Clearly not." She made a point of setting her card in front of him, just in case he'd mislaid the last one she'd given him, and then placed the photo on top. "You can keep hold of this. It might jog your memory. And if this man or his mate do come in again, call me on either of those numbers."

"Do your own fucking dirty work. You'll be sat outside my shop anyway." Sadek shoved the photo away. "Are you finished?"

"No, I'm not." She turned to her first page of questions. "You may as well get comfortable. We're going to be here for a while yet."

❖

The newspaper left smudges of cheap ink on Eleanor's fingertips, making her look like a perp and adding further insult to the indigestion brought on by the story plastered across pages three and four. She chewed a couple of Rennies, grimacing at their chalky texture as she used a wet wipe to scrub her fingers clean. Her phone rang right on cue.

"My office, ten minutes," Litton said, and hung up.

She chased the antacids with paracetamol and dumped the paper in her bin on her way out. Ten minutes allowed her a trip to the bathroom, where she washed her hands thoroughly and repositioned the clip that had spent all day working loose from her hair. One of the toilets flushed, and Sanne came out of the cubicle to join Eleanor at the sinks. She looked as knackered as Eleanor felt.

"Anything?" Eleanor asked.

"No. He 'no commented' the second half."

"Fucking hell." She balled her paper towel and launched it toward the bin, where it skipped off the rim and landed on the floor. "How long for the CCTV?"

"The request is in." Sanne shook the excess water from her hands and wiped her face with what remained. Several hours in Interview One had left her eyes bloodshot and her skin sallow, as if she hadn't seen daylight in weeks. "But who knows what calamity will befall the tape in the meantime?"

"It's unlikely to be our smoking gun, at any rate. Sadek is too smart for that." Eleanor hated the defeated note in her voice but couldn't knock it out in time.

Sanne turned her back on the mirror and leaned against the sink. Something in her neck cracked as she stretched it from side to side. "He seems to have every angle covered, doesn't he? Look at Miklos last night. If he and Sadek really are working together, he was careful enough to leave the shop with full bags, even though he knew nothing about the surveillance."

"Are you having doubts about Sadek's involvement?" Eleanor asked. She trusted Sanne's instincts, and Sanne had spent more time with him than she had.

"No." Sanne's answer was emphatic. "And not just because he gives me the creeps. He's a game player, boss. He'll look you right in the eye while he's lying through his teeth, like he's daring you to blink first."

"I think DCI Litton is about to blink," Eleanor said quietly.

"Shit. The *Sheffield Post* made it onto his desk, then?" She offered Eleanor a commiserative Polo Mint, and Eleanor sucked the sweet, its clear peppermint flavour helping to alleviate her heartburn.

"I imagine so. Keep it under your hat for now, please. I'll brief everyone as soon as I have a verdict."

"Will do." Sanne picked up the errant paper towel and then held the door for her. "Good luck."

"Thank you."

Despite Litton's summons and the deadline he had set, his secretary asked Eleanor to wait outside his office. Unwilling to shoot the messenger, Eleanor nodded her acquiescence and leafed through the latest issue of *The Billboard* as she listened to the secretary fielding phone calls with patience that defied belief. She hated being dragged down to the first floor, with its plush carpets and framed portraits. The darkened corridors seemed to stretch for miles, their office doors always shut. It was a far cry from EDSOP's previous home in a dilapidated set of portacabins on a Hadfield industrial estate. The refurbishment project that had centralised Sheffield's police admin had found a new home for EDSOP as well, bringing the department closer to the city and putting its staff right under Litton's nose.

When the secretary finally gave her the nod, she abandoned a half-read article on forensic podiatry and nodded politely in return, though she felt like kicking a hole in Litton's door and demanding back the twenty minutes of her day that he'd pissed away. He closed a file as she approached, but a sickly smell of artificial vanilla told her he'd been puffing on his e-cig only seconds ago.

"You wanted to see me, sir?" She locked her eyes on the window behind him, seeking out the floodlit flagpole in the car park and watching the material ripple in the breeze, until she was sure she wouldn't blurt out anything more creative. He'd buttoned the jacket of his dress uniform, his way of signalling that this wouldn't be an informal chat.

"I'm assuming you've received a copy of this?" He brandished a rolled-up *Sheffield Post* like a man attempting to swat a fly. Without waiting for an answer, he spread the newspaper across his desk, the page turned to a colour photograph of Rafiq Sadek, his mournful expression utilised to full effect as he posed with his equally anguished wife. The headline eschewed subtlety for impact: "Local Businessman Hounded by Police," underscoring its claim with a candid shot of Sanne and Nelson escorting Sadek through a crowd of irate onlookers. Sadek's request to contact a solicitor had evidently gone hand in hand with phoning the neighbourhood press office and arranging a mob to witness his alleged ill-treatment. He must have gone straight from Interview One to meet with the reporter.

"Yes, sir. I've read the piece." She didn't know what else to say. The article hit so many nerves—racial harassment, the persecution and unscrupulous police surveillance of an honest local lad, and the lack of viable evidence that had inevitably led to the police targeting an innocent victim—that she was amazed Litton wasn't rocking in a corner.

"The *Post* has contacted our press office asking for a statement," he said. "And *Look North* has requested an interview for tonight's bulletin."

Even though she could sense what was coming, he let the silence drag out until she was forced to ask him.

"What are you intending to tell them, sir?"

He closed the paper and folded it carefully in half. "That I have revoked the surveillance of Sadek Foods with immediate effect. That EDSOP will not contact Rafiq Sadek, his family, or his friends again unless new evidence comes to light. The press office is working on the wording, but I think that about covers the gist."

Eleanor struggled to hear his closing sentence above the rushing of blood in her ears. Litton had always been an idiot, but he had never interfered to this degree, not to the point of jeopardising an entire investigation. She wondered which promotion he currently had his heart set on and hoped it would take him as far away from Sheffield as possible.

"Rafiq Sadek is the best lead we've got," she said, keeping it simple. Litton had access to everything case-related, and if he hadn't been able to join the dots, she wasn't going to do it for him.

He picked up his pen, effectively dismissing her. "Find another one."

❖

Tempted though she was, Eleanor didn't call her team together immediately on her return to the fourth floor. After Litton's office, her own felt like a sanctuary, and she let its clean apple scent calm her nerves as she changed out of her sweaty blouse. Russ was the first to dare an approach, his hand appearing before anything else, waving a white paper towel.

"Safe?" he asked.

Eleanor sank onto one of the more comfortable chairs gathered around her small conference table. "As you'll ever be."

He shut the door behind him, placing an envelope on the table before sitting next to her. "How bad?"

"Bad enough."

He didn't push. He had worked with her long enough to read her moods, and she was sure he could fill in the finer points for himself.

"What are you going to do?" he asked.

She rubbed her temple with a heated palm. Litton would be preparing his sound bite for the local evening news, pointing out how distressing the case had been for everyone involved and acknowledging that mistakes had been made in its handling. Perhaps later he would call round with a sword she could fall on.

"We're going to carry on," she said. "Sadek's not playing the media because he's innocent. He's doing it because he dropped a bollock by having Miklos come to the shop and we've got him on the ropes. Litton's ordered me to pull the surveillance and stop the interviews. So I want our focus on the tangible—the evidence from Cheviot Road, digging Miklos out from whatever hole he's hiding in, and finding that fucking car." She let out a breath and rested her head back on the chair, waiting a beat as Russ did likewise. "You don't have to stay, Russ. It's bad enough that I have to ask my team to support me in this. You should cut and run while you can."

"Oh, you know me, El, I like to see things through. Unless I'm getting under your feet and that's your polite way of telling me to bugger off." He returned her smile and handed her the envelope he'd brought in. "Didn't think so. Well then, while we're on the subject of Cezar Miklos, Meg Fielding put a positive ID on these for us."

The photographs featured a young woman with shoulder-length brown hair. Naked and posed, she seemed to look right through the lens of the camera. She was so thin that Eleanor could count her ribs.

"The transactions recorded under her name indicate she was working at Cheviot until a week ago. There's nothing after that, and no note of what might have happened to her, but the cut-off tallies with her attendance at A&E last Wednesday, and it also ties Miklos in with the traffickers. We are getting there, El. Slowly but surely we're pulling it together."

She nodded, feeling the familiar rush as a cohesive pattern began to form. "Where the hell is this girl now?" she asked. There was a name on the back of one of the photographs: Mirela Costea.

"She could be anywhere in the country." Russ eased the photos from her hand. "My team are still working that angle, and I've already sent a nationwide alert to any hospital with an A&E. Without treatment for her burns, Meg said she'd probably be septic by now."

"She'll be no use to them if she is. She'll be another body on the moors." Eleanor felt the sudden weight of responsibility crash down on her like a wave. It stole her breath for the seconds she went under. "Jesus, this fucking case," she whispered.

"You need to speak to your team."

The direct instruction grounded her somewhat. She went back to her desk and fired up her computer. "Give me ten minutes," she said.

❖

Sanne had never played with her food. As a child, she'd polished off whatever was set in front of her, her hand the first to go up if seconds were available. Aware that the evening meal might stretch thinly around her family of five, she had made the most of her free school dinners, though the stodgy puddings and the semolina with its wallpaper paste consistency had been anathema to most of her classmates.

She didn't usually mind the meals in the hospital cafe, either, but the gravy encircling her shepherd's pie had formed a skin on its surface, and she'd busied herself dividing the mash and mince into chunks and arranging them in size order. Two tables to her left, an obese man in ill-fitting pyjamas stabbed a Spam fritter and began to devour it as if he'd slain it himself. The slick of grease dribbling down his chin made her push her plate away until she could no longer smell its contents.

"Here, try this instead." The quiet suggestion came with a bowl of chocolate sponge and custard, two spoons, and the scrape of the chair opposite as Meg sat down. They took a spoon each, Sanne getting stuck in properly when the taste hit home and stirred her appetite.

"Almost as good as Mrs. Orcey's," she said. "Do you remember her? There were so many stains on her apron she looked like a serial killer."

Sacrificing the last of the custard, Meg dropped a straw into her can of Pepsi. "I remember she rapped my knuckles with a spatula when I wouldn't eat my mushy peas. She was a nasty old bag, but she did make a mean jam roly-poly." She sucked on her drink and then let the straw go. "How long were you up there for?"

Sanne folded her napkin and placed her spoon on it. "About twenty minutes. He woke once and asked for a drink. I gave him some water, which probably wasn't what he'd meant. They're moving him to the GI ward tomorrow, and I wanted to ask when he might be coming home, but I couldn't." The spoon fell to the floor as she grabbed the napkin to blot her eyes and blow her nose. "Sorry. It's been a shitty day."

"I know. I saw the paper."

"Yeah. That picture didn't show the bloke who swung a punch at Nelson or the one who spat in my hair, but it's made the DCI crap himself. He's ordered the boss to leave Sadek well alone, just as we were starting to build a case against him." She sat on her hands so she wouldn't touch that side of her head. Sadek had painted the police as the aggressors, but she had been scared that morning, hemmed in and completely outnumbered. Despite her attempts to wash her hair, she'd felt dirty all day.

"Jesus," Meg hissed. "What about the photos I picked out? Does your DCI really think Miklos was at that shop buying basmati rice and garam-fucking-masala?"

Sanne pinched the can of Pepsi and swallowed a huge mouthful of sugar and caffeine despite the late hour, her sense of rebellion stoked by Meg's outspoken incredulity. "I doubt he can think of much with his head buried in his arse," she said. "And we're not giving up on Sadek. As far as the boss is concerned, he's officially a suspect now, though we can't tell anyone that, and we can't keep annoying him or his mates."

"Sanne Jensen, are you enjoying being all naughty and clandestine? Because that's really not like you."

"I know." She blew bubbles down the straw. "I probably should be worried about being dragged down on a sinking ship and all that, but the DCI has got this one wrong, plain and simple." She knew it might not seem that simple at three a.m., when the doubts began to set in and she started to consider the impact on her career prospects, but in a brightly lit cafe with bacon popping on the grill and Meg sitting in front of her, she had absolute faith in Eleanor's judgement.

"Speaking of sinking ships, I should get back to the grind." Meg leaned over the table and kissed her, lingering for so long that the obese man lost interest in his fried bread and simply watched the show. "Mm. I can't wait till I'm done with this set of shifts," she murmured.

Sanne opened her eyes and ran her tongue over her lips. "You really have to go?"

"'Fraid so. Somewhere in Minors there's an abscess I need to stick a big scalpel into."

"Oh God. I'm so glad you bought me custard." Sanne hooked a hand around the back of Meg's head and kissed her again. "Best of luck with your lancing, and I will speak to you tomorrow."

CHAPTER EIGHTEEN

The forecourt of Mukherjee Motors was nose-to-tail with clapped-out bangers, the banners in their windscreens reduced to listing features bordering on the desperate: "Electric Windows!", "Cheap Insurance!", "Working Air Bags!"

"Did you buy your Landie from here?" Nelson asked Sanne as they inched their way to the navy blue Toyota Previa on the third row. He brushed against a wing mirror held on by Sellotape, and it fell off in his hand.

"Vandal," she said. "And no, I have more sense than to purchase a vehicle from a bloke using a caravan for an office." She scanned the Previa's dash, to no avail. "Bloody hell, I can't see the VIN. We'll need the keys."

Knocking on the caravan's side sent a tremor through its plastic shell and brought a chubby Bengali man to its door. He spat a mouthful of betel onto the floor, narrowly missing Sanne's boot, and scratched his bollocks.

"You got a warrant?" he asked.

"Damn, here I was thinking we were incognito." She showed him her ID. "I don't think we need a warrant to look at your cars, sir. Do you have the keys for the Toyota Previa?"

"Yeah, somewhere. Would you not prefer the Micra at the front there? Very good bargain, and more suited to a woman of your size."

She wondered whether she'd look any taller with her Taser in her hand, but refrained from testing the theory. "Just the Previa, please."

He disappeared into the murky recesses of his office, and she listened to drawers open and slam shut as he maintained a muttered commentary in Bangla. She checked her list while she waited, crossing out the first address and rearranging the third and fifth to reflect their location. Working off adverts in the local press and on the Auto Trader website, she and Nelson were resuming a task previously sidelined by the Cheviot raid and the interviews of Sadek's associates. Common sense dictated that a potentially incriminating vehicle would be chopped into pieces, burned out on wasteland, or stashed away somewhere, but when she thought about it, hiding the Previa in plain sight seemed like the audacious sort of ploy Sadek might try. All he would need was a willing collaborator, a set of spare number plates, and perhaps a paint job, together with the hope that the police wouldn't come knocking to cross-reference the car's vehicle identification number against the one provided in his surrendered logbook. The initial enquiries, such as they were, had focused on Sharcliffe, but Sadek's possible links to Eastern Europeans had widened Sanne's early morning Internet searches and given her and Nelson plenty to fit into their day.

Her phone buzzed with a text from Zoe, who was out and about on the same assignment: *Offered a free valet by a chap at Jericho Street, but he wanted to nibble my ear in return. Why are men so fucking weird sometimes? The Previa there was a no-go. And it's pissing down xx*

Sanne struck Jericho Street off her list as the first drops of sleet rattled like shrapnel on the caravan's roof. She pulled on her hat and caught the keys the proprietor tossed to her.

"Post them through when you're done," he said, and shut the door.

She walked back toward Nelson, pressing the key fob, which made the Previa's indicators flash optimistically but failed to unlock it. "I think Mr. Mukherjee is guilty of false advertising if nothing else," she said, eyeing a windscreen banner that boasted "Central Locking!" She used the key the old-fashioned way and cracked open the passenger door, the gap between the Previa and its neighbour barely wide enough for her to squeeze through and spot the VIN on the jamb. Nelson watched from the front, cutting a pitiful figure with sleet glistening in his hair. She checked the number twice before she rose and shook her head.

"Never mind." Nelson offered her the wing mirror as a consolation prize. "There's still plenty of daylight left, and at least we'll be warm while we drive to the next stop."

"How very 'glass is half full' of you." She shoved the keys and the mirror through the caravan's letterbox. "Come on. Last one to the car buys breakfast."

Hailstones the size of gobstoppers were pelting the railway arches above Azzi Automobiles. Sanne swore as yet another umbrella capitulated to the winter weather, leaving her hat bearing the brunt of the onslaught. She broke into a run, leapfrogging a puddle and bursting into the sales office. Two young Asian lads in shiny polyester suits put phone calls on hold to stare at her.

"Sorry." She shrugged as Nelson joined her, stamping his boots on the mat. They displayed their ID in unison. "Police," she said.

The lad closest to Sanne hung up abruptly and came around the desk. "How can we help?"

"You had an '09 plate Toyota Previa listed on your website this morning, but it's not on the forecourt. Can you tell me what happened to it?"

"We sold it," he thumbed backward through a diary, "two days ago. We've not had a chance to update the site. Is there a problem with the car? We do thorough searches before we take any vehicle in part-exchange."

The rare glimpse of sincerity made Sanne smile. "No, I hope not. Could you give us the address of the buyer?"

"Of course. She lives just around the corner."

Double-parked cars lined the street to which the lad directed them, and Nelson pulled up at the end of it in time to catch the Previa returning from the school run. A dishevelled Pakistani woman hefted a toddler onto her hip and crunched the hail with her tapping foot as Sanne found the VIN and made sure it didn't match Sadek's.

"Thank you for your time, ma'am," Sanne said. She waved at the child, who popped a spit bubble. His squeals of delight were still audible after his mother had taken him into the house.

"At least someone was glad to see us," Nelson said. Pausing in the middle of the road, he peered heavenward as if all the answers were up there. "Where next?"

Sanne patted her pockets for her list but diverted to her ringing phone instead. Nelson carried on ahead as she answered it.

"Hey, Zoe. Don't tell me, free car washes for life for a zap of your Taser?"

"Don't give the buggers ideas. Whereabouts are you?"

An edge to the question told Sanne this wasn't a call to suggest meeting for lunch. "Cavendish Street, west side of Sharcliffe. Why? What's up?"

Zoe's voice faded as she passed the information to her colleague. Moments later, she came back on the line. "We've got a suss one at Tinder Hill. Gem Motors on Sydney Street. The Previa's red, and it's parked at the back with a big 'Sold' sign on it, but there's no visible VIN and the business owner—a Mr. Antonescu—seems to have misplaced its key. We're in civvies, so we didn't ID ourselves, just looked at a couple of his other cars and then withdrew. I wondered whether he might find you and Nelson a little more persuasive."

"Right. Or failing that, a warrant." Sanne dashed across the road toward her pool car, raising an apologetic hand at the taxi she'd forced into an emergency stop. "Can you see the Previa from where you are?"

"Yep. If he tries to shift it, we'll block the exit."

"Fab. Be careful. We'll see you in about twenty."

Out of breath, she fastened her seat belt and grabbed the A-Z as Nelson waited for an explanation.

"Tinder Hill," she told him. "Previa with no VIN and missing keys. Sounds dodgy as fuck. I'm going to call it in, in case we need a warrant."

"Okay." He still sounded slightly bewildered, but he started the engine. "Left or right at the end?"

"Straight on," she said, and hit "Boss" on her contacts.

Tinder Hill was flat as a pancake, its name an enduring mystery. A few independent artsy shops had started to appear on its main drag, but gentrification remained a pipedream, and its population was a melting pot of economic migrants from the EU, asylum seekers, and locals who couldn't afford to move away. Streets of empty houses stood awaiting demolition, and Gem Motors occupied a rough piece of brick-strewn land between a derelict primary school and a corner Polski sklep. Two men were milling among the cars outside, but neither seemed interested in making a purchase.

Sanne keyed Zoe's comms code and buzzed her radio. "We're here. Are either of those blokes Antonescu?"

"Negative. He's shorter and older. These two arrived about ten minutes ago and began shifting the cars around. The Previa's still there, but there's less blocking it in now."

"We need to move, then." She unzipped her jacket, freeing up her access to her Taser, handcuffs, CS gas, and anything else that might come in handy should Antonescu or his pals decide to play hard to get. "How about nose-to-tail in front of the exit?"

"Sounds like a plan."

Their cars arrived within seconds of each other, Nelson getting so close to Zoe's front bumper that a feather wouldn't have fitted between them. The two men reacted at once, one bolting toward the office and the other toward the chain-link fence at the rear. Zoe's mate set off after the fence-climber and hauled him down by his belt, cuffing him as he lay sprawled on the wet bricks.

"Call for a van!" Sanne yelled. There was no time to arrange backup; they would just have to make do.

At a nod from Nelson, she kicked the office door open, catching the second man full in the face and sending the door key flying from his hand. He yelped and clutched at the blood spurting from his nose, and then stuck his head down like a rugby player and tried to force his way out. While Nelson and Zoe presented a united front to block him, Sanne dodged past them and headed for the door marked Sales. She booted this one as well, bouncing it back against the wall and startling a middle-aged man into raising his hands and imploring her not to shoot.

"Mr. Antonescu?" When she grabbed his left hand and snapped a cuff around it, he lowered his other to make it easier for her. She had no idea what she was arresting him for, but she still wanted him secured. "I'm a detective with the East Derbyshire police. I need the keys for the Toyota Previa in your yard, please."

"Top drawer of the desk," he said. "I'll pay the money back, I promise."

All the hairs stood up on the nape of Sanne's neck.

"What money?"

He looked at her with big, wet eyes. "Five thousand to store it and say it was sold. If anyone asks, I phone the men outside."

Sanne opened the top drawer and found the key. "Oh, we're definitely asking," she said.

❖

The van bumped off the kerb, the officer at its wheel giving Sanne a cheery salute before accelerating away. Rocking heel to toe to work off some of the adrenaline still buzzing through her, she watched until he rounded the corner.

"The boss, SOCO, translators at the custody suite." She ticked them off on her fingers and turned to consult Nelson. "Are we missing anyone?"

"Nope. Zoe's about to leave with the fence bloke."

The second man had been taken away in the van, still trying to stop his nose from gushing. The men would undoubtedly have their stories straight already, but giving them extra time to compare notes was a bad idea, so they were travelling to the cells in separate vehicles.

"Hey, Scrapper!"

Sanne grinned as Zoe slung an arm around her. The difference in their height was so pronounced that she went up on tiptoe in a vain attempt to even things out.

"We're ready for the off," Zoe said. She kissed Sanne's cheek. "We have to do this again sometime. Or, failing that, lunch."

"Lunch, yes. Maybe next week?" Sanne suggested, optimistic that the case would be over by then. "I'll give you a shout."

"Shout loudly." Zoe tightened her arm but dropped it when Sanne squeaked. "Oops. Sorry. Did I crack a rib?"

"No, not quite. Go on, get gone."

Gem Motors had probably never been so popular. Minutes after Zoe left, Eleanor arrived, stalking toward the Previa like a hunter tracking fresh blood. Sanne met her at the passenger side and highlighted the VIN with her torch.

"No doubt about it. It's Sadek's car," she said. "The plates don't correspond, and he's obviously arranged for a spray job, but the VIN is a match."

"Is there anything inside?" Eleanor took Sanne's torch and shone it around the darkened interior.

"Nothing that's jumped out, apart from the smell of disinfectant and the fact that it's spotless. We did notice this, though." Sanne led her to the rear of the car and touched a gloved hand to one of the side windows. "See this glass? It doesn't quite match the tint on the others. It's close, but there's a slight discrepancy when you know to compare them."

"Which ties in with the fragments of safety glass you found on Old Road." A smile spread across Eleanor's face. "What about the men you arrested? Are they talking?"

"Not unless you count swearing and the odd bit of Romanian."

"I'm not waiting for forensics on this," Eleanor said, as two SOCO got out of a van and began to assemble their kit. "TAU officers are en route to Sadek's house and shop. Liaise with them regarding the arrest and the search warrant."

Sanne hadn't been expecting to be a part of the arrest, but she wasn't going to argue. She nodded to acknowledge the orders and scarpered in Nelson's direction before Eleanor could change her mind.

"Nothing? Jesus Christ. We'll meet you at the house, then." Sanne made a circling motion with her hand, indicating that Nelson should make a U-turn. She lowered her radio as the TAU sergeant disconnected. "Sadek's not at the shop," she said to Nelson. "The staff say he left about ninety minutes ago, told them he had a family emergency."

"What a coincidence." Nelson hit the kerb hard with the back wheels, jolting Sanne forward against her seat belt. He spun the car, its rear end skidding out before he managed to control it.

Sanne settled back in her seat and made no comment on his driving. "One of the Romanians must have given him a heads-up. I doubt he'll be at home either."

Sadek's home was a three-storey mid-terrace with a recent loft conversion and CCTV above its front door. The TAU were already inside, the sound of their boots on the hardwood floors mingling with that of a full-volume cartoon and a woman's high-pitched protest.

"We have a search warrant, ma'am." The TAU sergeant stood in the hallway, nose to nose with a woman Sanne presumed to be Sadek's wife. "That's what gives us the right."

As Sanne and Nelson ran up the front steps, the woman began to hit the sergeant's chest, her fists beating ineffectually at his stab vest. He ignored her until she raised a hand toward his face, her painted nails aiming for his eyes.

"Oi! Pack it in!" When he caught her hands in one of his, her screams brought a toddler into the hall, who threw down his bottle and set off wailing at the sight of his mum battling a stranger. Beckoning Sanne and Nelson forward, the sergeant shouted above the melee, "Sadek's not here. She reckons he's gone on a business trip."

"Couldn't even be bothered getting his story straight, could he?" Sanne knelt by the distraught child and picked up his bottle. "There you go, little one. Let's take you in here, eh?" She guided him back into a spacious living room, where a baby was sleeping in front of a massive plasma screen television. Removed from the source of his distress, the toddler slumped against Sanne's chest. She rocked him gently, listening to the TAU searching the rooms overhead. Shouts of "Clear!" rang out at uneven intervals, and the woman in the hallway fell silent. Her child was dozing in Sanne's arms by the time Nelson escorted her into the room. She seized the toddler and brushed off his clothing as if Sanne's touch had tainted him.

Nelson took out his notepad. "Where has your husband gone, Mrs. Sadek?" he asked.

Mrs. Sadek bared her teeth when she smiled. "No comment."

Sanne and Nelson exchanged a look.

"Tear the house apart," Sanne said. "Get someone to watch the kids. She comes in with us."

❖

"The neighbour on the right didn't see or hear a thing, but I got the impression there's no love lost between the Sadeks and the family on the other side." Nelson checked the notes he'd scribbled, giving Sanne time to bag the brightly patterned diary she'd just found in a bedside cabinet. The writing inside was in Urdu, so she put it with the evidence she'd been saving for the translators. Piles of clothing and personal effects covered the double bed, sorted into "his" and "hers" as if the room had been targeted by tidy burglars.

"Sadek arrived home at approximately nine forty-five this morning," Nelson continued. "The woman on the other side remembered hearing his car approach at speed. He ran into the house, set the kids off crying, and left again twenty to thirty minutes later carrying two holdalls. She knew his car reg—they've had an ongoing dispute about parking—so I've sent it across to HQ for an ANPR request."

"You're very efficient," Sanne said. "But I bet he's already on a flight to Lahore or Bucharest by now. And he doesn't seem to have left anything useful behind. No laptop or other electronics, and the filing cabinet in the study is conspicuously empty."

"Hmm, it's almost as if he's trying to cover his tracks, isn't it?" Nelson closed his notepad. "An auntie has arrived to babysit, Mrs. Sadek is going in the van, and the TAU are reporting nothing found at the shop."

The drawer to the bedside cabinet stuck as Sanne tried to shut it. Nelson helped her shove it back in, managing to topple a framed verse from the Koran onto the bristles of a hairbrush. Looking sheepish, he set everything back in place and tapped the top of the frame in apology. With nowhere left to search, Sanne sat on the floor and attempted to ease the ache in her lower back by drawing her knees up.

"I suppose we should feel satisfied that we had the right man," she said.

Nelson joined her, leaning against the wall and opening the foil on a packet of Rolos. They chewed without speaking for a few minutes. They had both missed lunch.

"I keep thinking about those women from the barn," he said. He retrieved a scrap of foil from the carpet and put it in his pocket. "Where they are now, and what's happening to them. Every time we get close to an answer, it slips right through our fingers."

"We'll find Sadek," she said. "Even if he has to be extradited, we'll get him eventually. And we'll find Miklos and his mate from the shop. They all have faces to put a name to, Nelson, and you know how much easier that makes our job."

"And we have the DNA from Nab Hey," he said, but he was shaking his head as he spoke. "Doesn't count for much, though, does it?"

"Not without someone to compare it to." She patted his leg and got to her feet. "The case might go across to SOET and Parry's MST now, especially if SOCO can put our vic in Sadek's car. The rest of it has gone way beyond our usual remit."

"True." Nelson almost sounded wistful, as if fondly remembering the simpler days of one-punch murders and interviews with idiots like Seamus and Daragh Thompson.

"Come on," she said. "Two more bedrooms, and we might get to go home before ten for once."

❖

Less than five minutes after walking into Eleanor's office, Russ steered her firmly out to his car and drove her to the nearest coffee shop, where she tore the lid from her takeaway cup and glared at him across the sugar-sticky table.

"I was fine at the fucking office, Russ. I've got a stack of things to do."

He removed the teabag from his cup with the little wooden stirrer and placed it on a saucer. His calmness made her want to throttle him.

"How many times had you called Litton?" he asked.

"Just twice," she said without thinking, and then tried to remember. She had left multiple messages with Litton's secretary, and Russ had caught her on the verge of marching down to his floor and demanding a meeting. "Maybe three," she hedged.

"Okay, so consider this an exercise in career preservation." Russ hid the stirrer, as if afraid she might try to stab him with it. "Litton knows he's fucked this one up. You pointing that out to him will only give him someone else to focus on. He made a shitty call, but it's still your name at the top of the case file."

"There is no way I'm taking the blame for this," she snapped, but she knew from recent experience how easy it would be for Litton to manufacture that outcome, especially if the alternative was him admitting culpability. "One day, one more fucking *day* on that surveillance and we'd have had that bastard. How the hell did we get to the point where a sob story in the local press determines our decisions?"

Russ shook his head, clearly at a loss. "From what you've told me, Litton's been running scared since the very start of this case, and Sadek took full advantage."

"Did you know that SOCO found blood in Sadek's car?" she said. "There were traces on the rubber around the rear window, and a few spots on the seats. They're running an urgent DNA comparison. It's fucking typical: we finally get some concrete evidence, and we're reduced to posting travel authority alerts and hoping we get an ANPR hit, because we let him out of our sight."

"Refocus on the family. They've helped him once, so there's a good chance he's reached out to them again, maybe for a car or a place to lie low."

"We're already on it. His wife and the three men arrested at Gem Motors are in custody, pending interview, and we're still looking for the Romanians from the shop surveillance, although SOET have been making noises about taking them off our hands. I managed to hold a teleconference and a team briefing before I locked myself away to have a paddy."

Russ beamed at her. "Atta girl. Do you think it's safe for me to take you back now?"

"You mean, have I quashed my murderous impulses?"

"Yes."

She held up his car keys. "Just about."

The stuffiness of the office was starting to make Sanne feel sleepy. Hiding a yawn, she tried to concentrate on the list of names in front of her, but they were all starting to merge into one.

"Move him into Priority." Nelson tapped the relevant line on the Excel table. "He forgot to 'no comment' his first interview and lied through his teeth instead. We can probably do him for assisting an offender and perverting the course."

Sanne made the edit, scheduling Sadek's mate for an early morning raid. Given the number of people who had corroborated Sadek's "my car's been taken to London" story, EDSOP were going to be keeping the TAU very busy for the next few days. She hovered the mouse over the lower tool bar and groaned at the time: 7:17 p.m. Sadek's wife had demanded a solicitor more than three hours ago. At this rate they'd be interviewing her at midnight.

"Aha, saved by the bell," Sanne said, as Nelson's phone rang.

He reached over the desk to answer it, leaving her with a view of his armpit and arse, and only able to hear odd words of a conversation that ended with, "Cheers for that, boss."

Fearing the worst, she crushed her stress ball until he retook his seat.

"Is the solicitor here?" she asked, digging her nails into the pliable foam.

"Nope. And he's no longer on his way. Mrs. Sadek has apparently developed a migraine. The custody suite doc says she's unfit for interview, and the boss has just sent us home."

Sanne let the ball go. "You're having me on."

"I am not."

"We really get to go home?"

She didn't believe him even when he saved their document and closed her computer, though hope kindled as he collected his jacket.

"Please don't be pulling my leg," she said, tentatively reaching for her coat.

"I'm not. Be in tomorrow for a briefing at seven, and we're to interview Mrs. Sadek at nine." He hit the lights, throwing the office into shadow. They were the last ones out, as usual. "What's Meg cooking for your tea?" he asked, as the lift doors opened at the ground floor.

Sanne sighed. "Nothing. She's on a twilight. I'll be home alone with a plate of beans on toast."

They reached Nelson's car first, and he paused at the driver's side. "You could always invite that rooster of yours in, if you're that desperate for company."

"Ha ha. No." She waved at him as he drove away, but his comment prompted her to pull out her phone, where a reminder appeared alongside a tiny jpeg of Git Face. "Bugger," she muttered. Resigning herself to a detour, she jogged over to her Landie, her relief at finding it unfrozen diminished by the flake of snow that drifted onto her nose. The Landie started first time, however, improving her chances of outrunning the weather. After the day she'd had, the last thing she wanted to do was hike down to her cottage in the dark.

CHAPTER NINETEEN

The usual Peak District winter cycle of frost and thaw had formed deep pits along the track to Black Gate Farm. Lighting the way with her high beams, Sanne held her breath every time a rut rattled the Landie's suspension. She hadn't bothered to phone ahead this time; she could always collect the chicken feed from Trudy if Ron was at the pub. The snow was petering out by the time she entered the yard, bolstering her hope that the Snake Pass would remain open until she got home. She slid into the spot next to Ron's Landie and dropped her wallet into her pocket before venturing outside.

She could see a light in the kitchen, but no one answered her knock. Her feet grew numb as she peered through the window, the wind blasting off the high fields to chap her face and lips. Clasping a glove in her teeth, she knocked harder, loath to simply walk in. None of the nearby outbuildings showed any signs of life, though, and a couple more minutes of standing freezing in the dark made her decision for her.

"Ron? Trudy? It's Sanne," she called from the doormat, shaking off the instinct to show her ID and declare her reason for trespassing. The AGA's warmth eased over her, restoring sensation to her toes, and she closed the door to keep the cold out. The scent of the fresh bread on the kitchen counter reminded her how long it had been since she'd eaten. She'd brought more than enough money for a loaf, if Trudy had any to spare.

Wiping her feet on the mat, she shouted again but heard nothing in response beside the wind and the tick of a clock. Indecision halted her halfway to the living room.

"Crap," she muttered. For all she knew, the couple were upstairs in bed, and she certainly wasn't going to risk interrupting anything. On the verge of turning to tiptoe back out, she hesitated as a thud sounded behind her. She spun around, hearing a second, louder bang coming from the far wall. "What the fuck?"

Half expecting a cat to leap out at her, she crept over to the length of chequered cloth hanging on the wall and drew it aside to reveal a wooden door. It would have looked like the entrance to a traditional larder, were it not for the heavy sliding bolts securing it top and bottom. Afraid that the farm had been targeted by thieves, she pushed her back against the wall and searched her pockets, coming up empty on weapons. She had nothing with which to protect herself; her stab vest was safely stored in her locker, and she never wore her carry harness to drive home. Snarling at the "no signal" message on her mobile, she cast about the kitchen but couldn't see a house phone.

She tapped on the door and kept her voice low. "Ron? Trudy? Are you in there?"

A frantic cacophony set off in response, the dull bangs seeming to come from somewhere below her.

"Shit. Hang on, I'll get you out." She slammed the first bolt back but left the second one shut until she'd grabbed the biggest knife from the block on the counter. The door opened on well-oiled hinges, and the banging stopped. "Ron? It's okay, it's Sanne."

There was no light switch, so she used the small Maglite on her keyring to pan around the cubbyhole, her heart rate doubling when she saw a flight of rough wooden steps. Keeping the knife out in front of her, she edged down the first three and then stopped and crouched. The blade quivered as her hand shook, but she managed to aim the torch in the direction the noises had come from, the light glinting off a metal chain that she slowly traced to its source.

"What the hell?"

The metal moved, its links rising as the foot they were tethering kicked out at the wall, and for a split second nothing made sense to Sanne, as if the synapses connecting her vision to her brain simultaneously misfired. She shook her head, her breath coming in short gasps as she stumbled down to where the young girl was cowering.

"It's all right. It's all right. I'm with the police. Oh God." She peeled off the tape sealing the girl's mouth and began to work on her bound hands. As she freed the girl's wrists, the Maglite rolled, its beam falling on the cuff around the girl's ankle. Sanne swore quietly and rocked back on her heels. There was no way to release the cuff without a key. The girl began to panic, pulling at the chain and then snatching the knife to try to hack at her ankle.

"Shit! No, stop!" Sanne wrestled the knife off her before she could inflict any serious damage. "I'll find the key, okay? I'll find the key."

She tucked the knife into her belt and sprinted up the stairs, but at the top she suddenly bent double as if poleaxed. She couldn't do this on her own. Ron and Trudy might not be in the house, but they must be close by, and they'd spot her car at some point. She needed to phone for help before she did anything else.

The sound of the girl's whimpers faded as Sanne ran into the living room. Despite the risk of discovery, she switched the light on and darted to the phone that sat by the sofa. She'd dialled two of the three nines when something cold and solid pressed into the back of her head.

"Put the phone down, Sanne." Trudy's instruction came in the same pleasant singsong she would use to offer cake, but she added emphasis by knocking the object hard against Sanne's skull.

Sanne dropped the receiver into its cradle and slowly raised her hands. She could feel both barrels of the shotgun bruising her where they dug into her. Trudy snatched the knife and threw it onto the carpet.

"Why are you snooping around at this time of night?" she snapped. "Is anyone else with you?"

Sanne started to shake her head but thought better of it. Looking down, she could see Trudy's bare legs sticking out from a pink dressing gown, and the daft fluffy slippers on her feet. Smears of shaving foam were clinging to her ankles. Sanne licked her lips, but her answer still came out in a hoarse croak.

"I'm on my own. Ron said my chook feed would be in today, so I called on my way home. I thought you'd been burgled and trapped in the cellar."

The fucked-up simplicity of her explanation shocked a laugh from Trudy. "That little bitch make a noise then, did she? Come on, outside. I've told Ron umpteen times to lock the kitchen door when he's in the far shed, but he never bloody listens to me."

With Trudy continuing to mutter behind her, Sanne staggered into the yard, passing so close to her Landie that she could have reached out and opened its door. Her palms itched. She had the keys in her pocket.

"I'm a good shot, Sanne," Trudy said, and Sanne heeded the warning, keeping her hands in view. Trudy jabbed the gun into her back. "I know what you must be thinking of me. It's all right for you, sitting pretty with your well-paid job and your doctor girlfriend. But I did what I needed to keep my husband happy and my farm in profit. And Mr. Sadek made us a generous offer."

"He did?" Under other circumstances, Sanne might have been thrilled to hear confirmation of his involvement. "What did he offer? A child to abuse, and cash in hand for local storage?"

Trudy dug the barrel in again. "I had no choice. Ron was losing interest in me, and the farm was losing money."

"Right." Sanne wasn't stupid enough to argue the point. As they neared one of the outbuildings, she glanced from side to side, judging distances and obstacles and the amount of light afforded by the full moon, but rational thought proved impossible and she was prodded over the threshold before she could come up with a plan.

The sound of footsteps brought Ron out from beneath a John Deere, his welcoming smile faltering as he spotted the shotgun.

"What on earth?" He wiped his hands on his overalls. "Trude?"

"She found her," Trudy said. "I was in the bath with the radio on, and I thought I heard something. I came down as she was trying to call the police."

"Bleedin' hell. Trude...we can't. Oh, bleedin' hell." Ron's face had gone grey. Leaning heavily on the tractor, he mopped his brow with an oily rag.

"We're not losing all of this, Ron. And we're not going to prison. Put her up at the barn and let them decide what to do." Without waiting for his accord, she stepped in front of Sanne. "Strip."

Sanne shook her head, astounded. "It's freezing, Trudy."

"That's the idea. It'll make you stay put." Trudy aimed the gun at the centre of Sanne's chest. "Strip, or I'll get him to do it for you. Leave your underwear and T-shirt on. Trousers and boots go. Ron, find something for her hands."

As he turned away, Sanne began to unfasten her laces, her fingers already thick and clumsy. She kicked out of her boots and socks and then fumbled with the fastenings on her trousers, trying to get them off before he came back. Goose pimples instantly covered her exposed skin, and her teeth chattered so violently they made her jaw ache. She threw down her coat and sweater as he approached her with a length of thin wire in his hands.

"Please don't," she said. "Ron, just think about what you're doing for a second."

He ignored her, wrapping the wire around her wrists and pulling it tight. She felt a trickle of heat on her palms and realised he'd drawn blood.

"Use her Landie," Trudy told him. She shook Sanne's clothes, listening for the telltale jingle, and threw the car keys to Ron. He shoved Sanne's shoulder, urging her toward the door, but she dug her feet into the clumps of manure and tried to stall. She didn't want him to dump her at the barn. She had a terrible feeling she knew who was up there.

"You gave them Nab Hey, didn't you?" she said. "How the hell did you get involved in all this, Ron? How did you end up keeping a *child* in your cellar? What the fuck is wrong with you?"

He stared at her, his mouth open. Sweat was gathering again on his forehead despite the frigid temperature. "I don't—"

Trudy cut him off by slapping Sanne across the face, the blow hard enough to knock her sideward.

"No more," Trudy said. She righted Sanne and sealed a strip of tape over her lips. "Take her, Ron. I'll deal with everything else."

He nodded, obviously relieved to have orders to follow. He marched Sanne to her Landie and boosted her into the rear. Unable to steady herself, she landed in a heap, bashing her head on the bench seat and lying dazed as the engine started. She felt the car back out slowly, cutting a wide circle in the yard before picking up speed and heading away from the access lane. The wheels caught the edge of furrows and rumbled over divots, throwing her around as Ron took an uphill, off-road path. Shoving herself into the gap beneath the bench, she tried to calm down, abandoning her attempts to free her hands and concentrating instead on the layout of Ron's land, the fields that stretched alongside Stryder Clough and gave way to the moorland on Brabyn's Tor. Although she didn't know the farm well enough to map it accurately, visualising the route stopped her thinking about Meg or her mum, or about what was likely to happen to her once Ron handed her off at the barn.

The Landie eventually bounced to a halt, and she tensed, listening to his footsteps and then to a low, heated argument. Minutes later, a torch beam hit her full in the face, blinding her and hiding the person who aimed it.

"Get her out." A man's voice, his words thickened by an Eastern European accent.

The metal floor bucked as someone clambered in next to her and dragged her out by her T-shirt. She managed to stay on her feet, but her legs collapsed the second he let go, her knees smashing into the hard ground. Trying to blank out the pain, she looked beyond him to the shadowed bulk of the tor and the full moon slipping behind thinning clouds. He yanked her up, propelling her forward, and stones and ice-covered puddles began cutting into the soles of her feet, forcing her to watch where she was walking instead. He steered her into a stone barn, where she was glad to be out of the wind, if nothing else.

Ron had followed them across, but he stopped a few feet inside the barn. "I'll phone him from the house," he said, his hands wide in supplication. "I'm sure he'll come and sort this. I've got room for her Land Rover in my shed." He couldn't look at Sanne, and he almost ran to the door, slamming it shut behind him and leaving her squinting and petrified in the glow of two torches and a pair of paraffin heaters. She could just make out another man waiting by a small pen at the far end of the barn.

The man still holding her arm tugged on it, marching her over to the pen, where he stopped and ran a finger down her cheek, skimming the bruise that Trudy had left her with and clucking his tongue. He smiled and said something in a language she assumed was Romanian. His companion, whom she'd only ever known as Cezar Miklos, ripped the tape from her mouth.

"I don't care if you scream," he said. He touched his thumb to her abraded lips, his gaze roaming over her body. "You were in the newspaper. I think Mr. Stanton is right, Mr. Sadek will come and sort you."

"Bring him here," she said, before she could consider the consequences. "We've been looking for him."

Miklos barked a laugh, rattling off something she couldn't

understand and pushing her into the pen. She managed not to fall, and glanced around to see four young women huddled beneath blankets by the wall. Although filthy and haggard, they were unbound, and they had divided themselves along racial lines. Two Pakistanis were clinging to each other a short distance from two white women, one of whom was obviously sick, her eyes glassy and unfocused, her hair stuck to her face with sweat. Tattered bandages covered her hands.

"My God," Sanne whispered. Not only had she found Miklos, she'd found Mirela Costea.

❖

The mother of the twenty-three-year-old moaning in cubicle two bathed his face with a flannel she'd apparently brought from home, as she scrutinised Meg's every move. So far that had amounted to taking a quick check of the lad's baseline obs and providing him with a vomit bowl he had yet to fill.

"Will he be all right?" his mother asked. She stroked his hand, almost in tears.

"He'll be fine." Meg's eyes wanted to roll right out of her head, but she suspected the woman was a complaint waiting to happen, so she glued on her best reassuring smile. "He has a virus. Very common at this time of year and absolutely not life-threatening."

"But he's terribly dehydrated. And look at him shiver."

"Yep." Meg removed the blanket that the woman persisted in drawing up to his chin. "He's shivering because he's hot, but he kept his paracetamol down, and he's not been sick since arriving in the department, which is very encouraging."

The woman smoothed a crease out of the blanket and advanced it an inch. "You can't possibly be thinking of sending him home! He can barely walk."

Meg's smile began to slip. Ambulance crews were queuing almost out the door, and all this lad needed was a stat dose of Man-the-Fuck-Up. "I'll keep him here until I get his temperature under control," she said. "And then, yes, I'll be sending him home."

"I don't think I like your attitude," the woman snapped. "I want a second opinion."

"That's no problem." Too tired to argue, Meg threw her gloves into the bin. "I'll ask someone else to come in."

For once she was glad to find Donovan lurking at the nurses' station. "Number two's mum would like to see you," she said. "She's not happy that I plan to discharge her son."

Donovan peered at her over his glasses. He might be a pain in the arse, but he didn't take kindly to his staff being second-guessed, unless he was the one doing it.

"Diagnosis?"

"Mild gastritis. No red flags. Passed a fluid challenge with flying colours and tolerated a gram of paracetamol."

He snorted and adjusted his tie. "Leave her to me."

She waved him off, waiting until he'd disappeared behind the curtain before she checked her phone. One glance confirmed what she'd suspected: it was late, and Sanne still hadn't been in touch.

"Something up?" Liz asked. Meg had thought her occupied with blood bottles, but she'd always had eyes in the back of her head.

"No, probably not." Meg moved her mobile to her breast pocket, where she'd definitely feel it vibrate. "I was hoping for another sneaky restaurant rendezvous with San, but I've not heard from her."

"Is she with her dad? GI might've let her in if they know she's a bobby."

Meg picked up one of the desk phones to call the ward but put it down again without dialling. "It's just not like her. She's usually sent me a text by now."

Liz finished labelling her last sample and sat next to Meg. "Do you want me to call them?"

"No." Meg smiled to soften her refusal, but she didn't want to start chasing Sanne around, checking up on her every hour or demanding that she post regular status updates so that Meg always knew where she was. As friends they hadn't lived in each other's pockets, and she didn't want their relationship to change in that regard.

Liz touched Meg's hand. "Are you worried about her?"

Meg nodded, the simple question cutting through all of her rationalisations. She and Sanne had fallen into the habit of texting to say good night, and, while she'd never remarked on it, she'd always felt better knowing Sanne had got home safely.

"She's probably in bed," she said. "Her phone might've done a bunk. I'm sure she's fine."

"Could she still be at work?"

"I doubt it." Meg faltered, however. Last-minute late night surveillance duty was a possibility, but it wouldn't have stopped Sanne from sending a message. "I have Nelson's number somewhere. It's for emergencies, though. She'd kick my arse if I mithered him for nothing."

"You're giving me a bloody headache," Liz said. "Look, why don't you try the ward, and if she's not there, leave it another hour. I'll be worried about her by then, too, and I'll mither Nelson if you don't." She handed Meg the phone. "Extension four-four-three-seven."

"Thank you." Meg blew her a kiss and dialled the number.

Sanne had lost track of time. She sat by the other women, all of them as still as statues, their knees drawn to their chests to preserve what little warmth the heater emitted. Like her, they were all half naked, and they had clearly decided her presence meant trouble. None of them would make eye contact with her, and no one spoke. Too scared to try to make inroads, she strained to listen for the slightest disturbance outside. Every clatter the wind sent through the barn made her curl into a tighter ball as if that might somehow be enough to protect her. Eventually, with hyperventilation beginning to hook her fingers into claws, she found something to count, concentrating on the blanket that covered the woman next to her and numbering its multicoloured squares until the pins and needles began to abate and she no longer felt so dizzy.

She let her head fall back to the rough stone wall and stared upward, though she could see nothing above the rafters. The walls around the pen were equally solid, with no sign of weak spots or previous escape attempts, which left the door as the sole point of access. She closed her eyes, sketching a mental plan of the barn and what she had seen on the way in, but she couldn't recall anything that might be useful as a weapon, and the men seemed content to play cards and double-up on guard duty. Unless one of them left, she had no chance.

She jumped as something touched her arm, her feet kicking out and her eyes flying open. The twitch of her wrists against the wire tore a thin cry of agony from her.

"Shh." The woman next to Sanne carefully shifted one of her blankets to cover Sanne's bare legs. The oldest of the four, she was probably in her early twenties, though fatigue had carved sharp lines into her face. A scrap of dirty lace held back her hair, and bruises encircled her slender arms. She glanced across at the men, checking whether they had heard anything, but they remained engrossed in their card game. The fingernails on the hand she laid on Sanne's chest were bitten to the quick. "Is better," she whispered. "Not so fast."

"No." Sanne fought again to slow her breathing. "Not so fast. Thank you."

The woman's eyes widened. "English?"

"Yes. Police."

"There are more?" The woman looked toward the door as if expecting an imminent rescue, until something in Sanne's expression told her there wasn't going to be one. "No more," she said. "Just you."

"Just me. I'm sorry." Sanne choked down the fear that was threatening to overwhelm her again. "My name is Sanne Jensen," she said, sounding the words out carefully. She wanted the woman to remember them. If she died, she needed someone to tell Meg what had happened to her.

"Sanne," the woman murmured, pronouncing it "Senn-er." She hesitated. "My name is Dorina," she said at length, bowing her head. "He says he will cut off our hands if we untie you."

Sanne's vision dimmed, and she thought she might be sick. She could feel every inch of the wire that bound her. Her fingers were hanging swollen and useless, and her wrists burned in distinct lines. There was no way she could get free without help, when the slightest unguarded movement crippled her.

Dorina tucked Sanne's blanket more securely around her, the gesture bringing their faces close together. "Later, one goes next door, to sleep or to fuck," she said. "We wait. Yes?"

Sanne nodded, ignoring the needles of doubt telling her that Sadek was on his way, that she couldn't afford to delay. Dorina's offer was far better than nothing. Unseen beneath the blanket, though, Sanne twisted her hands, fighting to loosen them and only succeeding in splattering her palms with blood. The smell of cigarette smoke drifted over from the card table, followed by the hiss of a ring pull. With tears streaming down her face, she rested her cheek on her knees and waited.

❖

Meg eased her foot from the accelerator as the speedometer arced past sixty-five and chevrons warned her of an upcoming bend. Her shift seemed to have stretched on forever, her anxiety levels climbing beyond mere concern and hitting frantic as text after text went unanswered and the nurse on the GI desk confirmed Sanne hadn't visited.

The lay-by closest to Sanne's cottage stood empty. Using it as a landmark, Meg turned off the Snake and belted down the access road, still undecided whether to kiss or kill Sanne when she managed to find her. She stopped on the deserted driveway and stared at the darkened cottage.

"Shit."

She didn't want to go inside. From the lack of fresh prints in the thin layer of snow, she could tell Sanne hadn't been there. When she finally plucked up the courage to let herself in, the cottage was cold and silent. The dish and mug Sanne had used for her breakfast were still sitting on the drainer, and nothing apart from a relative's birthday was written on the calendar. Meg checked every room in case Sanne had got a lift home, and then she sat at the kitchen table and phoned Nelson. To his credit, he answered within three rings, no trace of sleep in his voice as he stated his name.

"Nelson, it's Meg," she said. "Sanne's Meg. I can't find her, Nelson. She didn't come home. Is she with you?"

"No," he said. "I'm not at work. She left with me just after seven. Where are you now?"

"At her cottage." Unable to sit still, Meg paced to the window. The kitchen light reached as far as the untouched snow covering the grass around the henhouse.

"Could she be at yours?" he asked.

"No, I don't think so. I've been ringing and ringing my house, and even if she had gone there, she'd have stopped here first to feed the chooks, but she hasn't. I contacted every A&E in the area before I left the Royal, and no one fitting her description has been admitted."

She heard rustling and the jangle of a belt as Nelson started to get dressed.

"Okay, well, that's good," he said, but his voice was as tight as a drum. "Why don't you go home and make absolutely sure she's not there? Give me a shout when you arrive, and in the meantime I'll start making a few phone calls."

"Right." Meg wiped her nose on her sleeve. "I'll speak to you in about twenty minutes."

"Take care driving."

"I will."

She hung up and was about to head to her car when she remembered the damn chickens. Sanne would never forgive her if she let them starve. She shook the last of the feed into a bucket and jogged over to the coop, where a chorus of indignant squawks greeted her.

"Okay, okay, keep your feathers on. I'll find your mum. She's much better at this than I am," she said, spilling half of the pellets around the trough. The chickens were too hungry to notice her lack of finesse. She left them to scrabble and ran back to her car.

❖

Eleanor hurried into the office, half expecting to be confronted by a maelstrom of activity: phones ringing, her team bustling around following leads or exchanging theories. Instead, Fred and George sat at their desks looking pale and upset, Scotty nodded at her but continued to type an e-mail, and Nelson—no doubt accustomed to the sound of her heels—didn't even notice she'd arrived, thanks to the trainers she'd thrown on with her jeans. He finished a phone call as she approached.

"Where are we up to?" she asked.

He waited for the other three to pull chairs over and join them in a tense huddle around Sanne's desk. Eleanor spotted a clip-framed photograph of Sanne and Meg holding a newborn and each other's hands, only visible to someone sitting right in front of Sanne's computer.

"I've just spoken to Traffic," Nelson said. "They've confirmed a sighting of Sanne's Landie on one of the Sheffield cameras en route to the Snake Pass. It's timed at seven thirty-seven, so I think we can assume she was heading home or going to Meg's. According to Meg there's no indication she made it to either address. Traffic are checking the M67 cameras on the other end of the Snake but haven't spotted anything as yet. Meg's on her way here. She's already called around the local hospitals, and Traffic have got a couple of patrols doing a slow run of the route to spot for possible accident debris."

Eleanor took a copy of the summary he handed out. It ran to half a page, establishing a timeline that started with Sanne leaving the office at 7:23 and nearing the Snake Pass fourteen minutes later. Meg's first unanswered text had been sent at 8:15, and it was almost five hours after the last sighting of Sanne's Land Rover that she'd alerted Nelson.

Eleanor raised her glasses and rubbed the bridge of her nose. "What were you and Sanne doing before you went home?" she asked Nelson. "Had anything new come up?"

"No, nothing. We were killing time, really, prioritising suspects for TAU raids. We thought we'd be interviewing Sadek's wife, but then you phoned, so we packed it in for the night." He shook his head, almost in tears. "She was joking about that daft rooster of hers and having beans on toast for her tea."

"Check her files anyway. Notes in the margins, anything she might've spotted and not mentioned. I know it's a long shot, but we need to cover all our bases."

"What about Sadek?" Nelson asked. "He's been weird with her from the outset, and we've no idea where he is now."

"You think he's hurt her?" Fred said, sounding horrified. "Run her off the road or something?"

Eleanor intervened before his imagination could go on the rampage. "It's very unlikely that Sadek has anything to do with this. He seems far too disciplined to risk acting on a personal grudge." She held up her hand to cut off the argument Fred seemed about to launch. "I'm not ruling it out entirely—of course we'll have to consider it as a possible scenario—but we can't do much in that regard without an ID on his current vehicle, and the dearth of ANPR hits on the one he left his house in suggests he switched cars soon afterward."

"I'll start chasing down local CCTV," Fred said. "See if I can spot San's Landie and check out the cars behind her."

"Good. Thank you," Eleanor said. It was a long shot, but it would give him a task to focus on, if nothing else. "George, help him out with that, please. Nelson and Scotty, you take Sanne's files and liaise with Traffic. Jay and Mike can fit in with you when they arrive."

"Should we start organising search parties?" George asked. "Mountain Rescue, or get out there ourselves with some unis?"

"Get out where?" Eleanor countered gently. "If Traffic find the slightest trace of her car on the Snake then we'll go out to search with every available resource, but we need a place to start. We can't just wander around in the dark on the off-chance that we'll fall over something."

"Or slip in something," Nelson said.

"Yes, or slip in something." She smiled, remembering how bad Sanne had smelled after her encounter with the sheep. She pushed her chair back until she could see everyone. "I know you're all worried about her, but she's probably the most capable person on this team in terms of looking after herself in the Peaks. Try to stay focused, and give me a shout if you hear anything or need anything."

Russ met her on the way to her office. He followed her inside and shut the door. "You okay?" he asked, looking as shell-shocked as she felt.

"Not really. Fuck. No, not at all. Where the fuck is she, Russ?"

"I have no idea. What does your gut say?"

"It's not saying much." Eleanor slumped onto the closest chair. "But my guilty fucking conscience is reminding me that I put pressure on her to be bolder, so I can't help thinking she's gone off investigating something on her own and got herself neck-deep in trouble. She attracts shit like a fucking magnet."

Overlooking her dubious grasp of physics, Russ sat beside her. "How likely is that? Score of one to ten?"

"Seven?" Eleanor was trying hard to be logical, but common sense was difficult at two in the morning, when her youngest team member was God only knew where, and everyone was looking to their DI for answers. "I don't know, Russ. Nelson says zero, but I just don't know."

"She's probably been in an accident. Which is bad enough, but better than anything you're imagining."

"I know." She laid her head on his shoulder for the briefest of moments. She was more frightened than she'd ever admit. "Litton won't authorise much; she's not been missing for long enough. He asked that I keep him updated, but I don't think he was planning to get out of bed."

"We're better off without him. What about Sanne's family?"

"Meg's coming in. Otherwise there's really only her mum. Her dad's been in hospital for the last few days." She stood up, restless. "I can't stay in here."

"So go and sit with your team."

"And do what?"

Russ didn't seem to have any answers either. He opened his hands in apology. "Make them a brew and hope for the best."

❖

Meg clipped her visitor's pass to her coat, smacking her hand on the button marked "4" the second she stepped into the lift. She spotted Nelson from the door to the EDSOP offices, head down in conference with Eleanor, Parry, and a detective she didn't recognise. When he came to meet her, embracing her in front of them all, she buried her face in his shirt and clung on.

"Anything?" she asked as she pulled back.

"Not yet." He brought her a chair, placing it on his side of the desk so that she didn't have to look at the family photos on Sanne's. "Traffic are still out on the Snake, but the weather's playing havoc with them."

"I'll bet." She'd driven in through showers of sleet and snow, visibility dwindling to almost zero over the Snake summit, before the clouds cleared as the wind picked up. "God, Nelson, if she's stuck out there in this…"

He didn't tell her that they'd find her, that everything would be okay. He simply put a hand on her arm.

"I phoned her mum and her sister," she said. "Keeley hasn't seen her in a few days, and there was no answer at her mum's. I left a message on her mum's mobile but didn't go into detail."

"Is it worth sending a patrol round?" Parry asked.

"Yes, it is," Eleanor said. "Could you organise that? Thanks."

Meg shifted her chair into the gap he left. "I've brought Sanne's address book, but most of the people in it are Christmas-card friends and relatives. There's a couple of neighbours that she swaps veggies and eggs with, so we could try them, and I was wondering about calling Ron as well."

"The chap at the farm?" Nelson said. "Where we went up to Greave Stones?"

"Yes, that's the one. He supplies San's chicken feed. I just used the last of hers, and I was thinking on the way over, what if she called in for some at Black Gate tonight? She's stupid about those chooks and far too organised not to have ordered in good time. The farm's only a couple of miles from her house. If we can establish that she got there safely, that would rule out a huge part of the search area. I could've knocked on when I went past, but I was in fucking Sheffield by the time I put two and two together."

"Go ahead," Eleanor told Nelson, and he almost snapped the address book out of Meg's hand.

They watched him dial. The phone rang out and switched to an answering machine, and he left a brief message before redialling immediately.

"We should go in person," he said, having hung up and tried a third time. "It's much harder to ignore a knock on your door, and we're not getting anywhere with the other stuff we've been working on." He aimed his appeal directly at Eleanor, who nodded her assent far more readily than Meg could have hoped.

About to suggest accompanying them in a medical capacity, Meg clapped a hand on her breast pocket as her mobile buzzed: Teresa. She moved across to an empty desk, with no idea what to say even as she accepted the call.

Teresa spoke before Meg could. "Meg? I just got your message. Is everything all right?"

"No, not really." Meg began to distinguish sounds in the background: beeping and a distinct give-and-take rasp. For an instant she had a horrific image of Sanne lying in the ITU, before she grasped the more plausible explanation. "Are you with John?"

"Yes, love. The hospital phoned to say he'd been taken badly again. I've been trying to reach Sanne, but I think she must be at work."

It never just fucking rains, Meg thought. "I'll come over," she said, unwilling to take the coward's way out and break the news remotely. "Will you be staying there for a while yet?"

"I think so." Teresa's voice wavered. "They said it's a matter of time."

Everything seemed to be splintering, the pieces flying apart too violently for Meg to stop them.

"Christ. I'll be there as soon as I can."

❖

Eleanor gave Traffic's four-by-four a wide berth as she drove past it. It continued at a crawl, a light on the nearside trained on the verge as its driver examined the hedgerows and stone walls for signs of damage. So far, Eleanor had only spotted two makeshift shrines to accident fatalities, both coming out of hairpin bends, but she was well aware of the Snake Pass's grim statistics.

"It's on the right, in about"—Nelson held his fingers apart, using them to judge the scale as he moved his torch over the map—"half a mile."

"Thanks." She didn't bother to note her current mileage; it would be far easier just to look out for the sign warning of the farm's concealed entrance. Nelson had always been task-orientated, though, and giving him the role of navigator had kept him occupied since leaving HQ. Sharing his urge to be out of the office, she had assigned herself to driving duties and asked Russ to oversee the rest of her team.

A mass of waterlogged potholes and patches of snow covered the yard of Black Gate Farm. She parked by a pile of gravel and opened her door to find a lake beneath her feet.

"Fucking hell." Her trainers slipped on the far edge of the puddle, splashing muck up the back of her jeans. "Someone had better bloody be in."

Nelson thumped hard enough on the farmhouse door to send flakes of old paint flying into his hair. With no letterbox to shout through, they had to rely on knocking, but a light finally came on, and an amorphous pink mass moved beyond the glass.

"Who is it?" a woman asked.

"Police, Mrs. Stanton," Nelson shouted. "Could you open the door, please?"

A key turned and a bolt grated back, and Mrs. Stanton appeared, bleary-eyed, with rollers in her hair and pillow creases down one cheek.

"Is something the matter?" she asked. "Is it Ron?"

"No." Eleanor paused, confused. "Where is Ron?"

"He's just gone up to one of the barns. We've had a cow took poorly."

Eleanor put her ID away. "Right, well, no. It's not Ron, it's Sanne

Jensen. She went missing yesterday evening, and her partner thought she might've stopped off here to collect a feed order on her way home."

"Oh! Sanne and her chickens. Of course. Lovely lass." Mrs. Stanton's face fell. "She hasn't been here, I'm afraid. We still have her pellets in the store. Do you need to see them as proof or anything?"

"No, thank you," Eleanor said. She could see lines tautening on Nelson's throat as he clenched his teeth, and she put a hand on his arm in case he decided to hit out at something. "No, that's fine. We're sorry to disturb you so late."

"Sorry I couldn't be of more help." Mrs. Stanton watched them to their car, and the kitchen light went off as Eleanor reversed.

"Damn it! She could've just answered her phone and saved us the fucking trip." Eleanor whacked the car into first, accelerating hard enough to spin the wheels.

Nelson didn't seem to notice her outburst or her driving. His eyes were glued to his wing mirror, and he didn't speak until the farmhouse had disappeared from view.

"She's lying," he said quietly.

Eleanor braked, wondering whether she'd misheard him. "What?"

He urged her forward. "Keep going until we're out of sight."

She did as instructed, pulling into a nook before she reached the Snake and turning off the engine.

"Nelson?"

"Sanne's been at the house," he said. "The keys to her Landie were on the kitchen counter. She has a Maglite on her keyring. It's chipped all over because she tosses her keys around. They were definitely hers, boss."

"But why?" Eleanor folded her arms, trying to make sense of what he was saying. "What reason would that woman have to lie?"

"I don't know. Maybe San hurt herself while she was here, and they're trying to cover it up." Agitation quickened Nelson's speech. "We need to request the TAU for a search."

"Or Firearms," Eleanor said. In her experience, farms meant shotguns, and the TAU weren't an armed division. She reached for her radio. "Are you sure about this, Nelson?"

He nodded. "Absolutely positive."

CHAPTER TWENTY

Sanne slowly rotated her shoulders, straightening and bending her legs at the same time to keep her circulation moving. If Dorina ever managed to free her, the last thing she wanted to do was fall on her arse. The men were packing up their cards, the grating of their chairs along the concrete jangling her nerves. One of the Pakistani girls buried her face in her blanket and began to sob, the other attempting to comfort her by increasing the fervour of her murmured prayers.

"They give no help," Dorina whispered. Her eyes were flickering from the girls to the men and back to Sanne. "They do nothing but *Allah, Allah.* Maybe they come with us, maybe not."

"They have to come," Sanne said. The girls were barely in their teens, and she wasn't leaving them for Sadek. "We all go."

Dorina shrugged. "You get them. I get Mirela."

The men approached the pen, cutting off the discussion, and Sanne hid her legs in the shadows as Dorina jerked her blanket away.

"Eenie, meenie…" Miklos's companion pointed to the women in turn, his finger coming to rest on Sanne. He started to laugh, and Miklos walloped him on the shoulder, their rapid-fire exchange incomprehensible.

Desperate for translation, Sanne threw a wild look at Dorina, who pretended not to even know she was there. Sanne pushed back on the rotted hay, preparing to offer whatever resistance she could if the men tried to touch her, but they walked away instead, their conversation loud enough to cover the yelp that Sanne let out as Dorina wrenched her around.

"You do not want to know," Dorina muttered, before Sanne could ask what the men had said. Her fingers skimmed the wire binding Sanne's wrists. "Fuck. This is very tight."

Sanne was painfully aware of that, but she managed to keep quiet as Dorina found the point where the wire was twisted into a knot and began to unravel it. A sudden gush of blood and a strange dragging sensation on Sanne's arms told her that Dorina had succeeded, but Dorina had already moved away, stalking silently toward the door with the wire outstretched between her hands.

"Shit. *Wait!*" Sanne hissed. She got to her knees, lost her balance, and tried again. Her hands wouldn't grip anything, so she slammed her fists like claw hammers onto the top of the pen wall and used them to lever herself to her feet.

The barn door banged shut behind Miklos's companion, shifting the light and giving her a snapshot of Dorina a hair's breadth from Miklos, her arms raised and parted. Sanne tore across the filthy concrete, aiming straight for Miklos and colliding with his torso as he grappled to get his fingers beneath the wire Dorina had wrapped around his throat. He lashed out, catching Dorina hard in the face and throwing her into the wall. Sanne evaded a second furious punch, kicking him in the groin because her hands were still useless. He wavered but stayed upright, and his backhand battered into her jaw. She didn't see the ground until she hit it, the impact knocking the breath out of her and peppering her vision with sparks. She heard a crack and then another, and managed to drag herself up again as Miklos crashed onto the floor. A small form followed him down, child-sized hands gripping a dark object and smashing it into his head. Blood spurted as his skin ruptured, the rich metallic smell of it filling the air. He grunted, lying still beneath the impact of another blow, his breathing becoming erratic and laboured. An acid stink mixed with the tang of copper as he pissed himself.

"*Stop!*" Sanne yelled. "You'll kill him!" She grabbed the girl, lifting her easily and tearing her off Miklos. The girl kicked and wailed, the rock she'd used to attack him dropping from her hands. Dorina helped Sanne guide her to the floor, cooing at her and stroking her hair when the girl burst into tears.

"He raped her yesterday," Dorina said. She spat on Miklos's face and then began to strip him.

"Jesus," Sanne whispered. She didn't know whether he would live or die, but getting help for him wasn't an option. She ran back to the pen, the girl right on her heels, and gently lifted Mirela to her feet. "Blankets," she said, poking one with her toe in lieu of translation. "Come on, quick."

The girls gathered whatever they could carry, one of them stopping to collect bars of chocolate from the card table. Their mouths were stuffed within seconds. Mirela leaned heavily on Sanne, her eyes closing in gratitude when Dorina put Miklos's coat around her.

"Here." Dorina threw a sweater and a long-sleeved T-shirt to the girls, and an apologetic look at Sanne. "No keys. Nothing else, unless you want?" She lifted her foot, the boot she'd stolen rattling loose around her ankle.

"No, but thanks." Sanne peeked through the door onto the pitch-black field. A Range Rover sat between the barn and a smaller building she assumed the men slept in. She couldn't see Miklos's companion anywhere. "Stay here and get them wrapped up as best you can," she told Dorina.

She sprinted to the car and ducked by the driver's side to try the door handle. It clicked open, flooding the cab with light and forcing her to dive inside to hit the switch. Still sprawled across the leather seats, she searched for the keys, her efforts becoming more frantic as the usual hiding places came up empty.

"*Fuck!*" She beat her fist on the dashboard, splattering it with blood, and crawled out of the car to see two sets of headlights creeping along the lane from the farm. "Oh *shit*."

Dorina had seen the lights as well. She met Sanne outside the barn, propping Mirela up with one arm and holding the two girls close with the other. She'd managed to rip holes in the blankets, and they were wearing them like ponchos. "Car no good?" she asked.

"No." Sanne widened the tear in the blanket Dorina offered her and shoved her head through it. She reckoned they had about five minutes, which wasn't much of a start. She closed the barn door. "We go up. Hopefully they'll think we went down."

No one argued with her. She took one of the girls by the hand and led the way across the field, keeping to the edge of the dry stone wall until she found a crumbled section low enough for them to climb over.

"Go, go. That's it." She boosted the smaller of the girls, the other clambering whippet-fast and unaided. Mirela struggled, swaying on the far side and leaning low to vomit. She sagged against Dorina, who shook her head at Sanne.

"No, we can't stop. *Move*," Sanne said. She threw Mirela's arm over her shoulders, her ruthlessness shocking Dorina into taking the other arm. They staggered but then found a rhythm, supporting most of Mirela's weight between them.

The sound of car engines and slamming doors spurred them on toward the top of the field. Sanne climbed the boundary wall first, thankful to see rough moorland and the pronounced dip of Stryder Clough. She knocked out the wall's loosest coping stone and half-dragged Mirela over the top, catching sight of torch lights bobbing by the barn and then dividing as the men began to search.

"Head for that bump." She pointed to the clough, trying to remember how far they were from the tor's summit. Too far, she thought. They would be lucky to make the clough. She set off again, the rough ground sending spikes of pain through her feet.

"Where...we...go?" Dorina asked between gasps. "A road?"

"No, we'd never make it. We have to find somewhere to hide." Sanne had a plan, she just hadn't had a chance to share it.

"Then what?"

"Then I'm going to run."

❖

Standing at a safe distance with Nelson, Eleanor watched the firearms unit and the TAU split into teams and advance on the farmhouse. Their enforcer ram made quick work of the door, battering it into pieces that they threw into the yard. She counted time as the first officers disappeared into the kitchen, no more than three minutes elapsing before Mrs. Stanton was marched out, her hands cuffed behind her, her slippers falling off her feet.

"Just clearing the rest, ma'am," one of the men said. "No trace of your detective, and this one isn't saying anything."

"Thank you." The words stuck in Eleanor's throat. "How many outbuildings?"

"Five or six in the immediate area. We're through the first two." A yell from the kitchen made him look around. "Ma'am, they're asking for you in there."

"Shit." Eleanor reeled, her hands reaching for the van behind her. She'd tried to prepare for this the best she could, but denial had overridden everything.

Nelson moved first. "I'll go, boss."

She shook her head and walked in step with him to the kitchen, where the smell of perspiration and aftershave mingled with home baking. An officer directed them to a door previously concealed behind a patterned curtain.

"It's not Sanne," the TAU sergeant said. "But I think Sanne might've found her."

"Found who?" Eleanor asked.

The answer came tucked in the arms of an officer: a young girl, her eyes bulging with terror, and a severed chain hanging from her ankle.

"What the…" Eleanor stared at the girl as the officer carried her past. "What the fuck is going on?"

"We're not sure," the sergeant said. "She can't speak English, ma'am. She's most likely Polish or Romanian. Judging by the mess, she's been down there for weeks if not longer. The rest of the farmhouse is clear." He pressed his earpiece, listening to reports. "Alpha team have found Sanne's Land Rover in one of the top sheds. There's a small amount of blood in the back, and there are fresh vehicle tracks heading along a lane behind the farmhouse."

"Right." Eleanor focused on those three facts, setting everything else aside to deal with later. "That's probably where Ron is hiding out. Get at least two teams of armed response up there. We'll organise SOCO, a translator, and medics."

"Yes, ma'am." The sergeant ran outside, leaving her and Nelson alone in the kitchen.

"I'll phone Meg," Nelson said. He went to the cellar door, his face pale as he looked down the stairs. "San just came here for chicken feed, boss."

"I know." Eleanor pulled her radio from her belt but held it without dialling. "Jesus bloody Christ."

❖

The peat hag formed the lip of a deep grough, a random spot in a maze of similar trenches, where the bite of the wind lessened and an overhang provided a modicum of shelter.

"Here." Sanne lowered Mirela onto the damp heather and bent double to catch her breath. "I don't think we're getting any farther."

They had crossed Stryder Clough and the Pennine Way high on Brabyn's Tor, avoiding the obvious safe haven of Greave Stones and happening by chance on this tangled labyrinth. Had it come with a roof, it would have been perfect.

"Close, close. Good," Dorina said, ushering the girls together and pulling the blankets around them. They were shivering, the cold hitting them hard now they'd stopped. She eyeballed Sanne in the faint threads of moonlight. "You are a runner?"

"Yes, I run up here on these hills." Sanne took off her blanket and added it to the ones covering the girls. The smallest girl was already dozing. Sanne had lost count of the number of times she'd lifted her from the peat.

Dorina's eyes narrowed. "Without shoes?"

"No. Never. Always a first time, though, eh?" Sanne looked up, using the stars to orientate herself. "Don't move from here, okay?"

"But what if the men...?" Leaving the question unvoiced, Dorina pulled Mirela into her arms. "Okay. We do not move."

"I can't hear them," Sanne said. "And there are no lights anywhere. Just stay close like this. I'll be as quick as I can." She couldn't afford to second-guess her decision; they weren't making any headway as a group.

"I have socks," Dorina said, fumbling beneath her blanket. She'd obviously hidden them within her stolen boots. "Here. I give."

"No, it's all right. Keep them." Sanne smiled. "They'll be too big, and I'll only go arse over tit when they get soggy. You stay warm."

"You stay safe."

The grough tracked in roughly the right direction, and Sanne kept within its sloping walls at first, her pace steady but slow by her usual standards, her progress hampered by exhaustion and cold and the gritstone shredding her feet. The clouds broke apart in unpredictable patches, glimpses of Orion and the Twins guiding her across the undulating summit of Brabyn's Tor in search of another clough to follow down to the Snake. She cursed every new bump, every new climb that leeched away her strength. For the most part she couldn't see the groughs until she hit them: black walls of soaking peat with heather crusted along their edges. Unable to rely on her legs alone, she took to crawling up them, her hands buried deep in the gnarled stems of the heather while her knees battled the slope below. She collapsed at the top of a particularly brutal one, her belly aching and a stitch pulling at her side. As she lay there, a heavy shower of snow passed over and coated everything in white. She caught flakes on her tongue to quench her thirst and then scraped up handfuls, swallowing the meltwater and spitting out the gravel. It was enough to get her moving again, dropping gracelessly into the next channel and scrambling up the other side.

She found a clough heading the right way, but it came out of nowhere, stealing her legs from under her and sending her sliding down its rock-strewn slope. This close to the top of the tor, the gradient wasn't too steep, and she got back to her feet, shaken and sore but otherwise whole.

"You're fine. You're fine," she whispered, needing to hear something other than the eerie shriek of the moors. "Go. *Go*."

She set off again, a deadened patch on her thigh making her limp slightly. The wind burned into her lungs, her pulse hammering in a constant protest against the exertion and the elements. Shadows played tricks on her, creating forms that moved and drifted ahead, making her halt in fear until the moon came out to reassure her she was safe. There was no path for her to follow, just a stream that she kept skidding into, and loose rocks underfoot. She was forcing her way through a thigh-high thicket of dead bracken when she hit the fence.

"Bloody hellfire."

She dropped out of sight, thrown into an unreasonable panic by this first sign of civilisation. Seconds ticked by, then a full minute. No one came for her. She climbed over the fence and landed, shivering, in the field on the other side. It was empty and too far from Black Gate to belong to the Stantons. She ran through the middle of it and scaled a dry stone wall, narrowly avoiding an unsuspecting sheep snoozing in the next pasture. Its irritated bleat set off a chorus that brought tears to Sanne's eyes. She was almost there.

❖

The TAU sergeant hadn't gone into detail. His command had been succinct and not at all in keeping with radio protocol: "Ma'am, we need you here. There's no sign of Sanne, but it's a fucking mess."

Eleanor and Nelson travelled with an armed unit. They'd been warned to be on the lookout, although for what, no one seemed sure. The sergeant met them where the track entered a field, and Eleanor could see the glint of torches, evenly spaced in a search formation.

"Three vehicles," the sergeant said before she'd even got out of the car. "The rear pair probably came up in convoy. Their engines were still warm when we arrived, so you must have just missed them at the farmhouse. The Land Rover belongs to Ron Stanton, but we haven't found him. The two Range Rovers are long-term rentals from Sheffield." Without waiting for comment, he led them across to the larger of two stone barns. "Looks like Sanne and a number of other vics were held in here. We think they got free and did a runner."

Eleanor caught his arm at the barn door. Her brain felt as if it was being pummelled. "What makes you think that?"

"Well, he does, for a start." The sergeant used his torch to pick out an unconscious man, bleeding from multiple head injuries and covered by a police blanket. "He's been beaten to a pulp and stripped."

Eleanor moved closer. She recognised him despite the swelling and lacerations obscuring his features. She covered her hand with her sleeve and nudged a chunk of rock to expose the blood on its underside. "He's one of our main suspects," she told the sergeant. "How many were here? How many vics?"

"We're not sure. There's a pen at the back where the flooring is scuffed and worn in several places, but it's impossible to say for definite. We, uh…" He coughed, obviously ill at ease. "We found clothing in the next building. Some of those Pakistani-type trousers, a couple of skirts. But there was a coat with Sanne's ID in the pocket, and there are other things in her size."

Eleanor heard Nelson swear and walk away, but she couldn't afford the luxury of reacting. There was too much she needed to do.

"Chances are we have at least two perps in the vicinity," she said. "At a guess, Ron Stanton panicked and contacted someone to deal with Sanne. Meanwhile, she's apparently orchestrated a fucking prison break, and now everyone's running around in the bloody dark."

"Including us," the sergeant said. "Most of the field's too frozen to hold a print, so we've no idea which direction any of them have gone in, but we're covering ground quickly."

"Good." Eleanor found her notepad; she preferred to bullet-point wherever possible. "Have we got an ambulance coming for him?"

"We've requested one, but their dispatch said they're stacking calls. Mountain Rescue are en route, though, with a doctor on the team."

"What about the helicopter?"

"Busy at present. We're their next priority."

"That's terrific." She threw up her hands. "I've got a half-naked detective in the middle of nowhere, in this weather, and we're in a fucking queue for the chopper?"

"Yes, ma'am." He pressed his earpiece, his expression shifting to something that resembled relief. "On the bright side, we've just arrested Ron Stanton three fields over. They're bringing him in now."

The last time Eleanor had seen Ron Stanton, he'd cut a distinguished figure in his Barbour jacket, a complete contrast to the snivelling man currently being shunted into the police van. He cowered into the far corner of the bench seat as she approached, his wellies squeaking on the metal floor.

"I'd lost a cow," he said, pre-empting anything she might ask. "I was just looking for a cow. I don't know what's going on. These handcuffs are pinching me. Can you take them off?"

"No," Eleanor said. "Did you hurt Sanne?"

Ron shook his head. "I was just looking for a cow," he whispered. "I don't know why you're all here."

"You're a lousy liar." She watched his face crumple, but he stayed silent. "And you're fucking pathetic." She left him to the TAU officers and went back to Nelson.

"The rest of EDSOP are on their way," he said, "and the unit I sent to collect Meg is about ten minutes out."

"Good. At this rate we might need another medic." Eleanor looked at her watch: 3:21 a.m. "I think I'd better get the DCI out of bed."

❖

Sanne heard the Snake Pass before she saw it: the thunder of a heavy goods wagon taking advantage of the early hours, its rear lights as bright to her as solar flares after so long in the dark. A hawthorn hedge stood between her and the pass. She squeezed below its tangle of branches, crawling out onto the verge and simply lying there for a moment. Cold nipped at her and then made her drowsy. She closed her eyes, trying to block out an oncoming glare of light and a din that seemed to rattle her bones.

"Stop pissing about," she muttered. She needed to get up. Clawing onto the hedge, she made it halfway to her feet, her white T-shirt and her movement enough to bring the petrol tanker screeching to a stop. She waved, fell on all fours, and waited for the driver to come to her.

"Jesus fucking Christ, I could've killed you!" the man yelled from a few yards away, but then broke into a run and knelt by her. "Hey, are you all right? Christ. What happened?" He took his coat off and used it to cover her.

"Police," she told him. Her voice sounded weird, the muscles in her cheeks frozen stiff. "I'm with the police. I think they'll be looking for me."

"What? I don't—what are you doing out here?"

"*Please*," she said. She didn't have the strength to explain. "Please call the police."

"Okay, okay, I'll call them. Hang on. God, you're bleeding." He patted his trouser pockets, fumbling for a mobile. "Bloody hell, no signal." He looked around, obviously trying to remember what he'd just driven past.

"Don't go to a farm," she said. "Don't take me to a farm."

He shook his head. "I won't, love. Not if you don't want me to. Come on, let's get you up." When she couldn't manage, he lifted her carefully and cradled her against his chest. "How about the Snake Pub? They'll have a phone."

"Mm." The warmth of his tanker cab enveloped Sanne like a feather quilt. She fought to keep her eyes open. "I need a pen, paper."

He gave her an empty McDonald's bag and a pencil, and she drew a sketch of the tor, marking an X where she thought the women were hiding.

"Ask for Eleanor Stanhope." She scrawled a note, holding the pencil in her entire fist, her fingers too numb for dexterity. "Tell her to phone Meg. Tell her I'm fine."

"Meg." The man scribbled that down as well and reached across to fasten her seat belt. "San-ner Jensen," he read from the bag, getting the name right first time. "You just rest, love. I'll have you at the pub in a jiffy."

❖

Meg was out of the car before it had completely stopped, splashing down into slush and mud and throwing her kit bag over her shoulder. Her armed escort ran with her, guiding her through a rutted field. Nelson waylaid her at the door of a barn.

"Have you found her?" Meg tried to push past him, but he held firm. "Is she in there?"

"She's not here, Meg. We have teams out searching, and we're waiting for the chopper from Sheffield. The Stantons are already in custody."

"Searching where?" Meg couldn't see anything other than darkness stretching for miles. She let her bag drop and looked up at him. "Searching *where*, Nelson?"

"On the moors. We think Sanne got away, but—"

A sudden commotion cut short his explanation. Meg whipped around to see an Asian man being frogmarched between armed officers, one of whom fisted the man's jacket at the back of his neck to keep his head angled low.

"Boss?" Nelson said urgently into his radio. "Bloody hell, boss, we've got Sadek."

Meg started at the name. "Is he the one? Did he do something to Sanne?" She watched the officers shove Sadek into a police van, slamming the security grille shut when he tried to spit at them.

"He was sneaking back round to the farmhouse," one of the officers said, as Eleanor hurried over. "And he's saying fuck-all."

"I don't need him to say anything. It's enough that he's up here. Get him out of my sight." Eleanor sounded dreadful, and her hand was trembling as she lowered her face mask. "Meg, I hate to ask you this, but we have an injured man, and our closest ambulance gave an ETA of twenty-five."

"A man," Meg said quietly.

Eleanor nodded. "It's Cezar Miklos."

Meg didn't stop to think. If she had, she would probably have walked in the opposite direction. She picked up her bag and followed

Eleanor into the barn, where the wet sound of an obstructed airway drew her attention from the forensic stepping plates that formed a path to one of the animal pens.

"What happened to him?" She knelt on the plastic sheet newly placed beneath Miklos's head and began to set out her equipment.

"Someone hit him with a rock," Eleanor said.

"And tried to throttle him," Meg murmured. She lowered the police blanket to get a better look at the ligature mark around his throat.

"Apparently so." Eleanor held up an evidence bag, its clear plastic window showing a length of bare copper wire. Although Miklos's skin was unbroken, there were beads of crimson glistening along the metal, and Meg had a sudden sickening flash of what else it might have been used for.

"I should leave you to die, you piece of shit," she said, her mouth so close to his face she could smell the stale cigarettes on his breath.

She slid a cannula into his wrist and injected an anaesthetic, waiting until his breathing had faded to nothing before she cranked his mouth open with the blade of her laryngoscope. He was a straightforward intubation. The tube passed without incident, and the resultant breath sounds were clear and equal. His colour improved immediately as his oxygen levels began to climb.

"Fuck you." Meg started to sob, her tears splattering onto his mutilated face. "You fucking arsehole."

The plastic sheet rustled as Nelson crouched beside her and gave her a tissue. "Mountain Rescue just arrived," he said. "There's a doctor with them, so they'll be able to transport him."

"Thanks." She wiped her nose one-handed, the other still squeezing the ventilation bag. She'd done as much as she could for Miklos, and she wasn't going anywhere without Sanne.

The team took over from her with subdued efficiency, and she shuffled out of the way once Miklos was stabilised and strapped to a stretcher.

"Come outside." Nelson took her by the hand, leading her to the door with gentle insistence. She didn't speak until they were back in the field, shrouded by the night and with the wind stealing her words.

"I don't think I'd do very well without her," she said. Nelson didn't reply, but she felt him tighten his hold on her hand. "We always joked about growing old together and hobbling up on the hills with our arthritis and our gammy hips, and I never believed for a second that there was a chance it might not happen."

"I think it'll be gammy knees for San," he said. "They don't half creak and crack."

Meg smiled. "Occupational hazard of fell running, or so she reckons."

"She can still outpace me without breaking a sweat." He nodded toward the police vehicles, where Eleanor had a map open across one of the bonnets and was speaking into a radio handset. "The boss is organising a search grid for us. I thought you might want to keep busy."

"Would you stick with me?"

"Of course." His radio buzzed, the noise accompanied by the blare of a car horn. When he looked across, Eleanor was flashing the car's headlights at them. "Boss?" he said into his mike.

"Snake Pub," Eleanor said over the radio. "Sanne's at the Snake Pub. Get Meg over there ASAP. They're screaming for an ambulance."

Chapter Twenty-one

Two men in pyjamas and winter coats had assumed sentry duty by the Snake Pub. They began to wave their torches when they spotted the blue lights, signalling Nelson into a car park mostly taken up by a petrol tanker abandoned at an angle.

"She's in the snug," one of the men shouted. "We'll stay out and wait for the ambulance."

Meg scarcely heard him. She left Nelson to collect her kit and ran into the pub, almost colliding with a bearded man carrying a woolly hat and a box of paracetamol.

"We're shut, love," he said. "We're having a bit of an emergency."

"It's okay, I'm a doctor. The police are with me." She didn't have any ID, but Nelson had caught her up, and he showed his badge over her shoulder. The man immediately gave her the hat and the tablets, as if anxious to relinquish responsibility to an actual medic.

"She's not been able to tell us much," he said, ushering them ahead of him. "She's more awake than she was, and we've done our best, but we can't get the poor lass warm at all."

The room he took them into was so hot it made Meg's head swim. A log fire was blazing like a smelting furnace, and a man in a Texaco uniform was kneeling by the sofa with a mug in his hand. He moved away to allow Meg through, and she caught a glimpse of Sanne, buried beneath a mound of bedding and propped up on pillows almost as white as she was. She didn't realise Meg was there at first, but when she did she started to cry.

"Hey. Shh, don't get upset." Meg crouched beside her and placed a hand on her forehead. Despite the stifling heat, her skin was cold, and she was shivering uncontrollably. Meg used the hat to dry the tears. "Come on, love, you're scaring Nelson."

"I'm so sorry," Sanne whispered, her words tumbling together. "I didn't mean to. I didn't do anything daft, I didn't. I went for chicken food."

"I know, I know." Meg touched her fingers to Sanne's lips. "You're safe now, and you're not in any bother. Stop fretting."

Sanne tried to push herself up, but she couldn't get her hands out. "Did you find Dorina and the others? Nelson, I drew a map on a bag."

"The helicopter's already looking for them," Nelson said. "The chaps here gave some rough coordinates when they phoned in about you, and we've arrested Sadek."

That was enough to settle her. She sagged against the pillows and closed her eyes. "I've buggered my legs up," she mumbled. "Trudy took most of my clothes off me. And my boots."

Meg rocked back, hitting the table and sending a glass of brandy to the floor. She'd thought she'd prepared herself for the worst when she'd seen the blood on the wire, but no one had warned her that Sanne had been forced to undress and had then crossed miles of frozen moors in that state. She wiped the sweat from her face, glad that Sanne wasn't watching her.

"How buggered is 'buggered'?" she asked.

"Pretty buggered. They hurt like the dickens."

The simple admission helped Meg focus. Pain was something Sanne rarely acknowledged, and it was something Meg could fix. She fished out her obs kit and IV pouch. "Right, then, let's top-to-toe you."

Sanne seemed too done-in to protest. Her nose did wrinkle when Meg stuck the thermometer in her ear, but it was a token effort.

"What's my score?" she asked.

"Crap." Meg showed her the screen, which just read "LOW." She tossed Nelson a bag of saline. "Do me a favour, Nelson: warm this. Sit it by the fire or something. And put a bloody rocket under ambulance control."

He nodded briskly, heading for the hearth with his radio in one hand and the IV bag in the other.

She waited until he was out of earshot and then perched on the sofa, stroking Sanne's cheek. "It's just you and me now. I'm going to uncover your legs, okay?"

Sanne looked at Meg, her hazel eyes a bright contrast to the bruising below. "They didn't touch me," she said. "They knocked me about a bit, but it could've been worse."

Meg nodded, still too distraught to appreciate this. She wanted to switch off the lights and hold on to Sanne until everything mended, but that was as unrealistic as wishing the night's events had never happened. Sanne fumbled a hand out from the blankets and took hold of Meg's. There were deep lacerations encircling her wrist, but her grip was strong.

"I'm not letting you out of my sight again, Sanne Jensen," Meg said.

"Mm." Sanne smiled. "Does that mean you're going to come running with me? Once my legs are better, that is?"

"Still going to be running, are you?" Meg didn't know why that came as a surprise. Sanne had never let anything knock her down for long.

"I hope so. I'll stick to wearing trainers, though."

"As your doctor, I would advise that." Meg sighed. "I don't suppose you fancy swimming instead? Something safe and indoorsy?"

"I like the hills, Meg."

"I know you do, love." She wasn't going to argue a point she'd never win. She placed Sanne's hand on top of the bedding and put the woolly hat on her head. "How about I fill you full of morphine and you have a nap?"

"You really need to work on your pickup lines."

"Yeah, well, I'm not on top form." Meg tightened her tourniquet around Sanne's arm and ripped open a cannula. "It's been a hell of a night."

❖

Eleanor banged twice on the side of the police van and watched it pull slowly away, keeping within the fresh tyre tracks carved into the field as it made a U-turn, with her fifth and hopefully final perp locked in the back.

The unidentified Romanian photographed with Miklos at Sadek's shop had been discovered nursing a twisted ankle on the nearside of Stryder Clough. For the price of a cigarette and two ibuprofen, he'd confirmed that Sadek had travelled to the farm alone, which left the four women who'd escaped with Sanne the only people unaccounted for. Mountain Rescue teams were focusing their efforts around the area of moorland that Sanne had described, and several ambulances were waiting in the yard of Black Gate Farm. Though little remained for EDSOP to do out there, Eleanor wasn't budging until the women were found, and none of her detectives had uttered a word about going home.

"It's official: I am definitely a city boy." Russ stomped thick clods of crap off his boots and wrapped his arms across his chest. He had to shout past the scarf he'd raised over his nose. "Speaking of useless urbanites, what time are we expecting DCI Litton to grace us with his presence?"

"We're not," Eleanor said. "DCI Litton has gone directly to HQ to address the media. I'm to notify him of any developments."

Russ scoffed, sucking his scarf inward. "Did he at least have the decency to admit he was wrong?"

"No."

"What a prize twat," Russ said, and then stood quietly as Eleanor answered a radio query. "Any sign of them?" he asked.

"Not yet."

They looked in unison at the sky, watching the shaft of light streaming from the underbelly of the police helicopter. It was some distance away, the beat of its blades inaudible.

"I wonder whether its thermal imaging will work if the women are severely hypothermic," she said.

"I have no idea." He stamped again. "How on earth could Sanne stand this? I've only spent a couple of hours out here—fully dressed, mind—and there are parts of me I doubt will ever defrost."

"I don't imagine she stayed still long enough to think about it."

"No, probably not." His eyebrows knit together. "What's the latest from Meg?"

"That she's stable and heading to theatre, to debride the wounds on—and I quote—'legs that look like they've been through an industrial fucking shredder.'"

"Ouch."

"My sentiments exactly." The barn loomed in the periphery of Eleanor's vision. She hadn't been inside again since the arrival of

SOCO, happy for once to let them tease apart the details of what had happened in there. "Knowing Sanne, she'll drag herself to work in a bloody wheelchair, but I'll have to get something in place for her. Counselling or peer support, or," she shook her head, "or, I don't have a clue, Russ. What the hell do you put in place for this?"

"Probably not a counsellor," he said. "Sanne doesn't strike me as one who'd open up to a stranger. She's more likely to talk to Nelson, or to you, or maybe just to Meg."

Eleanor watched the helicopter circle, its searchlight outshining the moon, before it swooped and hovered above a precise spot.

"You might be right," she said. "She'll have to give a statement, but we'll cross that bridge later."

Her earpiece crackled, delivering a bolt of static that made her wince. As the transmission cleared, she recognised the pilot's voice and gave Russ a thumbs-up halfway through the concise account. Relief made her knock-kneed, and she sat heavily on the back step of the SOCO van, longing for a Scotch and a week's worth of sleep.

"Three walking and talking, one poorly but stable," she repeated for Russ's benefit. "A Mountain Rescue team found them—almost fell on top of them. They should be down in a few minutes. The chopper's just looking for somewhere to land."

"Bloody brilliant," Russ said. At her nod, he put out an open-channel message to recall the search teams. He was still fielding enquiries when Fred approached her. One glance at his face set her on edge; even in the torchlight, he looked green around the gills.

"What is it?" she asked.

"We found something in Sadek's car," he said. "Probably easier to show you."

George was waiting at the rear of the Range Rover, a crowbar and a screwdriver by his feet. He'd hung his jacket over the tailgate and rolled his sleeves up.

"The floor of the boot seemed weird," he said. "It didn't quite sit right, and we found a lock box where you'd expect a spare tyre. I just jemmied it open." He collected his jacket and let Eleanor step into his place. He'd shut the box again, but its contents were neatly arranged across the boot's interior: heavy-duty bin bags, a plastic tarp, three Tyvek suits, disposable gloves, a saw, and a machete.

Eleanor tasted bile at the back of her throat. She closed the boot and walked around the corner of the smaller barn, where she knelt and vomited until there was nothing left but dry heaves and sour spit.

Russ found her eventually. He gave her a Polo Mint and helped her to stand.

"Come on," he said. "I'll give you a lift to the hospital."

❖

In flagrant violation of Sheffield Royal's "no flowers" policy, Meg arranged the daffodils in a spare jug and put them next to the roses on Sanne's bedside cabinet. The nurses were turning a blind eye, and Meg was determined to make the room as cheerful as possible for Sanne, whenever she decided to wake up. Late morning sunlight was streaming through the blinds, casting warm hues on the sterile equipment, and the cadence of Teresa's knitting needles sounded to Meg like a lullaby.

She retook her seat, wrapping her fingers over Sanne's. Sanne continued to snore softly, rendered insensible by a cocktail of anaesthesia and pain relief. Given her low tolerance to drugs, she'd probably be out for the count halfway into next week. Meg stretched out her legs and swallowed a mouthful of Cherry Coke from the can she'd bought hours ago. It had lost all its fizz, but the caffeine provided a welcome kick.

"She came home looking like this once," Teresa said. The tap of her needles slowed and then stopped. Every now and again she would touch Sanne as if to reassure herself that Sanne really was there. "Those girls had ripped her school bag from her and thrown her books in a puddle, and the meanest one belted her when she went to pick them up."

"I remember her coming to school with a split lip," Meg said. "But I'm pretty sure she told me Keeley had done it. I'd have bloody leathered them if I'd known." She reconsidered. The girls in question had been notoriously vicious, and at least two of them now had criminal records. "Well, I'd have given it a damn good go."

Teresa neatened the edge of a blanket, aligning it with the one underneath. "She didn't want anyone fighting that battle for her. Even our Michael offered to have words, but she wouldn't let him."

"Headstrong little soul," Meg said, more to Sanne than to anyone else. She would never understand the contradictions inherent in Sanne, why Sanne would kowtow to authority yet choose to face down seemingly impossible odds on her own. "That stubborn streak probably got her through last night, Teresa."

"I'm sure it helped."

"Far more than I did." She had lowered her voice to a whisper, but once the words were out she couldn't take them back, so she kept going. "I was so bothered about smothering her or mithering her that I left her for hours with those men. If I'd contacted Nelson earlier, the police would've gone to the farm, and she might never have ended up in here."

Teresa adjusted her chair until she faced Meg properly. "Stop talking nonsense. How on earth is any of this your fault?"

"Because I'm supposed to keep her safe." Meg pressed the point when Teresa didn't answer. "*Aren't* I?"

"You can certainly try." Teresa's even tone was a direct contrast to the challenge in Meg's. "Lord knows I've tried since she was a babe, but it doesn't always work out. You know that as well as I do. She'd be as nowty as a wet hen to hear you talking like this."

"Don't mention those sodding hens," Meg muttered.

Teresa laid her palm on Meg's cheek. "Sanne's never asked anyone to protect her. Not as a child, and especially not now. And she's been happier than I've ever seen her, these past few weeks. The last thing she'll want is you blaming yourself."

"I suppose."

Teresa rapped the back of Meg's hand with a knitting needle. "Suppose nothing, Megan Fielding. You're being an idiot, and you've made me drop a stitch."

Meg smiled at her indignation. "Sorry about the hole," she said. "But thank you."

"You're welcome." Teresa resumed her knitting, signalling an end to the discussion. She didn't speak again until she paused to watch Meg wipe a trickle of saliva from Sanne's chin.

"I'd almost given up on you two ever seeing sense," she said. "I can't count the number of times I've wanted to knock your bloody heads together."

"You can't rush these things, Teresa."

"Rush?" She gave Meg the look she traditionally reserved for the naughtiest of Keeley's brood. "You've been courting each other since you were eleven."

"That's not true." Meg took Sanne's hand again, brushing away the dried flakes of blood that mapped the lines of her palm. "We didn't have our first kiss till we were twelve."

❖

Sanne had no idea why she was sleeping on her back. She'd just choked herself snoring, and her chin was wet with drool. She coughed and attempted to turn over.

"Oh, hey, no! Don't do that."

The bed dipped as someone sat on it. Hands pressed on her shoulders, keeping her in place but being careful not to exert too much force.

"You've slept for long enough. How about you wake up instead?"

It took Sanne an age to make sense of the question. Meg's voice was the only thing she recognised. The bed and the smell of the room were unfamiliar, her pyjamas didn't fit her, and her body felt as if it had been steamrollered and then dipped in lead. She groaned, coughed some more, sucked water through the straw that was pushed between her lips, and finally opened her eyes.

Two relieved smiles were the first things she saw. She smiled back, even though her face throbbed and the pain in her legs was making her bottom lip wobble.

"Morning." Meg kissed her forehead and, ever practical, proffered a cardboard bowl. "Think you might need this?"

"Maybe," Sanne conceded. She could only bend four of her fingers to grasp the bowl, drawing her attention to the bandages covering her wrist. Her fingernails were caked with dirt and blood from the barn. She gagged and abruptly brought back the water she'd just drunk. "Shit."

"Here, I've got it. It's all right." Her mum moved the bowl out of sight, returning with paper towels to wipe Sanne's face clean. Not trusting her stomach to behave itself, Sanne lay still and let her mum fuss.

"This will get better, I promise," Meg said, tapping Sanne's contrary finger. "You've had a tendon repaired in your wrist, that's all."

"Mm. Ron tied the wire really tight," Sanne said, too groggy for subterfuge. She blinked against the sunlight, trying to organise her scattered thoughts. "Dorina?"

"Safe and sound," Meg said. "Mirela is here in the Burns ITU, and Dorina is at St. Margaret's with Paree and Fadiya. They're all doing okay."

Sanne murmured the unfamiliar names. She'd marched the girls out onto the moors, compelling them to trust her, but she'd never asked what they were called. She wondered which of them had saved her life by attacking Miklos with the rock.

"Nelson, Zoe, and Eleanor have visited," Meg continued. She held up a packet of chocolate HobNobs. "Nelson reckoned you'd appreciate these more than flowers."

"He was right," Sanne said. The thought of being able to dunk biscuits with Nelson and go home with Meg tightened her throat. She sniffled and rubbed her nose on her bandages. "Can I save them for later, though?"

"Of course you can." Meg was watching her intently, no doubt reading something into every crease on her face. "How bad is the pain?"

"Pretty bad." It had started to make Sanne clammy, sticking her loose hospital gown to her chest.

"Hang on, love. I'll go and find your doc."

The door closed behind Meg, shutting out the clatter of a breakfast trolley and a ringing phone, everyday sounds that Sanne could have listened to for hours. She shuffled around until she could see her mum properly.

"You should get to bed, Mum. You look shattered."

"I am," her mum said. "I feel as if I've been out there with you, running in the dark. You frightened me half to death."

"I'm sorry, Mum. I really am." Sanne didn't think she'd ever be able to apologise enough. "Did you tell Dad?"

"I couldn't, love." Her mum took a deep breath. "Your dad died, Sanne. About three hours ago. He'd been poorly all night, and they couldn't do anything to fix it this time."

Sanne bent her left foot until the bite of the stitches and torn skin cut through the fog of the drugs. She was terrified she'd wake up and realise she'd been dreaming.

"Were you with him?" she asked.

"No. I was here with you." There was no remorse or grief in her mum's tone. "Your dad didn't need me. He hasn't needed me for years, but you did. A nurse came to tell me when he'd passed, and I signed some paperwork."

Sanne stroked the back of her mum's fingers, smoothing across the raised scar from the slip of a potato peeler and the slight swelling where arthritis was beginning to take hold.

"If I believed in a god, I would've bargained your dad away in a heartbeat," her mum said. "But I didn't have to, in the end."

"I'm not sad that he's gone," Sanne said.

"Nor am I. I'm just glad that I got you back." Her mum unfolded the pile of wool from her lap, revealing a long red sock. "Here, I've been making these for your poor feet."

Sanne pulled the sock closer, admiring the double thickness of its sole. "Oh, they're perfect."

"She's making me a pair as well," Meg said, coming in at the tail end of the conversation. "For the next time you leave the damn heating off." She took a syringe filled with clear liquid from the tray she'd put on the overbed table. "This'll probably knock you out again, San. Is that okay?"

Sanne nodded, sure now of what she would be waking up to. She started to count as Meg injected the drug into her IV. Her eyelids were heavy by nine. She didn't make it to ten.

CHAPTER TWENTY-TWO

That man, that man." Dorina Ivas touched each of the mug shots, the sleeves of her sweater riding up to reveal finger-shaped contusions on her wrist. She looked at Eleanor, one eye closed by bruising, the other unflinching. "And that man."

Eleanor collected the photographs and turned them face down as Dorina sipped from a mug of black coffee. Though the heating in Interview Two was on its highest setting, Dorina wrapped both hands around her mug as if the chill from the moors persisted more than seventy-two hours later. A specialist SOET detective had assumed the lead in the interview, and she waited until Dorina set her mug on the table before asking her next question.

"You identified Vasile Enescu as the man who arranged to bring you over to England. Could you tell us how that process worked?"

Dorina turned to her translator for clarification. Her English was reasonably comprehensive, but there were gaps in her understanding, and she replied in Romanian. The translator jotted a couple of notes and spoke once Dorina confirmed that she had finished.

"She applied for a childcare job from a website promising good wages and prospects. She arrived in Manchester last Tuesday, and Enescu met her at the airport. He gave her flowers to welcome her, but he took her luggage and her passport from her. He stopped at a house close to the airport to collect Mirela, and then he drove them both to the barn. He told her it was temporary, that she would be moved somewhere better, but she didn't believe him. The two younger girls were already there."

"It all went to shit," Dorina said, with no small amount of satisfaction. "Mirela ran from a sex house, and they burned her to punish her. I was to go to that house in her place, but I heard the men talk of the police closing it down."

"Yes, we raided it on the Monday evening," Eleanor said, "which explains why they had to keep you at the barn."

"Very bad timing for the men," Dorina told her. "Enescu and the Pakistani were angry that we couldn't earn money for them, so they fucked us instead. The Pakistani said it was pity to let us go to waste."

The translator blanched and drank half a glass of water, no doubt relieved that Dorina had reverted to English.

"Would you be willing to testify, Dorina?" Eleanor asked. "To tell a judge and a jury what you've told us?"

Dorina seemed to shrink back, her body language closing off and her eye contact slipping. It was the first time Eleanor had seen a crack in her façade.

"My parents cannot know. They think I am childminder."

"We can withhold your name, and you may be able to give evidence via a video link so you wouldn't have to be in the courtroom." Eleanor paused to allow for translation. However reluctant she was to pressurise Dorina, she knew the case against the men would be weaker without her.

"If I do this, those men go to prison?" Dorina asked quietly.

"Yes," Eleanor said with absolute conviction. "For a long time."

Dorina inclined her head as if considering the truth of this. Her poise returned as she came to a decision. "Okay. I will do as you ask."

"We very much appreciate that." The response seemed inadequate to Eleanor, but Dorina showed all her teeth as she smiled.

"Officer Sanne," she said, "she will speak in court?"

"Yes, she'll be called as a witness, just like yourself." Eleanor didn't see the harm in deviating from the script now that the formal part of the interview had concluded. "I visited her in the hospital yesterday, and she asked me to thank you for helping her."

"We helped each other, I think."

Eleanor nodded. Dorina had provided a vivid account of Sanne's time in the barn, including details of a discussion between the men that Sanne hadn't been able to understand, details that were now recorded as part of Dorina's statement. They would be transcribed, included in the case file, and repeated in court, but Eleanor would do her damnedest to keep them from Sanne for as long as was feasible.

She stated the time and stopped the tape. The translator escorted Dorina to the lift, allowing Eleanor to return to her office. Her skin itched as if there was a layer of scum clinging to it. She was towelling cold water from her face when Russ toed the door open. He was carrying a large cardboard box, and a laptop bag swung from his shoulder.

"Ready for the off?" she asked.

"As I'll ever be." He hefted the box. "Although this makes me think we might be crossing paths again in the not too distant."

"I hope so." She kissed his cheek. "We got most of the way there in the end, didn't we?"

"We did, and my lot will keep plugging away at the rest of it."

"Keep us updated."

"Of course."

She held the door for him. "I don't really…" she began, and then shook her head, cut adrift. She felt as if she was losing her closest ally. "I'll see you soon."

He smiled at her. "I'll bring the bacon butties."

❖

Five floor tiles separated the bed from the chair. From her vantage point on the edge of the mattress, Sanne pondered the distance and concluded she'd probably end up on her arse.

"Let me get this for you. It's almost run through." Meg twiddled with the connections on Sanne's IV port, removing the antibiotics prescribed for a newly spiked temperature. The irony that Sanne was now too warm hadn't been lost on either of them. "All done. Are you ready?"

"Yep." Sanne slung her left arm over Meg's shoulder, her right manoeuvring a crutch into position. Her new socks cushioned the impact of her feet on the floor, and she ventured forward before she could chicken out.

"Four more steps and you're there," Meg murmured, her lips close to Sanne's ear.

Walking on fresh stitches and inflamed wounds hurt, but it didn't hurt as much as Sanne had feared, and she tightened her arm around Meg, happy to be mobile after three days in bed.

"Okay, sit your bum down," Meg said.

Sanne obeyed without protest, her one-and-a-half metre expedition enough to leave her out of puff. Unaccustomed to being ill, she'd forgotten the all-encompassing lethargy that came with an infection.

"Bloody hell, I was running eight miles last week," she said.

Meg used the chair's remote to raise Sanne's legs and draped a thin blanket over her knees. "You've taken a proper wallop, San. You're going to feel wiped out."

"I didn't sleep well last night." She had insisted that Meg go home and had regretted it as soon as she'd turned out the light. Her room was never really dark, but its shadows had spooked her, and every little noise had made her jump. If she had been able to find the emergency buzzer, she would have pressed it and asked for her door to be left open. "It was lucky you put the bed rails up."

"Did you try to do a runner?"

"Yeah, I woke with one leg stuck through them." She picked at a tiny rip in the chair's armrest. "Do you think I'm jinxed, Meg?"

The water Meg was pouring spilled all over the cabinet as she jerked the jug upright. "What? Do I 'eck as like, you silly sod."

"But I keep getting in shit," Sanne said. Worrying about this had kept her awake for the rest of the night, once she'd convinced herself that no one was hiding in her cupboard or under her bed. "And it doesn't seem to happen to anyone else."

"Carlyle got his throat slashed," Meg countered. "And if I remember rightly, Nelson fractured his skull."

"They were both with me at the time, though, and they got hurt because of decisions that I made." On some elusive level, Sanne knew her argument was groundless, that Nelson and Carlyle had understood the risks involved, and that she hadn't come out unscathed either, but the doubts persisted, and she couldn't seem to shake them.

Meg edged her chair across the floor until it touched Sanne's. "How many lives did you save?"

Sanne frowned. "What do you mean?"

"These last three cases, the ones where you've been hurt. How many people would have died if you hadn't had the balls to make those decisions?" Meg made a show of ticking them off on her fingers. "I'm getting eight. Nine if you count plugging Carlyle's neck with nappies."

Sanne hadn't thought about it like that. All she'd been able to see were the negatives. "I decided to hand in my notice," she said quietly. "At some point this morning, when I couldn't reach the light. I decided I'd leave EDSOP and do something else, something safer."

"And now?"

"Now I want to stay." She held out her hand to Meg, who took it in both of hers. "Would that be all right with you?"

"You don't need my permission, San."

"No, I know. But you're the one who has to pick up the pieces, aren't you?"

"Would you rather work nine-to-five in a nice comfortable office?" Sanne shook her head. "I'd hate it."

"Keep doing what you're doing, then," Meg said. "And if there are pieces to pick up, well, that's part of my job as a doctor and as your long-suffering better half." She tugged on a tuft of Sanne's bed-head. "Do you want me to sort out this mop of yours before your visitors arrive?"

What Sanne really wanted to do was throw her arms around Meg and smother her with kisses. She passed her the brush instead. "Thank you."

"You're welcome. Duck down a bit so I can reach."

Hair deemed presentable, Meg managed to wrestle Sanne into a pair of loose jogging bottoms and a clean T-shirt. Sanne flattened the creases from the shirt, self-conscious about its rag-tag appearance, despite being glad to get out of her pyjamas.

"You look gorgeous," Meg said. She laughed at Sanne's sceptical expression. "Okay, maybe 'gorgeous' is an overstatement, but you look less like you've been smacked around and dragged through a grough backwards."

Sanne peeked into the handheld mirror Meg had left on the cabinet, and pressed the tender swelling on her jaw. "I do still look like I've been smacked around."

Meg prised the mirror from her fingers. "Do you want me to cadge some foundation from that nurse with the orange face?"

"Thanks, but no. I think I'd rather stay pallid and purple."

"Wise choice." Meg spotted Nelson and Eleanor through the

door's slatted blinds. She stood on tiptoe to kiss his cheek and then shook Eleanor's hand. "I'll make myself scarce. I need to bend my boss's ear about exactly what constitutes a 'family emergency.'"

As the door closed, Nelson set a box in front of Sanne. "Everyone sends their love," he said.

"Crikey. That's not all they sent." She rummaged through assorted bags of sweets, boxes of chocolates, and a pile of cards.

"There's a Victoria sponge in there somewhere," Nelson said. "Courtesy of Fred and Martha."

"I'll ask for some plates and a knife when we've finished." She eyed the file on Eleanor's lap. "So, what have I missed?"

Eleanor smiled at her eagerness. "It's only been three days, Sanne." She left a pause perfectly timed for dramatic effect. "But quite a lot, as it happens."

Sanne shoved herself higher in the chair, forgetting all about her improper attire and the oddness of the setting. The impromptu bedside briefing had been a brainwave of Meg's, a compromise between keeping Sanne in the hospital until she was fit for discharge, and stopping her from climbing the walls through lack of information. She stifled a yelp as her battered heels reminded her why she was still an inpatient.

"Did you speak to Dorina this morning?" she asked, when the discomfort had eased.

"Yes, and she's agreed to testify," Eleanor said. "She identified each of the men we arrested at Black Gate as having raped her and the three other victims. From what we can gather, the raid on Cheviot and our obvious interest in Sadek put a dent in the plans as far as those particular vics were concerned. He had buyers in Sheffield lined up for the two girls, but he didn't dare move them on. The barn at Black Gate was a last-minute, temporary holding place."

"Sadek hadn't wiped the hard drive on his laptop," Nelson said. "We think he was intending to lie low and then resurrect his business once the fuss died down. Looking at his administrative records, he was small-scale in comparison to Bashir, but he certainly didn't lack ambition."

"Did you find any link between Sadek and Bashir?" Sanne asked. She'd been making mental notes all morning and was now regretting not asking Meg to write them down.

"We're still working on that angle," Eleanor said. "Sadek's laptop contained victim profiles, flight information: essentially a shopping list of the women he'd arranged to ship over. He and Bashir would trade on occasion, but he doesn't feature on Bashir's payroll. They seemed to have done business on more of a freelance basis."

Sanne murmured her understanding. Even through the fog of her mild fever, she could see the benefits for the two men. "They each had access to something the other wanted, didn't they?"

"Exactly. They were dealing in completely different countries, and it seems Sadek wasn't keen to lose his Eastern European connection; he put feelers out to Vasile Enescu—that's Cezar Miklos's real name— soon after Bashir's arrest. They must've hit it off, because Enescu had taken Dorina and Mirela to Black Gate that same day you spotted him at Sadek's shop. Enescu was one of Bashir's main suppliers. I suspect his computer will keep the MST busy until DI Parry reaches retirement."

Unofficial hospital briefings were all very well, but Sanne would have given a lot right then for the office flipchart and a marker pen, or at the very least a breakdown of the key points and players. "The girl in Ron's cellar, would she have come from Bashir, then?"

Eleanor checked her notepad. The page she turned to was filled with names and arrows, and she'd resorted to multiple colours to keep everything in order. "Originally, yes. He also provided a number of women for Sadek's enterprise at Nab Hey."

"How the hell did Ron get involved? He just...Jesus, boss, he always seemed like such a decent bloke."

"He liked young girls," Eleanor said with brutal simplicity. "His computer was full of underage porn, and we found records of webcam use, the type where the client can direct the abuse of remote victims. We think he met Sadek through a forum and tipped him off about the property at Nab Hey as part-exchange for the girl in his cellar. His bank records show that the fee he paid for her was refunded when he allowed the use of his own barn."

Sanne sipped from a glass of iced water and rubbed her cheeks with her chilled fingers. She couldn't tell whether it was anger or the infection that was raising her temperature. "Is she okay? The little one?"

"She needed surgery." Eleanor hesitated but didn't elaborate. "We've traced her family, but we're not sure if they were complicit in her being trafficked. SOET are working on that. They're actually working on the lion's share of the case now, alongside Manchester's

MST. They raided a brothel in Ardwick yesterday and found three of the missing Cheviot vics, but seventeen remain unaccounted for."

She opened a bag of boiled sweets, popping one into her mouth before she offered them around, as if keen to rid herself of a foul taste. Sanne let hers dissolve slowly, while Nelson, more of an instant gratification type, crunched his and pinched another. He smiled at her as he unwrapped it, obviously happy to have things back to a semblance of normality.

"Are any of the men talking?" Sanne asked.

"No," he said. "But they've all been charged. I can tell you the counts, if you want us to be here till midnight."

"You're welcome to stay. I have cake." She made the offer lightly but then sobered. There was only one obvious loose end, and it was the one that had initiated the entire investigation. "What about the girl at Greave?"

"Her name is Halima Hashiba, and she was fourteen years old." Eleanor flipped to a different page of her notepad, though she didn't seem to need the prompts. "One of the vics rescued during that last SOET raid had been held with her at Nab Hey. Apparently, Sadek brought her over with her older sister Nabila, whom we haven't yet been able to find. There's no mention of either of them on Sadek's computer—he's not that stupid—but Interpol have managed to contact their family in Pakistan. The labs have confirmed it was Halima's blood in Sadek's car. She probably cut herself going through the window."

"Sadek told the family all the right things," Nelson said. "That the girls would get a good job and the chance to learn English. He was a dab hand at getting these people to trust him."

Sanne took the printout that Eleanor held out: a colour photograph of Halima, embarrassment flushing her face, and her clothes pristine, as if her mother had insisted she look her best. The woollen bracelet around her wrist now sat in Evidence.

"We'll probably never prove who was driving Sadek's car that night, will we?" Sanne said.

"Not unless we find a witness." Eleanor took the photograph back but didn't put it away. Perhaps that would have felt like admitting defeat. "Sadek will go to prison for umpteen other charges, but he may never be held accountable for Halima's death. Not in a court of law, at any rate."

"Wanker," Sanne muttered.

"Of the highest order." Eleanor regarded her closely. "I've asked one of the SOET detectives to take your statement. There's no rush. Just give me a shout whenever you feel up to it."

"Thanks, boss." Sanne hadn't broached the subject with Eleanor, but the prospect of describing her abduction to one of her EDSOP colleagues had filled her with dread. "I'm loads better than I was. My doc promised to let me out tomorrow."

"In which case," Nelson delved into the gift box and emerged holding a large, round tin, "I think that calls for cake."

"There aren't many aspects of my life that don't call for cake." Holding the chair's remote in her good hand, Sanne lowered her legs and grabbed her crutch. "C'mere, Nelson."

He stooped obediently and allowed her to hang on to him. "What's your plan?" he asked as they stood together.

"Find a nurse. Acquire plates and a knife."

"Sounds doable." He settled his arm around her waist, hugging her close. "Ready? On three…"

EPILOGUE

Sanne hadn't been bluffing. She'd felt bright and chipper that morning, raring to go. Her trainers had pinched a little after her warm-up exercises, rubbing on a couple of sore spots, but she hadn't been planning on a long run, just an easy circular jog to get her back into the routine.

"Hey, you."

Meg's voice made her jump. She stared at the floor, ashamed for a reason she couldn't articulate. Meg didn't seem to notice, though. Still in her pyjamas, she perched on the kitchen counter, brandishing a postcard.

"Your mum's been sledging with huskies and fishing for king crabs, and she's seen a pod of beluga. She sounds like she's having a whale of a time," Meg said, and laughed at her terrible pun.

"That was disgraceful." Sanne threw a grape at her. It missed. "I'm surprised the card beat the ship."

"Me too. The Norwegian post must be highly efficient." Meg passed her the card, waiting in silence for her to read it. "You're not very muddy," she said, once Sanne had turned the card over.

Sanne studied the picture: the aurora borealis swirling above a snow-capped mountain, its waves of fluorescent green mirrored in the fjord below.

"I only got as far as the garden gate," she said, her toes curling on the cold tiles. She'd left her trainers on the mat, her running socks stuffed in them. "I opened it, but I couldn't go through it."

"Are you worried about going back to work tomorrow?"

"No, it's not that. I don't…" She raised her head. "I just couldn't."

Meg drummed her fingernails on the counter and then hopped off it, a decision apparently reached. "Make some butties. I'll be ready in ten."

"Ready for what?"

"I'll have egg on mine!" Meg yelled, pounding up the stairs.

Half expecting Meg to come down in purloined running gear, Sanne was relieved when she reappeared toting rucksacks and woolly hats. She chucked trousers and a fleece at Sanne, and added a bag of sweets to the picnic laid out on the table.

"How's about Blackden Brook?" she asked, and Sanne stopped chewing the skin from the side of her thumb for long enough to nod.

They parked in a lay-by at the base of the route, a steep and little-used path that followed the track of a stream onto the northern edge of Kinder Scout. It was one of Sanne's favourite scrambles, the path disappearing in places to merge with rock-strewn waterfalls. Standing by the lay-by's kissing gate, she peered up at the deep cleft splitting the hillside. Patches of snow still nestled in sheltered high spots, but the lowermost vegetation showed the first signs of spring, speckling the dull brown with dabs of fresh growth. It was a typical Peak District big sky day, with a vigorous breeze sweeping clouds across the blue, promising showers one minute and warm sunshine the next.

Sanne pushed her wrists through the straps on her hiking poles and stabbed the poles into the ground, dispelling the jitters that had been tempting her back to the car.

"All set?" Meg asked.

"Yep."

The path was narrow, obliging them to go single file. Meg offered Sanne the lead, letting her dictate their pace, any attempts at conversation hampered by the roar of the stream in spate and by their laboured breathing. As they climbed higher, a thick mist settled in the clough, blanketing everything in grey and dappling their clothes with dew. Sanne persevered for another half mile, her eyes on the ground rather than the ghostly shapes floating across the brook. Then she stopped short, forgetting to call a warning and making Meg skid on loose stones to avoid a collision.

"Jesus, San!" Meg flicked droplets from her hair, the brusqueness of her actions softening as she looked at Sanne. "Do you want to go home?"

Sanne shook her head, almost in tears.

Meg raised Sanne's chin and kissed her damp lips. "Do you want me to go first?"

"Yes," Sanne said. "Maybe just for a bit."

The chaos of rocks at the top of the brook provided the perfect distraction. Busy picking a safe passage, Sanne began to enjoy the burn of effort in her chest and the scrape of gritstone on her fingertips. She hauled Meg up a particularly dicey section, teetering with her on the brink of a stone slab until Meg urged her to carry on. They reached the summit together, climbing onto the tallest of the rocks to catch their breath. The sun gradually broke through the clouds, banishing the mist into the valley to leave the Peaks clear. Sanne turned a slow full circle, but she couldn't see another soul beside Meg. The Snake, its steady stream of traffic, and the farms scattered along it were all hidden away.

"Top of the world," she murmured.

"Aye." Meg spread a plastic bag on the rock, and they sat down, stretching their legs out. "How are your poor battered tootsies?"

Sanne knocked her boots together. "Slightly damp but otherwise sound."

"And what about the rest of you?"

Sanne paused to take stock. Although Meg hadn't put much weight behind the question, her expression was solemn as she waited for an answer.

"I think I'm okay," Sanne said. She wasn't one hundred percent, but completing the ascent certainly felt like progress. She kissed Meg's cheek. "Thank you for not letting me hide in my kitchen forever."

"It'll keep getting easier, San. Consider this a first baby step. Soon you'll be crayoning on the walls and sticking your fingers into plug sockets."

Sanne smiled. "If you ever get tired of medicine, you'd be ace at motivational speaking." She stood and pulled Meg up. "Come for a wander with me."

"Did you have a destination in mind?"

"Not as such." Sanne jumped down onto the peat. "I thought we'd plod north for a bit. Find some more rocks, eat our butties, see what we can see."

"So basically you're leading me astray."

"Yes, I am."

"Splendid. Which way's north?"

"T'other way." Sanne gently tugged her in the right direction.

Meg squinted at the compass, her attempts to orientate herself sending the pointer haywire. "Damn. This is why I never became a brain surgeon."

The path was wide enough now for them to walk side by side, and the mild warmth of the spring sun began to dry their clothes. A skylark soared overhead, its song mingling with the cackled "g'back" reproach of a nearby grouse.

Sanne had no intention of going back. She clasped Meg's hand in hers.

"Stick with me, love," she said. "I won't let you get lost."

About the Author

Cari Hunter lives in the northwest of England with her wife, two cats, and a pond full of frogs. She works full-time as a paramedic and dreams up stories in her spare time.

Cari enjoys long, windswept, muddy walks in her beloved Peak District. In the summer she can usually be found sitting in the garden with her feet up, scribbling in her writing pad. Although she doesn't like to boast, she will admit that she makes a very fine Bakewell Tart.

Her first novel, *Snowbound*, received an Alice B. Lavender Certificate for outstanding début. *No Good Reason*, the first in the Dark Peak series, won a 2015 Rainbow Award for Best Mystery and was a finalist in the 2016 Lambda Literary Awards. Its sequel, *Cold to the Touch*, won a 2016 Goldie for Best Mystery.

Cari can be contacted at: carihunter@rocketmail.com

Books Available From Bold Strokes Books

A Quiet Death by Cari Hunter. When the body of a young Pakistani girl is found out on the moors, the investigation leaves Detective Sanne Jensen facing an ordeal she may not survive. (978-1-62639-815-3)

Buried Heart by Laydin Michaels. When Drew Chambliss meets Cicely Jones, her buried past finds its way to the surface. Will they survive its discovery or will their chance at love turn to dust? (978-1-62639-801-6)

Escape: Exodus Book Three by Gun Brooke. Aboard the Exodus ship *Pathfinder*, President Thea Tylio still holds Caya Lindemay, a clairvoyant changer, in protective custody, which has devastating consequences endangering their relationship and the entire Exodus mission. (978-1-62639-635-7)

Genuine Gold by Ann Aptaker. New York, 1952. Outlaw Cantor Gold is thrown back into her honky-tonk Coney Island past, where crime and passion simmer in a neon glare. (978-1-62639-730-9)

Into Thin Air by Jeannie Levig. When her girlfriend disappears, Hannah Lewis discovers her world isn't as orderly as she thought it was. (978-1-62639-722-4)

Night Voice by CF Frizzell. When talk show host Sable finally acknowledges her risqué radio relationship with a mysterious caller, she welcomes a *real* relationship with local tradeswoman Riley Burke. (978-1-62639-813-9)

Raging at the Stars by Lesley Davis. When the unbelievable theories start revealing themselves as truths, can you trust in the ones who have conspired against you from the start? (978-1-62639-720-0)

She Wolf by Sheri Lewis Wohl. When the hunter becomes the hunted, more than love might be lost. (978-1-62639-741-5)

Smothered and Covered by Missouri Vaun. The last person Nash Wiley expects to bump into over a two a.m. breakfast at Waffle House is her college crush, decked out in a curve-hugging law enforcement uniform. (978-1-62639-704-0)

The Butterfly Whisperer by Lisa Moreau. Reunited after ten years, can Jordan and Sophie heal the past and rediscover love or will differing desires keep them apart? (978-1-62639-791-0)

The Devil's Due by Ali Vali. Cain and Emma Casey are awaiting the birth of their third child, but as always in Cain's world, there are new and old enemies to face in Katrina-ravaged New Orleans. (978-1-62639-591-6)

Widows of the Sun-Moon by Barbara Ann Wright. With immortality now out of their grasp, the gods of Calamity fight amongst themselves, egged on by the mad goddess they thought they'd left behind. (978-1-62639-777-4)

Arrested Hearts by Holly Stratimore. A reckless cop who hates her life and a health nut who is afraid to die might be a perfect combination for love. (978-1-62639-809-2)

Capturing Jessica by Jane Hardee. Hyperrealist sculptor Michael tries desperately to conceal the love she holds for best friend, Jess, unaware Jess's feelings for her are changing. (978-1-62639-836-8)

Counting to Zero by AJ Quinn. NSA agent Emma Thorpe and computer hacker Paxton James must learn to trust each other as they work to stop a threat clock that's rapidly counting down to zero. (978-1-62639-783-5)

Courageous Love by KC Richardson. Two women fight a devastating disease, and their own demons, while trying to fall in love. (978-1-62639-797-2)

One More Reason to Leave Orlando by Missouri Vaun. Nash Wiley thought a threesome sounded exotic and exciting, but as it turns out the reality of sleeping with two women at the same time is just really complicated. (978-1-62639-703-3)

Pathogen by Jessica L. Webb. Can Dr. Kate Morrison navigate a deadly virus and the threat of bioterrorism, as well as her new relationship with Sergeant Andy Wyles and her own troubled past? (978-1-62639-833-7)

Rainbow Gap by Lee Lynch. Jaudon Vickers and Berry Garland, polar opposites, dream and love in this tale of lesbian lives set in Central Florida against the tapestry of societal change and the Vietnam War. (978-1-62639-799-6)

Steel and Promise by Alexa Black. Lady Nivrai's cruel desires and modified body make most of the galaxy fear her, but courtesan Cailyn Derys soon discovers the real monsters are the ones without the claws. (978-1-62639-805-4)

Swelter by D. Jackson Leigh. Teal Giovanni's mistake shines an unwanted spotlight on a small Texas ranch where August Reese is secluded until she can testify against a powerful drug kingpin. (978-1-62639-795-8)

Without Justice by Carsen Taite. Cade Kelly and Emily Sinclair must battle each other in the pursuit of justice, but can they fight their undeniable attraction outside the walls of the courtroom? (978-1-62639-560-2)

21 Questions by Mason Dixon. To find love, start by asking the right questions. (978-1-62639-724-8)

A Palette for Love by Charlotte Greene. When newly minted Ph.D. Chloé Devereaux returns to New Orleans, she doesn't expect her new job and her powerful employer—Amelia Winters—to be so appealing. (978-1-62639-758-3)

By the Dark of Her Eyes by Cameron MacElvee. When Brenna Taylor inherits a decrepit property haunted by tormented ghosts, Alejandra Santana must not only restore Brenna's house and property but also save her soul. (978-1-62639-834-4)

Death by Cocktail Straw by Missouri Vaun. She just wanted to meet girls, but an outing at the local lesbian bar goes comically off the rails, landing Nash Wiley and her best pal in the ER. (978-1-62639-702-6)

Cash Braddock by Ashley Bartlett. Cash Braddock just wants to hang with her cat, fall in love, and deal drugs. What's the problem with that? (978-1-62639-706-4)

Lone Ranger by VK Powell. Reporter Emma Ferguson stirs up a thirty-year-old mystery that threatens Park Ranger Carter West's family and jeopardizes any hope for a relationship between the two women. (978-1-62639-767-5)

Never Enough by Robyn Nyx. Can two women put aside their pasts to find love before it's too late? (978-1-62639-629-6)

Love on Call by Radclyffe. Ex-Army medic Glenn Archer and recent LA transplant Mariana Mateo fight their mutual desire in the face of past losses as they work together in the Rivers Community Hospital ER. (978-1-62639-843-6)

Two Souls by Kathleen Knowles. Can love blossom in the wake of tragedy? (978-1-62639-641-8)

Camp Rewind by Meghan O'Brien. A summer camp for grown-ups becomes the site of an unlikely romance between a shy, introverted divorcee and one of the Internet's most infamous cultural critics—who attends undercover. (978-1-62639-793-4)

Cross Purposes by Gina L. Dartt. In pursuit of a lost Acadian treasure, three women must work out not only the clues, but also the complicated tangle of emotion and attraction developing between them. (978-1-62639-713-2)

Imperfect Truth by C.A. Popovich. Can an imperfect truth stand in the way of love? (978-1-62639-787-3)

Serious Potential by Maggie Cummings. Pro golfer Tracy Allen plans to forget her ex during a visit to Bay West, a lesbian condo community in NYC, but when she meets Dr. Jennifer Betsy, she gets more than she bargained for. (978-1-62639-633-3)

Life in Death by M. Ullrich. Sometimes the devastating end is your only chance for a new beginning. (978-1-62639-773-6)

Love on Liberty by MJ Williamz. Hearts collide when politics clash. (978-1-62639-639-5)

Taste by Kris Bryant. Accomplished chef Taryn has walked away from her promising career in the city's top restaurant to devote her life to her six-year-old daughter and is content until Ki Blake comes along. (978-1-62639-718-7)

Valley of Fire by Missouri Vaun. Taken captive in a desert outpost after their small aircraft is hijacked, Ava and her captivating passenger discover things about each other and themselves that will change them both forever. (978-1-62639-496-4)

The Second Wave by Jean Copeland. Can star-crossed lovers have a second chance after decades apart, or does the love of a lifetime only happen once? (978-1-62639-830-6)

Coils by Barbara Ann Wright. A modern young woman follows her aunt into the Greek Underworld and makes a pact with Medusa to win her freedom by killing a hero of legend. (978-1-62639-598-5)

Courting the Countess by Jenny Frame. When relationship-phobic Lady Henrietta Knight starts to care about housekeeper Annie Brannigan and her daughter, can she overcome her fears and promise Annie the forever that she demands? (978-1-62639-785-9)

Dapper by Jenny Frame. Amelia Honey meets the mysterious Byron De Brek and is faced with her darkest fantasies, but will her strict moral upbringing stop her from exploring what she truly wants? (978-1-62639-898-6)

Delayed Gratification: The Honeymoon by Meghan O'Brien. A dream European honeymoon turns into a winter storm nightmare involving a delayed flight, a ditched rental car, and eventually, a surprisingly happy ending. (978-1-62639-766-8)